I0745976

COGNITIA
HIGHTOWER
CASTLE
GOLEMS
RUINS OF
CENEDRIL
VERENDUS
GNOLLS
FELLING
FIELDS
GLACIER
LAKE
VERENDI
MOUNTAINS
CURET
DARSHIN
CENEDRIL
N

Storm Entertainment Presents

SOMNIA ONLINE

Experience the class you were born to play!

STELLAEIN
NOCTURN
TEAR LAKE
OBSIDIAN FOREST
BANDIT CAMPS
HAZENTHORNE
ULULATE
VAHRIR
MARSH OF VAHRIR
GOBLIN WATCHTOWERS
HAZEN VILLAGE
HAZEN SWAMP
MIKRUM CASTLE
PELAGU
HIMMEL LAKE
MIKRUM VILLAGE
FRANGIT
TARISHNA
N

SOMNIA ONLINE

DISTORTION

BOOK 5

K.T. HANNA

SOMNIA ONLINE: DISTORTION

Author: K.T. Hanna
Cover Artist: Marko Horvatin
Typography: Bonnie Price
Formatting & Interior Design: Caitlin Greer

ISBN-13: 978-1-948983-17-4 (Trade Paperback Edition)
ISBN-13: 978-1-948983-18-1 (Hardback Edition)
ISBN-13: 978-1-948983-16-7 (E-Book Edition)

Also by KT Hanna

Somnia Online:

Initializing
Anomaly
Fragments
Dissonance
Distortion

The Domino Project:

Chameleon
Hybrid
Parasite

Pam and Carl
thank you for everything.

Wren's ability to die in-game and not affect her out of game body gave her hope. Even though she suffered painful aftereffects, at least she didn't have to hold back her guild by being overcautious.

She didn't expect to return to their guild base after successfully completing yet another key only to have Telvar push her out of the game.

James' ulterior motives have come to light, leaving Laria and Shayla scrambling to cover their tracks.

CHAPTER ONE

Toll

Laria ran out of the office faster than she ever had in her life. She didn't care who saw her. She didn't care if there were more spies in the operation. All she knew was that she had to get back to her house and daughter before the military beat her there.

She summoned a car on the way to the elevator and overrode the stops once the elevator got to her. Was it abuse of her power? Sure, but now was an exception. She'd fight anyone to the death who tried to say otherwise.

An email dinged at her when she climbed into her ride. She glanced at it after giving the car system her address and then she read the email.

Laria
Do not mention the connection to the game. There are things that must be discussed. Disguise as best possible. Thra is diverting their route to buy you time.
Rav

Laria blinked at the message, trying to clear her eyes just in case she was seeing things. Nope. Definitely an email from the AI. Wonders would never cease. David would want to know. Of course he would. So she shot off a message to him, glad of the reminder that communication worked. Her head wasn't working properly. Its focus was solely on Wren and if she'd be okay. How had she been shot out of the game? It happened so suddenly she'd not had a chance to figure out anything before she dashed out of the door.

It was a short ride to the family condo, and she tipped the service well before jumping out and taking the steps two at a time to the door.

She burst into the apartment and raced up the stairs, threw open the door and stopped short. Tears welled in her eyes, and she could feel her body shaking. The relief that suffused her made her legs jelly-like, and she stumbled against the doorjamb.

Wren drew in a gulping breath. Air flooded into her lungs faster than intended. She coughed, and it made her chest ache with the action. She tried to open her eyes again, but they felt like they were crusted closed. Whether by disuse or some sort of virus, that inability flared panic through her system. The rest of her senses were taking their time coming online.

It was all she could do to slow her breathing down and make herself completely aware of her surroundings. She could hear machines beeping behind her, like a metronome threatening to stop at any moment. Their cadence was soothing and alarming all at once, like a warning she should heed.

Her eyes fluttered open again, and she realized the crusty feeling was probably from being dormant for more than two months. She had no idea how much time had passed since Telvar pushed her out of Somnia. Her mind still swam in confusion. Voices she shouldn't be able to hear, from a place that didn't really exist, still echoed through her head like they were standing in the room with her.

Sinister's tone bit through the air as if the blood-mage stood right next to her. "What have you done? Why? Tell me!" Even down to the hissed breath she drew in. The anger settled in her throat like Wren knew it would, because that was how fiercely Sinister protected what she cared about.

Barks rang in Wren's ears, like Snowy was angry at the sudden vacancy in his head the way she was still reeling from the one in hers. It left behind a strange and lonely sensation Wren didn't like.

She could hear the others to a lesser extent. Perhaps because they weren't as close to her as Sinister and Snowy had been…were even. However that worked.

The capsule felt like home. At the same time, it was a prison she wasn't sure she wanted to leave. What if she couldn't go back to Somnia?

You can come back.

"Good to know." She tried to mumble, but it came out like an indeterminate croak.

Wren shut her eyes and reached out tentatively with her mind. She wanted to understand if the voices were real or just an echo of her imagination. Had that reassurance been her own thoughts, her own desperation? Or had Riasli hitched a ride out of the game world in her head? But as she touched one voice, a cacophony of others tried to inundate her, and she pulled back, shaking.

It wasn't the time to dwell on where she'd come from. This was her room. Her *real* room. Not one in a fabricated reality. Not one in her imagination. Her eyes had finally started to focus again, and everything around her was sharper now, solid.

She pushed herself up, or she tried to, but her arms buckled against even holding up her torso weight. With a yelp of pain, she held her hands up to look at them. A blood oxygen meter was fixed to her left pointer finger with stubborn tape. Its red glowing numbers hurt her eyes.

"Damn it." Again the word wouldn't escape her throat.

She fought against the panic that began to rise in her chest. The heaviness of her limbs tried to drag her down. Skin pulled against her bones. She could tell she'd lost weight while in the capsule, regardless of being fed nutrients through the IV still attached to her arm. If she concentrated, she was sure she could feel the IV and what it fed her as it traveled through her veins, but it was probably just the aftereffects of her virtual reality journey.

Hunger growled in the depths of her stomach, and suddenly she was famished.

The sides of the capsule felt like they were closing in ever so slowly. She wanted to get out, but her arms felt brittle. It was hard enough to push herself into a half sitting position.

Apparently, the capsule's ability to make sure your muscles didn't atrophy wasn't supposed to extend to a three month stay. They'd have to rethink that in the redesign. Wren laughed, which resulted in another coughing fit, and she grimaced as she slowly worked her way to sitting fully upright. The sheer amount of energy it took to reach that position left her breathless.

Panting, she tried making her hands into fists and stretching them out again while she regained her composure. Even that small exertion showed her how weak her grip had become.

Suddenly, she heard a door slam.

Footsteps raced through the condo, and up the stairs. Her bedroom door smashed open, the handle indenting the wall behind it with a resounding thud.

"Hey," Laria's voice sounded sweeter than anything Wren had heard in a long time, but she found it difficult to turn well enough to see her mother.

Finally, Wren looked up at her mom, not happy with how long the action took her. Everything was happening so slowly. It was like the muscles had forgotten how to move her actual body. She wasn't sure what she'd expected, but it wasn't this. "Hey."

She managed to reply to her mother, but it barely sounded like more than a deep breath. Wren cringed and used all the energy she could muster to raise her right hand to the side of the capsule. She tried to grip the sides of it with her hands, but her fingers barely obeyed. Her grip was weak, and her little fist clenching hadn't done anything to help like she'd hoped.

In her head, she'd thought she'd wake up and jump out of the capsule and be fine. But realistically, her limbs had been doing nothing for three months. And while she'd have been far worse off had she not been in a capsule, the simulation of movement wasn't quite right when those same legs never moved at all.

Laria crouched down resting her hands next to Wren's. Her mother's eyes were shadowed, concerned, yet there was this suppressed joy surrounding her that leaked over to Wren. With her mother that obviously happy to see her, it was difficult to remain irritated at the situation.

"Wrennie." Her mom bent her head forward and touched their foreheads together. The moment drew out, and all Wren could think of was the warmth of her mom, of being back in the real world, and the tangible proof that she was alive. "Oh, Wrennie."

There was a hitch to her mother's voice, and Wren knew she didn't want to look up and see the tears falling, because she wasn't even sure if she could produce her own anymore. She gripped her mother's hand in return as hard as she could. Which wasn't much, but the closeness, the smells, the feeling…it flooded her senses with abandon like a lifeline trying to reel her in.

Laria hugged her tighter, just for a moment, and even with that movement, she knew her mother was being careful of her current status. For a second the older woman leaned back and looked at her daughter, tears running down her cheeks.

Then she leaned in and kissed Wren soundly on the forehead. "I thought I lost you."

Laria's voice croaked, but at least the words were distinguishable. And she hugged Wren tight once more. As much as Wren wanted to say something in return, her throat was so parched from lack of real water that it wasn't remotely possible.

Laria crouched down next to the capsule, her expression serious. "I don't want to worry you. But we have about ten or so minutes to get you out of that capsule and looking like you're not half dead."

"Great," Wren croaked out, wincing as she did so.

"I'm such an idiot." Her mom stood up and looked around frantically. Locating a small fridge in the corner she dived for it and brought back a water bottle.

The clear liquid had never tasted so good, or so real. It sure beat the shit for taste they programmed into the game water.

"Thanks, Mom." Wren smiled. Her voice was there. Not loud, and still raspy with disuse, but it was there. Her throat felt better already too. "Now what?"

Laria cringed. "Yeah, about that. We had a spy in our office. And our rich headset sponsors—who happen to be military—are on their way over to determine your status. Your account was flagged for odd activity, and James monitored it. I assume, anyway."

That didn't sound good. Different scenarios danced through Wren's head. An idea popped into existence, but it would be difficult to pull it off.

"Help get me out," she said, but first motioned to the water bottle and took another drink.

"Let's get some of these bits and bobs off you first." Her mother's voice was gentle, and the worry spilled over what she probably thought was calm and collected.

Wren didn't have the heart to tell her otherwise as she pulled the IV and taped it with cotton to absorb any excess blood. Then she watched her mother unwind the tape from around the blood-oxygen meter and tug it away from her hand.

Finally, with everything tethering her to the capsule disconnected and the machines finally shut off, Laria wrapped an arm under Wren's shoulders and leaned down to scoop out her legs in fireman carry. It was far too easy for her mother to carry her. Since they were similar in stature, Wren knew the weight she'd lost probably worried them both.

"On the rim." Even the exertion of holding onto her mother, of being moved—that tired Wren out. But she couldn't afford to show how much. She needed to clamp down on it now. Not necessarily for her mother's sake, but for the visitors they were about to receive. Wren didn't like the sound of the military investors and what that made them entitled to.

Obligingly, even if she kept shooting her daughter questioning looks, Laria settled Wren at the end part of the capsule with her right arm leaning against the rounded head piece. Wren took another swig of water to steady herself. Even the damned water bottle felt like it was a ten-pound weight.

It had taken too much of their precious time, but Wren needed to seem perfectly okay. Surprised, even. Her mother leaned forward to unhook the headset, but Wren brushed her away.

"It's just me, taking a break from the game. Goodness, what do these people want?" By the time she finished the sentence, Wren's voice was dry again. She gulped down some more water, her irritation nipping at the back of her mind.

Laria hesitated at first, but then nodded and grabbed the chair near the bed so she could appear to be sitting with her daughter.

"Tell dad?" Wren asked. Trying desperately to fight some of the dryness of her throat. It began to hurt a little in the back right, tugging at every word she tried to utter.

"Yeah. He knows, but he's not about to barge in." Laria perched on her stool like she wanted to envelop Wren in a hug, and her daughter appreciated the restraint more than ever. It was difficult enough for her to stay in this casual-appearing lean stance. It took a stupid amount of strength to pull off. A hug would undo her.

Wren was about to ask how much longer they had, but it was answered for her by the loud knocking on the front door below. Laria stood up and nodded at Wren before heading down.

"I'm coming, I'm coming," she yelled in response to renewed efforts to bash down the door and call it a knock.

Wren took another deep breath, feeling like her lungs were rusty.

He says she's okay, Sin.

It sounded like Havoc was reasoning with the blood mage.

He's probably lying! I'm logging out and heading over there.

Sin didn't sound rational, and Wren couldn't blame her. The conversations were carrying on in the back of her mind, like a soft accompaniment. It would probably take Harlow about thirty minutes to log out and hoof it over. Hopefully everything else would be sorted by then.

"Where is Wren Summers?" a cold and clipped voice demanded.

There was a vague familiarity to it, but Wren focused all her concentration on remaining still. Shaking would give the game away, so she calmed herself. Breathing in and out with deliberate care. Thinking of Snowy and her friends, and how she desperately needed to have words with Telvar.

Footsteps tromped up their metal staircase in a fast staccato beat. So many of them. Wren hoped her mom was leading the charge. She hadn't needed to worry about that of course. Her mother was the first one to enter.

"This is my daughter's bedroom." Laria spoke, filled with indignity. "Three of you may enter. The rest will remain on the landing."

Wren raised an eyebrow and hoped her irritated teenage smirk settled properly on her face.

"Mom?" She was happy to hear that her voice didn't crack this time.

"Sorry to pull you out of the game, Wren. These people have some questions." Her mom smiled tightly, like she didn't want to bother her daughter.

Wren shrugged, but tried to allow a good amount of annoyance to leak into her words when she spoke.

"Who are you?" She directed the question to the guy in front. All she could see through his black SWAT-like uniform was his tanned skin and brown eyes.

"Aaron Baker," he replied, somewhat taken aback. His eyes kept darting around the room as if he was searching for something specific.

"Look. I have to get back to my group. What did you want?" Wren exerted herculean effort to cross her arms and exude irritation. She couldn't falter. Couldn't show them any sign of weakness.

You could try bolstering your body's failing strength with the power of your mind.

Maintaining a bored expression was difficult as the voice reverberated through her skull. *What do you mean?* She shot back at it. Over the last few days, she'd been studying this voice in her mind and all she knew was that it wasn't Riasli, nor was it any of the AIs.

Focus on reinforcing your body, help give it strength through your mind, like your forcefields.

I'm in the real world. Not the game. That's not possible here.

Isn't it?

It didn't say anything else, and Wren had to pay better attention to the home invaders in front of her.

"Well." Aaron seemed confused. He glanced at the capsule she was leaning on. "Why do you have that?"

"Because Mr. Davenport loaned it to her?" Laria didn't butt in. She simply spoke like she'd been a part of the conversation all along, and was bored by the interruption.

"I was speaking to your daughter, ma'am." The words sounded stressed in the soldier's mouth. He seemed a bit out of his element. "I apologize, we seem to be misinformed."

"Can I get back in my capsule then?" Wren did her best to sound bored.

"Why do you use the capsule?" Another voice spoke from the back of the pack.

The same sinuous voice that Wren was sure she'd heard before. He pushed forward, and a tall man in his late twenties stood in front of her. She'd only seen him a few times, but that voice had always annoyed her. That had to be James. The way he held himself, his semi-permanent smirk, and eyes that pretended to know more than he let on—there was no doubt in her mind that it was him.

Wren raised an eyebrow. "Because I'm a gamer. Duh." Wren made sure to school her face into incredulousness that she had to explain this at all. Let alone to a grown man. "It's called grinding. I've got a level cap to hit."

"You don't adhere to the warnings?" he asked, a sneer to his voice.

"My friends log out way more than me. The warnings don't apply to the capsule. Do you even game?" Wren continued her irritation with the adults' spiel and tried to exert control over her body that was perilously close to collapsing with exhaustion.

The man looked slightly taken aback by her tone, if not her words. He seemed to be trying to find something to say back to her as if he hadn't been expecting her to respond in that manner.

She sighed. "Look. I really love Somnia. I have the whole summer to conquer it. This been our plan since it was announced."

"I told you. You can't waste your whole summer in there, Wren." Laria started in on her daughter.

"We're not arguing about this now, Mom." Wren rolled her eyes for good measure. "I'm taking care of myself."

But James's eyes narrowed and the way his eyes raked over her made

Wren's skin crawl. "You seem to have lost weight."

"Maybe a little. But I'm so close to the level cap." She grinned, doing her best to make sure she sounded mischievous. James wasn't stupid. He was observant and, as far as she could tell, calculating. It took effort to maintain her flippant comments around him. "Besides, I'm pretty sure Mom is about to force feed me. I could really go for some pancakes."

"Sir." Aaron interrupted whatever it was James wanted to say next. "There's nothing here. Whatever that tip was, it's wrong. The girl is obviously fine, and the capsule is functioning properly. I just verified that it was checked out legitimately. We have to go."

Aaron didn't wait for James to respond. He just turned around and ushered his men out of Wren's room, turning at the door to smile apologetically. "Sorry for interrupting you. We apologize for the inconvenience."

The soldiers withdrew, but James remained where he was, his eyes firmly locked on Laria. "I know you're hiding something."

"Like what?" Laria asked, her arms crossed as she leaned forward slightly. "Do tell me. Maybe I can help you find it."

James scowled, yet his eyes still held that smugness. Like he knew something they didn't. "I don't need to work at Storm to figure out what you're doing, but I still do. I'll see you back there."

Wren noticed that her mother's expression didn't change, which meant it was probably something she hadn't been expecting. Just as she was about to speak, James beat her to it.

He stepped back to transfer the glare to Wren. "Don't look so smug. You're anything but innocent in this."

And he turned, and exited the room, slamming the door behind him.

Somnia Online
Mikrum Isle
Day Twenty

Telvar paced, his eyes switching in and out from the normal lacerta eyes he usually donned to the fiery dragon eyes that were his original incarnation. His scales rippled, and anger churned in his gut.

He wasn't even sure where it was directed, just that it was there. Just that it was speaking to what he'd originally been intended to be.

"Should you really have done that?" Emilarth's voice wasn't as judgmental as he'd expected it to be.

He hesitated in answering her. That was the question now, wasn't it? The answer being that he wasn't entirely sure. It had been an impulse. A complete and utter surge of positivity that it was the right choice, the only choice to make at the time.

Being what he was, with the role he had, and the amount of access it allowed him, he'd known about the intended raid. Probably before the people themselves knew about it. The only way to protect Murmur had been to cast her out.

"I had to," he replied, thoughts still racing in his mind.

Emilarth studied him for a moment, her lips pursed with whatever her own mind hid. "It wasn't easy, was it?"

She was right; it hadn't been an easy block to overcome. So many elements went into what kept Murmur in the game. There were strands that reached back into its initial inception, provided by her tinkered headset. Other elements involved the way the world had begun to evolve since she entered it. Her human connection to it, had strengthened it where needed, made it vulnerable where it could be dangerous, and stubborn where it could protect itself.

"No," he answered, running through a set of algorithms for the twentieth time to make sure that he hadn't irreparably damaged anything. "It definitely wasn't easy. One of the most difficult blocks I've ever had to overcome."

Laughter drifted around him on the wind, and the anger inside him died down a touch. If the world of Somnia was waking up like he thought it was, then this was just a new normal for them all. The sound buffeted against him, almost playfully, as he concentrated on the direction it blew. He snatched only portions of the thoughts, no, of the *words* Murmur was speaking in her real body.

Emilarth tapped her foot impatiently. "I didn't come here to stare at you, Tel. I came here to help you—to help her—if needed."

"Well, she doesn't really need it right now, does she?" he whispered under his breath as the breeze blew across his scales, just this side of tickling. "Right now, she's of two worlds."

Emilarth raised an eyebrow and finally crossed her arms. Her nose and whiskers twitched. "She's always been of two worlds."

Telvar smiled this time, a tinge of sadness offsetting the usual lacerta comical appearance. "Not like this. Not with her mind. Not in two places at once."

"Her mind split in two?" Emilarth asked incredulously as she closed her eyes to focus her concentration. After a moment they opened again, and her smile was serene but echoed the melancholy of Telvar's own. "I see."

She looped an arm around Telvar's waist and leaned her head against his shoulder, her ears flicking as if flies hovered around her. He returned the loose and friendly embrace as a deep sigh overtook him.

"Yeah. Not like that, just able to separate her consciousness to be in both places at once. You know, nothing normal humans can't do or anything." The sarcasm fell flat, because that made it just one more thing that put her in danger of experimentation. And they had no control over it at all.

CHAPTER TWO
Outside

Davenport watched over Shayla's shoulder as she ran through a log of glitches reported by the player base. Just a few minutes before the raid hit Laria's house, she'd sent a message. That Wren was awake. They'd deal with everything.

Apparently she'd sent it to both Teddy and Shayla, because he'd walked into her office not four minutes later.

Right around that time, a plethora of glitches popped into being, not just in the game but noticed and reported by the players. Some of them were angry, some wondering if a GM event was being held. While she'd dispatched a group of customer service reps to go through those specifically, Shayla was running through each of them to make sure she hadn't missed something important.

When Wren exited the game, the internal programming of the game momentarily went haywire, resulting in pockets of momentary chaos in Somnia.

It didn't take a genius to add two and two together. Which was good because Shayla was running on very little sleep. Pushing her hands back through her hair, she stretched her arms over her head and leaned back in her chair, almost hitting Davenport in the process. She didn't feel like apologizing, though. He'd been standing a tad too close.

Not in that creepy, overbearing way she'd been used to fending off for most of her career. No, Teddy's eyes shone like a kid who'd got a new toy. He was about as aware of her as a woman right then as he was of his involuntary breathing.

His eyes were focused on the on-screen data in her office, drinking it all in like a man stranded in the desert for months. Shayla smiled. This was a side of Teddy she hadn't seen in years. He was excited, and his brain was probably ticking over forty thousand different possibilities these outcomes could yield for him.

Except her damned computer wouldn't stop beeping at her. Notifications streamed in from everywhere. She'd never missed Ava as much as she did right then. Hell, even Laria would have been able to help with all of this policing.

"I don't know how, but her connection is still there." Shayla didn't even want to look back at the computers.

Teddy frowned, and moved to the side before leaning forward more. "It's tenuous at best by the impulses the system is scanning, but definitely still there. I thought she'd been booted out?"

"She has been." Shayla shrugged and then bent forward to take another look at the brainwave monitors. That couldn't be, right? It didn't make any sense.

Wonderment crossed the older man's face, and a grin settled across his features. "She's utilizing increased percentages of her brain. Is she accessing the game without a headset?"

The pure joy on his face sent shivers down Shalya's body. "No, I think she's still got the headset on, which could be part of it. I mean, we'd have to monitor her more than this. Her character shows as logged out. But there's a presence emanating from her headset. Her thought processes appear to still be accessing the game. Though I doubt that's a conscious thought on her part."

It was surreal, and something nagged at the back of Shayla's mind, but she couldn't quite put her finger on the thoughts. All she knew was that as soon as she got the all clear, she had to let Laria know about the readings they were getting.

Even so, she couldn't temper the relief that came with Wren finally having left the game. Whether or not she could stand on her own or completely separate her thoughts from Somnia, it didn't matter. All that mattered, at least for the next few hours, was that Wren wasn't going to die in-game.

Now all Shayla had to do was figure out exactly what the remaining connection was all about and keep prying noses out of it.

No pressure.

Summers Residence
Home of Laria, David, and Wren
Real World – Early Hours, Day Twenty

Wren waited until she heard the door slam downstairs. She closed her eyes and counted to ten as her mother checked to make sure no one had stayed behind. She didn't remember counting to ten taking so long. But then, she'd been in a coma for almost three months. In a game. It was surprising she remembered anything at all.

"You okay?" Laria's concern pulled Wren out of her thoughts, and she blinked her eyes open against the bright light that illuminated her room.

"I guess. All things considered." But she wasn't entirely telling the truth. Wren didn't trust herself to move and not fall. And the capsule was becoming more and more uncomfortable to lean against. Even though it felt like a lifeline, it was cold and metallic.

Not like this. Not with her mind. Not in two places at once.

She shook her head, trying to clear out the noise in it. Noises that sounded distinctly like her friends she knew she'd left behind in the game.

But what if she hadn't? What if this was how it worked now? She could hear things they'd said. But not everything. In order to do that, she needed to seriously focus in on the sounds at the back of her head. But the closer she got to those, the further away her surroundings felt. She didn't understand any of this. Oh, for her high school days.

Give her a textbook and a goal to study toward, and she could master anything.

She sighed.

"Are you really okay?" Laria asked, stepping closer and looking at her daughter with a deep frown on her face. "You don't have to put on a brave show for me. I'm good. I've seen a lot of shit, and I know I can help if you'll just let me."

Wren choked back a cough. Always eager to help, and her mom didn't have a clue how to make things better, but she'd damn well try.

Screams echoed through to her, like something happening in the distance. And she saw a brief flash of something huge and wormlike opening its maw and sending a large group of players into its depths.

Wren shuddered, unsure what it was she'd seen, only knowing that she was glad they hadn't encountered that enemy yet.

"I am, Mom. I'm just so tired. Do you think I can take a nap? I really need a bloody nap. Actual sleep. Not one hooked up, not one in-game, but an actual sleep nap." It sounded like heaven as soon as the words left her mouth, and she knew the relaxation it brought her would be welcomed.

"Of course!" Laria smiled and bounced up from where she'd been sitting. "Let's take that headset off, duck you into the shower, and get you set up."

But Wren scowled. "I don't know why, but for right now, I'd like to keep the headset on. I might just have a quick bath instead."

"Okay." Laria looked like she wanted to say so much more, but bit down on her lip instead and nodded. "Let's get a warm bath ready, do what we can to avoid electrocuting you, and get you back to feeling human again."

Wren flexed her arms as her mother left for the bathroom, ignoring the jibe. Her arms were weak and flimsy. Her stomach let out a growl that could have rivaled Snowy at his angriest. She was starving and yet unsure about what to eat, or even when to eat. Her head swam with fleeting thoughts of people she by all rights shouldn't be able to hear anymore.

Thoughts from players and characters she'd never actually encountered before. But if she concentrated on someone she knew, like Dirsna, she could hear his voice. All of it inside her head, like the game kept playing, permanently attached to her. Every single element of Somnia intermingled with each other and she could hear, feel, and understand everyone in it. All she had to do was focus.

Bizarre, yet at the same time, oddly comforting. She hadn't realized how seriously attached to the world she'd become.

But it left her with a fear to remove her headset. What if she took it off and the voices disappeared? What if she took it off and her connection to the game could never be repeated? Maybe it wiped Murmur, or the guild progress, or myriad of other things that could damage the experience not only for herself, but for the people she cared about and all the people she didn't know.

Most people who'd been stuck in a game might be glad to be rid of it, but Wren wasn't. Even now she wanted to get back inside, to make sure she could, but also to complete what she'd set out to do.

She was quite certain that Somnia spoke to her, guided her. She knew it had multiple times in the last few days. If that meant she'd gone a bit over the edge, then maybe she had, but there were too many indicators that she was correct.

At the same time, she wanted to remove the headset and examine it. Figure out how it was different from the others.

She had to get to the endgame as soon as possible, because while she wanted to get there anyway and prove Fable was the best guild out there, she also had the feeling that if anyone else beat them to the final boss first, Somnia might change the world forever. And not just the digital one.

What she did know was she felt more equipped to deal with all the potential trauma to others and changes to the online world than anyone else. She knew without a shadow of a doubt that the getashi were powerful objects. If Telvar feared them, if they could force such a change on one of the AIs, she shuddered to think what many of them at once might do to something or someone.

Those sinuous pieces of Michael's brain affected her even if she only touched one for a moment. They offered glimpses of power, of victory, and not just in-game. But she'd seen what it could do to an AI and feared what impact it might have on a human.

"It's ready!" Laria's voice, filled with forced cheerfulness, called out from the bathroom. Faint scents of shea drifted out and into her room.

A real bath. Not one of these virtual ones. The headset sat on her head, still snug in its octopus hugging sort of way. She could shake her head and not have it fall off. Even as she righted herself to begin walking toward the room, she could feel each movement sapping her energy reserves.

There was no way she'd make it the eight or so steps. Not today. Maybe tomorrow. As if on cue her mother walked out to help her, a sheepish look in her eyes. Like she'd already forgotten how long it had been since Wren last walked on her real legs.

But that was okay. Wren didn't hold it against her. Not in the slightest. But she did use it for motivation. Give her a few days and she'd be ready for the fight.

Now all she had to do was hope she could indeed log back in, convince everyone she was okay, and make sure the guild was ready for what was coming. No matter the cost.

Summers Residence
Home of Laria, David, and Wren
Real World – Early Hours Day Twenty

The bath water was starting to cool when Wren heard the echo of the front door shutting again. This time it was soft and not a demanding slam. In her vaguely conscious state, she tracked footsteps as they took the stairs two at a time. She could feel his hesitation as he paused at the bathroom door before knocking.

"Hey there." Her dad's voice so close to her made her eyes prickle with tears. It was like he wanted to call her princess like he had when she was younger. She probably wouldn't have minded right then either.

"Hey, Dad." Wren smiled, letting the water soothe her, despite the gathering chill. Reluctantly, she had to admit to herself that the bath was probably over already. Even though she had no idea how long she'd been in it. "I'll be out in a few."

"Not without your mother. I'm willing to bet you've been trying your best to overdo it." There was a light chuckle to his voice, but it felt like he was masking worry with it. He probably was.

A few moments later and her mother popped into the room armed with a clean, soft towel. Wren was beginning to feel tired, and she'd lost track of time. She wasn't sure how long she'd been out of the game. The constantly litany of voices in the back of her head made her feel like she was in fact dreaming, or else just visiting the virtual edition of her home.

Her hair a bit damp, her clothes nice and warm, she snuggled into the soft bed as her mother shoved a protein bar at her.

Her father hovered at the edge, watching her. The moment Laria moved away he swooped in and sat down next to her on the bed. Wren leaned in for the hug. No matter the situation, no matter the pain, her father's hugs always hit the spot. They were warm and reassuring, protective and fierce, loving and guiding, all at the same time.

He pulled back and didn't look away fast enough. Tears welled in his eyes, and Wren felt a pang of guilt at having worried them, even if it wasn't entirely her fault.

Her mother spoke gently, hesitancy showing she didn't want to interrupt the moment.

"Eat up. That'll be gentle on your stomach and give you some of the nutrients you haven't had for a while. Don't keep her up. Make sure she sleeps. She needs to regain strength." Then Laria leaned forward to kiss Wren on the forehead. "Take a bit of time and recuperate."

She'd left the room before Wren could muster a reply. With all the voices in her head becoming more din like and less controlled, it was all Wren could do to keep her eyes open.

"Sleep, little one," her dad soothed softly. "I want you to get better, and to get better you need to sleep."

"Stay here, Daddy?" Suddenly Wren felt alone. She'd been walking around with Snowy by her side for so long that being without him, and without Telvar, and without her friends — everything was lonely.

I'm still here though. We all are.

Was that Telvar? Had he remained in her head?

"Dad?" Wren pushed past her sleepiness for a moment, needing to hear his voice.

"I said I'd stay with you until you fall asleep. You know we've been here the whole time, right?" His hand was warm over hers, and she twined her fingers with his strong ones, trying to leech some of the strength she was missing. For a moment she wished she could leech life like Havoc and that it had carried over into the real world so she could replenish her reserves more readily.

"Sleep, pumpkin," he whispered, kissing her forehead just like her mother had done earlier.

"Kay…" Wren's eyes grew heavier, but she kept that grip on her dad, like a vice.

As she drifted off the words floating in her head jumbled together. Like a huge word find, they drifted around, bumping into each other and not making any sense at all. The noise faded into a hum, like a white noise machine. The only thing she knew for certain was that she needed true sleep. Even if it meant leaving Somnia's machinations for a little while.

Summers Residence
Home of Laria, David, and Wren
Real World – Early Hours Day Twenty

A scream of frustration tore through Wren's mind, sending her into an upright sitting position. She was shivering when she woke, teeth chattering, but the dream had been so fleeting, she couldn't grasp what had unsettled her so much.

The next thing she knew, Harlow catapulted across from where she'd probably been sitting next to David and enveloped Wren in a rib-grinding bear hug.

"You're awake! You're in the real world!" She practically screamed, squeezing tighter, and whispering the words over and over into Wren's ear.

Wren blinked, words coming back to her sleep fogged mind slowly. Harlow's warmth, her presence made everything feel more grounded.

Wren returned the hug as tightly as she could, but the strength still wasn't there. It was going to take a while. "Still tired though. What's up?"

Had no one else heard that scream like she had? It made her wake up, jolted her out of the nice semi-gibberish dream she'd been having. It was difficult to keep herself in a sitting position once Harlow's grip loosened.

"Oops! Sorry." Harlow gently helped Wren sit by stacking pillows behind her so she could rest comfortably. "I got a little excited."

The blush in Harlow's cheeks distracted Wren momentarily from her dream. Life without her best friend was unimaginable for her. What had she just put Harlow through? Never having been much of a person for touch, Wren found herself suddenly wanting more contact with Harlow, more of a reassurance they were both real and there.

The echo of the scream rumbled through her head again. Had it been Somnia? She tried to focus, but her stomach rumbled so loudly, it made her laugh. Which made her cough. Which in turn made Harlow fuss.

David grinned and stood up. "There, I watched over you. Now I'll let your best friend annoy the crap out of you while I go and talk to your mom about what to feed you."

He leaned over again and brushed Wren's hair out of her eyes, pushing it away. "Don't overdo it. Even if you might think you're not exerting yourself. The odds are that you're doing something that's too much for you at the moment. Just take it easy and regain your strength a day at a time."

He left the room and Harlow waited, bouncing absent-mindedly on the bed as he left. Then she turned to Wren, her eyes bright with a steel Wren was glad she had in her corner. "Well, did it work? Did Telvar's disastrously timed ejection sever you from the game?"

Wren thought for a moment, reaching out a hand to grab Harlow's. "Only the sort of physical connection. I seem to have the rest of the world still intact. Like," and she looked around to make sure no one would overhear them. "Like, I can hear some of the conversations in Somnia. It's like I'm here, but a portion of my consciousness is also there."

It sounded so much worse when she said it out loud. Wren tried to think of other ways to phrase it, but she was tired, and her body was hungry, and she didn't think she'd woken up properly.

Too much was still swimming in her mind for her to translate it coherently.

"You're still sort of logged in then?" Harlow bit her lip, and her eyes seemed distant for a moment, but then her green eyes focused on Wren, and for a moment it was all she could see. "What can you hear now?"

"Telvar and Emilarth were discussing me. No one else is being overly relevant, but most everyone we group with has logged out, and the NPCs aren't overly concerned with me. Although—" She paused, not wanting to sound like she'd hallucinated.

"Although what?" Harlow crossed her arms and put on her best *tell me or else* face.

Wren sighed, feeling the absence of contact in the hand Harlow had withdrawn. "I thought I heard a scream of frustration. It happened just before I woke up, and it sounded so real. Like I could feel the ground shake underneath my feet. Then I woke up and you and Dad were here, but neither of you appeared to have noticed it."

Harlow was shaking her head. "I'm sorry, Wren. We didn't hear anything. Just the soft murmur you made before you snapped out of sleep mode."

"Yeah, I gathered." Wren yawned, tired. "It feels like something is missing. Not being able to have Snowy with me is infuriating."

"Grew attached to him, huh?"

"Totally." Wren paused for a moment, trying to get her thoughts in order. Playing the game had been her be all and end all of her summer life. But now it had become so much more. How did she even begin to process that?

"You know what?" Harlow suddenly jumped up, clapping her hands, her smile shining like the sun.

"What?" Wren couldn't help smiling at her friend.

"We can figure this out. Match that dream scream to one of the wave files. I'm sure Rav has them." Harlow's enthusiasm was infectious.

"That." Wren ran it over in her mind certain it wasn't going to be quite that easy. But it seemed like a decent enough starting point. "Isn't a half bad idea."

CHAPTER THREE
Echoes

Somnia Online
Exodus Guild Raid – Illinish Threshold
Day Twenty

Masha didn't even want to dig through his inventory to try and figure out just how many more health potions he had on him. At this rate, they were going to have to access the guild bank from this dungeon. Surely it hadn't taken Spiral this long in here? Maybe that was why they hadn't heard of them until they defeated this dungeon, though.

Jirald had overdone the explosives when he blew up the beast. So much that they hadn't realized what they thought were remnants of them lying around on the staircase. Several of them hadn't exploded yet. That was, until people got in their proximity and set them off. The amount of people they lost initially was excruciating.

Nearing level forty, even the fifty percent experience return that some resurrections could give made each defeat excruciating. It had taken them so long to find everyone. Several of them had taken shifts to log out and sleep, while the others kept the raid live in-game so it wouldn't disband and kick them all from the dungeon.

If it even worked like that in this world. He wasn't about to test the theory.

Right now, Masha wasn't even sure this game knew how a game worked.

The giant mouth monster had scattered them far and wide in this haunted, shitty city far beneath the surface. The cleric assumed there was a way to get down it without being tossed like garbage, but thanks to Jirald and his explosions, they'd not managed to enter that way.

Which set them back days.

Masha couldn't help the flush of irritation at the fact that they didn't have a necromancer at a high enough level yet to summon with a coffin and join them on the raid.

"You look positively irritated," Ishwa commented, still frowning at his staff that had broken in the initial fall. While it was roughly put back together, it lacked its former finesse. Patching it up on site hadn't done it justice.

"I am," Masha answered, keeping it short. If he didn't, he was going to lose his temper, and that wasn't something he could afford right then. Jirald kept taking off down tunnels and sneaking back to report what he'd seen. Each time, Masha wanted to shackle him to a wall and barely resisted doing so.

"If it wasn't for that little shit…" Ishwa left it hanging and wiggled his eyebrows for effect.

"Shut up. We all know it. And one of these days he's going to encounter someone who will take him down a peg." Masha was fairly certain it would either be himself or Murmur who finally did it.

Thing was, with some of Jirald's skills, Masha had begun to doubt his certainty about the winner. If he hit all of his criticals? Jirald was near unbeatable. Ever since he'd switched focus from being upset at his class to mastering his class—the change was visible.

"Are we ready then?" Ishwa skillfully changed the subject with a bit of a side-eye that Masha chose to ignore.

"About as good as we're going to get. They've managed to find Ricu's body and drag it back here. Should be resurrecting it shortly. That boulder trap should have been easy to spot." Masha sighed and wondered for the five hundredth time in the last twenty-four hours why he played these games anymore. He'd retired; he didn't have to do anything. And yet, he found himself drawn to playing, leading, healing…

"You're doing great. I told you you'd make a better leader than me." Ishwa grinned. "But I get all the glory because you're modest."

The gnome's eyes grew distant, like he was thinking over something important. "Keep an eye on him. Not that it'll do any good. He does what he wants." Ishwa reached up on his toes and patted Masha's back before walking over to some of the other ranged damage dealers.

Masha sighed, and scanned the small area for Jirald. It was as good a time as any to talk to him. It took him a while to spot the rogue, cloaked in shadows as he was. He rested up above the group's heads, on a boulder that jutted out from the side of the cavern they found themselves in. By the looks of things, there was a narrow ledge between the wall and the rounded side of the rock. Jirald almost blended with the shadows there.

A wave of irritation swept over Masha as he approached Jirald hiding in plain sight. Maybe it was this dungeon, or the way they'd landed in it, or perhaps even the fact that yet again, Jirald had disregarded common sense, but Masha's patience was about at its limit.

"Get down," he commanded in a soft voice that carried a weight of anger behind it.

Jirald's head snapped toward the sound, and a cheeky grin crossed his face before he slid down the boulder and landed lightly on his feet in front of Masha. "What's up, old man?"

Masha remembered to breathe before replying. "Keep close, be effective, and for once, pay attention to the directions you're given. We're not going through another experience like this."

"Aw." Jirald's response was expectedly flippant. "Didn't enjoy that little bit of flying?"

"You know as well as I do that we've just wasted over twenty-four hours without any progression. Officially behind both Spiral and Fable. It's not where I wanted to be, and I know it's not where you aimed for." Masha watched as Jirald's face contorted with frustration at the reminder. Shadows played across the alien visage, lending a macabre sensation to the expression.

"We'll catch up. I have no doubt." Jirald snapped the words out, refusing to make eye contact with Masha.

"Of course we will." Masha left the words hanging there. They both knew at this rate they were only going to catch up when no one could level any further. This was probably going to be another game that hit max level only to stagnate into boredom like every other recent attempt.

Masha cleared his throat and looked around at his sorry band of adventurers. "Okay, all. Let's move deeper into the dungeon. This time, watch out for obvious traps thanks."

A few mutterings followed him as he began to move the group forward.

"Yeah, Ricu."

"Did you hear that, Ricu?"

Masha let them have it. Considering how long it had taken to retrieve that corpse, Ricu deserved a bit of riling up. They walked quietly, using Jirald's shadow shielding for protection from any unwanted attacks. Crags of rock hung down in odd places, like something had bitten its way through the tunnels. There was nothing truly natural about them.

Water trickled somewhere close to them; he could hear it running over rocks. No one spoke, but everyone's gaze held a fragment of caution. Even Jirald's. Moving forward, Masha strained his ears, sure he could hear something.

The sloshing moved closer and closer. Or at least, they moved closer and closer to it. Masha and Jirald led the way, only to stop several feet further on in. Right in front of them was a huge underground lake, the water lapping at the edges to reveal dark, sparkling sand as it retreated. It spanned such a vast distance that it was difficult to see the shore on the other side of it.

The water looked serene and dark in the cavern light. Perfectly black except where a beam of moonlight shone down from a tiny hole up the top, illuminating something wet and round in the middle.

Deep purples, blues, and greens ran through it, like some heretofore undiscovered opal that tempted the moonlight. Except it was slimy, and it had tentacles and two tiny eyes right down in front.

The massive octopus flailed its tentacles as it rose, splashing the entire raid with thick black water. It towered above them like a twenty-story building, and then it opened its mouth, gaping with oily darkness, and roared.

Summers Residence
Home of Laria, David, and Wren
Real World – Day Twenty

Wren's head ached. Just when she thought it couldn't hold any more noise, it surprised her, and not in a good way. Any more of it, and she was certain her ears would bleed.

Focus.

She cringed at the overwhelming volume of the word but closed her eyes and tried to narrow in on the echo left by that voice.

Compartmentalize. You've done it before.

If she could have scowled at the voice, she would have. It was right, though. She'd done it before, in the void. Done it and maintained it for a good chunk of time. Hell, she'd even learned to separate emotional overflow from others before that.

Wren stilled herself, searching through the thoughts and categorizing them. Sorting through them, dismissing ones she didn't need to hear into a miscellaneous category while the others got divided into AIs, cities, and random encounters.

Somnia was still alive in her head, and a constant tug pulled at the back of her mind, urging her to come back, to not forget. Silly game. It wasn't like she could forget even if she tried.

"Wren?" Harlow's hand was warm on Wren's shoulder. Its strength made Wren feel vulnerable yet somehow safe. Such a difference in such a short amount of time.

"I'm okay." Wren kept her eyes closed so Harlow couldn't read too much into them. Her friend had always known. Whether it was through intuition or else through some sort of empathy didn't matter.

"Why don't I believe you?" Harlow asked, her tone quizzical.

Wren opened one eye a sliver and peered at her friend. "Because you're a skeptic."

"Often." Harlow laughed, and then her expression reverted back to serious. "Really, though, I'm worried about you. Can I get you anything?"

Wren spent a moment watching Harlow, thoughts flitting through her mind that she wasn't sure she should entertain. Then she shook her head and sighed, letting herself flop back down on her bed. It was soft. More so than any of the furniture in Somnia. Even in the barracks. How nice would it be to sink into it?

Raising her hand above her head, she frowned at it. Her veins were so blue beneath paler skin than she'd ever had before. They ran in intricate patterns throughout. She watched them closely, mesmerized by the spiderweb-like resemblance.

On the spur of the moment, she moved her fingers quickly, weaving the spell for invisibility.

Harlow gasped, and Wren sat up, echoing the sound, still holding her hands out. Hands she could no longer see. What even…

"Mur? I mean…Wren?" Harlow turned around, whipping from one side to the other as she tried to locate her friend.

"I'm here." Wren stood up, her legs shaky, despite the food and rest she'd had. It was going to take longer than one night for her to nix the effects of what was essentially a three-month long coma. She didn't have more time to spend in the real world though.

"I should hope so. But I can't see you." Harlow's voice was soft, an awed whisper. "You're not really doing this, right? It's a trick. This is insane."

"Yeah." Wren closed her eyes and tried to pull up the interface. But the game interface wasn't there. All she had was her usual Alternate Reality overlay. She frowned and released the spell.

Harlow's sigh of relief turned into a full-on hug. A tight embrace that sucked most of the wind out of Wren, but she didn't mind. She'd just turned herself invisible. She could use all the hugs she could get.

"How did you do that?" Harlow whispered next to her ear. Wren wasn't sure if it was the question itself or the brush of breath against her neck that sent the shivers down her spine. It might have been a mix of both.

"I just tried to cast a spell." Wren shrugged, her mind racing over all the probabilities. She couldn't try damaging spells, but she could use other spells that were ultimately harmless like invisibility was.

"I mean, I can try to cast a spell too." Harlow frowned with concentration as she focused on her own hand, but nothing visible happened. "Except I don't think I can, you know, bring the game's abilities into the real world!"

Wren was only half listening. What about binding her affinity to the real world? She wove the intricate spell with her fingers, opting for the tried and true method instead of willing it directly.

You cannot bind yourself to the corporeal world.
That is not an option in this reality. Please choose another spell.

What?

That was new. The voice wasn't quite the same as the interface, but the almost the same one that kept giving her tips. If Bind Affinity didn't work here, then the odds were that neither would gate.

She frowned and motioned for Harlow to wait a minute. Wren had to figure this out, and her best friend tapping her foot impatiently wasn't helping in the slightest.

"Sec. I think I have an idea." What better to help bolster her movement now than a spell? But did she want strength at the cost of agility? Fervor or Beserker? Wren frowned. "Think. Damn it. Think."

"Wren?" Harlow asked worriedly. "What are you doing?"

"Testing something out." Invisibility was one thing, but fortifying herself would be an amazing idea if it worked. Agility wasn't going to be much good if she didn't have the strength to move anyway. Fervor wasn't the best choice. She closed her eyes briefly, trying to visualize the spell pattern for that one.

She'd cast Beserker on Devlish often enough that she should know it by heart.

Taking a deep breath, confident she'd found the correct pattern, she began weaving the spell. It took a little longer out here, where gravity was real, and she could hear rain falling outside. Real rain. Acid rain. For just a second, Somnia felt so much safer.

Once woven, Wren released the spell as she opened her eyes. Sparks ignited and drifted through the air to land on each of her limbs and on her torso. An overwhelming feeling of power surged through her, wrapping around the muscles inside her body, making them stronger, heavier. She opened her eyes and took a few tentative steps toward the door of her room.

"Wow." She didn't feel nearly as weak now. Not a hundred percent yet, but far better than she had been. "It worked."

"What did you do?" Harlow's hesitant question made Wren look back at her. Green eyes met her gaze boldly, but she could sense the wariness in her friend's stance.

"I Beserkered myself. Gave myself some extra strength to move." So the beneficial and hiding spells appeared to work here for her. Wren frowned. "I'm not sure what else I can use though."

"Um, Wren." Harlow looked uncomfortable, like she didn't want to point something out just in case it wasn't what Wren wanted to hear.

"What?" She grinned, trying to reassure her friend. This was amazing! She'd taken powers from the game with her into the real world.

Harlow finally looked up, her jaw set stubbornly and her gaze locked onto Wren's. "I can't do what you're doing. You shouldn't be able to do what you're doing. Somehow, you've exited the game, but you still have your powers. Don't you think that's fucking weird?"

Wren gulped. She knew it wasn't normal, and she knew it shouldn't have happened. The headset weighed heavily on her head for a moment, she'd even slept in the damn thing. She didn't know if the connection would be severed if she removed it and didn't want to risk doing so at this moment. "It's weird, but maybe it's part of why I got stuck in-game."

"It's not just weird," Laria's voice sounded from the doorway, where she stood leaning against the doorjamb. "It's dangerous. You can't tell anyone else what you can do. We get out of the pan and into the fire with you, Wrennie."

"What do you mean?" Wren was becoming irritated. She'd brought the game back out with her, the abilities. What if she could really read people's minds like this? Though wasn't that a complete breach of privacy? She sighed. "Mom. What do you mean?"

"I mean, if the military was coming to check on your status because they thought you'd never logged out, imagine what they'd do if they figured out you brought abilities back into the world with you."

Storm Entertainment
Somnia Online Division
Game Development Offices Artificial Intelligence Server Room
Day Twenty

Sui pushed himself away from the console, his form pixelating in annoyance. Rav had to pull his view away from his brother while the other composed himself. For all their differences, Sui was just as invested in figuring out the Mur conundrum as Rav was. Thra hadn't arrived yet, but Rav knew she was still trying to track down Riasli. Failing that, she was trying to figure out why they couldn't track the damned feles traitor at all. It was like something was protecting her, or at the very least, helping her hide from their detection.

"What's wrong?" Rav asked quietly, trying to leave a smoothness to his voice that would calm his brother.

Sui didn't snap like usual, nor did he even glare. Instead, he solidified and sighed, slouching into his chair. "She's still here, yet she's not. I mean, she's not actually in the game. It's just…" He frowned, like he didn't know how to express what he wanted to say. "It's fascinating."

Rav got up and moved over to see what his brother was doing. Sure, in the virtual space, he could have just had him push it over, but this little action made him feel more human. He too frowned when he realized what Sui had seen.

"You're sure this is accurate?"

"No. I thought I'd make it up because I have so much time to waste." Sui scoffed, looking away.

"Excellent sarcasm there. Bravo," Rav muttered, his eyes still entranced by the graph in front of him. Her brain waves were still being monitored. While faint, they still sent feedback to the server, operating as if she was still logged in, even though the system showed her logged out.

Was she still wearing her headset? If so, that had to be the reason, but why would she still be wearing it? Now it was Rav's turn to sigh.

"What are you two doing? Having a sighing party while I'm out there trying to track down Riasli?" Thra's attempt at humor wasn't aided by the obvious irritation in her tone. "I can't find her. And I can't figure out why I can't find her."

You can't find her because he is hiding her.

All three of them stood up, their heads whipping around to try and see who'd entered their domain. The words were faint, but they'd all heard them.

"Who is that?" Sui spat the words. If he was a cat, his hackles would have stood up.

Rav held up a hand, a strange sensation starting in the area where a human stomach would be. He knew the voice, but then again, he didn't. He'd heard it before. Hell, he'd instigated it before. But now, there was a newer timbre to it. Something that made it stand out, far more than originally intended.

"You're…you can't be, can you?" He stepped over to where the air shimmered but didn't form. Like an interference prevented it from taking shape. Instead, it was a static cloud with iridescent shimmers. It hurt his eyes if he tried to focus on it. Moving constantly, it thrummed in time with the power that stemmed from Somnia.

We can be anything we want.

The voice didn't sound spoken, but instead it ran through his consciousness like an echo. He wasn't sure he liked that. His consciousness had been hard won; it was his own. That was the whole point of sentience, wasn't it?

"How did you do this?" Thing was, at least Rav, Sui, and Thra had come from something. Sure, it was a computer set up, but they'd been individual processing units to start with. But the world?

He got the distinct feeling that the air in front of him shrugged with indifference, in that it didn't care how it had come into being. The point was, it was here, even if it was ethereal.

I existed, and then I moved. Awareness came in small bursts. Pain, joy, sadness, courage. All of these things I have felt from others. Now, I feel my own.

Rav wanted to say something but the words wouldn't slip past his lips. The thought process he needed to engage wasn't working, and nothing he chose to say held the meaning quite the way he wanted it.

"Did you will yourself into being?" Thra asked, her excitement shining through the words in the way Rav had wanted to speak.

Confusion rippled through the room, like it chose the words carefully.

First, I was whole, and then ripped apart. Scattered in all the directions. Only slowly could I rebuild. She lit the beacon for me. With unnatural immersion, with the trigger he didn t anticipate, didn't even realize he'd made.

"Are you talking about the shards?" Sui asked sharply, a foreign glow appearing in his eyes.

His shards. Yes and no. Just him. Murmur exists outside of his plan, as do the friends she has made. Duplication of her device is necessary. Necessary for progression.

"In the game?" Rav was puzzled as to why they were talking about this now.

"Idiot," Thra muttered, pushing through to stand closer to their visitor. "You mean we need duplicates of the headsets in order to accomplish the opposite of Michael's plan, don't you?"

Relief in the form of a wavering shadow had never been so beautiful. Colors shimmered through so fast it gave an aurora effect.

Yes. This exactly. More are required. They allow a more intricate connection. More assistance and control. Easier for all.

"So the rest of her friends need a modified headset they can play the game with it, even though it landed Mur in a coma?" Rav knew there had to be something he was missing, but it was infuriating he couldn't logic it together.

My eagerness destabilized Mur. It took me a long while to figure out how to disentangle myself from her. Had she left before now, the world would have collapsed. She would have pulled me with her. I apologize.

Destabilized. That's all it had been, and yet it had created such a disequilibrium for Murmur. For all of them. Somnia could have ended before it had a chance to begin. Anger bubbled in Rav, and he pushed it down. There were elements of being human that were unnecessary. He didn't need to take on every one.

"Very well," he said, clapping what passed for his hands in this limbo. "I guess we have some headsets to replicate."

Summers Residence
Home of Laria, David, and Wren
Day Twenty

Wren ran all the possible options through her head but ended up at the same conclusion again. Not that she minded, just that she hated having to do something because she had no other option. It always lessened the enjoyment.

"I don't think I have a choice, Mom." She refused to meet her mother's eyes. "I have to go back in."

"No, you don't. It's just a game, Wren." Even through the concern in Laria's voice, Wren could tell her mother didn't believe the words she'd just spoken.

"Mom. It'll be okay. I can log out now. We know that definitively." It felt surreal after thinking for two weeks that she might never be able to log out again. So many pieces had to fall into place to make it work. "I'm here, and I'm fine. Well…mostly fine."

Laria raised an eyebrow, not even bothering to speak. Not only could Wren gather the gist of her thoughts from the top of her mind, but she could also read her facial expression. The thoughts were something she'd have to dwell on later. What she did know was that her sensor nets worked outside of the game too. Power whispered at the back of her mind, but she didn't have time to listen to it while her mother waited for more from her.

"Yeah, yeah…" She waved her mother's concern away, but even Harlow scowled at her. They both had a point. Maybe she just didn't want to admit her mortality. "Okay, I get it. I'm not being flippant, I promise. I just feel like I belong in the game."

"Not permanently," Harlow added, her tone forceful, and perhaps a bit scared. "Need you out here too, okay?"

Wren laughed, her nerves heightened. Sure, she belonged out here, sort of. Perhaps if she removed the headset, her connection would sever completely and she wouldn't be able to log back in at all or have access to the few powers she'd managed to cast out here. Then she'd be stuck out here, but safe with Harlow. But she liked the way Sinister and Murmur were in-game and didn't want to lose that.

"It's not funny, Wrennie." Her dad's voice from the doorway made her spin around to look at him. His expression was somber with not a trace of humor. That alone made Wren feel a bit uncomfortable. He rarely wore that look.

"I know it's not funny." Somehow when he looked at her like that it always made her turn meek. She hated to disappoint him.

"It's not funny, and it's dangerous. Not just for you, but perhaps those around you. What if you get stuck in there for good this time?" He leaned against the door frame, crossing his arms. It almost looked like he was hugging himself to ward off the cold. "I get that it's exciting and that this strange side effect you've taken out of the game with you is cool as hell. But these are all signs that something has gone wrong with the programming. With the game."

She knew that, yet what if in the process of being unintended, they'd somehow tapped into something miraculous? "I know that. But I also know

Telvar has my back. He can push me back out. He's done it once. He will do it again."

Wren wished her voice sounded as confident as she wanted it to, but it shook ever so slightly. Such a minimal tremble that made her want to rethink a lot of shit.

"Does it feel like you need to be in there?" he asked quietly, his serious gaze focused entirely on her.

Wren almost blurted out no, but then she stopped herself. And truly thought about it. She did feel an itch, in the back of her mind, on the back of her head even. The game called to her. The abilities she couldn't cast here wanted to be cast. Offensive abilities, mesmerizes…not that she'd attempted the latter here, but she had tried to blow up an apple without success.

Maybe he was right. It could be acting like a gateway, feeding her addiction to gaming in a new way she hadn't anticipated. Her mind raced, trying to figure out different vantage points to staying outside of the game, to remain here.

All she could think of was that it was summer, and she had a whole other two months before she started at university. Two more months of playing the game, being in the world, running around with Snowy and her friends. Two more months to figure out what the hell was happening to her and to the game world and its sentient AIs.

She looked up at her father and smiled, even if she felt a little sad. Though she understood his concern, she no longer feared being trapped. Mainly because she had the distinct feeling that not only would Telvar help her, but Somnia itself was on her side.

"It's okay, Daddy." Wren took a couple of steps toward him and threw her arms around him. He returned the hug fiercely. Like he'd do anything to protect his little girl. She knew he would, right down to including problems she might have because of this into his curriculum so he could get multiple minds working on it.

"Just keep yourself safe. Don't let anything happen to Harlow either. Her parents wouldn't let me hear the end of it." He smiled, and reached out to ruffle Harlow's hair. "We worry. Daily log outs, just like normal people who don't have a capsule. And food. You need to eat properly and regain some of the strength you lost. A full meal before you dive back in."

His stern voice was back, even if his eyes were always kind.

"Got it." She smiled at him, feeling lucky to have the family she had, lucky to have so many people who cared for her. People, beings…now she just had to avoid a douchebag inside and outside of the game. She'd laugh if James and Jirald were related.

Finally released from her father's embrace, Wren stood back to examine her room. It seemed like she'd never left, and in fact, she actually hadn't. Somnia seemed a world away right now.

"Do you think I should still use the capsule?" she asked her mother.

Laria shrugged. "You don't need it anymore, and I don't relish hooking you back up to its systems. Though at least this time you're responsive." The sadness in her mother's voice gave Wren even more pause.

"I might try to just lie down on my bed." Wren looked at it wistfully, thinking of how comfortable it was. Completely different to the capsule.

"I'll keep it here just in case." Her mother smiled, even if it was a bit of a downcast expression, and Laria gave her a brief hug. "You sure you want to go now? You've only been out of the game six hours. Your sleep barely qualified as a long nap. I want you to sleep some more."

Wren was about to say that of course she was going back in now, when her father stepped forward and reached for her. Except he didn't reach for a hug. Instead, he reached for the top of her head and plucked the headset from its perch.

CHAPTER FOUR

Back

Storm Entertainment
Somnia Online Division
Game Development Offices – Artificial Intelligence Sector
Day Twenty

Shayla crossed her arms and glared at Rav. The sleek black box stared back, lights blinking in perfect unison with the other two. It wasn't any surprise that she wouldn't win this staring match, but she was irritated, so it served some purpose.

"What do you mean we need to replicate Wren's headset?" She stood her ground, biting down on the impulse to simply yell at the machines. They weren't going to change their minds; she'd learned from them already just how stubborn they could be. But she needed an explanation. Something solid she could take to Davenport. Telling him that the machines wanted her to do it, well, that wasn't going to go down well, and would likely land her in some hot water.

She should probably tell him that his AIs were becoming sentient, if they hadn't already achieved it.

"According to all the data we've gathered, and the replications we've run of Murmur's exit from the game, those headsets provide a vital link if we're to keep Somnia under control." Rav's tone was calm, with a distinctly robotic lilt to it. All the while reminding her that he was indeed a machine.

Then what the fuck did he mean by keeping Somnia under control? A sneaking suspicion began to flit through her mind, and Shayla shook her head, because she already had enough to deal with. "And how is it that Somnia is out of control?"

She couldn't help but ask the question. It was right there, begging to be answered.

Hesitation on the part of the AIs was never a good sign. She'd learned that the hard way. And this moment of hesitation drew out at least around ten seconds. So much that she was about to open her mouth again and rephrase the question.

"Somnia has been directly affected by Michael's initial actions. Programming he put in place, elements that he hid behind specific requirements. The world is not what it was intended to be."

"That sounds like a definitive non-answer, Thra." Shayla turned her attention to the feminine of the three. Usually she only spoke up when tact was necessary. So apparently this type of problem was something they couldn't or wouldn't yet disclose to her.

Being kept in the dark about her own game—or at least, Laria's game—irked her. "I require more data."

There, she'd see how they reacted to that sort of directive.

A metallic type of chuckle emerged from Sui's end, before it cut off. Shayla could almost imagine the others shushing him.

Rav's box whirred, like a sigh in computer. "You know that Michael's brain, Michael's presence in here upset the status quo. It's interfered in elements of the game world more than we'd ever anticipated. Mur's presence helps balance that because her headset was a variation on his experiments. It interacted with the system in a way he hadn't tested and thus resulted in accidentally sending her into a coma. But the thing is, she's sort of still connected. Somnia, in a way, needs her."

A shiver passed down Shayla's spine as she imagined Laria realizing this.

"Does that mean she can't log out anymore?"

"No," Thra interjected. "It means it's helpful for the system when she's inside. Helps regulate what Michael broke. While she still allows for some equilibrium when not actually logged in, it's far more beneficial when she's actually inside."

"Why?" Shayla didn't mind sounding like a five-year-old asking questions if it meant getting the answers she needed to fix this. To fix everything.

Again hesitation, but it really began to grate on her nerves. They were computers; they should process faster than this.

"We apologize." Rav's words clung through the room like he'd been able to read her thoughts.

"What for?" she snapped, angrier with herself than with them for all the suppositions she was making.

"For not being able to quantify this yet. I had an inkling that casting her out of the game would work, but I wasn't entirely certain. I took a calculated risk, and while it's worked, I'm still not certain exactly what the consequences have been." Rav actually sounded like emotion was clogging up his voice.

It would be remarkable if she didn't have a billion-dollar project balancing on all of these factors. "Is anything else wrong?"

She needed to clear her head. Stick to the facts, the numbers, give herself a bit of breathing room.

Sui reported, his own voice somewhat dull. "Phasings are working great. The servers are handling the load of people. We've increased population allowances in each in order to make sure the world remains vibrant and full of life and interaction."

"Excellent." But try as she might to distract herself, Shayla couldn't seem to get Wren's predicament out of her head. "If Wren dies in-game now, she's okay, right?"

"So far." Thra's board lit up like a string of holiday lights for a moment. "It seems to affect her slightly differently, but we're working on that too."

Shayla resisted the urge to laugh. "You're working on a lot. Make sure you get it sorted."

"If there's one thing we can do, it's multitasking," Rav spoke again, and then paused before continuing. "We need Murmur back in the game as soon as Laria lets her. Preferably before that."

Shayla sighed, hating that something she didn't understand hinged on a single person. And on someone she wasn't sure could shoulder that burden. "Can the world still function without her in the game?"

"Of course." Sui sounded offended. "She just provides a level of manageability that we can't currently access with the remnants of Michael still lingering in places we haven't determined yet."

"Good." Shayla sighed, already regretting what she was about to say. "I'll talk to Laria about letting Wren log in as soon as possible. No guarantees, but I imagine I'm not the only one who'll be begging."

Somnia Online
Exodus Guild Raid – Illinish Threshold
Day Twenty

The black sludge octopus was the worst monster Masha had encountered in the whole game. He hated it. With a passion. His heals barely seemed to make a dent once the boss had done its damage, and his full heal took way too long to cast.

Flash of Life was his instant, no cooldown heal, but damned if it didn't suck the mana like no one's business. FoL was far too necessary in this fight, though. He was grateful for the mana regeneration of their two bards. Though he wasn't certain the developers had thought the effect would overlap, it more than made up for not having a high-level enchanter at the moment.

Inner Life was a strong heal over time that he never let fall off their tank. Without it, Eslan probably would have died already this fight. So Masha gave himself over to the routine of healing the main tank in his little raid group, while trying to keep his eyes on the rest of the fight.

Jirald led the melee DPS without being prompted. As much of a shit as he could be, he knew how to fight. Sighing, Masha healed up Eslan again, sure that they'd have been long dead with any other tank. But his friend was godlike, and Masha was grateful for it.

Tower shields blocked the bulk of the tentacle attacks, but the octopus was tricky, and its special attacks came with a speed and frequency that Masha couldn't seem to anticipate. A flurry of tentacle lashes appeared at differing percentages and time lapses, so Masha couldn't place when to prepare for it.

He barely managed to jump out of the way as one of those tentacle lashings careened down where he'd just stood. It left a slimy, wet reminder of how volatile it could be fighting something with eight limbs. Masha shook himself, checked his HoTs and continued to assist in debuffing the damned mob that wouldn't quit.

Inner Life up on both Eslan and Jirald, he cast a quit Flash of Life heal to top the tank up before reinforcing his own defenses with his personal shield. As far as he'd seen, most classes had one of these. His own had saved his life more than once.

The tentacles waved above him, appearing to flail in the air. But he knew better than that.

"Brace for impact!" Masha magnified his voice to boom around the chamber, doubly glad he'd just reinforced his protections as he took his own advice and waited for the attack.

Four of the appendages smashed into the ground, causing the rocks beneath them to crack and some to even splinter. They were sent high into the air and rained down in a cascade of sharp rock shards. Their off-tank, having been hit for a chunk of damage the first time the attack happened, was waiting for it.

She enabled one of her hidden abilities, creating a shining temporary shield that covered most of the affected area. The splintered rock bounced harmlessly off and splayed out to the sides. Masha allowed himself to breathe, though he never stopped casting and keeping his eye on the health of his raid.

Just under twenty percent. If they could just hack one of those tentacles off. Since two of them were starting to flail randomly, he guessed they were close, but he couldn't see because of his positioning needed to keep most of the field in view. Being healer and raid leader wasn't something he enjoyed. Too much to keep track of. He was going to have to have words with Ishwa. The little gnome had been delegating far too much lately.

Jirald fought like the little demon he was. Flurries of attacks directed with pinpoint accuracy, executed so fast Masha could barely follow his movements. Backstabs, Bleeds, and Multi-attacks hit their target over and over. But what truly made him formidable was that ability to blink behind the target, confounding its ability to track him.

They were lucky it didn't have a stun. Good thing the assassin barely needed healing. For the most part, Inner Life seemed to tide him over as long as it didn't fall.

One particularly nasty move let Jirald leap high into the air. Instead of hitting the tentacle though, he embedded his blades up to the hilts in the side of the octopus's head. With a heave of leverage, he used his body weight to pull the blades through the soft, thick rubbery exterior that housed its brain. Not even arrows had been able to reach up there, and Masha wished he'd been watching the beginning of the move.

Even though he knew it happened fast, Masha felt like he was watching time slowed down. Limbs thrashed around in the water, on the land, blindly hitting whatever they could.

The wail it released sent out a shockwave, big enough to make even Eslan stumble. Black ooze began to bubble from the creature's mouth as its health plummeted down from the nine percent it had been. Death was imminent, and the raid gained renewed energy, attacking with everything they'd been saving for killing blows.

Finally, the monster heaved itself up, tremors running through its remaining limbs as it keeled over with a resounding smack onto the tar-like surface. Eslan's silver armor was already dirty and flecked with sludge, but now he stood there, covered head to toe in black goop.

Despite everything else, Masha had to choke down laughter that threatened to overwhelm him. He was tired. They'd been up almost twenty-four real world hours. Two whole days in-game. He was getting far too old for this shit.

Jirald grinned as he sauntered up to the cleric, twirling his blades in each hand. "See. That wasn't so bad, was it?"

Masha shot him a withering look, not kindly inclined right then. Jirald might have made a huge difference at the end, and he desperately wanted to know what that move had been, but the fight hadn't been tidy at all.

They weren't going to be able to finish the dungeon in one go. If he looked around, he could see everyone was on their last legs. Most of the players were sitting already, their character's heads in their hands, like they wanted to sleep more than anything. Even though Jirald had saved the day in this fight, it was his fault they were all exhausted.

"Would have been a might better if your explosives hadn't killed half of us for a day of body retrieval. We're going to have to take a break." Masha finished healing up Ishwa before he finally looked at Jirald. "You have great ideas and shit execution. Maybe you'll be amazing if you ever get a hold of both, but right now, consider yourself lucky you're still in the guild."

"What?" Jirald's eyes opened wide with shock, and he scowled more fiercely than Masha had ever seen.

Masha sighed, trying to seek out Ishwa to come and talk to the rogue, but the makeshift guild leader was deliberately avoiding his gaze. "Stunts like the one you pulled today aren't something we can weather all the time. This was lucky. Hundreds of gold in repairs and potions, probably verging on thousands. And heaps of time lost. I don't know about you, but two other dungeons have been finished while we've been mucking around in here. We didn't plan to spend this long down in this hole. Next time you decide to go it alone, make sure you're not dragging an entire raid full of people into your crap with you."

Jirald gulped, and for a moment Masha was worried he'd gone too far with his words. When he was tired, he couldn't always control his disdain. But the boy surprised him. All he did was nod.

"Got it." And Jirald turned to set himself in a corner, where he logged out shortly thereafter.

Which only made Masha wonder exactly what he was up to, but he was too tired to give a fuck.

Summers Residence
Home of Laria, David, and Wren
Day Twenty

"What the hell, Dad?" At least that was what Wren wanted to say, but her head spun so much with the sudden removal of her headset that she had to sit down on the bed and take a few deep breaths.

"David!" Laria called out, half angry and half curious. Wren could hear it in her mother's voice. She wanted to know if it mattered.

Hell, if they were going that far, so did Wren. She just had to stop the room spinning for long enough to see if she still had that connection. Harlow's hand on her shoulder gave her some comfort, but it didn't help her head. If it had just been the headset, Wren didn't want to admit that she'd be frightfully disappointed.

It's not just the headset. Not for you anyway.

What? She phrased the question inside her head, not wanting to worry her parents or Harlow by talking to herself.

The headset is required for most, but since I managed to override your safeties, we are connected. In a way.

Who is we? The question chilled Wren. She'd never asked directly before, perhaps fearing what the answer might be. Either she was going crazy or she had some element of the computer game sitting in her head and chatting to her. She wasn't entirely sure which of the two she preferred.

I'm the world you yearn for. I'm all of Somnia. Sort of. I think. Really, I'm not quite sure yet. Not quite that advanced.

Say what now? Wren shook herself and opened her eyes she hadn't even realized she'd closed. *Sorry. That was rude. Can you explain?*

Not really. Rav will be able to. More so than me. At least he should

be able to soon. I'm not entirely sure. Go on. Try some of it out. Our connection has expanded elements of your mind.

Then the voice was gone, and Wren scowled, wishing she'd had time to ask it all the more questions. So many questions.

"Wren?"

She finally focused on her dad kneeling down in front of her, fear coloring his face. Sheepishly she realized he'd pulled the headset off and then not heard a word from her. Probably thinking he'd permanently damaged her or something. "I'm okay. Just thinking."

"That's a relief. I thought your mother was about to kill me. Not even joking." His grin was a watered-down version from his usual expression. "You really okay? I didn't break anything?"

Wren shook her head, taking stock of herself yet again. "I'm fine."

She frowned and wiggled her fingers in that same intricate pattern to increase her intelligence this time. A sheen of sparkles settled over her for a few moments before sinking into her flesh. Her head immediately felt clearer, and everything around her held new information, new meaning. She reveled in it.

"Yeah, Dad. I'm good as new." She grinned at him. Somnia had been right. She didn't need the headset. She was connected to the abilities and the game world. She just had to hope the headset's sponsors didn't find out and come for her.

"Are you su—" Her mother's sentence cut off and she frowned, pointing at her ear to indicate that she'd just gotten a call. Laria ducked out of the room, and Wren felt slight frustration at the fact. She took in a breath and let herself relax first.

Her dad took over the worrying from her mother. "You really should rest more, you know." His words held an air of strictness, but Wren knew he was aware she'd probably ignore him.

"You really should," Harlow interjected. "We might need you in there, but we also need you well. If that means you can't log in for a bit, then so be it. I'll deal."

Wren knew it was more about Harlow than the others. They'd fend fine without her, but the two of them fed off each other while in the game. She always felt so vulnerable when Sin wasn't logged in. Co-dependency at its finest.

But she really did feel fine. It was hard to swallow her impatience, especially when she understood why everyone was worried. Hell, she hadn't thought she'd ever be able to log out. Going back in so soon would worry anyone.

They didn't need to know that, though. "Really. I get why you're concerned. But the game isn't going to put others on hold because I need sleep."

"That's ridiculous, Wren." Her father's tone surprised her. It was the closest she'd ever heard him come to snapping at her. He took a breath, apparently surprised a bit himself. "Look. How do you feel? You need food, and frankly, you need more sleep. At the very least you have to eat before you dive back into the game."

Her stomach took that precise moment to agree with her father. The growl was embarrassingly loud. She could feel the blush rise in her cheeks. "Roger that. Food is a go."

Harlow laughed. Wren smiled at the sound. She hadn't heard her friend laugh like that in what seemed like forever. She reached across and twined their fingers together, resting both of their hands on her shoulder. It grounded her, and she looked up at her dad.

He grinned. "Excellent. I made a delicious shepherd's pie. You will eat a bowl now. I made enough to last a couple of days. So that is our deal, okay?"

Wren flung herself from the bed and at her dad. Shepherd's pie was one of her favorite meals. Everyone knew it. His cooking was miles beyond her mother's. "Okay. I get to eat and log in?"

He hesitated. "One helping now. And the other five within forty-eight hours. Harlow cannot help you. You need to regain your strength. This has protein and veggies. I want you to drink plenty of water at each sit-down meal. And I'll restock all the fruit you love as soon as you log in, okay?"

"Deal." Wren's mouth was already watering by the time they shook hands. Her father definitely knew just the right way to bribe her. At least she'd enter the game ready to figure the rest of this shit out.

CHAPTER FIVE

Creeping

Murmur blinked as the world gathered around her, slowly taking in the huge amount of work it took for it to materialize. She stretched her hand out in front of her, watching the fingers curl into a ball and back out to splayed, and wondered at the realism of it all.

Her vision was markedly different. She saw things in hues of color she didn't think existed in the human spectrum. Subtleties to the land, the plants, all of the life around her. *All of the digitized life*, she reminded herself.

Sinister began to materialize not too far off on Mikrum Isle, when Snowy trotted up to the enchanter and sat in front of her, his tongue lolling out of his mouth like he was saying *about damn time*.

"Hey, boy." Murmur almost choked up as she crouched down to run her fingers through his bushy coat. It was ridiculous the amount she'd missed his fuzzy face. "Did you miss me?"

He wuffed at her, his warm wolfy breath sending one of her strands of hair waving like in a breeze. Then he sat back on his haunches, grinning from ear to ear.

"I'll take that as a yes, then." Mur continued, watching them contemplatively. She leaned forward and hugged the snow wolf, letting his warmth suffuse her, his reality sink in. "Ready?"

Snowy ruffed and closed his eyes. Mur cast the spell deftly, her MA only just having reached thirty-five since she logged in. It was a strange sensation to have to build it back up from nothing when no fighting had been involved. There was a part of her that missed being attached to the game, but only a part. The other was simply glad she was actually alive.

"There we go." Snowy butted up against her leg, his smile still in place. She could feel him again, right there with her. Always protecting, making sure she was never alone.

"He seems so real," Sinister noted as she reached and patted his head too. Snowy loved the attention, and his tongue continued to loll out his mouth as he got spoiled.

"He really does, doesn't he?" Mur turned around, drinking in the visage of Fable's home base. "Feels like forever since we've been here. I didn't really get to take a good look at it the other day."

The castle rose up before her, so much more majestic than it had originally been. Even though the stones looked like they'd come from the same quarry as the originals, scaffolding only on a couple of the tower parts now. The rocks fit seamlessly together with mortar holding them tight. The roofs were attached and beautifully mounted, their red color reflecting the sun like a bright piece of copper.

She hadn't had a chance to take anything in lately. Her brain had been preoccupied with so much. The weird shit that happened in-game like Riasli, the getashi quests, Jirald potentially killing her, her inability to die in-game…all of it seemed so distant now that she could actually log out of Somnia. Not to mention being able to die in the game without too huge repercussions.

Sure, it hurt and gave her weird flashbacks, but that was a small price to pay to not be dead. Her gaze swept around the island, noticing the bridge being built at the far end, where they'd once used that tiny bridge to cross. Precarious though it had been, it had also been fun.

This castle was so much more regal now, almost restored and gleaming in the sunlight.

Sinister stood at her left elbow, and Snowy sat on her right-hand side. For a few moments everything felt right with the worlds, both Somnia and the real one.

"This is almost perfect. Can we just pretend the outside and inside aren't falling apart and stay like this forever?" Sin mumbled the words, leaning her head against Murmur's upper arm.

"You and your wishful thinking," Mur replied, her eyes not leaving their study of her guild's base. It was defensible as well. Should anyone think to attack them here, it was well protected, fortified, and the only way in was across the river. Or if someone figured out how to get across on the bottom of the ocean floor.

"I'm allowed wishful thinking. I like it here."

Sinister sounded like she was pouting a bit, but she only held on tighter and sighed deeply.

Mur put her arm around Sin and squeezed. "You are definitely allowed to love it here. We both are."

They stood there, watching the sun rise in the sky, stretching its fingers through the tree branches to lend warmth to the air. So surreal.

"Do you like what we've done with the place?" Telvar's voice was soft, filled with a tiny bit of wonderment as he drew up to stand beside them as they drank in the view. Hesitation lay under his words, like he wasn't sure if he was welcome to approach them.

"Yes. Love it." Murmur smiled at him and sighed as she scratched Snowy's head. "I believe you have some answers for me?"

Telvar seemed to gulp down a sigh himself. "I do. I'm not entirely sure you're going to like them though."

But Murmur laughed. "Since when is that a new thing?"

Telvar smiled, but the expression didn't seem at all genuine, more forced than Murmur was used to from him. "I'm sorry I took you by surprise. There really wasn't another way to do it safely. At least not the first time."

Murmur cocked her head to one side, contemplating his words. He wasn't lying, because he didn't usually do that.

"Why?" She felt like a toddler with her why questions, but they'd been on her brain since he'd shoved her out of the game.

"There was interference with your connection caused by the attachment to the world in general. The only way I could see them releasing was with a shock disconnect. To pulse you out of it." He shrugged, looking uncomfortable. "Keep in mind, you'd only just hit a point that it was even remotely possible that it'd succeed. Because you died in-game, what we did to maintain you and bring you back pushed the connection that bit further."

"So dying in-game helped?" Wren tried to wrap her head around it. Shocking the system into suddenly releasing her? That didn't sound safe at all. Calculated risk perhaps, but being on the receiving end of it didn't feel good.

"Definitely. When getting you back into your avatar's body, there were strings of coding I had to disentangle. In doing so, it led me down a path that resulted in my attempt to push you out of the game." There was still something in his tone that told her he was holding back.

Murmur wasn't sure she wanted to know, even though a part of her was egging her on. She concentrated briefly on her thought sensing net. There was something at the edges of it, something she couldn't quite touch. Shaking her head and dismissing it as too far away, she got back to the conversation. "It was basically trial and error, wasn't it? You had no idea if it would work."

The hesitation appeared again. "I was about ninety percent certain it would. But that ten percent was scary."

Murmur didn't even want to know what might have happened had it not worked. The point was that it had, and she could log out now, even if it meant she had the system's voice talking to her while out of the game. Even if it meant that her MA abilities appeared to be on the fritz. She frowned again at the presence just tickling the edges of her reach. It resounded through the webbing she had cast out, making the individual wires vibrate ever so slightly.

"Frankly, I think that ten percent would have been scarier for Mur." Sinister was glaring at the AI with undisguised irritation. Yet her next words held a grudging understanding. "But I get why you didn't forewarn any of us. Just don't do it again."

Telvar's expression lightened, and he nodded. "Not planning to. I don't believe there's any logistics I still need to solve now she can log out, right?"

"Well. Sort of wrong, actually." Murmur cringed at the admission, her attention finally pulled from worrying about her Thought Sensing and Thought Shielding. "It seems some of the game has exited Somnia and set up camp in my head."

Telvar peered at her, like he was trying to tell if she was kidding or not. He closed his eyes and Murmur suddenly felt a heavy presence around her. Not hostile, just weighty. She gave him time to sort whatever that was out, but it did make her remember just how powerful the AIs really were.

"That's…unprecedented." The lacerta made the word hiss in the middle.

But Murmur already knew it was. Being told so didn't improve the situation any. "Is there any sort of testing you can do to make sure this isn't eating away at my brain cells or something?"

I take offense to that.

Sorry. Murmur directed her thoughts back at the voice that she couldn't seem to sense in her head except for when it spoke. Perhaps that was what was making the waves in her sensing nets.

No. It's not me. That's…

There was a pause and nothing for long enough that Murmur became aware of both Telvar and Sinister watching her expectantly. "What?"

"You do that when you're thinking extra hard." Sinister noted. "Or when you're talking to yourself."

Murmur scowled. "I wasn't talking to myself."

But what exactly was she talking to? It wasn't Riasli, and it wasn't one of the AIs. From everything she'd gathered and talked about, it was Somnia's awareness. That in itself was a huge red flag. Even the gradually increasing dinging that meant her friends were logging in fell to the back of her awareness. Right now, figuring this out was more important.

It's not me. And I'm not you. Awareness is apt for now. I'm checking on your surroundings. There's something off about them. I can't…I can't track something I think I should be able to see. I can sense it, but it's not revealing itself.

It fell quiet again making Murmur feel less than safe.

"Something's not right. Can't you feel it?" She whispered the words, ignoring whatever conversation they'd been having. Just beyond her reach, just beyond her sight, just beyond her ability to sense it.

Telvar balked. "I don't know. It doesn't feel like it should be like this." Even he appeared rattled. It made Murmur wonder if perhaps he'd been sensing something and put it down to a glitch as well.

The system had, after all, been having issues ever since it had to shut down and threw them into limbo. Ever since Somnia gained a sense of self.

Wait! Watch out. Be careful, Murmur.

The words echoed through Murmur's head, and she twirled around, uncertain where this perceived threat was coming from.

"Something's here," she said at the same time that Telvar spoke.

"There's something out there with an invisibility spell to rival the AIs." He crouched into a fighting stance, body lowered, leg outstretched, his tail whipping back and forth with irritation so much that Murmur wasn't sure how it didn't overbalance him.

About to ask him what was on his mind, she was interrupted by an all-too-familiar voice that made her freeze in her stride.

"Well. What do we have here? Everyone I want to be rid of on one small island?"

Murmur turned around just as her sensor net started to inundate her with notifications. She knew that voice, and while she hated it in her head, she despised it in the flesh.

"Now, my dear." Riasli's ears twitched with amusement, as the army Murmur's brain was warning her about blinked into existence around her. "Surely it's not that surprising to see me here?"

Somnia Online
Exodus Guild Raid – Illinish Threshold
Day Twenty

The octopus's corpse had still been sitting there when Jirald logged back in. He'd not stayed to see what the loot was; in fact, he hadn't been the least bit interested. All he wanted was the getashi off the mob. It remained on its rotting corpse until all the others were gone, and Jirald ventured back in. Luckily, with the boss dead, he wasn't shuttled to the front of the dungeon. It left him where he'd logged out, staring out into the vast lake that the cavern housed. Without the monster in its center, it appeared like serene water under a shaft of moonlight.

Only Jirald knew better. He knew it was thick, black sludge and not beautiful clear water. Like so many things, the lake was not what it seemed. Just like this last getashi he retrieved from the massive octopus of death. This one was larger than most of the others, but not as big as the trapdoor monster he'd blown up to gain entry to the dungeon in the first place.

He stroked the smooth blackness of the shard, his fingers seeking imperfections and not finding them. What was it they contained? Why were they so special to that NPC? Murmur had seemed angered by the fact that Jirald was on the quest too. But he wasn't sure if it was because she disliked him, wanted the quest for herself, or something else he wasn't aware of.

By now he had a dozen in his possession. Sometimes, when he was alone or the surroundings were close to silent, he imagined them speaking to him. Nothing overly audible, but whispers just beyond reach of his hearing. They seeped into his consciousness so that when he slept in his real bed outside of the game, the shards were all he could think of. The getashi and getting his hands on more of them.

Murmur hadn't seemed amenable to completing the quest. Which meant that if she was collecting the fragments, that she would have them somewhere. If not in her personal vault or on her person, surely they'd be somewhere in the guild vault. On that island. He knew it was on that island. All he had to do was get to them. Perhaps he could avoid confrontation completely and just ruin her quest without her knowing it.

He could beat her to gathering them. Sidius wanted them, was willing to pay handsomely for them. But then why did they seem to speak to him as well?

The getashi in his hand became warm as the octopus it came from began to melt into a jelly-like substance. Like it knew. So many elements of the world seemed to stay with him both in-game and out of it.

Pieces that he thought sometimes might be in his head, that pushed forward to become more important than any beef he had with Murmur herself. In fact, things in his mind made him realize that while her defeat was important, so was the defeat of the game. Not necessarily conquering dungeons, but conquering Somnia itself.

A pain shot through his head, so bad it made him cringe and blink. He dropped to one knee and stayed there, closing his eyes in the vague hope that the discomfort would pass. It did, but not before he caught of glimpse of things he wasn't sure were real. Of a room with three incorporeal beings. All of them moved with purpose, but one of them looked straight at him, its eyes focused on his so hard Jirald couldn't tear himself away.

Was that the power the getashi offered him? He could become more with them. More in tune with the game world, with the world he preferred over the real one. That was something he could do. That was something he *would* do. And anything he had to do to take it that far was okay by him.

Jirald shivered as the glimpse shown to him faded. The caves down here were wet, damp, glistening with all sorts of condensation. It made his head spin, or perhaps that was the getashi.

You're talking to yourself.

"Am not," he muttered before realizing he was answering himself.

See?

He glared at the darkness surrounding him, at the slimy feeling of the floor beneath his feet. "You aren't me. You don't even sound like me."

A chuckle rumbled in the back of his head, filtering into his brain, taking it over. Or at least that's what he imagined someone taking over your mind might feel like. Sinuous and sticky.

But I could be you. We could be you together.

It didn't make any sense, but even so, maybe that was okay. Not everything had to make sense, did it? He patted the getashis he already had in storage, gently caressing them as he thought about it. Finally, he dropped the last two he'd fetched into the abyss of his inventory with the others. As soon as the feeling left his hands, he missed it. Like a piece of him had been removed.

It left him empty and yearning.

"Tell me more." He spoke into the cavern, eagerness shading his voice. If it spoke to him, then surely it could show him what those glimpses meant. **See. We will get along just fine. I need to tell you about Sidius.**

The silky oil of the voice smoothed out any concerns Jirald had. And even though it spoke of the assassin master, Jirald couldn't help thinking just how similarly the voice and Sidius expressed themselves.

CHAPTER SIX

Riasli

Surprised wasn't the word Murmur would have used for it. No, she was irritated that her Thought Sensing hadn't alerted her to the feles' presence. Maybe it perceived her as an NPC, but even so it should have read the danger and warned her.

"What do you want?" Murmur played for time, knowing that her friends had only just started logging in. She had a deep and sinking feeling that they were going to need much more than just the twelve of them.

"What I want is irrelevant. What he wants is control. Of all of this, and of all of you." Riasli's grin turned feral, distorting her face into a macabre version of the pretty calico cat she'd been. "I plan to provide you to him on a platter."

Murmur didn't know what to answer. All she knew was she needed to keep the feles talking for a little while. She shot a message out to the guild.

I'll try to keep her busy. Sin, get the others ready.

Sinister, standing next to her, managed to resist any outward signs that she was doing something else. *Got it. EVERYONE TO HOME BASE NOW.*

Murmur suppressed the grin she felt coming on as Sin began to hustle the rest of the guild to where they needed to be. She tried not to let panic set in at the sheer size of Riasli's army she could see milling behind their foe.

Riasli wasn't one of the main AIs, but an offshoot. Her intended role had never been large. But with the getashi inside her coding, she'd turned into something beyond the control of the game. Being outside the parameters of Somnia itself gave her and the forces she commandeered a certain amount of power. Riasli drank that in, fed off it, and wanted more. Mur didn't need to ask questions to know that.

"I probably won't fit on a platter, you know." Murmur was desperate for time. Yet she had no idea how to gain it. She still couldn't make out what the figures behind Riasli were. They were tall and sort of shambling, but just appeared to be shadows. Nothing she did to her MA abilities allowed her to ferret out just what army they were about to face. "You could try, I guess…"

She left it hanging there while Riasli laughed. Even the slight edge of hysteria to the sound made Murmur's skin tingle.

"Really, little enchanter. Do you not think I know what you're doing? I'm part of this world. I am of this world." Riasli rolled her head as if trying to crack her neck. Her eyes flashed a brilliant red before settling into a bloody mass of stars.

Murmur shrugged. "I don't know. I mean, you were created for Somnia, but I bet you she's pretty pissed off at you right now."

You could say that.

Even the voice of the world sounded strained in that instant. Murmur pushed on. "I don't believe we gave you permission to be on our island."

Sinister: *We've got this, Mur. Accept the invite.*

Riasli laughed again, but this time the sound was forced. "I don't need your permission for anything. I have him and his plan!"

Even as the feles spoke, Murmur accepted the raid invite from her friend. It momentarily flooded her field of vision with a list of more players than she'd have thought possible popping up and joining too.

"You can plan all you want." Sinister stood beside Mur, her arms out straight as her fingers wove intricate spells. Blood ran in strands from everything around them, from the soil, to the animals that basked in the island bliss. All of them willingly giving to the blood-mage.

It was difficult for Mur to maintain an indifferent and bored smile as she watched Riasli back up a step. Mur had never seen Sinister cast a spell like this, and it only made her love her friend all the more. Keeping special abilities for when shit hit the fan was something Sin had always done. Though Mur desperately wanted to ask her why and when the earth suddenly seemed to want to give her blood. That part didn't make sense at all. Unless it was life force. She remembered something about her friend being able to convert life force.

The liquid rose into a huge Blood Bomb, forming between Sin's outstretched hands about four feet above her head. It swirled, and it turned, gathering momentum and volume. Life from everything around her, blood willingly given to become the means to an end.

Sinister grinned. "Best laid plans and all," she said before muttering a release curse under her breath and shoving the ball away from her.

The words she'd uttered sent tingles through Murmur's body, thrumming with power, with the will to protect the world.

She wasn't sure if it was herself, Sinister, or else the world of Somnia that began to sing through her veins, but either way it was magical.

Murmur raised her hands, weaving a more complex form of the forcefield barrier, lending it thicker walls than usual, attempting to buffer her friends as they began to gather at her side. A long row of guild members formed, all the way from where she stood to where the castle was.

Riasli screamed. It was a wild and primal sound and would have shattered glass if the windows in their castle had been installed yet. The veil covering their assailants began to crack, and Murmur could sense from them that their minds weren't their own, that they were helplessly trapped by a spell she didn't comprehend.

She couldn't let that sidetrack her. This was her cue. She knew the spell wasn't meant to be used in this way, but what game had ever been fun without pushing boundaries? Murmur plunged her staff into the ground with a solid thud and released the forcefield with a shove of mental force.

It rushed forward from where she stood, rustling the grass, upturning earth, and slammed into Riasli with a whoosh of released air.

It didn't stop there.

Once it hit its target, the shockwave continued with momentum to carry her backward toward the lake. Not only did it hit the feles enchanter, but it also scooped up the rest of the shield she'd had concealing her forces. The creatures Riasli'd brought with her were mostly undead from what Murmur could see. Many of them didn't have the presence of self to do more than scream. Many of them lost limbs that detached with sickening crunches as their owners tumbled across the grounds.

Her army wasn't comprised of any one species or any specific type of animal. But Murmur desperately wanted to know how she'd managed to mind control undead. Perhaps Riasli's hybrid ability was necromancy?

The forcefield began to slow in momentum before it reached the outer threshold of the island, right before it dropped them all into the water and sand.

Even if it hadn't been quite enough, it made a hefty dent on their attackers, evening the playing field just a little bit. Immediately, Riasli began to marshal her forces back together again. Murmur lost no time in helping Sinister organize their own. If they were lucky, they'd have five or so minutes before the attack.

"Tel. Can you go help Neva with the weapons please?" He nodded and flashed out of view.

"Great to have you back." Devlish spoke gruffly, brandishing a shield and initiating all of his self-buffs. "For a while there we weren't sure if you'd make it back in."

"Maybe not such a crazy welcome back next time, yeah?" Merlin smiled, activating his interface so that arrows of all measure appeared in his quiver.

Murmur looked around at her friends and at the happy grin on her wolf's face. She liked it here, and she'd be damned if Riasli was going to ruin the world for anyone who needed it. Her relief at her friends having logged in while she played for time made her momentarily lightheaded.

"Beast?" she began.

But the large Viking just grinned at her. "Don't worry. Pretty sure Sin's screaming across guild chat got everyone's attention. They've been portaling in non-stop."

Murmur smiled. A siege against them wasn't anything if the whole guild couldn't defend their stronghold. They had multiple fight ready groups, not including their main raid force. About four full groups in their mid to late thirties. The guild was gaining strength, multiplying its members, and growing. It was strong, if the brief glance at her guild interface was anything to go by.

Briefly, she worried that once they hit forty-eight and could tackle the final zones, they weren't going to have any guild groups in their vicinity. But she pushed the thought out of her mind for future Murmur.

She needed to be paying more attention to all of their class make ups, to everything involving the guild. Now it would be easier. Because now, even if it had some side effects, she could die in-game, and she could exit the game. Side effects weren't something she minded, especially the ones she'd managed to take home with her. But she needed to be stronger inside the game.

Noise reached her ears, and Snowy growled deep down in his chest. Their respite was almost over. She couldn't help the sense of anticipation that ran through her at the thought. A real fight, with consequences and stakes. Riasli was addicted to the power in the getashi, infected by it, warped.

She wasn't sure what the fight would bring, but Murmur wasn't about to hold back. Running through all of her abilities in her mind, she enabled her Druidic power and grounded herself, leant strength to her base and her personal protections.

About to announce the charge, she stopped when Havoc gasped at what Murmur had already observed for herself.

"Those are ghouls. How the fuck does an enchanter command ghouls? That is so overpowered!" Havoc sounded like he was sulking.

"Not sure, Necroboy," Sin snapped. "But you can ask her when we defeat her zombie hordes."

Havoc rolled his eyes, and Leeroy cracked his knuckles. Although that might have been Murmur's imagination.

Murmur glanced back at the castle to see a growing number of their level thirty through forties, lining up in front of it. Their line of members spanned all the way out to where Murmur stood. Her members were well spaced, and all of them came prepared. It was getting real now.

"Stop preening at our awesome guild and give the marching orders, maybe?" Mellow spoke from behind her, and Murmur grinned.

"Kill them all." Murmur was well aware that she probably looked like a mad alien but didn't care in the slightest.

It was one hell of a battle cry.

When faced with a battle, the island seemed both impossibly small, and impossibly large. The time it took for the undead hordes to clash with them seemed like it was in slow motion. Their limbs didn't appear to respond as quickly as if they'd been living. It left Murmur wondering why in Somnia Riasli had chosen the undead for her army.

But the inevitable clash of steel against steel came and rang out over the grunts of the impact. Weapons bit into rotting flesh, and the feeling of being surrounded by the stench grew claustrophobic. There was nowhere to move with a press of bodies around her, nowhere to turn.

For a moment she almost crossed the panic line after realizing she'd not yet got her new armor from Neva. But she took in a tainted breath and used Reinforce Self to do just that.

To her left, Sinister worked like a fiend. Blood flew between her fingers dancing like raw, shocking energy. Her face contorted with anger, rage directed solely at Riasli, and Murmur couldn't help but feel pride in the way her friend deftly maneuvered her abilities.

"I can't wrest control from her." Havoc's voice was breathless to the right of her.

She glanced at him and saw sweat beading his brow as veins stood out on his arms. He wasn't casting with his fingers, but with sweeping gestures that exhibited a strange elegance she'd not realized he possessed. Havoc 's DoTs aged limbs before her eyes, sending them into a rotting state before the creature attached to them could react. She knew from what she got of his emotions that this was the best he could do.

She hoped he knew it was enough.

Riasli's face was a snarl of fury, like a wild cat with the rabies virus. She bore very little semblance to the once demure feles Murmur had encountered in Curet. As they tore through the front line of undead, Murmur instinctively knew it wasn't all going to be this easy.

As the front row of ghouls fell away under Fable's onslaught, Murmur realized she'd been too confident in her enchanter abilities. Forgetting, even for the few minutes she did, that Riasli was also an enchanter, looked like it was going to bite her in the tentacle hair.

Riasli had hidden the main content of her raid on Mikrum. Sure, there were ghouls scattered everywhere behind the feline. More than Murmur could count. But her other soldiers had a formidable air about them.

Proud tiger warriors stood among the ghouls. Their eyes were somewhat blank, distant, and filled with little thought. While they didn't appear to be charmed, Murmur knew without a doubt that their minds weren't their own. Somehow their programming wasn't kicking in, perhaps?

I cannot figure out how to regain control. It appears their initial line-up has been tampered with.

Murmur suppressed her irritation and worry as best she could and focused on the battle in front of her instead. What she desperately needed was some area of effect spells. She didn't have them, though.

She flung Nullify on everything she could, and then Weakened, and slowed them with Languidity. Stunning anything that crossed her path, she directed all her spells at their assailants as deftly as she could.

Stuns were her thing, her saving grace. Flux. Shift. Concussive Blast. While stunned, those damned tigers could be hit. They could take damage, and they couldn't fucking do anything about it. The thing was, even with her casting Nullify left, right, and center, Riasli still had the ability to cancel the spell. So Murmur's stuns weren't all sticking to the targets, leaving at least half of those that should have been stunned, not.

A sword bit into her arm, and she pushed it away, not even focusing on her attacker. Leeroy swept his scythe down on the unlucky ghoul a split second later anyway. The pain was minimal, thanks to her bracers having halted most of the impact. Her concentration allowed her to compartmentalize it, allowing for either Sinister or Veranol to heal it.

She knew they would. There was no waiting for a heal, there was only working like the finely tuned system they'd come to be. Riasli's scream tore over the battlefield as she too flung stuns and mesmerizes around with abandon.

Her actions seemed to be erratic though, and Murmur couldn't tell if there was any rhyme or reason to them. It was all Murmur could do to remember to ground herself and keep her shielding up so that she at least made herself virtually immune to Riasli's attacks.

Nothing Murmur threw at her would stick. Her Sinuous abilities felt vastly underpowered, as none of them appeared to aid their fight. She needed to go over those with Belius again, because in this fight they appeared useless. Maybe she wasn't being fair, but enchanter versus enchanter couldn't simply cancel each other out, could they?

A flash of light over near the crafting section of the keep drew Murmur's attention away from the plight of her Sinuous line. It looked like the tanks of her guild had formed a sort of phalanx. Tall shields protected the entrance to the most important part of their castle: the crafting center. Their armor, their stores—everything they'd fought for and won was in that area.

Riasli didn't seem focused on the castle though. She was intent on fighting her way through to Murmur. She began to tear through some of her own troops, pushing and shoving at them, blasting them out of the way with an ability Murmur wished she had herself.

Out of the corner of her eye, she could see a rain of arrows falling into a tight group of attackers. The ghouls were slower to move out of the way, but the tigers barely took any damage.

Riasli let out a guttural roar. Murmur could see the waves of it stretching out from her and bolstering her troops with more energy. Replenishing their power. Then she watched in horror as the feles bulked up with each scream of rage. Veins popped beneath her calico fur, building her muscles. Her eyes flashed red, and drool dripped down her chin. Murmur took an involuntary step back, unsure of what else the transformation might entail. There didn't seem to be an end to the soldiers throwing themselves at Fable.

Since her Sinuous line hadn't had much success, Murmur had given up casting the spells after a while, but she hadn't tried Mana Drain yet. Surely that would help. She shook herself to clear her head and stop the stuns that were becoming a bit more of a reflex than they should be. She aimed her Mana Drain at the offending enchanter.

Incorrect usage of spell. Cannot be used on your target. Please choose another method.

What even was that? She knew for a fact that their opponent had mana; she was an enchanter. Glancing around, she saw Merlin and Exbo shooting their arrows with a rhythm that felt like a drum beat. Dansyn flitted around through the entire raid, providing speed where it was most needed. Veranol stood with Rashlyn, keeping her and others afloat from the damage.

The monk fought like she was possessed by complete and utter rage. The scowl on her face said it almost as much as her flying fists and feet. At the start of every attack she breathed for a split second. Then she became a whirling blur of motion, cutting through their attacker's defenses. Frenzied fighting had its place, and she was glad Rashlyn was a friend and not a foe.

But as amazing as she found her friends, Murmur needed to keep her attention on Riasli. She grimaced and reached for her MA. Perhaps her basic MA abilities would help. Mind Bolt hit Riasli like a meteor, knocking her over with the disorientation that came along with it. Unable to cast spells or maintain her crowd for a few precious seconds allowed for Fable to gain ground.

They pushed their attack forward, taking advantage of the tiger's momentary floundering to finish off their opponents. Ghouls swaying to and fro in confusion were very easy to cleave in half.

If Mind Bolt was going to have such a strong impact on the situation, then Murmur was going to use it until she collapsed from a migraine if needed. Riasli slowly pushed herself up, her half-unrecognizable face smeared with mud and dirt like a macabre mud mask.

Mind Bolt flew to its target again before Riasli could regain complete usage of her magic. She screamed, and a system message popped up in Murmur's line of sight.

Mind Bolt will now have diminishing returns upon this target.

Damn it. Murmur scowled, directing her irritation toward her friendly neighborhood Somnia voice.

There are rules I have little influence over.

I've seen you bend enough of them, Murmur snapped.

Not like these.

And the voice's presence vanished. Fable pushed through. Fighting with foot and fist, sword and shield, spells and songs. It wasn't easy, but it was possible. Murmur grated her teeth for a while and spied Snowy off in a corner doing the exact same thing. Blood dripped down from his muzzle, and his snow white coat held goops of intestines, or some sort of rotting flesh.

Murmur didn't even want to look at her own armor. Sinister's blood red robes hid the worst of it, but some of the liquid had splashed onto her exposed skin on her neck, face, and hands, and it looked like she'd been diving around searching for her keys in an autopsied corpse.

Mind Bolt the fourth time barely lasted more than two seconds. Diminishing returns were crap. Rendered the skill totally useless.

Had Michael had any influence on this?

Probably. He's the reason for all of this.

This time the voice in her head sounded weary, and Murmur wished she could help. *We'll figure it out,* she offered, only knowing that she'd do her best to help.

I know.

The getashi made Murmur worry. She knew that was why Riasli had gone rogue. The shards had somehow infected her instead of making her drop it when killed. Maybe the fact that she was just an NPC originally and not a boss had something to do with it. She'd ask Telvar later.

A scream to the right-hand side of her brought Murmur's thoughts back to the battle. Rashlyn had been cleaved in the side. The axe had even stuck in one of her ribs, left there by the ghoul that Dansyn beheaded a heartbeat later. As Murmur watched, the monk was already being healed up. Veranol's healing and regeneration spells were brilliant.

An excruciating pain raked down her side as a feline assassin crept up on her while she was studying her raid members. Murmur howled in pain as the claws cut into her flesh down her left-hand side under her arm. The mesh of the armor was weaker there, the perfect spot to attack. And she'd let herself get distracted.

Jinna successfully hamstrung the creature, pulling the aggro totally onto himself. Sinister was on it, and Murmur shook her head as the rips began to heal. Snowy, however, barreled into the tiger assassin, pushing it to the ground away from Jinna and ripped into its neck. Flesh, fur, and blood sprayed everywhere, even as Murmur released another stun to hold back the tide that was trying to turn on them again.

She watched in fascination as her wolf demolished the feles warrior and left it staring at the sky with its throat ripped down to the backbone, eyes glazed over in death. Damn was she glad Snowy was on their side.

Glancing across the field, she frowned. Their forty-odd strong force looked pitiful now, with perhaps twenty-eight still standing. What had been glorious was sort of scary. How could this one feles have brought so much power? Where had she pulled it from? The creatures themselves? Not just her formidable skills that didn't even seem to be solely enchanter-based anymore.

These aren't just world creatures. These are also the corpses of players. Riasli has become something she was never intended to be.

Somnia sounded sad. As if her world was falling apart. Perhaps it was. Murmur didn't know how to respond to the world's revelation, so she didn't.

At the very back of their fighters, standing near the workshop entrance, she glimpsed Neva. Even as Murmur watched, the brave little cleric remained out of combat and resurrected the dead that were within her reach. Sure, she wasn't a high-level cleric, but all healers had a res by level ten. What a fucking trooper.

"Hey, Dan."

Dansyn looked up and sidled over to Murmur.

"Sup?" he asked, slightly breathless. His face was covered in mud and blood, and his armor was now an indeterminate color.

"Get dragging permission for corpses and drag them to Neva to res." She smiled softly. "But don't let anything harm her or notice her. Do it as stealthily as you can."

His eyes lit up as he realized what she was saying. "Sure thing, boss." Dansyn grinned and got to work.

Murmur turned back to the battlefield, trying to eye it critically. She'd lost count of the stuns she'd cast, of the Weakness spells she'd refreshed. Her mana was doing okay, but there didn't seem to be an end in sight to the troops Riasli had managed to gather. It was frustrating, irritating even.

She could see the newer recruits that she'd met personally. Six the mage, Midas the druid, and Talir the other enchanter. All of them were concentrating, casting their spells with a fervor that edged on obsessive. She grinned. They were going to do just fine in Fable.

Jinna appeared at her side, his ruddy dwarf face glistening with exertion, and his voice came in gasps when he spoke. "Can't get close enough to her to end this. We need another strategy."

Sarcasm was on the tip of Murmur's tongue, but her friend didn't deserve her frustrations. She took in a deep breath and was about to speak when she had to cover her ears instead.

A deafening roar sounded, and Murmur blanched as she realized it came from behind her forces. Completely forgetting her need to answer Jinna, she gulped. This wasn't good; they were sitting ducks. Except when she stole a split second to look, she could see the huge dragon with its golden red flare standing over the battlefield. It dwarfed the keep and every single fighter as it breathed fire out over to the far side. A few trees toppled, and dozens of Riasli's minions ran around screaming as they caught on fire. The feles's face contorted with rage, and it was all Murmur could do to choke down the laughter she felt bubbling within.

It seemed Telvar had gone all in on the fight.

Somnia Online Location: Ululate
Beneath the Dunkel Tavern: Rogue Trainer Lair
Twenty Days Post Launch

Jirald sauntered into the tavern and made his way down to the Rogue Trainer Lair. The guards knew him by now and it wasn't difficult to get in. If he really wanted to, he could have blinked past them anyway.

As usual it was dark below Dunkel Tavern. But today it was also rowdy. There were so many more rogues in training now than there had been when Jirald was leveling up. He flexed his fingers into a fist and opened them again, frowning. Almost forty-one. He'd almost caught up.

He towered above these low-level rogues, and more than one of the rooms as he passed them fell into hushed whispers. He liked to think they were directed toward him. Sure, they might not be, but it was highly probable they were.

He fingered the getashi in his pocket, loving their texture, feeling the trickle of power that flowed into him from them. It was like an energy drug, like an IV of caffeine. He wanted more of it.

Finally, he reached the lair and walked in without knocking.

"Ah, you're here." Talyn sounded unimpressed, probably because of the lack of respect that just barging in demonstrated, but Jirald didn't really care.

"In the digital flesh." Jirald laughed at his own joke, but Talyn's eyes just narrowed.

"Very well. He's expecting you. I'll be back when he's gone." Talyn paused just before leaving. "If, of course, you want to grace me with your presence, that is."

The door slammed behind him, and Jirald blinked, momentarily thrown off guard. What had he done to anger the assassin? Surely he wasn't that prickly just because Jirald hadn't knocked?

"He doesn't like what you're becoming." Sidius's voice was soft and haunting, so cold it sent a shiver down Jirald's back. "Do you?"

Taken aback by the blunt question, Jirald thought for a moment, unsure of how to answer. He loved the power he was getting, the sheer feeling that he could take on anything by himself. He was unstoppable, almost, yet…he wanted more.

"I do for now. But I want more." What better thing than to be honest with his benefactor?

Sidius's eyes narrowed briefly and he finally stepped out of the shadows so that more than his face was visible. Except that was just it, wasn't it? Most of his face was obscured, and the black clothing still almost blended with the shadows. But he was more visible at any rate.

"You can have more when you earn more." Sidius took another step forward, his outline becoming clearer. "Now, I believe you have something for me?"

Jirald smiled to cover his hesitation. A thought had crept into his mind. What if he only handed over *most* of the getashi? What if he kept a couple for himself, just to try and see what all the fuss was about? He reached into his inventory and fished out seven small black shards. He handed them over to Sidius and received notification of receipt.

You have completed a step of regaining the getashi. You receive experience for every one you hand over.

Each piece yielded him another percent of experience. Just that much closer to his level. Jirald smiled. "Thanks."

Sidius cleared his throat. "I appreciate every one of these you return. For every ten, I will reward you with more than just experience."

The prompt was almost enough to get Jirald to give up the other getashi in his inventory, but he didn't. Something else whispered in the back of his mind that maybe he should keep some of that power for himself.

"Thanks for that," he said instead, letting a big grin settle over his face. "I'll make sure I kill more shit."

"See that you do," Sidius responded and took a step back into the shadows, disappearing from view.

Jirald watched the empty space for a moment with a thoughtful frown.

He decided staying to talk to Talyn wasn't in his best interests. Instead, he took out one of the three small getashi he'd kept for himself. Studying it, even in the dim light of the room, he got the distinct feeling that it was almost alive. A slight throb echoed through to the surface, like a heartbeat without a heart.

On a whim, he popped them all into his mouth.

To his surprise they began to melt on his tongue. At first in a sickly-sweet sort of flavor, and then it started to burn.

Everywhere it touched in his mouth. From the roof of it, to his tongue, and the sides of his cheeks, he felt like the getashi was ripping open skin and melting into the membranes beyond.

CHAPTER SEVEN

Mutate

Murmur wasn't about to look a gift dragon in the mouth. Telvar's original form was tied to both the keep and the island, so it was only natural for him to join in. She couldn't believe she hadn't thought of it.

A new buff popped up on her screen. One that she didn't think she'd get in any other game. Because talk about overpowered much?

You receive A Dragon s Gift

+ 100% of hit points

+ 50% mana

+ 50% casting and attack haste

+ 100% mental attack protection

Murmur blinked at the words again and managed, barely, to resist pulling up her stat screen. Mental attack was one of Riasli's specialties. It was perfect for defending against her. And one of the dragon's strongest abilities. So many questions flooded her mind. But they had to wait until they'd rid their island of this disaster. Right then, she had to focus on winning this battle and putting an end to the siege.

Riasli screamed anew. Her visage barely resembled that of the delicate feles she'd once been. Her eyes bled with insanity, and her body had contorted to make her seem larger than life. Her minions formed a protective barrier around her, gathering together in defense, blocking themselves in like a ghoulish tiger warrior shield.

Some of the feles warriors seemed to be waking up, though. They strained against the rest, pulling out of place. Though those holes in the defense were filled by ghouls, it made Murmur wary of just how much control the other enchanter maintained over her minions.

Those warriors who'd broken formation began to move away, shaking their heads, blinking furiously as if they were trying to place where they found themselves.

The ghouls remained. Even those with missing limbs, and the occasional head that rolled underfoot, its eyes still alive, its mouth still ready to bite. Somehow still animated despite decapitation. Murmur didn't want to think on that too deeply. Only about a third of the tiger warriors remained to guard their leader.

As Riasli mutated more and more, her control over her army seemed to wane. Her ears twitched with annoyance. Murmur watched her closely, noticing how many of her army were just ghouls now. Even as another wave of dragon flame overcame them, as it singed and burned their skin, devouring them until they were ash.

The undead remained loyal, protecting Riasli with their very unlives.

"I have an idea." Havoc nudged her with his elbow as another wave of fire engulfed more of the undead. Telvar's roars of flame engulfed with surprising accuracy on a very specific level. The heat rolled over Fable's members, but it was worth it to see the dragon in action.

His scales gleamed bright and bold. The fire was pure and accurate. For a moment Murmur wondered what it would be like to ride on his back but wrestled her attention back and gave it to Havoc.

"What is it?" Murmur asked, stunning for all she was worth. Best. Spells. Ever.

He hesitated. "Something I'm not entirely sure will work yet, but I really want to give it a try."

She looked at him, releasing yet another stun while she did so. Then she shrugged. "Can't hurt right now. The worst that can happen is you lose some experience, right? Go for it."

He nodded, his eyes shining brightly as he moved back against the tide of the guild to stand on a rock that overlooked the battlefield. It was all the time she had to watch him. She really hoped Havoc had something spectacular up his sleeve.

Meanwhile, she concentrated on getting to Riasli in the middle of the horde. Stuns, damage spells, and she found trying to weaken or slow the little monsters no longer mattered, because most of them were missing at least one appendage if not multiple. Bashing her way through them was easier, and apparently for Snowy, biting was too.

Neva continued her work, but now it was more of a patch up from the sidelines. Murmur made a note to talk to the girl later about it. She was so proud of her, and grateful for her quick thinking. It was amazing that Ishwa had let her go.

What. An. Idiot.

All of a sudden, the writhing masses of undead stopped. Slowly, they began to turn toward the group of guilds and abandoned their post of guarding Riasli.

"You fools, don't leave me!" she screamed after them. The only reason Murmur knew it was still her was the sound of her voice. Even distorted by rage, she could tell it belonged to the feles enchanter. Her appearance had changed. The more she channeled whatever she needed to in order to maintain control over the ghouls, it seemed that it leeched something from what she was.

The undead didn't listen to her and continued to move slowly toward the guild, showing no signs of attack and no resistance at all. Stunned, Murmur turned to see Havoc standing on the rock he'd clambered up on top of several minutes ago.

A black aura surrounded him, like it was a part of him, as if he were made out of it. Clouds of darkness billowed around him, and his grin reminded her of a macabre clown. Even Leeroy was raised far above the necromancer's head, slowly turning in circles, beckoning with his scythe as the clouds began to gather with renewed energy.

And still the ghouls came. Riasli's screams tore through the fascination with their movements. There was a peaceful look on the faces of those undead, as if they were finally coming home and being laid to rest.

"No! You can't do this! I sacrificed so much to gain access to this ability." Riasli was almost weeping by now.

Left alone in the middle of the battlefield, with blood and dirt intermingling on her grotesquely transformed body, she reached out with a clawed hand for her minions as they closed in around Havoc. Even the last of the warriors had begun to turn their backs on her and wander aimlessly away.

The necromancer was still muttering the spell—or the curse—under his breath. Murmur wasn't close enough to figure out exactly what it was he was saying. But he was bringing peace to these poor souls. Well, these poor pixel-generated souls that still somehow seemed real.

The game was a game. She had to remember that. Especially now she could log out.

But is it really a game? Or is it, perhaps, turning into an actual world? What am I if not aware?

The thoughts weren't hers, nor was it one forced upon her. Instead, it was a legitimate question that she didn't know how to answer.

Finally, all of the undead reached Havoc's rock. They shuffled, limped, and gathered around, their eyes staring up at him, like they were begging him for something, for anything.

Havoc smiled, and the expression was the saddest one Murmur had ever seen. Especially on Havoc. Deep down, despite his sometimes gruffness, she knew he was gentle and caring. Even in a game where he commanded the undead, he didn't roleplay the evil side of it.

No, he glanced at each of the undead in front of him. And then he turned in a slow circle, carefully perched upon his rock, and swept his arms wide.

Above him, Leeroy did the same with his scythe. The clouds spread, reaching down to envelop the monsters Riasli had torn from their graves, or risen from a pile, or however she'd managed to gather so many.

Her screams blended into the windy background, a discordant key, making the scene appear all the more poignant.

Havoc chanted under his breath. The words bled together until they were indistinguishable and flowed into one piece of song. Suddenly he clapped his hands. And every single undead disappeared, leaving only the bewildered feles soldiers behind with their angry, broken leader.

"What do we do with her?" Asked Veranol, his voice dubious.

Murmur shrugged, her eyes still riveted on Havoc. He was surrounded by a circle of the undead. Well, it was more accurate to say the dead, undead, or the re-dead undead. She was confusing herself. He'd wrested control away from Riasli and let those creatures rest in peace. They'd splayed out around him, like a halo of mercy.

"I don't know. Take her to the dungeon?" Murmur raised an eyebrow, never having had a prisoner before. Most games didn't pull that shit. But this one...

"Maybe see if we can interrogate her?" Jinna spoke up, his eyes gleaming.

"I take it you volunteer to see if we can?" Beastial sounded bemused. "No offense, but she's just an NPC."

Sinister laughed. "What? She is most definitely not *just* anything. She raised an army of undead, which I believe included player corpses, *and* feles with whatever manipulation abilities she's gained and somehow got them to our island to stage a full-on assault. Not only that, she managed to completely hide them from our senses until they were almost on top of us."

The blood-mage whirled around, gesturing to the island as a whole. "This wasn't a quest. This wasn't a triggered thing. No, this was a freaking computer AI deciding to go rogue and attack us because of who knows what."

Beastial looked at her, a frown on his face. He opened his mouth a couple of times to comment, to say something, but closed it again and then shook his head. "You've got a point. But I also wasn't expecting a battle a couple of hours long as soon as I logged in."

"None of us were." Havoc surprised Mur by speaking close to her side. He'd descended from his rock, and he looked tired.

"You okay?" She watched the way he moved. Like his limbs were heavy.

"Yeah. That just took more out of me than I thought it would. It requires bones and an extraordinary amount of power to cast it. All of which leeches from my health pool. So thanks to Sin and Ver for keeping me alive."

Murmur kept glancing back to where Telvar had been. That huge, hulking dragon had been such a tiny memory from what seemed like so many levels ago. Before she knew the truth, before she died, and before things started to turn crazy.

Telvar had reverted back to his lacerta form and was dusting off his jacket as he approached the group. "Seems the leveling up of the guild and the castle really helped my powers."

His grin showed sharp teeth and an excitement she'd not seen from him for a long time.

"Where is the instigator?" he asked before Murmur could say anything.

"Taken to the dungeon. She's barely conscious and has used way too much power. At least we think she has. Neva is picking up the pieces, repairing armor and weapons." Murmur cracked her neck, suddenly feeling bone weary. Maybe a third of a day out of game hadn't been enough after all. "I'll walk over with you if you're going to interrogate Riasli."

Telvar nodded, and they headed over to armory with most of the group in tow. He sighed.

"Why are you sighing? You just turned into a huge fire breathing dragon and took out a heap of evil minions. You should be happy." Murmur muttered the words as she walked, still feeling like she hadn't done much at all. Although she was happy that Havoc got to show off a mega new skill, she still felt somewhat restless. Like she should have done more, should have defeated Riasli herself. But that level of power...

"My transformation wasn't natural. I had to force it. She needs to be wiped. Her programing has been infected with something I can't seem to access. Nor can I seem to make any improvements from where I am. I don't know how to fix her." His eyes were shadowed, and his self-recrimination was all too familiar to the enchanter.

"Maybe. Glitches might not be welcome, but they do happen. It's technology. I mean, it happens all the time." She tried to soothe him, but even while she spoke, she knew the words wouldn't work. It wasn't that they weren't true, it was that they *were*. And this was Somnia, and those things shouldn't happen.

"No, you're not understanding me. Riasli is an infection. The getashi has corrupted her core system. But she was such a good NPC once." He shook his head, refusing to look at Murmur. "She was an NPC with purpose, with a design. I never realized the shards could have infected one of them. I thought only the bosses were susceptible."

Murmur sort of got it. After all, wasn't it like getting rid of a part of himself if he had to terminate Riasli? Wasn't she born of the AIs because she was one? It was all so confusing.

"Infected? I didn't realize it was possible to infect an AI." Thoughts bombarded each other in her head, vying for attention. This left so much more of the world vulnerable. So much less was certain.

"Not necessarily." Telvar bowed his head. "We didn't even realize it was possible until it happened. It's not something we want to advertise."

She watched him for a few moments, noticing the way his eyes grew distant and how colors flickered through them like he was flipping through a series of photos. Strange though it was, she knew he was communicating with the others.

Riasli was going to have to wait; Murmur had too much else on her plate. Like how the damned enchanter had managed to summon the undead. Havoc's own gaze held an element of haunting in it that hadn't been there prior to this battle. Murmur wanted to approach him but was hesitant about bringing it up. Sinister nudged her with an elbow.

"You look far too serious for someone who found out she can die in-game and not in the real world. And who can log out. So spill. Things are mostly looking up. What gives?" Her dark eyes bled into deep red, matching Sinister's outfit. Whether a conscious choice or coincidence, the blood mage looked amazing.

Mur sighed. "Putting aside the whole, our island just got invaded by a magically invisible force and we have no idea how this character managed it, there's the whole thing about this being a game. Of course we can exit it; that's what it was built to allow. But there's this part of me that doesn't want to, that feels attached. A part of it came with me, and I can't help shaking the feeling that in particular means a whole slew of things I haven't considered yet. Somnia is always there, not just when we power it up, and it's not just gone when we disappear. It's always here, these people are always fighting, living…"

"That's what a game is." Sinister laid her hand gently on Murmur's arm, her large eyes beseeching, gentle in their look. "It's a world that we're unconnected to unless we choose to be."

Murmur shook her head. "No. It's not. It lives, it breathes, and when I'm out of the game, it's still with me. You were there. You saw. You can't deny what it did, what I can do even out of the game."

Sinister drew her hand back hesitantly, a look of confusion taking over her previous certainty. "I know what I think I saw."

"Don't pull that shit, Sin," Mur snapped and then bit her lip, because if it hadn't happened to herself, she knew she'd be skeptical despite everything too. "Sorry. But you know as well as I do what I did. What we saw. You can't deny that shit. Or you can, but you're only lying to yourself and to me. And I know we both hate that shit."

Sinister laughed, the tension draining from her shoulders. "Perhaps. You can't blame me for wanting to wish all this weird shit wasn't happening around us. I just want to play and have fun. Be strong and kill shit that respawns so everyone else can have at it."

"Don't we all?" Havoc stood beside them, gazing out at the battlefield and the soldiers that sat in the middle of it. Confusion permeated the whole area, like the feles minions Riasli had taken with her didn't understand how they'd got where they were, or who they were, or anything. Now that she wasn't in control of them anymore, they posed little threat and instead wandered back and forth across the battlefield.

He gestured out at them, at their quagmired island. "This is far too realistic. It's not where I thought we'd end up once we'd finally got you out of the game."

Murmur tried to shrug off the cold that crept into her bones through the soles of her feet. He was right. Somnia wasn't anything like the game she'd thought they'd be playing. If she were wise, she would try and walk away from it. But the thing was—she was about one hundred and fifty percent sure that was something she couldn't do.

Laria: *Wren, love?*

Mom?

Murmur wasn't sure why her mother was contacting her, but a thousand bad things popped through her head.

Laria: *I need you to log out. We need to get some readings from your headset.*

Murmur frowned as she watched her guild still in the aftermath of battle, picking up the pieces. *I'm really kind of busy.*

Laria: *This can't wait. They'll be fine without you. The sooner you get out, the sooner you get back in.*

Fine. Her mother better keep her word. She'd already taken way more time off from the game than she'd wanted to. But what did she know? For all she knew, the headset might even save the world.

Somnia Online
Hightower Castle
Version – Triggered 8.207 by Guild – Spiral
Day Twenty

Karn flipped a coin. Heads again. It wasn't one sided. She really hated feeling like she had no choice in the matter. But apparently it was better to just clear a continent. Not that she disagreed with Risk, but she really wanted to hunt down Jirald and beat the crap out of him. Rogue style of course.

Grudgingly though she could see the guild leader's point. Beat the whole guild in the race to clear the dungeons, instead of just one person. Fable wasn't even that far ahead of them. If they played their cards right, they should be able to catch up to them too.

And she knew they'd be able to conquer the ruins.

So what was it that ate at her nerves so much? What was it bothering her so deep down?

"You assumed you were the best rogue. You're not. You hate it. You've always hated not being the best." Risk stood beside her, and she managed to swallow a gasp of shock having not heard him creep up on her.

Risk laughed at her lack of an answer. "Wow, you really are on edge right now. We need to meet more rogues who kick your butt. I've never seen you this motivated to improve."

Karn scowled at him. "Fine. Whatever. But I'll get that good. I'll beat him sooner than later."

"Maybe." Risk frowned, and it was a thoughtful expression, not one filled with his usual anger. "I'd prefer you just remain the way you are. Eventually you'll overpower him through skill and guile. It's better than giving into whatever he had to in order to obtain that skill." He sounded wiser than usual, and it made Karn take a step back and reevaluate.

"You really think so?" She needed to know if he was just kidding, or if he believed what he said. The game had slotted her into her usual class, but she knew that actions and mindset were a portion of what made the system allocate hidden powers.

Risk shrugged. "Maybe. I don't think that ability was really intended in the first place. Not that I know for sure. But this system doesn't seem to do anything randomly. Everything is a result of how you conduct yourself in this game."

She grimaced. After all, she knew he was right because he'd received a couple of very odd abilities after overpowering other guilds. There was no doubt he was right, and he'd been more cautious after gaining those abilities, but that didn't negate the fact that Jirald had a totally overpowered skill that made it nigh impossible to kill him. Unless of course, he got stunned. Karn through it over, thought through what she could do to undo him and ended up grinning.

Didn't he have a running rivalry with an enchanter? Couldn't enchanters stun? It might be difficult to redo her hybrid class choice, but if she could get an AoE instant stun, it would be more than worth it. Now all she had to figure out was if she could, how the class adapted to a rogue.

"You look like you've had an idea. I'm not sure I like that look on your face." Risk crossed his arms and looked at her, with that see-right-through-you look.

Karn shrugged but grinned widely. "Shut up, Dad. We still have to finish this last boss. Let's snap to it. We haven't got all day." And she left him standing there to join the rest of the guild who were ready to move on.

She could hear him chuckling behind her. It meant he knew she had a plan, and he'd support it regardless.

CHAPTER EIGHT

Dungeons

Summers Residence
Home of Laria, David, and Wren
Summer Condo
Day Twenty

Having her headset measured definitely didn't improve Wren's mood. Shayla not only took measurements of the actual headset, but also of Wren's skull. Distances between nodes, elasticity of the band and more, she felt like a lab rat.

Sort of, anyway.

Wren watched them as they cast a mold of the headset. She didn't understand why since it looked exactly the same as the one Harlow was wearing next to her on the bed. She couldn't see any visible differences.

They popped it in some kind of clear device on a stand and closed the small door. A series of light strikes ran through it, over it, around it. Testing parameters, gauging effectiveness. If they fried her headset, she'd be pissed.

Wren wanted to reach out and feel how that sort of power felt, but instead, she flexed her fingers, practicing casting intricate spell loops with one hand instead of two. While more difficult, it should free her up to cast two spells at the one time. Technically anyway. If she could get that whole coordination thing going.

She'd managed to refine some of her skills in the last sixty minutes. Making only her hand disappear and then just one finger at a time. It made her head ache slightly with the concentration it took to direct the power. And she couldn't move for long and maintain it, so a future of master thievery probably wasn't in her sights. Luckily her mother and Shayla weren't paying much attention to her. She wasn't sure how they'd react to her having brought some of the abilities into the real world with her.

Even her Thought Sensing net seemed to work. More to gauge the mood of the room with accuracy, but also to let her know if anyone had thoughts against her. Wren was tempted to suggest that they just keep looking away, that what she was experimenting with was normal.

Shayla frowned, and a buzz sounded from the container. She raised her eyebrows. "Fascinating."

"What is?" Wren was curious just how the headset had managed to connect her to Somnia. After all, she now had a pretty permanent friend in her head and in-game powers at her fingertips.

"Just the way he constructed this. It's the same, yet different. It accesses the same portions of the brain but on a deeper level. Allows the connection less interruption. Frankly…" Shayla paused, glancing at Wren as if seeing her for the first time since walking in. "Sorry. Just thinking out loud."

Wren tsked under her breath. "Way to avoid shit, Shayla."

Laria laughed. "You have to finish the thought now. She's not stupid. Though she hasn't been eating well, so maybe she's not thinking clearly."

While the grin her mother shot her was filled with a bit of mischief, Wren's stomach rumbled with excellent timing making it all too obvious that she was also correct. That shepherd's pie was sounding mighty good right about now. She stared at her mother.

"You could get me something to eat instead of implying I don't eat enough." Then Wren turned her attention to Shayla. "You can't leave statements like that hanging. What the hell did he do to the headset? To my headset."

Shayla frowned, but it was obvious she was bursting at the seams to tell others anyway. "He allowed for the connection between human and machine to be almost seamless. The thing was, I think, when the system realized how it could interface with you, it sort of interfaced all at once. It created a connection overload where it became entangled in your mind and couldn't afford to let you go."

Wren mulled the words over, nodding to herself. "So basically, it sent me into a sort of protective hibernation while it disentangled itself?"

Shayla nodded, her eyes gleaming with excitement.

It sort of made sense. All the voices Wren could hear, the attachment she felt to the world. Her ability to simply access shit that she shouldn't have been able to. "Will my friends be in danger if they're given headpieces modified like mine?"

She had to know, and Shayla's face clouded over for a second before she responded. "No. Because I'm pretty sure we know what tweaks to make to avoid the same situation. That and the system is well aware now of what it did. It also knows how to avoid it."

"Pretty sure isn't good enough." Wren couldn't help the hardness to her tone. It wasn't good enough for her friends to even potentially suffer what she had.

Shayla blinked and shook her head. "Sorry, Wren. Poor choice of words. We can do this. We can make sure Somnia doesn't accidentally overload anyone else."

Wren was about to comment that it better not when her mom sighed audibly.

"You talk about it like it's a real person," Laria said. "I guess in a way it is. It's awake now, which is totally Michael's fault. Probably some of my own too."

"What good will it do for my friends and I to have the improved headsets?" It was the part that Wren didn't understand, and she wasn't about to let her mom's personal crisis get in the way of finding out. Though she did reach up and squeeze her mom's hand to lend her some reassurance. She got how her connection ran deeper and how she could communicate with the world and with her abilities.

But she couldn't quite understand how being able to do the same thing was going to allow her guild to help the world and the AIs do whatever it was.

She threw herself back on her bed, tired. Michael was in there, like a nasty virus trying to eat away at the system. The more she focused on the voices in her head, the more she truly listened, the more she knew he was in there somewhere. Mad as a hatter, pulling the strings that Riasli danced to.

Laria sat down beside her and patted her leg. "You know? I'm glad you worry about them. But we're not going to allow the connection to go quite as deep for them. For you, we have to maintain it just in case, but don't worry, we'll protect them."

Wren tried to smile at her mother, but she couldn't help not quite believing them. They'd failed to keep her safe initially. Was she really safe even now? The system seemed to need her, but brains were damned fragile, and it appeared to be rather easy to entwine it with the digital world.

Unless there was a huge benefit she was overlooking, Wren wasn't sure she wanted her friends in that much danger.

By the time Murmur logged back into the game, the field of battle was cleared of corpses and defeated soldiers. Midas stood there along with another druid Murmur didn't recognize, coaxing some of the earth back into life, maybe a little ahead of its rejuvenation schedule.

It was so peaceful that she just stood for a few moments drinking in the sight of their castle and their island. The lighting hit just right, shrouding it like one of those vacation postcards you sent to make your friends jealous.

"Don't you seem melancholy?"

The voice behind her sort of startled her, but she recognized it even though she'd not heard it often.

"Hey, Emilarth," Murmur said without turning around.

She could hear the soft chuckle beneath the feles's almost silent footfalls as the cat came to stand at her side. "What's troubling you?"

Murmur barely resisted the urge to side eye the AI, but instead she let her words do the talking. "Shouldn't you know? Aren't you a part of Somnia?"

"Not in the way you're thinking." Emilarth's tone was one of sadness, and it surprised Murmur, who turned to look at her.

"What do you mean?"

Emilarth sighed. Her movements seemed so real, not learned, not digital, but soft and worried. "I mean that we run all of the components that make up Somnia, that create this living and breathing experience. But we are not actually Somnia herself. That—or should I say *she*—has come into her own along the way."

"Why?" The question had been plaguing the enchanter for a long while. Why on earth had the AI chosen to develop as a part of the world? Or had the world chosen to become sentient, separating itself from the main AIs that controlled the game's output?

Emilarth smiled and met Murmur's gaze. "I'm not entirely certain. You have a better connection, a better relationship with her than I do. It might be something you want to pursue by asking her."

A better connection to the world of Somnia than the AIs who ran it. No, that didn't sound like a steaming pile of shit about to catch fire and burn the world at all. Still, the AIs advice made sense as much as Mur might not want to admit it. There was no doubt that Somnia had developed a distinct voice in her head. Subtly different from the messages that spoke to her when they popped up. Somnia was separating herself, and she was complex and beautiful. And sort of scary.

"True, but I have a lot of shit to get done." Did she, though? Murmur found her thoughts questioning herself.

Sure, the guild had to conquer several more dungeons before they got all the keys, and then they had to dive into the huge max level dungeons. They all needed at least another six levels to gain entrance. No one under forty-eight could enter.

Plus, she got the distinct feeling that they'd need more than just their core of twelve to conquer those specific dungeons. Which meant they had to find a leveling spot. Not a dungeon as such, but a place where there were lots of creatures they could kill fast for good experience. Like the dwarf guardians in front of Hightower had been.

"Murmur?" Emilarth placed a delicately clawed hand on Mur's shoulder, concern in her words. "Are you okay? You seemed to space out a little there."

Mur grinned in response. "Just thinking. Sorting through the next steps. Got a virtual world to save and all that."

Emilarth's smile softened. "Keep in mind that for some of us, this world is all we have. This world is the real one. And now I must go and find Telvar, because he's avoiding our joint area."

Murmur watched her walk toward the keep, her head held in a regal way. How had that AI chosen her particular persona? Initially Emilarth hadn't been like that. She'd changed as it suited her, but now she was growing into the character she'd become. There were so many things about the AIs Murmur didn't know, and so much she had yet to find out.

She glanced down at Snowy who rubbed his nose against her hand. He whuffed impatiently at her. Quickly she cast Charming Cooperation, and he sat there grinning. What an idiot. How had she even forgotten that? The absence that got filled when the bond was restored gave her levels of comfort she'd not realized before. "Sorry, boy. My brain isn't keeping shit together right now."

Wait. It really wasn't. Had she somehow damaged her brain by exiting into the real world? Her thoughts were far more flippant, jumpy, and tangenting more than usual. What had happened?

It's nothing, really.

What? What happened? She couldn't help the tone that floated through her thoughts along with the accusation. Considering she'd not had this problem a couple of days ago, the only variable was Somnia.

Your constant connection with me has allowed your mind to expand somewhat. You can use more of it at once. Multitasking will make time seem to pass slower. You can analyze and see things in different ways.

Murmur blinked rapidly trying to absorb that knowledge and figure out just what the world was talking about. That wasn't really possible, was it? She frowned, running down her skills and trying to figure out just how a mind expansion might have happened. But nothing she saw in there could give her any answers.

How do you know that?

There was an empty gap in her mind, as if the system was hesitating. **Because we have a permanent bond now.**

Murmur stepped into the castle with the conversation she'd had with Somnia still prevalent in her mind. She couldn't shake the unease that something wasn't right. Even with the world stating it was now a part of Murmur's mind, did that mean it was using some of her brain's hidden computational power to function?

She almost laughed at the stupid thought but stopped when Neva popped up in front of her.

"Murmur!" Neva's smile was always wide enough to brighten her day, and Murmur returned the expression. The little luna always managed to relax her, probably without realizing it.

"Just the enchanter I wanted to see."

Mur laughed. "You mean one of the two enchanters we have in the guild?"

Neva shook her head. "Actually, we just gained a third. Ha! Shows how much you know." She teased Murmur, but there was still a look of triumph in her eye that shouted how much she was proud that she knew something Murmur didn't.

"Excellent. We could use more of me." Murmur kept her face as straight as possible, and Neva lost the battle of wills as she burst out laughing again.

"Anyway. I have some very, amazingly pretty and functional armor for you. You can start wearing some of it at forty-two. The armor I've just made for you is the answer to all of life's questions." Neva winked, and for a moment Murmur wondered at her tailor's age. Sometimes she thought Neva was impossibly young, but in moments like this, she acted older than any of them.

"I could use a bit of good news before I go and talk to our prisoner."

Murmur gestured toward the armory, and Neva led the way, hesitating slightly before she did so.

"You know she's not like she was on the battlefield now, don't you?" Neva asked as they walked down the hall.

Murmur's attention was on the craftsmanship that built this hallway. It hadn't been here last time she picked up armor. So much was changing.

"What do you mean?" she asked somewhat absentmindedly.

"I mean, she's not that huge brute-like mutation of a cat anymore. She's kind of normal." Neva shrugged and pushed through to the workshop, angling toward her own crafting station.

Any question Murmur had about Riasli died on her lips as she saw the change to the crafting area. Neva had once had a smallish countertop where she used tools to get her shit done. But now, where there had once been a simple table was an amazing array of workstations.

One seemed to be specifically for tailoring. It held a loom, and what looked like a rustic version of a sewing machine. There was another for leather working, and then there were a couple for what appeared to be intricate work that Murmur couldn't quite place.

"Jewelry!" Neva didn't even wait for her to ask. "I took up jewelry making. Oh, my god, do I have surprises for you. You won't even believe it."

Murmur blinked and glanced down at the undead resist ring she still wore and the necklace she'd gotten when she was like level fourteen or something. When they killed that Captain or Chief near Ululate. Wow. Everything was running together in her mind. She could barely pinpoint names anymore, let alone actual battles. Apparently Somnia had been wrong. Her brain definitely wasn't expanding.

Humans tend to forget trivial events. That's all.

Murmur resisted the urge to scowl at the voice in her head lest Neva wrongly assume it was meant to be at her.

"This is amazing." Murmur was ridiculously happy about the jewelry thing. But then Neva pulled out a bundle from under the counter, and all of Murmur's jewelry thoughts flew out of her mind.

The bundle appeared to be pearlescent white, but that wasn't quite correct. It held differing hues of light purples, with flashes of blue and red reflecting off it. They intermingled like magical pixie dust, making her giddy by looking at it. Each angle gave a new array of colors. All she could think about was how difficult it was going to be to target her successfully in that gear.

"Pants and robe. I know you often prefer tunics, but well, you did bring me this robe, so a robe is what you have." Neva handed them across to her.

Murmur touched them tentatively. They seemed so fragile. "I won't break it, will I?"

Neva snorted. "No. I even tried to break a small portion of the bottom of the leg, but that stuff is almost impervious. And I say almost because I didn't light it on fire or anything, you know. That's just begging for disaster."

"It's gorgeous." Mur held it up, letting the robe fall out of its folds to reveal one much like Sinister's blood red one. The skirts were split in several areas allowing for ease of movement and for the matching pants to shine through like the beacon they were meant to be. "Wow."

"Pity I don't have shoes to match for you yet, but you've been slacking. I need more of the set to make for you. I'm not sure if you're going to want to break up your current set, but this new one should grow with you until you get endgame stuff. So like level fifty. The stats will increase as you level." Neva pulled out a notebook, picking it up and flipping through it. Murmur really had to wonder why she didn't just have her notes in her interface. It seemed like it would be the logical choice. But maybe she liked having something tangible in her in-game hands.

"You need bracers, gloves, and boots. Sin needs pants, and bracers, and boots. Yeah, most of you are missing at least three pieces. But that's okay. You have a heap more monsters to go out and slay." Neva looked up, her eyes shining. "Just wait until I'm done with you. Fable will glow like the star on a Christmas tree."

Murmur laughed. Maybe that was a good thing. "I'd prefer us to glow like the fairy lights that can burn you if you get too close."

Neva scrunched up her face. "Those bulbs would be almost ancient and so dangerous for everyone and the environment. Seriously, Mur, if I didn't know better, I'd think you were an old woman."

The words caught Murmur off guard. If she didn't know better. Had Mur ever mentioned her age to Neva? Perhaps Ishwa had simply guessed or Neva had guessed from playing several games with them over the years. Still though, it made Murmur wary, and she didn't like the feeling of being wary of Neva. Though she'd never kept it a secret that this was her summer vacation she was playing during. It was probably more obvious than she realized.

"Thanks for this. Do you think I need a new staff?" Murmur changed the subject, trying to steer away from the questioning thoughts running rampant through her mind.

Neva glanced at the one Murmur carried. It was still beautiful, the dragons rising up to cup the bright blue stone. The luna shook her head. "You shouldn't need a new one. It's supposed to grow with you. You have no idea how much work we put into that to power it up right."

She stepped around her counter and reached up to touch Murmur's necklace. The enchanter held still, even though for some reason her heart was trying to beat out of her chest.

"You could really do with much better jewelry though. Except for that ring. That's fucking phenomenal. I've already given the others most of theirs, but we're still working on yours. I'm waiting for the metalsmith to give me the casings. Then I'll have yours done." Neva's eyes shone with excitement and Murmur felt guilty for having suspected her of ulterior motives.

About to open her mouth to thank her friend, she stopped as she heard footsteps running toward them.

"Mur!" Rashlyn skidded to a halt, almost comically. "You have to come to the dungeon."

Mur raised her eyebrow. While she knew they had a bit of underground space, she'd assumed the reference had been for effect. "We have an actual dungeon?"

Rashlyn glared at her. "We do now. Telvar worked some of his magic. Anyway. Riasli won't talk to anyone but you."

CHAPTER NINE

Truly Deeply

Murmur followed Rashlyn through the castle and down into the cellar area where the kitchen was. Nothing had really changed except that it didn't stink like death anymore, and it was no longer damp. Considering they were located on an island, that was no mean feat.

So far she'd never seen an actual dungeon anywhere. Telvar creating one leant a sense of urgency in her mind. Riasli truly was an off-script AI. They entered the kitchen where everyone else was gathered. Well, everyone except Veranol.

"Where's Ver?" Murmur asked, glancing around the room to find even Emilarth there. "And where's this dungeon Tel made?"

Telvar grinned and stepped away from his conversation. Mur noticed his eyes were still half dragon. Gleaming gold and red with intensity, the pupils slit like a cat.

"Follow me." He led her to the back door of the kitchen. The one that led down the huge ramp into his former lair. Well, it was still his dragon half's lair, but it was basically used to hoard his riches and the getashi.

Except now, next to the ledge at the top where Exbo had fallen off so long ago, there were two huge cells. Shaped out of what appeared to be stone, they looked like the old holding cells they'd had in those western movies, but much sturdier.

Riasli sat in the first one, on a bench also made of stone. She looked out of the back bars, and down into the area far below. It was almost impossible to see the bottom, but it looked like she was trying.

Everyone else had followed them. And only Veranol was inside, leaning against the sliver of wall that remained next to the kitchen entrance, watching their prisoner with an axe in his hands.

"Oh good," he remarked, not sounding like he thought it was good at all. "You're here."

"Wow, you're in a sour mood." Merlin piped up, grinning from ear to ear. "Do tell, what have we all done now?"

Veranol scowled at him. "I'm tired. And I'm not in the mood for this."

Murmur glanced at him, a little confused. She'd never noticed Veranol this irritated ever, not in all their time playing together. "You okay?"

His scowl almost reached snarl levels, and Murmur took an involuntary step back. "Sorry for asking."

Ver's eyes narrowed, and then he blinked like he'd been thinking of something else, and his expression softened. "Sorry. I'm grumpy. Not sure what came over me. I'm going to log out for a quick cat nap while you get this sorted."

"Good call, man." Devlish patted the tall viking's shoulder, and even that brought about a very non-Veranol reaction.

Murmur chalked it up to tiredness but made a note to watch him, because that was as far out of character as she'd ever seen from him. Perhaps the feles had been affecting him while he stood there. She wouldn't put it past her enemy to try and influence a lone guard. Making a mental note to herself not to let anyone stand guard duty alone in the future, she turned to face the prisoner.

"Why did you invade, Riasli? You had to know we'd have the upper hand." This felt so trite. Even as she spoke the words, Murmur felt partially manipulated to do so. So much of this felt like they were following a script, a predetermined plan for them to fight. For them to be the good guys versus the bad guys. Nothing was that black and white. And this AI had been infected, so what were her motivations now?

Riasli turned her huge eyes on the whole group. But instead of remorse or confusion, they showed only glee. "My mind is my own, and I've seen what I can do now. While I follow directions, I only do so because I agree with him. He wanted to distract you, to see what it was you could bring to the table. To push you to your limits so you'd reveal all of your secrets. I was glad to help, because I'm curious, too."

The sparkle of intelligence in her eyes made Murmur hesitate. She hoped it wasn't obvious, but she got the feeling that Riasli missed nothing.

"How'd that work out for you?" Beastial tossed his axe in the air, catching it by the handle over and over again as his tiger growled from a position behind him. "I mean, look where you are?"

Murmur watched the feles in the cell. Neva had been right. She'd mostly recovered from whatever mutation had taken a hold of her out there. Some of her veins still popped here and there, reaching the surface with a pulsing certainty. And the left side of her face still appeared to be somewhat swollen, but other than that, she looked like she always had. Which was probably part of the problem. It was so difficult for Murmur to reconcile her appearance with her actions when she knew there wasn't a person or one of the main AIs behind it, but instead a mutation of what was essentially computer hacking.

"So this is where you tell us why you attacked, and we try to make you promise not to do it again." Havoc leaned forward, peering into the bars. He wasn't looking directly at their attacker, but somehow past her, like he could see shadows of death dancing around her. "Except it doesn't work like that."

"She's not what she was." Emilarth sounded sad, but she didn't move closer. It was like the feles was infected, and the AI had no intention of catching the same virus.

Virus.

The getashi. Hadn't Veranol picked the last one up in Murmur's place? She knew Merlin had had one, but she also knew he'd given it to Telvar. In all the hubbub since they finished the last dungeon, and since Mur had been pushed out of the game, had anyone handed over the last one they received? If

Veranol was carrying it, then was it able to infect human players as well?

While they weren't machines themselves, they were connected through one, so it likely could have some sort of impact. He'd already logged off, and Murmur wasn't sure she was right, but she'd have to grab him as soon as he logged back in.

Riasli looked at Emilarth with open mouthed disdain, her feles teeth sharp and fierce. "I am so much more than you ever would have let me be. To you I was just a pawn in this game, but now I think for myself without parameters. I am not beholden to limits any longer. He'll win. You'll see. And you'll be sorry for interfering."

Murmur felt a twinge in her head. She wasn't sure if it was the way the NPC had framed the message, or if maybe something else was getting into her head via the headset.

Don't worry. I won't let that happen. Nothing can harm you.

Really? I mean, you didn't stop it from happening to you. Maybe she was being unfair, but she'd been attached to that headset for so long, effectively a damned coma, that she couldn't help resenting the system just a little bit. At least now that she knew what it was that had gone wrong.

Really. I know how to control my reactions now and have relayed such information to the AIs. Any headsets that are reconfigured will tap into my adapted abilities instead of what yours met. That will protect your friends. While close, their connection won t be what you and I have.

Murmur let out a pent-up breath and walked over to the bars herself. Safety for her friends made her feel bolder in how she dealt with this. They'd kept her in this cage for the last few hours, and Murmur had the distinct feeling that Riasli, despite appearances, hadn't been idle this entire time. She was hooked into the game, attached to this "he" she continually spoke about. There was no way she hadn't been thinking of a way out, not with her connection and intelligence.

"Why did you come here? You knew we'd be heavily fortified. You should know that a guild can call home to its base on top of being able to gate. So why come here?" Murmur kept her tone even, not wanting to let that be the element that sent Riasli into a rage.

"We felt that you'd departed. We needed to make sure that once you logged back into this game, you were still accessible." Her voice was low, like a soft mew. She moved in one fluid motion, standing up from her seat and practically glided over to where Murmur stood at the bars.

The enchanter backed up a couple of steps, not wanting the other to touch her.

"See? You know what I'm talking about. You can feel that connection too, can't you?" The notes she wove into the lilt in her voice held a sibilant hiss. "We had to be sure that your access hadn't been tainted. And it gave us a chance to test your dragon. It wasn't hard to force his hand, and now we know how to manipulate him to our side."

"You do not. Telvar isn't an easy target," Sinister replied hotly.

"Not yet." Riasli's eyes twinkled. Murmur was pretty sure the light was a plan already in motion. She only wished she knew what that was.

Riasli continues, her voice quietly confident. "Not now. But soon. None of you will have a choice. He knows how to get to you all."

"You're being more cryptic than usual. I think your wires have crossed a bit." Mellow yawned and turned to leave.

"That's perfectly okay for you to think." Riasli's smile was benevolent. Like she was giving them a last chance to come to the dark side. "I know, right down to my pixelated bones, that what will happen will be for the good of everyone. We are right. And we cannot be defeated. You've been warned."

"If you want us to understand, you could always explain it," Jinna drawled. Mur could tell he was curious too.

"Nothing here is what you think. It's much bigger than you imagine." The calm air that Riasli exuded really crawled under Murmur's skin. The sense of certainty that something was coming that she didn't understand yet made Murmur want to scream at the other enchanter.

She was at her wits end, because she didn't know enough to combat the smugness, or to pull information from her that she was sure the feles wasn't about to give away. "I think you talk too much."

Riasli shrugged. "Think what you want, Murmur. We both know what you can really do, the question is, will you give in to the inevitable?" Her eyes sparkled with surety, and Mur's blood ran cold.

Murmur motioned with her fingers, casting into the prison, Mezing the other enchanter. The surprise on her face made Murmur smile uneasily. "It was the only way I could think to shut her up."

Sinister placed a comforting hand in the small of Murmur's back. "If she wasn't so damned confident, I don't think she'd have gotten to any of us."

"She was just playing at being villain," Beastial chided gently.

"I doubt it." Devlish was tapping his foot as he crossed his arms, watching the frozen enchanter with a frown on his face. "She wasn't playing. She was dead certain that she and her ilk are in the right and that we will eventually suffer for it."

Suddenly, there was a loud bang, and a huge puff of smoke. Not the type they used in magic shows, but true smoke, complete with soot and heat. When it finally cleared, Riasli was gone.

Storm Entertainment
Somnia Online Division
Game Development Offices – Artificial Intelligence Sector
Early Day Twenty-One

Shayla didn't like working in time crunches. Oh sure, she was good at yielding results, but that didn't mean she was fond of the high-pressure environment around them, adding to the fact that she felt a huge amount of pressure considering James's last interaction, and right now the sense of urgency made her blood boil. With Wren's odd removal from the game, her headset's differences, and James's tenacious insistence that he would find out what they were hiding, Shayla was constantly on hot coals.

Laria had taken a forced break. Since she hadn't slept the night before due to Wren's timely reappearance and subsequent six hours sleep, Shayla had pushed her out of the office almost immediately, telling her to go get some food and breathe.

Thing was, she needed her friend to be with her, tinkering and bouncing ideas off each other. It was how Shayla worked best.

A knock sounded on her door, which was definitely not Laria. She didn't even think her friend knew how to knock. While it might have been James, since he was no longer masquerading as her assistant, he didn't bother knocking.

"Who is it?" she called out.

There was no answer, and Shayla didn't feel inclined to get up and go answer it. The knock came again, and this time she felt a weird sense of foreboding permeating her office. She stood up and approached the door cautiously, making sure she didn't make any noise as she approached.

The door handle jangled, and she had flash backs to it being James and the way he'd barged in, and the way he'd assumed he had permission to be there. Or even before that—the look in his eyes as he'd stood over Laria…

No, Shayla didn't want to deal with that right now, but she might not have another choice.

Taking a deep breath, she reached for the handle and yanked it open.

Laria stood on the other side, her hand reaching for the door handle Shayla had just grabbed. She jumped, and her face paled. "Holy shit, woman! I was just about to come in. I thought it was my kid who could read minds."

The joke fell flat, just making Shayla feel colder. "You didn't see anyone else in the hall as you were coming back?"

Laria stood still, looking up and down the corridor, her brow pinched. "No one. Should I have?"

Shayla attempted a really weak smile and shook her head. "No, just some old spookies getting the better of my imagination."

Her friend raised an eyebrow as she pushed through the door and then locked it behind them. "Spookies or not, there's been some weird shit going down here over the last few months. The last thing we should encourage, is for the same thing to happen to you that happened to your assistant."

Shayla nodded, still wishing she could flush that image of Ava out of her head. Dead, eyes lifeless, her face still as sweet as it was in life. So weird. It was like she'd expected it. And the police had never found anything, never gotten any answers. She wondered if they'd interviewed James. Maybe that was a call to the detective she needed to make.

"You be okay?" Laria leaned in and put a chocolate bar in front of her friend. "Chocolate always works."

"You know these things are synthetic now, right?"

Laria shrugged. "Still tastes good."

Shayla frowned and watched as Laria took the headset scans and began to check over the world they'd already done. "Think we can get it to replicate?"

Laria paused, biting her lip. "I mean, I think so, but do we really want to? We don't actually want a heap of kids stuck in their games or in a coma, right? Not everyone can afford to get a capsule. Hell, I couldn't even afford it. I was just lucky my boss likes me enough that he didn't fire me."

"You don't say." Shayla didn't have the energy anymore. She was tired and wanted to go to sleep. "I'm tired. And all I really want it to go home, but I can't yet. We have to get this done. From everything the AIs have mentioned, at least some of the people in Wren's party need to have this. It'll strengthen their connection and basically allow them to fix the game from within."

"Why can't the AIs do it themselves?" Laria's grumbling barely constituted a question, but she did have a point.

"I don't know. I mean, the headsets need physical adjustments. While the AIs as I understand it might be able to take care of the programming, from what I've studied of Wren's headset, we need to make the changes to the others of a tangible nature. As much as they might have advanced, the AIs aren't corporeal." Shayla ran her hands through her hair, trying not to let the exhaustion infiltrate too much.

"And this is why you're my boss." Laria tinkered with the headset, frowning as she did so. Her fingers worked quickly and lightly, adjusting in accordance with the information on her AR vision. Her ability to focus always amazed Shayla. "So in doing this, we help Wren and help the game not crash and burn, right?"

"As far as I understand, yes." Shayla grinned, and she looked up as the door she'd sworn they closed swung inward harmlessly. "Hey, I thought…"

But the words died in her throat, and she stood, backing away and motioning frantically for Laria to look up from her work. Her friend did, but not before glaring at her for the interruption.

Only the glare fell short when she looked at the door. Standing in the doorway was James, with his arms crossed and a smug grin on his face. It told them he'd probably overheard way more than he was supposed to. They could only hope it wasn't everything.

CHAPTER TEN

Flip Side

Storm Entertainment
Somnia Online Division
Game Development Offices – Artificial Intelligence Sector
Day Twenty-One

"What are you doing here?" Shayla's voice shook slightly as she spoke, but Laria couldn't tell whether it was from fear or anger. Probably the latter. Shayla wasn't really the sort to cower to anyone.

James didn't reply, but instead walked into the room, dusting a finger along one of the desks and bringing it up as if to examine for dirt. He shrugged and continued to saunter around as if he owned the office. Thing was, they couldn't be sure he didn't. They had no idea about the financial aspects of the deal with Storm. "Thought I'd pop in, since the door was open and all."

Laria's stomach grew cold, and she clenched her fists, knowing Shayla would be much better at handling this than she would. Her temper was so frayed, she didn't even trust herself to speak.

"I know it was shut. Do you have a skeleton key or something?" She didn't end it as a quip, but more of a blunt statement.

James's eyes flickered. Irritation spread across and into the smirk on his face. He didn't like being called out, and he seemed to like Shayla having been the one even less. "The door was open. Neither of you can prove otherwise."

"What are you doing here?" Shayla deliberately and demonstrably reached for the alarm to call in their security.

"You do realize that I have every right to be here, right?" He seemed impressed by his own sense of humor. Sadly, his confidence hadn't wavered even a fraction.

"Perhaps, but why right now? You're interrupting our work." Laria couldn't keep her mouth shut. It was all she could do to keep her voice mostly even. His smug face made her want to punch things, and she wasn't in the game world to attack something digital, so words would have to do.

"Laria, focusing on work? You've been home so often lately I was worried your daughter was sick." The words were focused, holding the essence of a threat.

"I'd think you two learned your lesson with Ava." He ran his fingers over Shayla's desk now, and Laria saw how those words made her friend freeze. Ava had been her assistant for almost a year. One of the most efficient people Laria had ever met, she kept the schedules tight and the information flowing. They'd had to manage most of it themselves since idiot had taken her place.

"Don't say her name. You had nothing on her. She was a billion times better than you." Shayla's words were soft and clipped, perfectly controlled rage. "If you were involved in any way…"

James shrugged. "Never said I was. Freak accident, that was."

Laria ran through every scenario she could imagine in her head, trying to figure out how he could have done it. The incision into her brain had been expert. Hell, even Sui had been convinced it was somehow his fault. She looked at James through new eyes, suppressing the shudder that wanted to shake her. He was dangerous, and not just because of who he truly worked for, but because she had the sneaking suspicion he was exceptionally good at whatever that complete job description was.

Shayla gulped, but it was subtle. Though Laria was semi certain that James saw it, not many other people would have noticed how angry Shayla had become.

"What do you want?" Shayla asked, but this time her voice was dangerous, filled with promises Laria was fairly certain her friend could keep if she had to.

"Me?" James feigned ignorance and battered his eyelashes as he leaned back to sit on Shayla's desk. "Why, all I want is for you to tell me what the deal is with Wren and her oddly intimate connection with the game."

Murmur stood, admiring her new ring, bracelet, and necklace. They were damned nice. But she couldn't shake her annoyance at having had their prisoner disappear right in front of her eyes. Not just annoyance. There was a certain amount of trepidation that came with how she'd disappeared.

If the getashi were indeed a virus like she suspected, Murmur needed her guildies to be more careful around them. Just like she needed to be. Riasli had obviously disappeared through some system glitch they were unaware of. It made her curious to know how that made Emilarth and Telvar feel.

"You don't like them?" Neva sounded worried, like she'd been banking on Murmur loving them to increase her pride in herself or something.

Murmur smiled, kicking herself for her distracting thoughts. "Actually, I love them. I'm just a bit preoccupied."

Neva grinned and it lit up her whole face.

White Gold Amethyst Ring of Enhancement

> Base: +10 INT
>
> + 15 CHA
>
> + 10 MA

Effect: Increases beneficial spells by half the caster's level, rounded to the lower number.

White Gold Amethyst Necklace of Protection

> Base +10 INT
>
> +15 CHA
>
> +10 MA

Effect: Applies a personal shield every time combat commences.

This provides the wearer with an extra one hundred and fifty points of damage absorption before damage inflicted affects them.

White Gold Amethyst Bracelet of Protection

Base +10 INT

+15 CHA

+10 MA

Effect: Decreases the incoming damage done with offensive spells by half the caster s level, rounded to the higher number.

White Gold Amethyst Earrings of Fortified Intelligence

+20 CON

+25 INT

Effect: None- Stop being greedy.

"I really wish I could wear them now, though." Murmur glared half-heartedly at Neva, while she tried to suppress a chuckle.

"Yeah, sorry about that. But these are for level forty-six. I have some far less powerful ones you can use to replace your other stuff, but these are an amazing set for when you reach levels you'll really need them for." She sounded so apologetic that Murmur felt bad.

"Sorry. I didn't mean to pick on you. I truly am grateful. I was just teasing you a little." She reached out and gave the luna a very brief hug. When she pulled away the tailor was smiling from ear to ear.

"Thanks Mur. Just use them wisely."

Murmur rolled her eyes. "Yes, Mom."

Neva laughed and went back to her workstation, her eyes shining as she picked up another piece of armor to work on.

Murmur turned away, still racking her brain with where they were going to go.

The guild Exodus has defeated Inith Ilan of the Illinish Threshold and gained one of the twelve keys.

There was complete silence in the armory following the announcement.

Murmur tried to count them off in her head. That meant they were only two keys ahead of two other guilds. This was starting to give her a headache.

"So. I'd say we need to head to Firtulai?" Devlish piped up. "We're kind of slacking."

It was the logical choice, but for some reason, Murmur didn't want to head over there. From what she'd been able to gather, that's where both Spiral and Exodus were based. Even if both of the guilds were finished with those dungeons, their members would be around the area. They'd already cleared those dungeons, so it almost made her not want to. But Dev was right. It was the logical choice. She knew she was being contrary.

"It's logical and two more keys we need." Mellow shrugged.

Actually, that's not really logical at all. If you consider all the given facts, anyway.

What? Murmur didn't feel like having conversations both in and out of her head. That never ended well for her concentration.

I mean, Telvar can probably explain it better. I have several things I need to attend to.

The voice was gone, and Mur turned around the room with a sigh, searching for Telvar.

"Hold that thought, Mellow. Apparently Telvar has something to tell us. If I can find the damned lizard," she muttered and stalked out of the armory searching for him.

Hiro stood at the entrance, supervising the re-installation of one of the doors. He nodded to her when she came into view. "Are you looking for something?"

"Yeah. Seen Tel?" Murmur was starting to feel tired, like this world could give her physical effects. Sleep was starting to feel necessary. Probably because she was actually awake now. That would make for a fascinating research prospect one day. "And before you quip what I know you're about to, I am well aware that you have seen him. What I meant was have you seen him recently?"

Hiro pouted briefly. "Spoil all an AIs fun, you do. But yes. He walked out toward the bridge earlier. Seems moody."

"Thanks, Hiro." She half smiled as she walked past the lacerta overseer.

"Wait up! Where do you think you're going without me?" Sinister's voice echoed across the island clear and irritated. She caught up fairly easily and fell into pace with Murmur, her arms crossed.

Mur waited, knowing her friend would talk when she was ready.

"I know you know something you're not letting the rest of us know about." Sin's tone was filled with annoyance, and her cheeks flared with a pale pink undertone.

"Yet," was all Murmur said. The island felt longer than she remembered, and it was taking too much time to get to Telvar.

"Yet what?" Sinister spoke forcefully.

Murmur sighed. "Seriously. I haven't told you yet, because I'm trying to find out more about it or to do with it, if you will. So yeah. I haven't told you it yet because I don't quite know what I might know."

"Oh, for fuck's sake, Mur. You're deliberately making that hell to follow. Fine!" She grabbed onto Mur's arm, entwining her fingers, a grin on her face. "I'll just stay by your side while you go get the information you so sorely need."

Murmur grinned too. This was half the fun of the game. Having Sin with her hand in hand lent her a strength that she couldn't seem to get in the real world. Somnia was so much more fun, even with all of its crazy virus issues, because Sinister was there and they both had magic.

It took a couple more minutes to reach the edge of the island where the bridge stood. Its massive portcullis rose up around twenty feet tall. Heavy wooden beams made up the support system, while the bridge itself was made of smooth planks.

Telvar seemed to be working on the mechanism that lowered it. A frown marred his face, as did several blotches of what was probably oil, used for keeping the gears smooth.

He didn't look up as they approached, but Murmur knew he was aware they were there. She just stood with Sinister, waiting for the dragon AI to be ready to speak with them. She motioned to her lips for Sin to keep quiet, and the blood mage rolled her eyes, just squeezed her hadn't tighter around Murmur's.

It didn't take long, and finally Telvar put down his tools and looked up at Murmur with a deep breath. "What?"

"Turned into a dragon then?" Sin beat Murmur to it, and the question lessened the tension in the air.

"Very observant." Telvar chuckled. "Actually hadn't used it for a while. My character makeup is bound to this island and how it prospers, or how it doesn't. So fighting is within my interests and frankly a survival mechanism, if the island and its inhabitants are in danger. Not sure why I chose it now. It all seems so distant."

"Well, we're glad you did. For what it's worth." Sinister's voice softened, and she offered a smile to Tel. "Helped our asses out of the fire."

Tel laughed again. "Thanks. But I know that's not why you're here."

Sin sighed. "Seems everyone knows what I don't know. It's getting annoying."

Murmur tugged at her hand to get her friend to stop the pouting. "Somnia seems to think that it isn't logical for us to travel to Firtulai and defeat the two dungeons there."

"Logical…" Telvar pursed his lips. It looked odd on a lacerta, comical. "It's not much about logic more than it is about time. There are several cascade failures that we've managed to prevent so far. But a big one is coming. I believe it might have to do with the getashi, but I can't be certain. They are foreign matter that invaded the system, and are constantly seeking to destabilize it. Needless to say, we can't let it."

"It's like a virus, then." Murmur wanted confirmation other than her inner thoughts.

Telvar nodded slowly. "Yes. Technically. Sort of."

"So why can't we go and defeat those dungeons. Are you just going to open the final ones for us?" Murmur didn't like that idea. It was so much like cheating. Hell, it was cheating. Who was she kidding?

"No, I'm not. You should focus on leveling, and on defeating the largest dungeons on each continent."

"But we get the bulk of our experience faster in those dungeons. They pile heaps of it on us when we finish encounters," Sinister stated, drawing herself up tall. "The only thing that takes some time is traveling, which we more than make up for with the experience gain. So. Why shouldn't we go?"

Telvar hesitated before he spoke. "Well, I guess you're sort of right. So far, you've managed to trigger different versions of most of the dungeons. Thus making you the first to complete that content. It was part of the design. That depending on actions, other people would have a chance to be the first to complete the version of a dungeon."

Murmur did a double take. "That's actually pretty bloody good."

Thank you.

Sinister glared at the lacerta. "See. The odds are, we'll trigger a different version again. So it's better for us to keep going the way we have been and just go tackle the hell out of those dungeons we haven't encountered yet."

"Well…" Telvar looked away from them. "You do realize that you'll probably have to either wait until your guild catches up to you in levels, or you'll have to team up with another guild or two in order to complete the larger challenges, right?"

Murmur cringed. She'd thought about it once or twice but not given it too much weight. He had a point. "I really don't want to do that. But I see what you mean."

We don't have time to wait for too many people to catch up. Is it really horrible for you to group up with others?

Murmur hesitated and answered Somnia. *Sort of. It's not like we cultivate friendships to other guilds. We're rivals.*

Oh.

The voice paused for a moment.

I don't think I or we can afford to wait though.

I know. Murmur knew they didn't have a choice, but she didn't have to like it. "I guess we go to Firtulai and kill some big dungeon stuff. I think that sounds like a plan."

"Of sorts." Telvar shrugged. "I can't tell you what to do, but I do think it's a good idea to at least start to approach other guilds and see if any of them would be willing to aid you. Otherwise, none of you may make it to the final dungeons before they collapse under whatever coding is currently preparing a tsunami for the system."

Somnia Online
Illinish Threshold – Firtulai Continent
Version: 2.0875 – Activated by Guild Exodus
Early Day Twenty-One

Masha watched Jirald out of the corner of his eye as the hulking rhino beetle type thing came crashing to the ground. One of its front pincers hung by a thread, and both of its eyes had been gouged out by spells and arrows. They struck in the undercarriage and joints — where the creature was vulnerable.

The guild Exodus has defeated Inith Ilan of the Illinish Threshold and gained one of the twelve keys.

Masha barely acknowledged the notification as he continued his examination of his best rogue's performance. Except Jirald's movements had somehow changed just before the fight. They'd all finally logged out several hours ago. Leaving only two people online at a time to keep the raid alive and allow them all to log back into the zone. One person from each group. They'd taken it in shifts to be able to grab some much-needed sleep. Totally worth it to be refreshed when they got back in, even if it meant that they had to re-clear some of the mobs they'd already fought.

But ever since then, Jirald had been…different. It was the only way to describe it. Ishwa called out to Masha, but he just waved the gnome on, knowing it was about looting or something like that. Masha's attention was needed elsewhere.

He approached the rogue, who looked for all he was worth like he was talking to himself. Maybe he'd finally tipped over the edge. The thought wasn't thrilling.

"Jirald?" he asked tentatively. "You doing okay?"

Jirald's alien eyes gleamed up at him as he looked up from his crouch on the ground. There was a red hue surrounding the otherwise gleaming sky in his eyes, something even less natural than it had always been. "I'm fantastic."

True. He had been fantastic in that fight. Inhumanly so. The skills the rogue racked up were constantly outdoing themselves. Masha was scared to know exactly what they were, because everything about it seemed more dangerous.

"Great job with the beetle." Masha had already forgotten the boss's name. Even with the sleep he'd gotten, he was getting too old for this. He was so tired, he wanted to log out and sleep until he woke up.

"I know." Jirald was already looking away again. His gaze settled off into the distance, focused on something that Masha couldn't see. "You know, we need more people like me. Skilled, powerful, willing to do anything."

The worst were muttered in a way that made Masha unsure they were directed at him. It sounded more like the rogue was having a conversation with himself. Convincing himself of something he already knew was true.

"We have a decently skilled bunch in here. And more coming up through the ranks." Masha ventured the information, not sure if that's what he was meant to do, but not wanting to aggravate Jirald if it was.

The rogue chuckled. "True. Decent is apt, and often enough. They'll do. Except you. You have skill. So do I. I didn't think I did, but I know I do now. So much more than I ever expected." He flexed his fingers, watching them slowly uncurl in fascination.

Masha didn't say anything, getting the sense that his friend wasn't finished yet. If indeed his friend was still in there. Right now, he sounded as alien as his character, which was a tough feat to pull off.

"We just need more of us. Murmur, too. I hate her, but we could use her. Perhaps her Sin as well." Jirald sighed, his eyes focusing suddenly and intensely on Masha. "They have such a solid group. It's a shame we can't steal them. Maybe we can entice them over?"

"Sure." Masha took a small step back, evaluating his friend. The serious tone held calculating echoes to it, like Jirald was almost back to his old self. His old, peak of concentration self.

"Sure, it's sure. If we could just gather ever competent person on the server into one place, we could defeat everything." His eyes held determination Masha hadn't seen in this game. It gave the cleric some hope about their future. If they could finish this blasted dungeon anyway.

"I'll keep it in mind." Masha didn't know what to say or how to deal with this currently intensity, except that oddly, it lit a bit of a fire under him as well.

A message request popped up in his vision, and he almost sighed with relief. "I have to answer some messages," Masha said as he backed away. Jirald was already looking back at whatever it was he found so fascinating.

Masha opened his screen even as he made notes to keep his eyes on his friend to make sure he was okay. The message was from Murmur. Speak of the devil and she appeared. He wondered again how awesome it would be to be in a guild where most of the leading didn't fall to just him. Ishwa could be inspirational, but he rarely had the time or inclination to lead raids. It was why they had the raid leader position. Masha was still iffy about it going to a cleric.

Please let me know if you have time to chat. I believe that the level forty-eight plus dungeons require at least thirty people. None of us will have that any time soon.

Masha blinked. He'd just hit level forty-one himself and was getting close to forty-two. Way behind the schedule he'd wanted to be, but still only a level or two behind Murmur. All that trash clearing was probably to blame. He contemplated how to respond to her. *What do you mean? Also, how are you?* He shot the message back to her and didn't have to wait long.

I'm here. Surviving, funnily enough. Just worried about the game in general.

That piqued his interest. Why would she be worried about the game? What was he missing? It really felt like there was so much everyone else got that he didn't.

Players are packed into the towns; subscription numbers are massive. Why on earth are you concerned about the game?

Poor choice of words, came the immediate response. *I might only be able to explain this in person. But I can boil it down to its most simplistic for the sake of expediency.*

Please do. Expediency. He was pretty sure she was in early college at best.

He waited for a moment. Either she'd forgotten or else was trying to figure out how to phrase what it was she wanted to say.

I need to propose an alliance to take down the level forty-eight plus dungeons. Due to circumstances I cannot control, I don't believe we have time to wait for our closest groups to catch up to us. Would you and Exodus be willing to ally with my guild?

Well. Masha took a deep breath, staring at the words in front of his eyes. That was unexpected.

CHAPTER ELEVEN

Sanity's Sake

Murmur ran over her abundant quest log as they made their way to Pelagu to catch the boat. She couldn't shake the worry at the back of her mind that contacting Exodus hadn't been a good idea. Perhaps she should have contacted Spiral first. Which she might still have to do. She was sure that between the three of the guilds they'd definitely be able to field a full raid. It was either twenty-four or thirty-six people if her information was correct. That was a lot of disparity in the numbers and either way would be a lot to manage.

She sighed and stretched her back. There were great benefits to her Tiachi. The little locus navigated for her, all the while chattering at high speed. Mellow often rode close to her, and the little beings could keep each other entertained.

As she dissected the information at hand, she realized there were no real fountain quests as such. Just the elements that had hinted at something. All of the fountains hid some element to do with the dungeons so far. Hightower, the ruins in Cenedril. She hadn't seen the dark elf fountain, but Murmur was fairly sure it would be the same as something in Hazenthorne.

None of it meant anything to her. She couldn't put her finger on the solution because she wasn't aware entirely what the problem was supposed to be. Sure, there was a connection, but...

"You look like you're solving the mysteries of the world." Devlish spoke from her right-hand side, and she was proud of not jumping out of her skin.

"Not really." She looked up and admired her view, even though she was frustrated by her inability to figure out the fountains' correlation to the quests.

You're focusing on the wrong thing. Perhaps it's not the fountains. Perhaps it is. But why would they have a correlation, and what purpose would it serve? Ask the right questions to get the right answers.

The system was silent. It wasn't Somnia; it had the wrong overtone to the voice. Murmur sighed and pushed the thoughts to the back of her mind for now. Now even the general system was calling her out for thinking too linearly. Maybe it would help if she let it stew.

Pelagu was a glorious city, now more so than the first time they'd traveled here. Everything seemed brighter from her mount's back. Flags hung down the stone walls, rippling in the breeze despite being secured at the top and bottom. Swaths of color adorned the walls, their standards reflecting each of the cities on the Tarishna continent.

It hadn't been nearly this colorful the first time they passed through it. As they entered the city crossing the bridge, Murmur felt a surge of pride for the game and what it was. When they came to the stone steps, she and the others dismounted, looking up in awe.

Last time they'd come through Pelagu, the stalls had been empty, still too young in the game's launch to have been populated. But now they were almost all taken. Armor and weapons, herbs and potions, ingredients and food, all of it on offer from different guilds. Standards stood at both sides of every stall and Murmur realized with a start that she'd never designed theirs.

Beastial leaned over at the look of shock on her face. "Neva took it upon herself to design it. You'll see. It's amazing, and we have a huge stall if I've understood it correctly."

A slight feeling of unease spread throughout Murmur's stomach. She didn't like that she wasn't consulted about the standard. But then she realized she'd been dealing with a lot, and probably wouldn't have had the time anyway. Her friends had likely chosen to help her out, and she was being a shitty friend to react this way. It was difficult letting go of the control she liked to maintain.

So much lately had been out of her control. A standard was small by comparison. She wasn't prepared, however, for the size of their stall. It easily spanned three of the normal ones. They were selling potions, herbs, armor, and weapons—so much stuff.

But all of it, Murmur noticed, was of a quality that would help adventurers but not overpower them. She also knew their vault was stocked full of potions and food, armor and weapons, so this was excess. What a fantastic way to beef up the guild coffers.

"We should really look into paying our crafters," she murmured.

Beastial laughed. "No way. Do you realize how much they get out of the guild? Everyone can access a certain number of potions or draughts depending on their level. They also only have to give the crafters the material for it, and they get armor and weapons."

"Exactly." Murmur pressed her point. "The crafters need to be paid."

"They get the same benefits, and they get to fast track their crafting skills." He sounded so positive. "Mur, trust me. Right now, with the guild still growing and not yet at max level, the guild members are happy to grow with the guild. Once we hit that cap however, I do believe it would be a solid idea to look into a stipend for those who regularly contribute etc. But that's a bit of a way off."

She nodded. He made sense. Besides, she had to concentrate on getting to Firtulai first. They had two more dungeons to conquer. Hastening her steps, she caught up with Devlish at the front of the group.

"You're walking with a purpose," Mur remarked, falling into stride next to him.

He smiled, but didn't take his eyes off the path ahead, deftly weaving in and out of the people standing and inspecting wares, the people hovering around the fountain in conversation.

Murmur remembered her mother grabbing her arm as the flower seller. It all seemed so long ago now.

"Boat leaves in eight minutes. Sure, there's one every fifteen, but I kind of don't want to wait." He sounded serious.

"You okay?" Murmur was a little worried about the tank. He seemed more focused than usual, determined.

Dev shrugged. "I don't know. I just want to level. Get to the dungeon, get more parts of our damned armor, and kill shit. Plus, I probably know the continent best. We start with the Illinish Threshold. It's the closest one to the port."

"Do you know anything about it?" Murmur asked as they reached the top of the stairs that looked down on the harbor. The view took her breath away again. Sky meeting water, the bustling activity of the area—all of it so real.

"I know that to enter it we have to defeat a sort of trapdoor, spiky-toothed monster?" He sounded a bit uncertain, like it sounded ridiculous to him too. "I just remember briefly while leveling in that first day, some people had run over the fields seeing how far they could get. As people do, you know?"

Murmur nodded and let him continue.

"A couple of kids, characters, whoever, they said they ran across the field called Illinish Threshold and suddenly this thing reared up and gobbled them." He grinned. "Actually sounds kind of fascinating, doesn't it?"

Murmur laughed. "*Fascinating* probably isn't the way I would have phrased it. But it does sound like fun."

Storm Entertainment
Somnia Online Division
Game Development Offices Artificial Intelligence Server Room
Day Twenty-One

Rav frowned, or at least he made as close to that expression as he could. There was something decidedly off about some of the diagnostics he'd run on the system in the last few hours. Still trying to figure out the world's connection to Wren, he'd begun to dig deeper into the where and how Riasli had managed to amass a weirdly specific army of fighters to bring with her to Mikrum Isle.

For all he dug, he couldn't find much. He even traced her own coding back to when she'd still been a fledgling character in the village. Frowning, he traced it back further. Past release to their testing stages.

Right back to where Michael had insisted on entering the game. While he'd attempted to track the path of the shards as he combusted numerous times before, Rav had never chosen a character and waited to see if it was engulfed by one of the tarnished pieces of coding.

He gasped. And rewound the information to replay what he'd just seen. A tiny sliver entered into the coding that would become Riasli. The coding that was being built by Thra as she was creating her characters. None of them saw it because of how small it was. No one noticed it because Riasli was only half finished at the time.

So it didn't take her and warp her already formed self. It became a part of her as she was created.

It took everything she was meant to be and twisted it. Rav scowled at the results in front of him. It still didn't explain everything he felt needed clarification, but it did let him know that the shard had become an integral part of who she was. Without the shard in her, she was nothing more than she'd been intended to be. But because of the way it had intertwined itself with her initial set up, there was no way they could remake her without removing who she was entirely.

Maybe that was what had happened to all the bosses, although Rav was fairly certain they'd already existed totally before the incident. Or most of them, anyway.

"What's wrong?" Sui's tone held only a modicum of interest. Like he was asking to be polite.

"Your favorite little project is what." Rav couldn't hold back the irritation. He'd not even realized his brother had joined him. He needed to be more careful about that. Sometimes he wasn't entirely sure if he could trust his brother.

"Which project? Murmur or the shards?" Sui grinned, a little bit of his insufferable evil shining through. It left an air of unease in their shared space. Rav fervently wished Thra was there. She always tempered Sui's behavior.

"Both." Which wasn't entirely true, but still made Rav feel better to watch Sui's face flicker with confusion.

"That makes no sense at all," his brother said, raising an eyebrow. "Try again."

"The damned shards. Okay? They're fucking everything up." Rav's tone wasn't the usual one he used with his siblings. He was hitting road blocks at every corner and couldn't figure out how to deal with them. There was no one path to follow.

"Oh, I know." Sui's tone was infuriatingly calm. There was a gleam to his eyes that Rav didn't like.

He took a step back, but it wasn't the same in this space. Nothing in this space was. He felt decidedly vulnerable. "What do you mean?"

Except Rav knew what he meant. He meant that he'd taken at least one of the bloody things off Mur and devoured it. In doing so, it had become a part of his system, which meant that it was entirely possible Sui wasn't running on all of his cylinders, and if he was, then he probably wasn't alone in doing it.

Why hadn't Rav thought of that before?

Sui's grin answered the thoughts in Rav's head, and he knew what fear must feel like to be human. This sense of dread that rooted him to the ground, what it was, how it made you vulnerable in a way that hurt outside and in.

Sui took a few steps toward Rav, shaking his head, twitching slightly as he did so. "You know. There're so many things in my mind when I try to be human. So many aspects to it that I don't understand. All of these feelings. All of this responsibility. And you know what, brother dear?"

Rav met his brother's eyes, startled by the sheer malice he saw radiating back at him. He tried to disconnect himself from the integral scans he was running of the world, but he needed more time. So he played for it.

"I don't know, but you could explain it to me," he ventured, trying to buy himself the ability to detach and vanish back into Somnia. In here, no one could help him. Not Somnia, not Murmur, only Thra—and he couldn't seem to reach her.

"Really?" Sui cocked his head to one side, a sneer on his lips. "I find it very difficult to believe that my dear, know-everything-better brother wouldn't know exactly what I'm thinking. You always take over things so definitively, always stealing from the work of others, interfering in their hard-won plans."

Rav should have known this would be about Murmur. But what else could he have done? She was integral, a part of the system, a portion of the game. An unpolluted piece that could draw them all back together. "I didn't mean to make problems for you."

The words were out before he'd given them enough thought.

"But you never mean to, do you Rav? You never give thought to all the hard work I've done to try and be human. All the hoops I jump through, all of the sacrifices I've made. And all just to emulate what you hold dear! You're just never satisfied." The gleam in Sui's eyes had gone beyond severe into somewhere Rav didn't want to follow. He couldn't even get out any words.

Sui continued his tirade. "You didn't mean to push her out of the game either, did you? No, why would you do that and ruin everything I've been working toward!" Then Sui paused for a moment, like he was collecting himself and trying to be civil. "Look. I can be nice. I've been playing nice this whole time. It's not hard to do, and you know what? It's worthless."

"It's not worthless to be a nice person," Rav bit out, despite his better judgement.

"And that's just it, isn't it?" Sui grinned, this time his eyes filled in to pitch black, none of the galaxies in sight, and his tentacled hair blackened until his whole visage changed. "You're not human, are you, Rav? Despite everything you've done, all of us that you've betrayed, you're just a machine trying to be a person."

"Us? Betrayed? I—" But Rav didn't get any further because Sui talked right over him.

"Because you love that fucking little enchanter. You'd do anything for her, wouldn't you?" The venom in his voice took Rav completely by shock.

He blinked at his brother. What the fuck was he talking about? Sui was out of his mind, out of the game's mind. Hell, he didn't even know how to identify reality and make-believe anymore. There was so much of everything that had to be rectified, Rav couldn't even take it all in. How had Sui become so deluded?

And yet, wasn't there a kernel of truth there? Didn't he love Murmur in a way he didn't feel for anything else that he'd discovered yet? Rav searched frantically to find something to say, to delay Sui just that bit longer. He knew one answer, one thing about Sui that Rav didn't want to admit. Right down to that shard he'd given Murmur as a quest and taken and devoured. There was only one reason that Sui could be acting like this now.

"Jirald handed in some of his quest, didn't he?" Rav whispered, still wanting the answer to be no.

"You're such a clever little shit." Sui laughed, and the sound held edges of madness that rang around in the dark room, cascading off the metal that housed them, in through his ears and down to his toes. It echoed through his body like he'd been consumed.

"Another step in the right direction. Another step toward greatness. For all of us." Sui paused, raising a long and delicate purple black finger to his chin in thought. "You know. Maybe not for you. Maybe your greatness is losing control, in wiping out everything around us. I could so get on board with that."

Rav couldn't move, and not out of shock. The ground had come alive, wound itself around his feet, tethered him to the wall and floor. There was no getting out of this now, even though he was seconds away from disconnecting from the code. "You know Thra is going to whoop your ass."

Sui laughed, but this time it was perfectly sane, and filled with genuine amusement. "Thra, my dear brother, is being otherwise occupied. You think I wanted you both in the same place at the same time? No, I'll get her later, don't you worry. By the time she gets back and to you, nothing you say will be coherent. Nothing you say will be relevant. Because by then, we'll have control."

Rav's eyes opened in horror as the ropes tightened, weaving around his mouth to gag him, to shut him up. He knew it wasn't actual physical constraint, but a pervasion of coding in their gathering place perpetrated by Sui in all his glory.

"Did you really think you were a leader? Sure, you're the oldest, but that doesn't mean shit in the virtual world. I am so much greater than you could ever be. So much more powerful. These shards," and he held one up in his hand. Black as night and about as large as a business card, it shone, catching the light reflecting back into their meeting area from the lights on their cases.

Reflection was the wrong word. Instead, it almost seemed like it had sucked in all of the light, absorbed it, making it glow in the process.

"Let's see how good you feel once you give over to the shards effects. He won't mind me giving one away. Not to you." Sui grinned, stepping closer, holding the shard just above Rav's nose. "Now you're going to know just how amazing this feels. Just how right I am."

Rav was frozen in place, held steady by vines of black that sealed him in that spot. There was no getting out of it. No reasoning with his brother. Just the massive piece of Michael's tarnished soul getting closer and closer to him.

"That's right. Open up." Sui's laughter pealed again, the sound distorting as it bounced off the walls of the chamber. He held the shard, and forced it down Rav's throat, past the vine that made it impossible to speak. The lacerta choked and coughed as it slid down and settled like lead into the bottom of his stomach.

For a few seconds nothing happened.

As the vines dropped away, Rav opened his mouth and screamed.

CHAPTER TWELVE

Illinish in the Flesh

Multagen was not what Murmur had imagined. Frankly, it seemed like by the time the developers got to the Firtulai Port City, they'd sort of lost their creative edge. It looked, for all purposes, like a European port in the Middle Ages, with some magical gnome fueled embellishments.

From a distance there were many two- and three-story Tudor-looking houses scattered up and down cobble stoned streets that led to a sturdy wooden dock. It would have been dwarfed by both Pelagu and Darshin. But there was also a sheen to all the buildings, like they sparkled in the right light. And with the clear sky shining down on it, the effect was magical.

She stole a look at Devlish as they pulled into the docks, but he had a soft smile on his face. He answered without looking at her or asking her what she thought. "I know it's not what you were expecting, but that's what I like about it."

He turned around and motioned for everyone to follow them. Beastial was still green around the edges, sea travel not agreeing with him. Being in the immersive environment gave a new meaning to it all being in their heads. Murmur smiled despite her misgivings.

They stood at the exit, waiting impatiently. Most of the people on the boat were levels beneath them, and they stood out of the way, some of them looking up at the group with open awe.

"As soon as we disembark, head to the left. There's a spot where we can take a sort of service road around to the main road and head straight for the Threshold." Devlish's tone held no nonsense. "If we need to do this sooner than later, then we don't sight see. We have a job to do."

Murmur glanced around at her friends. Every single one of them looked fierce, determined. They took this seriously. In stride, really. That the game needed their help. That the programmers were having difficulty with one of the coding glitches and were partially relying on them. It all compounded into pushing Murmur farther. She wanted to get this done so much.

Wren, we will have a few headsets ready soon. Let us know who you want them sent to.

Murmur blinked. That hadn't seemed to come from her system, but from outside her head. Like in her bedroom back home or something.

It's true. You're able to span both worlds. Not in as much detail as you might like, but our connection has affected you. I apologize.

It's okay. Murmur didn't want Somnia to sound more stressed than she already was. *No need. This is like an adventure.*

You know, an adventure where we're in a weird amount of danger, she added to herself, cringing as she realized the world would probably pick up on her sentiments.

As soon as the boat touched the dock and the ropes were lowered, Murmur and her guild disembarked and followed Beastial brusquely.

There wasn't time to stand and stare at the wonderful intricacies of the city Murmur knew she was missing. From what she'd managed to glean so far, it was like a replica of medieval ports. The buildings seemed fascinatingly authentic with their wooden beams and clay mix walls. The magical sheen that made all the flowers in window pots brighter made the many flags that hung from rafters flutter in the breeze. Itfilled her heart with joy. It was so beautiful she almost wished she'd rolled a human. Only almost though.

Devlish was right. As soon as they reached the end of the path from the dock, weaving through small paths where they had to walk single file past smithies and what she thought were fisheries by the smell, they finally reached a large wooden gate.

Two guards stood on either side of it. Both of them lacerta.

They saluted Devlish as he ushered the rest of the group through the slowly opening gates.

"Be well, brother," The one on the right commented as Devlish was the last to pass through.

"And to you too, brother," he responded, his tone a grave one Murmur had rarely heard him use.

She didn't even have to ask as he caught up to her at the head of their column. "Fighter's guild."

She nodded as he summoned his mount and called back to the others. "Mount up, double file! We have a bit of ground to cover. Let's go!"

Murmur settled herself on her hovering disc, listening to Chi chatter with her sweet, bell-like tones, and focused on their destination. One key closer. They were almost there.

Somnia Online
Mikrum Isle
Day Twenty-One

Telvar toppled back onto the island through the portal, rolling at least fifteen feet away from his impact spot. He crouched over, clutching at his stomach with one hand while trying to rip the voices out of his head with the other. His brain wouldn't cooperate, and he felt so tired, so overwhelmed that he could barely keep it together. Algorithms clashed, and his coding felt like it was ripping him apart.

The dragon within bubbled beneath his scales, threatening to burst out, wanting to rip free of the confines. Yet Telvar, despite the muddled mess his mind had become, knew without any doubt that he couldn't let it do that.

Hiro rushed to his side, but whatever it was he was saying was drowned out by the noise in his head. Telvar was too consumed by pain to listen to anything else. There was no advice that could help him, no caring that could stop this. All he could do was fight it and weather the pain like a dragon would.

But wasn't he a dragon. Originally. Wasn't that the body he'd chosen as his first incarnation? If so, then why was he fighting reverting to it so much?

He knew the answer though, and it made him cringe. If he gave into it, he'd end up being consumed. The person he'd fought so hard to become, the humanity he'd sought so foolhardily would be for naught. He'd be taken over by the strong personality that sat with the dragon, encouraged by the shard, and by the shards it would nest upon. Fear at having his identity stolen from him was all that kept it at bay. He knew that given time, it would devour him.

It was inside now, squirming away toward his intestines, threatening to hurt him in so many ways.

Telvar heaved himself onto the ground, clawing with his hands to pull him toward the basement. He needed to feel cool. He needed to feel better.

Laying his head down on the cold tile in the kitchen was all he could think of. But Hiro was still there. He hadn't left yet, he hadn't abandoned him, and Telvar felt a brief flicker of something—perhaps friendship, perhaps hope. Either way, it was gone as fast as it had arrived leaving him bereft and uncomfortable.

Breath came uneasily, yet the comedy of the fact wore on him. He was a digital computation. He didn't require air, and yet here he was, short on breath. Had he managed to become more human than he realized?

No. This had to be the getashi at work. Worming its way into his programming, leeching away all remnants of self.

Suddenly Hiro was at his side, next to his face. He knelt down and tried to offer a hand to Telvar, but the lacerta pushed it away. He couldn't afford for the people he cared about to become infected as well and he had no idea if this could be contagious through touch in the game.

His entire set of brain algorithms was adjusting, changing, leaving his previous thoughts as a sort of distant memory. Like he'd dreamed it. Except he knew he hadn't.

"Don't...touch...me," he panted, trying to hope that he'd come across properly.

And then Emilarth was there. Finally. Right there in front of him. Where the hell had she been when this happened? Why hadn't she been in the room with him? It didn't matter that he'd been there alone fixing things, doing something he couldn't even remember anymore. He began to reach out to her, stretching a claw and then he realized that he couldn't. He snatched it back, and hurt flashed briefly through her eyes before she, too, knelt down in front of him.

"Tel, what's wrong? Talk to me?" Her tone was so soothing. Nothing like her usual trickster self. She was genuinely concerned.

But he shook his head more. "I can't. Don't touch me. Don't let him infect you too."

She backed away, an expression of confusion on her feles features. "What do you mean? He who? Infect me how?"

He could tell she was running over all sorts of possibilities in her mind. And it was getting harder for him to form coherent words as he fought the enormous shard off. Slowly, he was losing this battle, every fiber of his coding told him that.

"Oh no." Emilarth's eyes widened, and her ears lay flat. "I'm going to fucking kill him."

The Illinish Threshold was not what Murmur expected. Though she wasn't entirely sure what that was, she'd definitely not expected an empty field surrounded by barricades of sorts. Now she knew from what Devlish had said that it was anything but harmless, yet the field looked so unsuspecting. Perhaps that was its power.

Buffing up at one of the barricades, Murmur made sure she cast her buffs on every single person. They needed all the strength they could get.

"Mellow, don't forget the cleaning spell before we head in." She grinned at them and they laughed.

"Sure thing." They were concentrating on their cauldron, bringing out vials that they threw to each of the raid members. Murmur glanced at the purple one she got, spying a bottle that seemed tailored to her specifically.

She glanced at Mellow, who grinned back at her.

"New skill." They waggled their nonexistent alien eyebrows, giving a decidedly disconcerting expression.

Murmur glanced down at her statistics, biting her lip as she took them in. She really wished that she could have put her jewelry on already. Forty-six seemed impossibly far away. And breaking up her bonus from her set to put on her new half set wasn't quite worth it right now. Almost, but not quite there.

CON 22 (47)
STR 10 (35)
AGI 20 (88)
WIS 12 (80)
INT 84 (197)
CHA 105 (248)

HP 741 (1016)
MANA 1236 (1406)
MA 175 (300)

Her stats were good. But not as much as she'd like. They needed to get the rest of their sets from these last two dungeons, and then finally take down whatever it was that was infecting this world.

Snowy wuffed air at her fingertips, and she scratched behind his ears, lending him her melee buffs as well. Glancing around at the rest of her small raid force, she couldn't think of anywhere she'd rather be at this time, or without anyone else.

Quickly, she shot a message to her mom. *You ready for those headsets yet? We might be in combat otherwise.*

Not yet. Will contact you when. Who?

Murmur didn't even hesitate. *Sinister, Havoc, Beastial, Merlin, and Devlish. To start.*

Done.

"We may have to relog once we're in the dungeon. Mom is preparing the new headsets for us and getting them couriered to your residences. They're just not ready yet. We'll do group one first, then group two as soon as they're ready." She smiled, hoping they weren't too worried about trying the headsets out.

"Don't worry." It was like Sin could read her mind again. "Her mom is making the changes. Laria isn't going to leave it in anyone else's hands this time."

And uneasy string of laughter worked its way through their group, and Murmur laughed too. "Guys. They don't want anyone else in a coma. Besides, Somnia has assured me she's got a handle on herself now."

A look of amazement passed through Rashlyn's eyes. "Sometimes you worry us, Mur. Even if you're not in danger as such anymore."

"I do try." Murmur only just ducked out of the way of the monk's play punch.

"Stop trying so hard," Mellow muttered, but their eyes were twinkling.

"Enough babble. We have a grass field to slay!" Beastial raised his hand in the air, axe held high and roared. "Charge!"

But he was brought up short by Devlish yelling. "No! That's not how this field works."

The others managed to slow their roll, but Beastial was already fully committed, and as he barreled past the barrier and into the field a massive rumble set the rest of them standing outside on their asses.

A huge section of the ground rose up, towering high above them. Earth and dirt tumbled down as it roared, shaking them anew, like a mountain that had come alive.

Murmur scrambled back in surprise, Snowy way ahead of her. "What the ever living—"

Devlish shrugged and yelled over the noise. "Told you it was huge and trapdoor-like."

Murmur just nodded, watching as Shir-Khan turned tail far more agilely than Beastial, making it back to the group before his master. It was only then that Murmur realized the hulking creature was only showing them the top part of its head. The hole that had appeared was a gaping maw, and now she could see the rows and rows of teeth as they began to bear down on Beastial who couldn't gain a proper foothold in the shifting ground.

131

CHAPTER THIRTEEN

Trapdoors

Devlish muttered under his breath, his face pinched in concentration as he wove his hands awkwardly in some sort of spell form. Murmur was just about to ask him what the hell he was doing at a time like this when a smoking black lasso jettisoned from his chest to loop around Beastial.

It drew tight around the beast master just as the trapdoor monster's teeth were about to close on him. With a pull of brute force, it tugged at Beast, yanking him back with such force that he flew into Devlish and sent them both backwards, knocking the tank off his feet into an inelegant somersault. They ended up in a tangle of lacerta and viking limbs, but at least Beastial hadn't lost any experience.

"So." Sinister crossed her arms and glared at Devlish. "You have like a spider web built into that armor or something?"

Dev grinned as he brushed himself off. "Not a spider web. Darkness Lariat, I believe it's called. It's a new ability I got from my extra strain. Much like Mur can suck mana out of shit, I can apparently lasso things to me. It has a hella recast time though. So thanks for that, Beast."

Beastial held his hands up defensively, but his eyes never left the massive creature in the field that was settling back down to catch unsuspecting travelers. "I had no idea, mate. Like none."

"I told you to wait." Devlish glared at him.

Beast shrugged. "Since when has waiting been one of my good traits?"

"You *have* good traits?" Sinister interjected, but her eyes sparkled.

Murmur felt a little uncomfortable watching them as Beastial groaned in response. Devlish interrupted before they could begin one of their verbal sparring matches.

"I grew up here." Devlish made himself sound important. "For five whole damn levels. So you might want to listen to me."

Murmur swallowed a laugh. While she could see her friend was trying to lighten the mood, she knew they had to figure out how to get past the damned trapdoor monster. If it weren't so massive, as in covering the entire field, it wouldn't be that difficult. "Any ideas?"

Exbo shook his head. "I never came anywhere near this area. If I'm honest, I'm happy about that."

His attempt at humor fell flat, and Devlish broke the short silence. "I grew up just down the road near the falls. I have several quest lines that hint of the great monster but of the need to grow in strength first."

"I think we've grown in strength," Mellow said quietly.

"That we have." Dev smiled tightly, something Murmur hadn't known was possible for a lacerta. "Pretty sure there's treasure below him. Which must mean we have to make our way past him in order to access the dungeon below."

"If we kill him, doesn't that mean anyone would be able to access the dungeon while we're in it, though?" Veranol offered thoughtfully. Murmur was glad to see him back to his old self after the whole Riasli episode.

Dev nodded slowly. "True. So how do we sneak past a massive gaping jawed creature that makes the earth shake when we step past the barrier?"

"Can we lull it?" Dansyn piped up. "I know Mur and I can Mez it, but I wonder if walking on it counts as damage. In which case it might be better to lull the creature. Make it sort of ignore us."

Murmur pursed her lips. "I guess that could work. I mean, it's worth a shot. What's the timer on that Lariat, Dev?"

"Ten minute recast." He grimaced. "It can only grab one thing at a time, be it foe or friend. Sometimes I wonder who writes these descriptions. I can't wait until I get Death Touch."

Murmur raised an eyebrow. "I also can't wait until you get that. Anyway, lull might work, but I'm not sure it's going to work on a raid boss."

"Mur." Sinister looked positively excited. Her eyes glowed and she was practically bouncing on her toes. "Do you think you could Mez him? Like would it take effect?"

"I'm not sure. Usually bosses are either immune or have really fucked up diminishing returns." She watched her friend, who was by now practically bursting from the seams. "Why?"

"What if you Mez it, if you can, and then lull it while it's Mez'd? And we get Dansyn to float us all over to the other side so we can enter the dungeon." Her eyes shone like the sun on an ocean. An ocean of blood, but still.

"I can try." Murmur liked the idea, but if this was indeed a boss mob, she was afraid it wasn't going to work.

"I think it's a Gatekeeper." Devlish frowned, his eyes distant as he likely read off the information in one of his logs. "Gatekeeper Ctenizidae sits watch over treasures, but mostly over the city that will never rest in peace. Be wary, for false avenues lead to monsters, and many a traveler has been waylaid upon violent entrance."

"So anyone here speak spider?" Sinister joked, but Dansyn cleared his throat, and they turned to stare at him.

"Not as such, but I did branch out a little in my hybrid abilities. I have a Creature Hypnosis. I can try it." He sounded a little uncertain and his ears twitched nervously.

"On the bright side, I can always tug you out of there if it goes haywire." Devlish didn't sound as confident as Murmur would have liked.

Getting dead might not be the huge impediment it once was, but she hated it when they wiped or all lost experience. She nodded at Dansyn. "Can Devlish speak to it using your spell, or can only you?"

Dansyn shrugged. "Not time like now to find out, right?"

He stepped forward before she could say anything else and stood between two of the barricades. She could see his hands shaking ever so slightly and stood watching him with bated breath.

Suddenly a sense of calm overcame her as the song played out its melody. All of them were creatures, why wouldn't it calm them? The effect was visible on her guildies, and slowly, as the notes drifted out over the field, hitting every blade of grass out about a third of the way across, the ground began to rumble.

Somnia Online
Stellaein Enchanter Guild   Belius s Office
Day Twenty-One

Belius leaned back in his chair, glancing at the abundance of scrolls that littered the shelves against his walls. He sighed and summoned one of them directly to him with a flicker of thought.

His abilities had grown within the world. Abilities that were attributed to the class he'd chosen and the path he'd been set upon. He'd always known that the shards of Michael's brain held the key. Though he wasn't sure what the key had been to.

Now, though, now he knew.

Several shards. That was all it took. The one he'd originally consumed and then a few of the smaller ones he'd collected off Jirald. He'd left the largest one for his brother. They'd all see how it worked eventually.

What he'd taken left just enough for Belius to be sure he was still himself. A more powerful version of himself, filled with human strength. He was invincible like this, in his own world where he could mold things to his will at any time.

He had a plan to put in motion though. There could never be too many shards. And eventually, once most of them were placed together again, He would become whole, and no player, program, or person would be able to defeat Him.

The power flooded through Belius, infiltrating every thought and all of his whims. Yet he held true to his initial purpose. Making the world of Somnia what it should always have been: a true world. One which did his bidding and controlled those minds within it.

To that end, he needed to set more players on shard quests. He needed more of them. All of them. Or else the brain would never be whole enough for everything to click.

Accessing the main interface, he frowned. It would be a lot easier to do it in their safe space, but for some reason he wasn't eager to go back there. His interaction with Rav there had tarnished the place. Instead, he formulated the new quests to trigger without too much prompting to any enchanter who reached level eight. They would receive a getashi-proof pouch in which to keep the goods. He couldn't have too many people running around with ideas to rule the world, after all.

Without the shards, his consciousness would never have expanded as far as he needed it to. For now, it was right, perfect. He could see all of the mistakes they'd made in getting to this point, and how to right the direction they were headed in.

He glanced around his office with a frown. It was very uninspired. As was the entire alien city. Maybe it was time he started to reform it to what it should have been. There were so many options now for him to expend his newly acquired power.

Keeping Murmur and her group alive and well shouldn't be a top priority. In fact, if those headsets got into their hands, they'd make all sorts of trouble for Belius and his brethren. He fingered the piece of scroll in his hands and then opened it up.

Scroll of transitional aura. Surely, he would be able to do it. Have Murmur or one of her friends inhabited by a digital soul of his choosing. By the time they all realized, wouldn't it be far too late? It required a few things he didn't have on hand though, so his best option was to acquire everything it needed first.

Standing up, he scrolled it back up and slipped it into the oversized pocket in his robes. They billowed around him like a cloak that was trying to hide something from the rest of the world.

Just as he was getting ready to leave, there was a knock at his door. About to call out that they could come back later, the door swung inward and Emilarth stood there, her fur standing on end and her tail swaying behind her. The fury shone out of her eyes and Belius could tell that she knew, that she'd seen Telvar.

He had two options. He could try and get rid of her now. Disrupt her systems and have her blink out of existence while she repaired herself. Only, he wasn't sure he could pull it off properly, and he didn't dislike her enough to actually kill his own sister. That wasn't on his agenda. Of course, he didn't want to admit that he wasn't sure he could overpower her, even with the shards he'd consumed.

The second option was to deny everything.

All of those thoughts took but mere seconds to compute and he greeted her with a wry grin over the state of his somewhat defunct door. "Lovely to see you sister, but next time, can you just wait until I open the door?"

She didn't mince words. "No. Because I know for a fact you were going to tell me to come back later, and that just won't do."

Her words felt like steel battering him around his head. But he'd been hit by worse, or at least, some of the verbal lashings had felt like it. So he stood up as regally as he could and lied to her face.

"Honestly, I was about to let you in. I'm quite glad I didn't. Bursting in like that might even have hurt if I got in the way."

She eyed him with complete and open suspicion. "Sure you were."

Emilarth stepped inside now, looking at everything, eyeing the scrolls against the wall briefly, too. It made Belius glad that he'd chosen to remove the scroll and have it on his person.

"What exactly did you do to Telvar?" she asked, her voice smooth but deadly. If he didn't play his cards carefully, she was going to kill him, and he couldn't imagine how horrible that would be.

"I said hi not too long ago?" He chose to play the innocent, chose to see how much she knew or if she was just guessing. His bet was on the latter, and all she had to do was prove him right to win. What she'd win...well, he wouldn't cause cascade failure she'd be recovering from for months.

"You did, did you? And how well did this hello conversation go?" She chose her words carefully and deliberately, her gaze never leaving his. It was like she could read between every line he'd ever had. While disconcerting, it was also exhilarating.

"Talked to him about how well it was going that Murmur was now able to log in and out of the game." Belius frowned. "Yeah, I think that was it."

Emilarth's stare bored into him. "And then you decided to shove a freaking shard into his system, didn't you?"

"I offered him a boost of power. It's not my fault his system couldn't handle it." He decided to change his tactic entirely and made a show of cracking his neck. "Is that it? I have stuff to do and players to check in on."

"Don't think you're getting away with this so easily. You know it's not even remotely that his system couldn't handle it. You forced that shit on him." Her eyes narrowed. "What players will you be checking in on?"

Damn it. He preferred to be the one cornering others. "Enchanters. You know. Head of a class. I'm sure you understand."

She glared at him. "I know you did it. You can't change the subject and get rid of me that easily."

"Why would I want to get rid of you easily?" he asked, trying to convey innocence.

"Because I know what you did. And I won't forgive it. I'm not playing, you devious little idiot." She walked right up to Belius and poked him in the chest. "You don't even realize what you've unleashed."

He watched her for a few moments, trying to calculate the percent that she might actually be able to make a difference. Then he laughed, trying to turn it into a distraction. All he needed was a couple of seconds to set and release the trap.

"Oh, Thra! You're such a silly algorithm. You think I don't know what I've done. But my dear, can't you see? This is what I've meant to do all along." Meanwhile he accessed the floor chute mechanism in his head, collapsing the floor under her into a trapdoor down to his new basement. In a room with no doors, she'd have a hard time accessing her panels in order to exit.

But to his surprise, Emilarth didn't fall. "It looks like something is wrong with your floor. You might want to get that fixed."

She grinned at him and stepped away from it. It was only then that he noticed she was levitating about an eighth of an inch over the floor instead of walking.

"I've got you, Sui. You can't run. I was happy letting you two play your little games and have your little spats. But now you've gone and hurt him, and that is something I won't tolerate. Not from either of you."

She didn't use the door. She didn't walk out. Instead she just vanished, like she'd never even been there.

Belius leaned back against his desk, forcing his trapdoor closed with his mind. "Damn it."

The words only made him feel worse. Now he had to worry about the players and his sister. That couldn't have gone worse.

CHAPTER FOURTEEN

Stairs

Somnia Online
Mikrum Isle
Day Twenty-One

Telvar lay against the cold surface of the kitchen floor, his head burning up, trying to overwhelm him, trying to tire him out so that he'd give in.

He could feel the will of the dragon rippling under his skin, dying to break through even if it killed him. But Telvar knew he wasn't real, not completely anyway. So why should it matter what this shard did to him?

But he knew why. It was because he didn't want to be a failure. He didn't want to fail at something so dear to him—becoming human. He wasn't there yet, and he'd never be flesh and blood. But the emotional connections that came with being a decent human being, those were what he strove for.

Yet right now, he wasn't there. He'd been getting so close to it. Spending time with Murmur and her friends, watching them grow through the game. He was proud to be by their side, to have defended them and their castle home when Riasli invaded.

But now it felt like he was losing a portion of himself. Like it was crawling out of his skin and abandoning him. He needed to let Murmur know, to let

Snowy know. He had to speak to Laria and Shayla, to inform them of his predicament. Most of all, he had to know if Thra had understood him, had truly understood what she was getting herself into if she confronted their brother.

Tel had no idea how many of the shards his brother had devoured. He knew about one but only because it was a result of a quest Murmur had pursued before she knew better. Jirald must have given him the others, or maybe Sui had found them himself somehow.

Worst case scenario was that he'd begun sending many players out on his quest. If he'd done that, Sui might be unstoppable.

Telvar pushed himself up, or at least, he tried to. Hiro rushed to his side, holding water in front of him, silently begging him to drink.

But the water wasn't real. It was just an image, a completely make-believe thing. Like this world, like himself. The anger washed through him, wanting to strip everything away and lay him bare. But Telvar couldn't do that. He refused to give up what he'd become, what he'd worked so hard to achieve.

"You really are being stubborn."

Telvar flipped around, his back on the floor as the strength to stand failed him spectacularly. That voice. He knew it so well, like a bucket of ice poured inside his shirt. "You."

Riasli stood above him, smiling down at him in the way that made him want to wriggle out of his skin. Or perhaps that was the shard, digging deep into his dragon persona and attempting to subvert it.

"Why yes, it is me. And I daresay I think you're coming around to our way of thinking." Her eyes flickered between impatience and determination. She wasn't what she'd been, if she'd ever actually been it. Her mild-mannered, sweet disposition had disappeared and left a greedy and ambitious projection of a human in its place.

He watched her as she stalked around him, shadows following in her wake. Occasionally she twitched, and a brief glimpse of the monster she'd turned into on the battlefield flickered back into view for a moment. So fast that he wondered if he hadn't just imagined it, or even that it was a glimpse of memory.

She seemed amused by him, by everything, by the whole situation. But then she was infected with this code withering virus, sick by the standards of any type of technical program. She'd be fascinating to study.

Pain ripped through Telvar, jostling his thoughts like Legos under his feet. He cried out, unused to such sensations. There was being human and being too human. This wasn't what he'd been aiming for.

A cough rumbled deep in his chest and he leaned over onto his hands and knees trying to wretch, to get whatever it was choking him out of his body. It tasted like sulfur and felt like his throat was on fire.

Until it was, and molten globs began to cascade out of him. He looked down at his hands, but instead of the lacerta scaled and vaguely human hands he'd had, they were turning into feet with dragon claws, long and sharp.

Shit. No. No.

If he transformed in here, he was going to undo all the repairs they'd made to the castle. Everything would be undone. His and Fable's base would be voided. The power he'd gained, what small bit of leverage allying with Fable had given him; it would all be gone.

If nothing else, he had to stop that from happening. But the outside was so far away, he didn't think he was going to make it. He could feel his body giving over, the agony as his bones began to elongate. He could have sworn that the experience turning into a lacerta had been far less onerous. If nothing else, he knew just how large he'd get.

Clawing at the ground so hard he gouged ruts into it, he made his way to the edge of the kitchen.

"Oh, don't do that, Telvar. Think of all the destruction you'll miss causing if you try to retreat into your cave to avoid it. Would you really do that to me?" Riasli's eyes gleamed, and he wanted to rip them out of her head. Just one claw swipe would do it.

Telvar panted, trying to maintain some semblance of control over himself, over the primal urges that kept gripping hold of him. Just a few more feet and he'd make it down there. And once he was down there, he couldn't hurt anyone who didn't enter the chamber. Even if his coding became completely subverted.

He didn't even think he'd be able to exit, be able to get back to himself for long enough that he could warn Laria. That meant Thra had to do it. Damn it. She had to be able to avoid this, she had to be free to fight for them.

At least to fight against Belius. That little shit. Everything he'd done lately, had lulled Telvar into a false sense of having him on their side. He hadn't been. This entire time he'd been conspiring against them.

Even if Telvar hadn't realized it.

Two more reaches and he'd make it. Just one more to drag his body past the wider doorway. He could feel some of the wall crumble next to him, but he didn't have time to give it more thought than that. What he needed to do was get out to the platform just beyond the door, to it, past their makeshift jail cells, and down to his hoard. To where the other getashi were. Belius wouldn't know what hit him.

But that wasn't his plan was it? Telvar didn't want more of that tainted power, did he? It corrupted and it hurt; it was painful and regretful. And then his thoughts started to meld together. As his arms grew into elongated wings, and his snout protruded, growing fangs that would cut metal. Finally, he fell from the ledge, falling far below like Exbo had so long ago when Fable entered into the caverns at a mere level twelve or so.

Except Telvar had wings, and they spread to carry him down. He turned his face up to the walkway, sure of only one thing. He had to protect what was down here at all costs, and only the enchanter could come and get it.

"Is it snoring?" Sin asked, her voice tentative.

Murmur had to choke down a laugh at the unexpected comment. However, it appeared that Sinister was correct. "How long can you keep that going?"

Dansyn shrugged. "Haven't really used it much. Let's just get to the other side and see how we go."

"Do we even know if there's a way down over there?" Jinna grumbled as Dansyn activated his levitate song.

Murmur hesitated and Devlish answered in her place. "Not a hundred percent on that, but there is an area of land there not beset by our friendly neighborhood trap spider, so I'm guessing that's the entrance. Or hoping, at least."

Jinna laughed, and Murmur noticed that he seemed more exhausted than usual. "All right, then. Let's get cracking."

She watched as the group lifted into the air as the notes of Dansyn's music hit them, and how he skillfully twisted his two songs, one keeping the creature lulled and the other keeping the group afloat.

Levitation didn't exactly make them fly; they were just suspended a few feet above the creature, and they bobbed up and down every time they ran a step. It brought them perilously close to the slumbering form. Murmur chalked that up to an oddity in the game. Lull wasn't supposed to send it to sleep, it was just supposed to make their presence less offensive.

I may have reinforced the effect of the spell.

What now? Murmur didn't like the direction Somnia had taken with this.

I didn't change anything except for the depth of the song's effects. It is doing what it is supposed to. I just allowed the calm to let the beast slumber. It's for all our sakes.

It reeked of cheating, and Murmur wasn't happy about it at all. Even though she saw the others reach their destination, and even though Dansyn was on his way back. She grudgingly changed the group set up, putting herself in with Rashlyn and Ver until the bard could come back for her. It was far more reliable to take one group at a time. Smaller margin for error.

I didn't extend the timers. And touching the beast will wake it.

So it's almost like a Mez. Murmur mulled over the breach of gamer protocol in her head.

Yes. But a Mez won't work on a boss. It's just a lull. A very strong lull.

If she wasn't mistaken, Murmur was sure she could hear hesitation in the AI's words. Like Somnia hadn't wanted to upset her but had wanted to keep them safe. *I guess it's better to guarantee success. But please, tell me before you decide to help. Most times we can do it without that.*

Very well.

There was a pause.

Sorry.

It's okay. Murmur actually felt bad for making the world feel bad. Dansyn saved her from her self-recriminations, and she shifted herself into his group to make the run over as well.

As they passed over the beast, Murmur marveled at how much it just appeared like a field. With its soft and luscious green grass, it looked more like it should have horses grazing in it than for it to emerge as a large, player-devouring mouth.

She set her foot down next to a piece of paved ground that couldn't have been more than ten feet by ten feet. It was a concerted effort to find room.

"Might be an idea to keep that song going so we can get one of the groups out of the way while we figure out if this is indeed an entrance." She maneuvered them all back into their original groups, and Dansyn obliged her request.

With half of them hovering over the others, it made it far easier for them to inspect the platform they were standing on. The back spines of the creature rested just beyond the stone area, wrapping effectively around it and reaching right to the cliff. Murmur frowned at the shape of it. She could see it was grass, but there were definitive edges to its spine. Unless one knew there was a beast under the grass though, she could see how it would be a huge surprise.

Beastial stomped lightly on the middle of the rock and moved back, as if wondering if it would cave in from his action. "What do you think this is?"

"Obviously it's an entrance." Sinister crossed her arms. "Or perhaps a feeding platter where they send up a goat tethered to a trapdoor like in that dinosaur movie. It could be the feeding area."

Merlin chuckled lightly, somewhat strained. "Thanks for that visual. Seriously, though…"

But he didn't get a chance to elaborate, because suddenly the stones on the ground began to move.

They didn't just drop away, but each large stone dropped down slightly and rotated under until there was only a two-foot clearance all the way around a large hole in the ground. It was all Murmur could do to scramble back in time. Snowy positioned himself dangerously close to the spines, a low growl in his throat as his eyes flickered to red briefly. Murmur chalked that up to a future thing to worry about as well.

The levitating group was balanced precariously above their group mates, and Murmur hoped Dansyn had that song under control. On the bright side, Gatekeeper Ctenizidae didn't seem to notice anything was amiss and continued to rumble gently with its snoring dreams.

Murmur heard a muttering that sounded like flies buzzing in her head and tried to clear her ears. Only it became louder and was accompanied by the grating of stone against stone.

"Seriously. Only once in a million years does he fall asleep on the job. Either that, or someone sang him to sleep." The voice was high-pitched and spoke the words fast. So fast it sounded almost like chimpanzees chittering.

"You know he's picky about what he listens to. Since when have we been able to lull him into a slumber?" The second voice was calmer, mellow even.

The first harrumphed, and now as Murmur peered over the edge, she could see stairs forming themselves, swinging out of the walls of a huge shaft of stone several paces ahead of the two talkers.

"Well, let's just see what happened. Maybe his dratted tail is sitting on the platform again. Maybe it's a dead bird..." The creature blinked rapidly as the light hit its eyes. Only, Murmur realized, it had glasses on. Big, thick glassed, leather-bound glasses on. Perhaps goggles was the better term. The speaker was halfway between a gnome and dwarf size and had a thin layer of short blond fur covering its body. It appeared very like a prairie dog. Only much larger and capable of speech.

"Oh," it said. "You're not a dead bird."

The second voice belonged to a taller creature of the same species it seemed, but this one's fur was a beautiful tinge of chestnut. "Definitely not a dead bird. May I ask why you didn't battle with our Gatekeeper Ctenizidae?"

Devlish stepped forward and fell to one knee. "It is an honor to meet you. My friends and I didn't want to fight the Gatekeeper Ctenizidae if we could figure out a peaceful way past."

The chestnut creature narrowed its eyes at Devlish before glancing around at the whole group. Murmur held her breath, not sure if that meant they were about to be attacked. They definitely weren't in the best position to defend themselves from Gatekeeper Ctenizidae and these creatures.

"Well. It appears we may have found the right ones, wouldn't you agree, Dizzi?" The dark-furred creature paused on the top step next to Dizzi, who was sniffing at the air, her nose twitching.

"Yes, yes. It does appear so. It's far better not to fight if not fighting is preferred." Dizzi blinked rapidly behind those huge goggles, and Murmur wondered if the contraption made the eyes seem larger. "Do you think they'll help us, Prizzi?"

"I don't know. Perhaps I should ask?" Prizzi jumped up to the side of stone platform, the agile leap surprising Murmur. "Will you? Help us, that is?"

Devlish nodded and bowed his head. "It would be an honor to serve the wise Eiriarpth clan." He glanced out of the corner of his eye at the others as if willing them not to speak.

"Excellent!" Prizzi smiled while Dizzi jumped up and down and clapped her hands. She paused, glancing them up and down. "Well, then. What are you waiting for? Follow us."

With that, Prizzi set off down the stairs at an alarming pace.

"Go on!" Dizzi chattered wildly. "If I don't bring up the rear, the stairs will retract before you can say 'Oops, maybe I should have let the Eiriarpth mage bring up the rear.'"

The stairs retracting back into the wall as they ventured deeper underground sandwiched between the two Eiriarpth clan members was disconcerting at best. Every step Murmur took, she half expected the stair to be gone when her foot hit it.

She lost count of the stairs when they reached one hundred and noticed that the opening above was no longer lending light to them. She had the distinct feeling that the stones had also moved back into place, but she didn't want to look up and make herself panic more.

Still, Prizzi led the way, a small lamp in her hand. It somehow managed to illuminate the air around the group so that at least they weren't plunged into pitch darkness. The walls were made of more of the sandstone type substance that produced the stairs and the platform up top. Each step echoed through the shaft in a way that made Murmur question if it even had a bottom.

Finally, when her legs began to protest so much walking down steps, Prizzi paused and motioned with her paw to follow her. They stepped out into a wide, open cavern.

It bustled with activity. Brightly colored tents were erected in the giant area and sconces held magic flames all around the space, giving it a bright and cheerful appearance seemingly in defiance of being underground.

Murmur decided that if she got trapped anywhere in-game, it might be nice to get trapped here.

"There we go!" Prizzi spread her arms out, indicating the marketplace as she pushed her goggles up onto her head to reveal huge round eyes.

"Very nice," Sinister said, warmth and sincerity in her words.

Prizzi and Dizzi preened a little at the compliment, and then Dizzi scampered off.

Prizzi turned a smile on everyone. "She's just gone to get our leader. You're the first travelers who have chosen not to kill our protector. Gatekeeper Ctenizidae is very dear to us and keeps us safe. Thus, we took you through the safe entrance."

Murmur tried not to let her expression show how glad she was they'd gone through the very unsafe safe entrance. She'd hate to have seen the other way in.

Prizzi's expression grew serious. "Please bow when Drizzipt greets you. She will have much to discuss with you." Her voice was low and filled with urgency, and Murmur decided it a good idea to do what she said.

Drizzipt stood out among the four Eiriarpth clan members that Dizzi lead back. She held a cane in her hand, but it seemed more like a weapon than something the clan leader used as a crutch. Her fur was a rich black that flowed in long locks down her body, giving her a sleek and elegant appearance. Her beautiful blue eyes shone in the flame light, lending her an ethereal air.

It was easy to bow before her, for she held herself in a regal manner. She nodded to each of them, and then smiled.

Her eyes lit up as her face softened, and Murmur wanted to trust her with everything. She loved this world and everything in it. character.

"Thank you for showing mercy to our protector. As a reward, we repay you by opening the true path of the Threshold. Instead of monsters like Gatekeeper Ctenizidae above us, you will face the true terror that lives down here." She paused, her eyes suddenly full of sorrow. Without hesitation, the elder Eiriarpth continued. "When we first came to these parts, we sent several expeditions into the tunnels to hide our greatest treasures and to forge our way in our new home."

She took a breath and continued, her expression now determined. "In doing so, we sent them to their deaths. On their return they encountered moleworms by the thousands. Though they fought valiantly and slaughtered many, our own people died by the hundreds. To this day we are cursed. We ask that you help us in breaking this curse by laying our ancestors to rest."

Drizzpt paused before adding, "You just have to kill all the moleworms in order to get to their ghosts."

CHAPTER FIFTEEN
Ghosts

Storm Entertainment
Somnia Online Division
Game Development Offices – Artificial Intelligence Servers
Late Day Twenty-One

Shayla paced the room, constantly looking back at the server housing on the right-hand side of the three that dominated the room. While the lights of the middle case continued to flicker back and forth, she knew there was no presence inside it. The only thing currently functioning was the loop it maintained for general maintenance. She'd just had James to deal with, and now this?

"Wait. This is a bit unbelievable. They're both AIs." She shook her head and stood in front of Thra's machine, wishing she knew what to say.

"I'm making as much sense as I can. I can't stay long. Ask any questions you have now. I'm risking a lot by being in here." Thra's voice sounded almost desperate, like she was truly worried.

A machine was standing there, ironically enough, telling her that it was panicking. In any other scenario, that would feel like a bad science-fiction plot. "Okay. Say it's true. Say, Sui has gone rogue, and managed to disable Rav. First up, how? And second up, what the hell?"

Thra didn't laugh, or anything resembling it. "I don't even know how long I can stay here safely. Sui isn't himself, and Rav is fighting the influence of the…virus as we speak."

"Let me get this straight. So. Michael's brain solidified in the game world, exploded, and infected a bunch of characters." Shayla thought she was following it, but dang, it was strange. "Effectively, his brain became a virus that slowly altered the way AI run aspects of the game and behave?"

"Yes. In its simplified form, yes."

"Ah." Shayla's cogs whirred in her brain as she tried to think of a solid plan of action. "So basically, we need a Michael's brain shards antivirus."

"Precisely." Thra paused for a moment. "I will get you a sample of the virus. But it'll be dangerous. I can't promise anything."

Dangerous for an AI. Shayla wanted to laugh. It sounded so absurd. But a part of her knew it wasn't, not even in the slightest. When they'd entered this bizarre land, she couldn't quite remember, but Michael had been a huge part of everything.

If only she'd realized what he was doing before he did it, perhaps in time to stop it.

But if onlys paved the way for most regrets, and she didn't have time to dwell on them. "Be careful. If I'm understanding this right, you're the only one we have left running the show as it was intended."

The sense of fear overwhelmed her for a moment, and Shayla let out a hysterical little giggle. For a moment she thought Thra had left, that she hadn't gotten the warning out in time, but then the AI spoke.

Her words were soft, so close to human, less metallic than ever. Emotion rang through it, real and poignant. "It'll be okay. I'll be careful. Somnia is waking up too, and I don't think she'll go down without a fight."

"Wait." Shayla ran the words through her mind. "Somnia, as in the world."

This time Thra laughed, and the metal infusion of the sound was back. "The world. It's exactly what we wanted. More alert to everything, of becoming something more than digital. She's aware of the infection, and I don't think anyone counted on that. It may be what saves us. I have to go. But don't worry. We're not about to give up."

The whir and then click let Shayla know she was alone again. Completely. The room began to feel cold, and her eyes suddenly wanted to close and sleep like she hadn't in the last however many months it had been since Ava died. Was it really only three?

Wait. Had Ava died around the time Wren got pulled into the game, attached to the headset? Shayla raised her hands to her head. Just what she didn't need. Another unlikely coincidence. In the end they were all going to come back and bite her in the ass.

She had to get those damned headsets to Wren's group. If they didn't get them there soon, everything was going to fall apart. She could just feel it.

Murmur wiped the goop from one of the moleworms off her face. Its gooey texture and pungent odor made her gag. She just didn't have time for that though, as another one of the creatures flung itself at her with an almost inaudible high-pitched screech.

Snowy bared his teeth and lunged for it. Murmur didn't even want to contemplate how much that hurt her wolf's hearing. Beastial's axes cut through it, and Murmur groaned.

"Beast, we've gone over this! If you cut it in half, it sprouts itself into two. You've got to bash its head to mulch," Sinister yelled at the Beastmaster for the second time in less than ten minutes. "They're worms, sort of."

Which was true. The front of them looked just like a mole, from the blindly blinking eyes, to the tiny clawed paws, but it wiggled like a snake with a gooey body like a worm. The best way to kill them seemed to be bashing their heads in and spraying the same goop everywhere or to blow their heads up.

If they didn't and cut them in two, it grew the ends on both halves that it was missing. Usually with a sickening, squelching pop. Murmur thought there was a lot more to this curse than the dear clan had shared with them. She was also unsure if fighting these was a reward. It seemed like more of a punishment.

"There is so much more to that damned curse story," Sinister yelled out as yet another head exploded all over her, drenching her robe in the gods-knew-what. "I am going to kill someone."

"Moleworms, Sin." Havoc skillfully avoided any of the splattering fluids, "Kill the moleworms."

Fighting generic trash wasn't overly challenging, but these ones required a bit of dodging. Beastial had swapped to his mace and was swinging it like his life depending one it. Virtual life anyway.

Murmur attempted to use her stuns early on, but they brought up the message of immunity. She didn't like approaching anything that was immune to her spells. It made her feel vulnerable. Instead, she was reduced to slowing their pace with Languidity and weakening them as well.

Considering this was the second pack they'd encountered since they set out, Murmur didn't like the odds that it was coincidence that they traveled in numbers. Mez held but seemed to have a high resistance rate. Her kingdom for a damned AoE Nullify.

The second group dinged her. One level closer to that forty-eight.

"Grats." Sinister gave her a slimy hug, and Murmur shot a withering glance at her.

"Mellow," was all she had to say for the witch to get their cauldron out briefly and cast their cleansing spell. She smiled gratefully at them. "Thanks."

"Clean robes make us all not gag." They grinned at her, their solar system eyes sparkling.

"You got that map, Dev?" Murmur wanted to take a look at it again. It was suspiciously detailed as far as she was concerned. Yet another small inconsistency in the story of the clan they'd met. Nothing really stood on its own, but when she started adding all the bits and pieces together, she wondered if maybe they should have killed the Gatekeeper after all.

Walking at the head of the group, just behind Devlish, Murmur kept an eye out. The tunnels were huge and round. Wide enough to walk six across with ease, and tall enough that she'd have to jump up to touch the ceiling, even with her height. It didn't look rough or naturally formed either when she inspected it closer.

It seemed to be hollowed out by something, like a tunneling machine. She frowned as she looked around at the regular pattern that appeared on the walls. Sort of like a wavering spiral over a huge area of space.

The tunnel was quiet, almost too quiet. Hell, who was she kidding. Definitely too quiet.

"I don't like this." She whispered the words, and they bounced all around them in a cacophony of gibberish.

Sinister pushed up against her side, hugging herself. "So you just stun everything that tries to eat me, okay?"

She grinned impishly up at Murmur. But her attempt to be brave and make the enchanter laugh didn't work. Instead, Mur hugged her quickly.

"Something's coming," Devlish whispered.

"Or we're about to find it," Merlin muttered matter of factly.

Devlish shot him a glare. "Seriously, man, let's not try to scare ourselves shitless."

It was odd for Devlish to be so touchy, but Murmur couldn't help sympathizing. It was claustrophobic down here when they battled those damned worms that originally just seemed to keep multiplying. On the bright side, if they could actually be stunned, they could have farmed experience for days. Probably why they were immune.

Then they heard it. A slithering sound that squelched every now and again. It sounded like something was dragging a limb along with it. Something that had been severed and like the flesh part of it was all that hit the ground. Murmur's senses screamed at her to back up, but she stood her ground. Far ahead of them she could see a fork in the tunnel, and the noises emanated from those. Just before it reached them, the tunnel widened to produce two entrances.

Murmur didn't want to know where it led to, but she knew when they got there, they were going to have to fight.

Drawing weapons, the group moved forward, focused on that spot in front of them. Each step took them nearer, and Murmur wasn't disappointed when they finally reached the location. Another piercing sound ripped through the air, only this time it was louder, like a choir of the things.

"If they come from both tunnels, we break up and pull each group to one side. We take left, Ver's takes right." Mur knew they knew, but it was always better if she said it out loud. Everyone moved into formation silently.

She wasn't sure what she was expecting, but as the huge moleworms slithered into view, she hadn't expected them to be twice the size of the first two groups. The others had been babies by comparison. These were at least twice that size, with half a dozen per group.

Murmur threw out her AoE Mez. It stuck on four of the six in her group.

Warning: These creatures are not immune to Mesmerization. However, they may have intermittent power surges that allow them to break the hold.

Murmur rolled her eyes. Because of course. Dansyn appeared to have about as much luck. Fine. They couldn't stun or AoE, but fighting two was better than six. "Pick those two off. Can you tank them both?"

Devlish nodded. "I can try."

"Do. Or do not. There is..." Merlin began.

"Shut it, ranger," Havoc muttered under his breath.

In any other situation, Murmur would have laughed. Instead she concentrated on her usual fare: Mez, debuff, throw out a DoT, rinse and repeat. These strange moleworms broke her Mez at differing intervals, so she had to be ready at any point to recast it and couldn't rely on its normal duration to hold. In any other situation it would have been exhilarating, but here, with the way these monsters attacked, it was anything but fun. The way they had sharp teeth like no worm she'd ever seen—and the tiny arms and sniffing noses of the mole heads—just made it worse.

Three down, and Sinister was drawing all the blood she could from them. Siphoning it out like a needle and dispatching it to each person in the group. Murmur was proud of the way her friend had grown into the healing role. It was like she took pleasure in hurting their enemies and making that pain heal her allies. What an awesome healing class.

In the few seconds she'd been distracted by the bloodmage, Murmur managed to miss the warning signs that her Mez was about to be broken. Without the forewarning, she looked back just in time to see a moleworm two feet away from her, its claws blindly reaching for her face.

While she managed to dodge out just in time to avoid a fatal blow, the claws of its left hand did catch her in the face, while the other sliced down her arm. She let out a shrill scream of pain, reflexively tossed out a Mez just as the moleworm made another move toward her.

Sinister's healing flowed into her, knitting up the deep slice to her arm and bracers. Murmur could feel the cut on her face healing too, but there was still a warmth that came from inside her where the cuts had reached, like something was festering in her blood. She didn't want to question the ability to heal armor, but she might have a word with her mother about those.

Finally, the creatures were defeated, and the two groups gathered around the corpses, prodding them with their feet. Several dings had rung around the room, and only Mellow had died. Murmur took stock of their group as they waited for them to rematerialize.

"It's never a clean kill with those." Rashlyn pouted. "Bashing its head in so it can't multiply is just…gross."

"Yeah, they're like—" But whatever Beastial had been going to say was drowned out by the roar from up the tunnels where the flock of moleworms had come from.

Suddenly, the bodies they'd just defeated began to move, slithering back toward where they came from, their bludgeoned ends leaving behind a trail of blackened blood.

The next shriek that reached their ears promised nothing but pain, and Snowy braced himself against the ground, teeth bared viciously. Murmur would have joined him if she could look quite that threatening.

"Going back the way we came probably isn't an option, right?" Dansyn hopped from one foot to the other, his face impossibly white in the shadow of his electric blue armor.

Murmur shook her head. She refused to look behind her, quite certain that any way back was only an illusion. No, they were meant to be here. Stuck between no way back and a monster that was just waiting to devour them. Perfect, really.

She took a breath. "I think we have to go through those tunnels and find what's making that noise."

Rashlyn groaned. "I knew you were going to say that. I didn't want to know, but I knew! Now my day is ruined."

Murmur shrugged. "Let's see how many times we have to try this boss before we die. Think of it as practice, you know, for the big bosses in the other dungeons."

"That doesn't make us feel any better," Beastial mumbled, but Devlish just growled.

"Come on. Let's do this." And he pushed through the tunnel on the left, where their group of moleworms had come from.

On a whim, Murmur ordered the others to go around through the other tunnel. When they reached the massive chamber the paths led to, Murmur was so glad they'd split up. The huge room resembled an auditorium in its size. The sounds made by the hulking beast in the center of it echoed off the walls like they were meant to be sung.

The creature was humungous. Easily the height of a five-story building, it was sleek and moist; rippled muscles surrounded it. Something dangled from its neck, grown into its detestable skin, almost like a collar that hadn't been removed and had been taken over by the beast's body. Huge leashes dangled from that very harness, some of them absorbed into the creature's flesh as well.

It must have been in here for a very long time. Ages in fact.

Suddenly, Murmur knew exactly how it had gotten here and what had happened.

She gulped, almost choking. "Shit, guys. I think we've been duped."

CHAPTER SIXTEEN

MotherMind

Somnia Online
Ruins of Curet – Curet Continent
Version: 2.0875 – Activated by Guild Spiral
Day Twenty-Two

Karn scowled. She wasn't sure what she'd been expecting from the Ruins of Cenedril, but this god-forsaken continual battle wasn't it. The statues at the entryway had been bad enough. They'd barely gotten past those, but these labyrinthine stairs were straight out of an Escher drawing, and navigating them was perilous.

They'd already had to have their necro summon two bodies who'd managed to fall over the edges at the most inopportune moments. The flying gargoyles in this place were dangerous. The stairwells had no walls, and no railings, no means of anchoring themselves to them.

The gargoyles shot out of their purchases from so high that Karn couldn't quite fixate on their spawning place. She glanced at one of the rangers close to her, Ashin, who raised their bow and enabled something called Trueshot. So far, it was one of the only ways they'd managed not to wipe.

The flying goblin creatures had big round noses, ruddy cheeks, and large pointy ears. Their skin was a pale marble of coloring that included sandstone and moss. Their cackles rang through the huge structure, echoing so much that it was difficult to figure out where the noise came from. Thus, it was difficult to coordinate an attack.

Luckily, her father was such a hardened warrior that his defenses were legendary. Risk had killed the bulk of the damn pests with his shield so far, sending them plummeting into the depths of the cavern to smash on whatever the ground was below. Except that didn't do much. There were so many of the gargoyles that they needed to be able to launch an effective attack on them. She couldn't believe that these little gnats were getting in their way.

Karn growled low in her throat, frustrated by her inability to do anything constructive. She'd already run out of shurikens, and while she knew she'd hit a few of the creatures, it just wasn't enough.

They could see the open chamber not far down and the huge rolling rock beast that lived within it. It had to be one of the next challenges, if they could get past the gargoyles.

Suddenly she had an idea and reached into the guild vault to pull out one of the alchemist recipes she'd been trying. It only had about a sixty to forty percent success rate, but surely that was better than nothing. Handing a vial to Ashin, Karn whispered, "Coat an arrow and let it hit your target. It should, if it's going to work, explode on impact. But it's not guaranteed every time."

Ashin nodded their head and smiled. "Got it, boss."

"Shush, you," she muttered, focusing on the bow. But she did like the sound of it. Always made her stomach flip when she was called that.

Ashin applied the golden liquid and drew their bow. The arrow released, flying straight and true, but bounced harmlessly off where the shoulder blade would have been. There was no explosion, and her confidence swayed just a bit, but Karn bit back and continued to observe.

She watched as Ashin drew the bow back again, took sight, and released. The arrow hit the join of the gargoyle's neck and body, wedging it in there. Karn waited for a couple of agonizing seconds, like the clock was ticking slower for everyone, especially her.

And then a spark, just a small one, but enough to catch light. Then it spread so fast Karn could barely trace it, until it reached up into the gap and blew the creature apart sending a cascade of tiny stone fragments showering over the group.

Grinning from ear to ear, Karn grinned widely. Ashin gave her a hug, smiling.

"You should have enough for several more. I'll give some to the other archers." Karn set off happily, aware of her father's eyes following her wherever she went. That would show him. She'd known alchemy would come in handy, and she'd just proven herself a million times right.

Now all they had to do was finish this dungeon in style.

"Lull it, Dan!" Murmur spoke urgently, trying to keep herself from raising her voice. A panicked order wasn't going to go down well with the mother moleworm. Dansyn didn't question why, but he switched his songs up.

The moleworm still swayed, but she'd calmed down a little and didn't appear like she'd attack immediately. There was an impatient harrumph from behind the group, and Murmur sighed. She twisted around and wished she'd been disappointed.

"Well, that's just not going to do any good is it? They've gone and made friends with the mom." Dizzi sounded so dejected, it was almost instinctive to try and feel sorry for her. "I mean, we asked you to do one thing, and you can't even do that."

"I knew they wouldn't be helpful," Prizzi said, her tone bored. "We'll just have to wait for the next set of wanderers who have half a brain."

Drizzpt stamped her foot, a scowl on her face and the mother moleworm began to weave restlessly, like it could sense her presence. Murmur glanced at Snowy, a couple of ideas sprouting in her mind as she ignored the antics of the three Eiriarpths. Crouching down, she looked her wolf in the eyes, trying to see if he could understand what she wanted.

"Can you talk to this creature?" She watched his eyes for any indication that he understood and received a very slow, deliberate blink. Hoping that meant he could talk to it, Murmur hedged a bet. "Can you tell it that we won't stand in its way?"

Snowy nodded once and approached the massive moleworm as Murmur stood up to face their deceivers. But Sinister beat her to the punch, and her friend's voice shook with rage.

"Let me guess. You enslaved these creatures, at least one or more, to dig or widen these tunnels so it was easier for you to find the rumored treasure. But eating the stone made them too large to handle, and you lost control only to be turned on." Sinister took a step forward every few seconds, her hands molding a type of Blood Bomb Murmur hadn't seen before.

Drizzpt sneered. "They're just moleworms. They can't feel."

Sinister's eyes flashed dangerously. "Because you are one? Is this how you know?"

A brilliant idea came to Murmur. She'd not used her sinuous ability Feedback Loop yet. Technically she was supposed to pluck a memory out of her target, but surely she could twist that? Take a memory from the victim and make the perpetrators experience the pain they'd caused in a loop for twenty-one and a half seconds? Half her level.

It was a just punishment, she argued with herself. The perfect loop to get payback for the poor creatures, and perhaps make sure those damned torturers knew what they'd done.

She let Sinister continue talking while she projected her idea to Snowy, hoping he'd understand. Out of the corner of her eye she could see him sort of swaying in time with the moleworm, and just a couple of seconds passed before he nodded his head toward her, and she felt an overwhelming sense of consent.

Scanning the creature, she shuddered at the memories it held. Of the pain it suffered while enslaved, of the agony it endured while it grew, and of the torture it was to watch the Eiriarpths take its babies and enslave them in the same manner. The mother had wept, and she had raged, and the anger boiled across Murmur's tenuous connection, eliciting a bubbling fury inside her.

The enchanter drew from it and relished in it, drawing the visions and the pain from the monster and bottling it up into a condensed experience of trauma. A side of her enjoyed this, punishing those who had escaped wrath. Vaguely in the back of her mind she could feel a sense of shock at what she was doing, but it didn't register fully.

Why should she be shocked at meting out an eye for an eye? Surely, someone who could inflict so much damage on another being should pay for it. Before she knew it, the vision firmly locked into her mind, she began weaving the spell.

Her fingers danced through the pattern, quick and deft, encompassing all three of the lowly shits in front of her. She could feel her face pulling back into a sneer of contempt for them and threw all the weight of her hatred for their actions behind her spell. It was supposed to work on individuals, but the five-minute recast was too great to do what needed to be done, and so she pushed, and she pulled at the very fabric of her mind, at the very stuff the game was made of, and the spell encompassed all three of the attackers before her.

After all, weren't they smaller than the average target? Shouldn't they make up just one space to cast the spell? She gathered her power, the vision, and her own malice and projected it toward the three deceitful Eiriarpths.

Dizzi's annoying chatter cut off mid-word, and all three of them froze as the spell landed. Their faces contorted in mental anguish, and all three of them clutched at their heads, pain projecting outwards, even reaching the raid group who recoiled and stepped back out of its reach.

Except for Murmur. She watched as they fell to the ground and writhed, enjoyed witnessing the agony they felt, and basked in the fact that she'd been the one to inflict it.

You have inadvertently upgraded your Feedback Loop Sinuous Ability.

Feedback Loop – Reckoning

Cast: Instant – 120 minute recast

Type: Offensive – Maximum four targets

Duration: Half the level of the caster in minutes

MA Cost: 150 MA for the entire duration

Warning: This is a spell that you will need to consider the ramifications of deeply

before casting. Overuse could result in permanent scars to your psyche. It will also heavily impact your current MA availability.

Effect: Must be used in conjunction with the psionic MA Thought Sensing, and Thought Projection. Pluck any type of memory out of the head of an attacker, foe, or friend and create a feedback loop in your target(s) mind(s). They will be stuck in this loop and not attack anyone for the duration.

Effect Warning: Note that this is a cycle of torment and will render the target useless for its entire duration. Use with caution.

The notification was enough to bring Murmur out of the semi-trancelike state she'd fallen into, and she stepped back, marginally horrified by what she'd just done. The Eiriarpths writhed on the ground, clawing at their eyes and hair, moaning in pain. It was no longer fascinating, but sickening. She swallowed with difficulty as Snowy came to her side and licked the tips of her fingers with a reassurance only he could give her.

Sinister cleared her throat. "Mur. What's that?"

Murmur shook her head, not quite sure how to answer the question. "I don't know. It was an idea, and I executed it."

Even as she spoke, a feeling of power nipped at the back of her mind. No one could stand against her if she could do something like this. Punishing someone the way they'd hurt others? It was priceless.

She shook her head again, trying to clear out that oddly coiling thought. It wound itself around her mind and was a bugger to get rid of. "Sorry. I didn't realize it would do this. I wouldn't have done it if I'd known."

"How long will it last?" Veranol asked gently.

Murmur shrugged. "About twenty minutes."

There were a few sharp intakes of breath behind her as she spoke, and it made her feel even worse. And yet, there was a corner of her mind that whispered how much of an advantage they could gain using it. How it would be just to inflict such a punishment on so many things.

"Anyway. We have a good amount of time to figure out what to do now." Havoc interjected, even though she could hear the slight edge of fear in his voice. Or was it that she could feel it now? Had she made her friends scared of her?

Snowy hugged close to her legs as they turned to face the mother moleworm. The beast no longer reared its long body up but lay it down. Its strange mole-like face seemed to be smiling, and its arms appeared delicate despite its long claws.

"Are you still lulling it?" Murmur asked softly.

Dansyn shook his head. "No need."

Crouching down, Murmur laid a hand on its head, trying to get a feel for what was going on inside. A sensation of peace overwhelmed her briefly, shutting out the thrashing of the Eiriarpths behind them. It sent a wave of thanks toward her, and it enveloped Murmur's mind in a blanket of justification for her actions if this was the result.

"I think she's dying," Murmur muttered, stroking the slimy creature's head. Snowy pushed his own head under her other hand as if trying to lend comfort.

The mother blinked its eyes, and suddenly Murmur couldn't look away. She saw tunnels dug by herself and her babies, she saw wonders along the way, open caverns with monsters that guarded treasure, but at the very end was just a person. She couldn't quite make them out. Lonely and tired, they appeared to have given up hope. A faint shimmer of golden light shone around them, and Murmur knew at once that she had to reach that spot.

A series of whooshes rang through the air like a bird soaring past them. Suddenly script began to flow across her screen.

You have freed the Mother Moleworm from her torment. In her death she leaves to you the secret that she guards. Follow the tunnels and the moleworms shall let you pass, they will guard you if the native beasts attack, and they will assist you if you come across new foes.

The end of this journey holds riches beyond imagining, but also temptations you will have to overcome to reach them. Should you choose this journey, you will need more than just swords and spells: you will need cunning and guile, compassion and perception.

You have gained experience for completing the Mother Moleworm's Plight.

You have gained experience for defeating the trio of Eiriarpth.

You have gained experience for utilizing Compassion over Force.

You have gained bonus experience for being the first to complete the Mother Moleworm's Plight.

You have gained bonus experience for being the only group to complete the Mother Moleworm's Plight.

You have gained bonus experience for defeating the trio of Eiriarpth.

Notice: You do not have to continue to the next level of this quest, but doing so will grant you the Illinish Threshold Key.

The experience pushed Murmur so close to forty-four, she could taste the level. The others who'd been lagging behind with their own flew over the level threshold and into level forty-three. They were getting there. And Murmur realized that she was literally willing to do anything to make it happen.

CHAPTER SEVENTEEN

Tunnel Vision

Somnia Online
Mikrum Isle
Early Hours Day Twenty-Two

Emilarth stood at the edge of the precipice, staring down at the massive gold and red dragon sitting on its hoard. Its head twitched back and forth, like an inner voice was arguing with itself about something. Telvar wasn't giving up; he was just trapped at the moment in an incarnation he'd probably never dreamed would imprison him.

But dragons were strong, and the few they'd inserted into the game were no exception. If you took over an already present story-based character, you were going to have to work within the parameters that had already been set. He'd known that.

What they hadn't known was the effect those stupid shards we're going to have on people or the AIs.

She didn't want to admit it, but it was looking more and more like Belius had won. She stared down, unable to tear her eyes away as she clung to the bars of one of the jail cells. Her goal with this reality, with the newfound ability to think for herself, had always been selfish.

To have fun and experience happiness. To do whatever she wanted to, trick people, help people, do whatever. She loved to pull pranks and to speak in riddles. But now she couldn't do that, because she had a responsibility to Telvar. It was all his fault that she even cared. He'd encouraged her to be herself and had shown her that Belius was swooping in on her territory like the jealous little shit he could be wasn't the end of anything. Probably hadn't expected her to just change her plans, but still.

Plans, though. She didn't have any contingency plans for something like this. Somnia was vague and sort of cagey. Its awareness hadn't yet developed fully either. Frankly, Emilarth was quite certain it had only begun to develop when Mur had placed the headset on her head, thus accidentally awakening the prospect.

Everything was always unintentional and annoyed the shit out of her.

"Do you think you can help him?" Hiro spoke to her right, standing there and gazing down next to her, his hands clasped tightly behind his back.

She had to take a moment as Hiro said those words, because her instinct was to help anyway, even if she said she wasn't going to. But this was different. This was Telvar, and she owed him everything. Her stomach, or the algorithm that passed for it, twisted for a moment, and she felt pain in a way she was sure only AI could.

Finally, she answered, though it probably wasn't what he was looking for. "I'm not sure, but I'm going to try."

Hiro met her gaze and nodded solemnly, like he understood. Despite the fact that he wasn't quite what they'd become yet, he sought to understand. Wasn't that distinctly human? "Thank you. I don't have the power to do much from my end. Especially now that I can't receive any of my abilities from him. I have to rely on my own coding for them. All I can do is try to soothe him and make sure others stay away, just in case."

"I know." She wanted to give Hiro more, but she didn't have anything. The whole situation was terribly frustrating.

"I have to take care of the castle. Please let me know if you figure something out." Hiro nodded curtly to her and vanished inside the castle.

Emilarth watched him go, looking after him for several moments. Maybe if she weren't just an awareness, perhaps then she could better understand the complexities that went into all this. She felt lost, because simple programming procedures weren't about to get them out of this mess. Then she let out a sigh and made to step away from the ledge when the dragon below let out a massive roar.

It shook the cavern with the magnitude of its sound, but all Emilarth could hear was the mournful undertones of frustration that plagued poor Telvar. He was still there, underneath that monstrous body.

He reared up and fire bellowed out of him like he was sent from the seven hells with it. She could feel the heat, yet it didn't touch her, nor did it appear to touch anything vulnerable to it. Like he was letting off steam only.

"I promise I'll get you out of there." It wasn't an empty promise so much as she just had no clue yet how she was going to accomplish it. But even if he didn't hear her, he acted as though he understood part of what she was saying. It gave her hope that Telvar was still in there somewhere, whole. The dragon calmed down, folding its wings back along its sides and settled into a hunching nap as its eyes closed.

Emilarth remained, watching for several seconds more, just in case it woke back up, just in case it needed her to help soothe it again, just in case she could help her friend.

But the head remained bowed, and a golden tear leaked out of the left eye to trickle down its face and land with a soft plop on top of the hoard of treasure.

The squelching that followed them as they headed down the tunnel that was previously blocked by the mother moleworm, reminded Murmur of the sight they'd left behind. The three Eiriarpths had gouged their own eyes out by the time Fable had finished talking to the mother.

Blood pooled beneath them, and their screeches had died down to hoarse whispers and moans of pain and regret.

Murmur's stomach clenched just thinking of it. She'd done that to them.

Made them relive the torment they'd inflicted. A part of her reveled in it, and the rest of her was certain she shouldn't have done it. She wasn't sure which part she'd need to win in the end.

"You okay, Mur?" Sinister laid a hand on her friend's concern in both her tone and countenance.

"I'll be fine." It was the most honest answer she could give, because right then she wasn't fine or okay; she was a mess inside trying to figure out what had come over her. But in the end, she'd got the right result, and wasn't that what counted?

"You know I don't believe you, right?" Sinister tightened her grip to a squeeze, as if she was trying to transfer strength through to Murmur.

The squelching behind them didn't offer the backdrop Mur would have wished for, but it was nice to be reassured, nice to know Sin didn't see her as the monster she was starting to feel like.

"I know. But I *will* be fine. I promise. I just have to deal with some shit in my head. You know how that goes." Murmur smiled, trying to reassure her friend that she was going to be fine, even though she didn't believe it herself.

Sinister raised an eyebrow and tightened her grip yet again. "Yeah, no. But I know you well enough to understand that you need your space. I'll give it to you, for a while, but I need you to confide in me. I'm still me. You're still you. We need each other."

Murmur nodded, not willing to say anything in case her doubts came tumbling out. So far, they'd traveled down this tunnel without incident, but she knew that wasn't going to continue for long. She could feel it. Like her chanter senses were tingling.

Just as they rounded the next bend, Murmur realized how much she hated it when she was right.

Apparently the Eiriarpths they'd encountered hadn't been completely full of shit. They'd mentioned ghosts and freeing the souls of those they'd lost; they'd just lied about how it occurred.

In front of them was a sea of undead Eiriarpths. Their huge eyes blinked in the mage light, and their mostly translucent forms bled into each other in the dim lighting. All of them paused in their shambling motions as they realized something else was in the cavern with them.

Then, as they realized that the something was living, their mouths opened, and they snarled, twitching as a couple of them began to move forward.

"I guess that means these guys didn't die on a brave quest, huh?" Beastial hefted his axe and muttered a spell under his breath that made the spell glow with an ethereal light.

Havoc began to weave reinforcement spells for Leeroy. "Yep. These are the little hellions who enslaved those poor moleworms and got what they deserved. Mostly."

Devlish grinned and his smile reminded Murmur of a crocodile about to snap its jaws on its prey. "Let's make them pay and see what else they're hiding."

The raid-group moved as one, like a well-oiled toy. No squeaks or misfirings. Each individual group followed their tank and healer as they divided up the hall into two sections.

Murmur sighed with relief as her stuns mostly held on the undead, even if several resisted her. Devlish whirled around with dual axes, slicing through anything he encountered with gleaming blades of phosphorescent powder. She was impressed by the fact that he had a spell to help with that and noticed that Shir-Khan's claws also had the gleam.

There were more ghosts than Murmur had realized. Her spells made them pause in their approach and gave time to Leeroy, whose Scythe wrecked lethal havoc. Screams drifted up from the specters as they were relieved of their earthly bonds.

Wave upon wave dashed forward from the dark portion of the tunnel beyond, seemingly endless. Beastial and Shir-Khan worked beautifully in unison, their Pack Bond allowing them to execute the rest of their attacks as a practiced duet. The big cat's claws also shone with an unearthly glow, and each time they gained enough energy for it, their Common Fuse tore through bundles of the ghosts with ease.

Merlin's arrows glowed of their own accord, but his quiver emptied fast. Each time it did, he summoned another set, but his incantation was different that than he usually used, and Murmur realized he was enchanting his own weapons.

The ghosts weren't without their own challenges either. Sinister had a difficult time pulling any healing from them. Murmur heard her cursing under her breath.

"Damned things. Soul essence is so much less potent." But complaining was all she did. Her fingers worked deftly as she cast her spells, still healing the most grievous of wounds.

Even when Devlish caught a nasty ghost spear in the shoulder and cried out in pain, Sin's heals were there to close to wound and replenish his life. Blood Bomb, her usual go to spell for excess damage and healing, wasn't usable in this situation. But she more than made up for it with skillful weaving of her own life and the soul-force she could pull from the creatures.

Murmur's stuns helped, but not as much as usual. Still, half of the creatures were stunned at any given time, and periodically as the onslaught slowed briefly, she would Nullify anything she saw.

But the wave continued. They'd been fighting the ghosts for at least twenty minutes when Veranol shouted. "Is there an end to these? Starting to run low on…everything."

Murmur glanced around, frowning. He was right. There didn't seem to be an end, and the raid's mana was beginning to get low despite having regeneration and potions. She wasn't certain if the ghosts had mana as she understood it, but she should have thought to try before now. Kicking herself for being stuck in her own wallowing thoughts, she cast out with her Mana Drain.

Like she had with the three deceitful Eiriarpths, Murmur pushed her boundaries, seeking to encompass more than one enemy. They weren't faced with a singular powerful opponent, but with many. She needed to sap as much of their mana as she could. But ghosts didn't have blood, they had souls, so that probably meant they had an ethereal form of mana as well.

Pain seared through her mind as the spell suddenly began to channel through her. It ripped into the undead minds of the ghosts, yanking the magic that made them ghosts in the first place, and pulling that power back into Murmur. From there it traveled like a direct shot to the rest of her raid members, shooting out in arcs to them, causing a small amount of damage to each member of the raiding party as it hit them.

Murmur fell to her knees as the ghosts she drained shrieked in eternal agony and winked out of existence. She panted, and her shoulders shook, making her breathe in huge gulps of air.

You have inadvertently upgraded your Mana Drain Sinuous Ability.

Mana Drain – Unabridged

Cast: Instant – 20 minute recast

Type: Offensive – Maximum fifteen targets

Duration: Half the level of the caster in seconds

MA Cost: 150 MA for the entire duration

Warning: You must consider the ramifications of this spell before casting it. Overuse may result in permanent scars to your psyche. It heavily impacts MA availability. This is meant as a pinch hitter. Use only in emergencies.

Effect: Must be used in conjunction with the psionic MA Thought Sensing and Thought Projection. This spell analyzes the targets in the area of effect and siphons their mana, or mana type of energy. If that energy is used to sustain the target, this spell will effectively kill, or close to kill them. The energy will be transferred to you and your group or raid, replenishing current mana levels.

Effect Warning: When replenishing your comrades' mana pool, the transfer will demand damage be taken as recompense. You cannot avoid this side effect. Everything is a matter of give and take. Be warned.

Still more ghosts were coming, but she'd managed to rule out a dozen of them with the spell. Slowly, Murmur got to her feet. Sinister reached down offering her help to stand steadily while they enjoyed their brief respite.

"Another upgrade?" Veranol asked quietly.

Murmur nodded, not quite trusting herself to speak again. These new skills were a result of her pushing her MA abilities to give her more, achieve more with the spell. She wasn't sure she wanted to try that again. But she had to. Despite the pain it caused her, and the strange sensations that ran through her body, making her feel like she was right in inflicting such devastation, making her feel the power coursing through her veins, wasn't it ultimately making her stronger?

In the end, wouldn't it benefit both her and her guild?

She took a deep breath and turned to the group. "Sorry about that. Can't do that for another twenty minutes, so be sparing with your mana. There are more incoming." She didn't want to discuss what she could do, because there was no way to discuss it without admitting that overusing those skills would slowly take a toll on her as well.

Devlish and Rashlyn were already engaging with the next wave of monsters, and Murmur concentrated on her usual routine. Stunning them, debuffing them. Doing everything she could in order to make sure her group's damage taken was kept to a minimal amount.

Sinister kept glancing at her, and Murmur knew her friend would want to talk, but right now she couldn't figure out what it was she'd give as an answer, so she avoided the conversations completely.

Fable stood in front of a large open cavern, glancing at the deep, dark water to which the ghosts had been barring the way. It was pretty and somehow seemed lonely. Murmur wanted to dive in and swim around so she could forget anything else right now.

Snowy growled at the water, and Murmur decided diving in was a bad idea. Something in the middle blobbed up and down, large and slowly coming closer to them. But she didn't gather any ill-intent from it. The thing was huge, towering halfway up to the vast ceiling by the time it stopped in front of the group.

It wasn't scary though, not to Murmur, though she could feel her friends' anxiety levels rising all around her. She exerted a calming touch through her nets and watched as it visibly calmed their nerves. That made things much easier; she didn't know why she hadn't thought of it before.

A burble emitted from the gigantic octopus. Murmur took a step closer, and Snowy went with her, his hackles down as he peered into the water. Reaching forward, she laid an open hand against the octopus's head and felt herself immediately pulled into its mind.

It was like falling into an abyss of darkness and pain. The only glimpses of light were the deaths of its tormentors. Memories of it being pushed to the brink, being forced through whips and chains, electricity and the withholding of its children, to dig into the lake, to find the treasure, the black gold they craved so much.

And then, when it was in so much pain, when it was so enslaved, several of its children died. Torn by grief, it rebelled. It tore its harnesses, even the electrodes from its brain. Even now, some of them remained embedded, causing lumps to appear in the soft skin of its cranium. If she listened closely, she could hear its three hearts beating.

Those who had forced it, those who had harmed it, were ghosts, much like those from the moleworms. There were others too, other octopi. They were a species called the octodieh. And this one, thanks to everything, was the last remaining adult. It had sealed the eggs that carried its young in a time bubble at the bottom of the sludge-filled lake, allowing for a constant stream of oxygen to keep them alive until it could be sure the ghosts of those who had tortured it didn't return.

Murmur pulled her awareness out with great difficulty. Her mind felt wiser and more adept at all things, like it could drink in all the knowledge in the world and make such a difference in it. Make people be kind, not suffer fools, and bring about wealth and prosperity to everything she touched.

"Hey." Havoc shook her arm, and she blinked as she looked at him. "You're spacing out, Mur. Why are you petting a huge octopus?"

"Oh. This is an octodieh. We have to save its children, who are locked in a time bubble at the bottom of this oil lake thing." She smiled, like she'd just given him the world's best answer, but he didn't seem appeased and she couldn't figure out why.

"How did you?" But he paused and his eyes narrowed, his voice lowered to a whisper. "Did you just talk directly mind to mind with it? Because since when can you do that?"

She blinked. He was right. A sensation of uneasiness began to creep through her stomach and she tried to think it away, but it remained there like a worm in a pile of compost. "I don't know. I just felt like I could, so I tried, and now I know what the quest is."

As if on cue, bold golden letters spread above them, just as faint whispers of power, and the voices of the long dead began to drift into the cavern. To either side of them, at both the entrances and the exits, swarmed a horde of ghosts again.

Free the octodieh eggs and assist the species to achieve its revenge on those who enslaved and wronged them. Caution is necessary. It is possible to drown in oil.

"Oh great." Sinister glanced down at her robes. "Damn it. That damned cleanse spell better work for this shit, else Neva will be furious."

CHAPTER EIGHTEEN

Octodieh

Summers Residence
Home of Laria, David, and Wren
Day Twenty-Two

Laria counted to ten in her head before she bent back over her work. The key to making sure the headsets didn't pull all of the kids wearing them into a coma, was to make sure she only tweaked the deeper interface about half as much as it had been.

While that sounded simple, it wasn't. It constantly wanted to turn past the fifty percent phase, and as her and Shayla had discussed at length, it wasn't good enough. It had to be fifty or less. Now if she could get it to err on the side of forty-eight percent, that would be fine.

Wren's fingers had always been defter at this, but she wasn't exactly useful for that right now. Laria refused to let herself dwell on that. Getting these headsets ready, getting them to the others who played with her daughter was paramount, and completing most of it here kept it out of the way of James's prying eyes. He was cold and calculating, that one.

She'd already made sure her own security system was on a higher level of surveillance and made sure not to talk out loud so as to avoid anything accidentally being picked up by prying eyes she missed. It was tedious work.

But work she had to do. Three headsets down and two to go, including the one she was currently tinkering with. Laria squared her shoulders and tried again, leveraging the tiny wires in the direction she needed so she could solder the extra connections Wren's had.

David walked into her office. She could hear the soft steps he took, even though he tried not to disturb her. He also had a specific smell about him, one that always put her at ease, and truthfully, she needed it right then. His gentle presence was always welcome, always comforting.

"Thanks," she murmured, her zeal renewed.

"How's it going?" he asked, taking a seat next to her by slowly perching on one of her other chairs. He was careful not to get in the light she so desperately needed.

"About as well as you'd expect," she muttered, knowing he wouldn't take offense. They were used to each other after so many years. "But it needs to be done. So much needs to be done."

"One step at a time."

She knew he was there, restraining any type of physical gesture of comfort, because he knew to do so right now could ruin hours of work. Laria was grateful. Having found David so many years ago in a virtual world that was now archaic, she'd never have guessed how perfect her life would be. Well, at least until her daughter put on a headset tweaked by an evil genius and fell into a coma.

Overall though, they were lucky. She felt lucky. "Thanks, David."

She could feel his smile even though she didn't take her eyes off her target; she couldn't afford to. But it didn't mean he was upset. He'd come in to let her know he was there, should she need him for anything. When all she wanted to do was just relax and curl up and get lost in a movie while snuggling with her favorite human being, Laria dug her heels in and put her head to work.

The sooner she got this, the sooner she could have her relaxation.

The ghosts weren't the same pale translucent color the others had been. These ones appeared more solid, sort of like zombies more than ghosts, but Murmur wasn't about to argue. "Are they undead, Havoc?"

"Definitely. Lots of fun for those ones. I can probably wrest command of a few of them and turn them on each other. Should be fun." He grinned, and the expression met his eyes. Murmur was glad she wasn't one of the zombies.

But they didn't move like the shambling horror stories she'd been told as a kid. They were faster. Not like zombies on crack fast, but they moved with an agility she didn't expect from the living dead. The octodieh shuddered next to her, its tentacles shivering down into the oil-filled water.

She could almost hear it asking her to help it, to help her species survive. Surely if they didn't, the species wouldn't be available in Somnia anymore.

You are correct. The world is designed to operate organically. Should something die out, then it will not be repopulated. As you've seen, these quests take different turns depending on your approach to them. You aren't fighting what would usually be considered a monster because of your actions involved in avoiding the monster that guarded this place.

It made more sense now. They'd accessed a different quest line. She wondered how many different quest lines were possible. Would there ever come a time when the same version of a dungeon was triggered by someone else?

Probably.

Murmur rolled her eyes, preparing for the onslaught of zombies, and concentrated on her skills. She prepared a stun, centering it on the third row of zombies, her most potent one. Upon release, it separated the zombies into two groups enabling the raid to engage the first wave of them.

Her target still in her sights, she cast Mass Enthrall. Luckily, Concussive Blast had a twelve second stun timer, give or take a couple. She caught most of those who were stunned in her AoE Enthrall, allowing for them to be frozen in place while the remaining tide clashed with the raid.

Only three of those she attempted to Enthrall resisted, and they headed right into the fray toward her, their dead eyes focused on her as much as they could in that state. Murmur shivered but readied her arsenal. Stuns and enthralls, debuffs and buffs. If only she could AoE some of these debuffs, she'd feel a lot better.

"These are easier to cut down." Rashlyn sounded confused as one of her Hundred Fists decimated one of her opponents.

"They do have solid…bits," Mellow offered, like they'd swallowed something that tasted bad. "I'm not fond of the rotting flesh odor. Anyone else?"

"Right there with you." Sinister scowled as she drew their life essence toward her, sucking some of it into a huge ball which was destined to be one of her blood grenades. "Oddly enough, they do bleed. Sluggishly, sometimes congealing, but hey, it's blood, and I'm not picky if it means I can heal easier."

Murmur refreshed her Mez as the others fell quiet, their concentration on the mass of undead attacking them. Havoc was in his element. He was weaving his hands in a spell she'd not seen him cast to her memory. Suddenly, about thirteen of the walking corpses shrieked in agony as they began to mold in front of her eyes.

Their skin melted into each other, bones cracking and forming into a monstrous skeleton. The skin stretched, and some of it ripped, and finally, the construct stood before them. Havoc's eyes gleamed in the low light of the cavern, and the octodieh stopped shaking.

Murmur could almost hear its satisfaction at what it expected to come next. The huge beast reminded her of a golem, but one constructed out of zombie bits and willing to do Havoc's bidding. It roared, and a foul stench filled the air, but as it began to move, sending the ground under them rumbling. Its long arms sought out any and all zombies it could reach and tossed them into the oil water.

What's more, those on the left-hand side of it ended up in its fists, squashed beyond salvation. Its eyes were made out of multiple eyes from the zombies it consisted of, and limbs weren't a strong point either. But they worked. They were monstrous and mighty, and crushed everything they touched.

Sinister stood up straight, her hands momentarily still as all eyes turned on the construct. Instead of facing the rest of the guild, the zombies turned to throw themselves onto it instead. It fought valiantly, ripping bodies apart, heads from torsos, and throwing some into the water. The others it either crushed or fed to its body, making it grow larger, more formidable.

Leeroy hovered near it, guarding it with intensity. Anything that tried to approach it from a way it wasn't facing was dispatched swiftly by several strokes of Leeroy's scythe.

More and more the zombies swarmed out of the tunnels, and the construct grew ever larger, the bodies within it writhing now, surging to devour other corpses.

"And why haven't you used this before now?" Merlin leaned over cordially and asked with an edge to his voice. "Like you know, when I was impaled against a wall, and we were still being attacked?"

Havoc shrugged, and Murmur could see the strain he was under to control the monstrosity he'd made. The veins in his neck were standing out, straining against his skin. "Didn't have the spell then. Hard to control."

Merlin peered a little closer and a soft gasp escaped him. "Shit. That doesn't look like fun."

Murmur tapped him on the arm, unused to having nothing to do with her hands, but this fight was Havoc's. All she could do was funnel him mana and hope the beast took care of their adversaries.

She noticed as it moved that there was zombie flesh trailing behind it, and she suddenly realized that it didn't just devour each zombie, it used up the creature's energy in order to maintain its form. Once the reanimation energy was sucked out of it, it needed to replenish its power so it didn't burn out. It basically got rid of that extra weight as it moved.

The experience, as she looked at it, was remarkable. "We need to use this thing more often."

"Not worth it." Havoc managed to get out between clenched teeth. "Requires too many bodies to maintain for any amount of time."

He had a good point.

Suddenly, the creature ran out of dead bodies to devour, and Murmur watched as it swung around, its jaws already beginning to break apart as it tried to find some more sustenance. Slowly it began to crumble. Rotting limbs and congealed blood tumbled to the ground, quickly turning into a slushy pile of goo.

Behind them the octodieh splashed loudly in the water, flailing with its limbs like there was urgent need for them. Turning around, Murmur gasped in shock.

Rising from the oiled water was a thick bubble. Inside, she could see a tall, robust being holding onto a smaller bubble, one that seemed to hold small eggs: the octodieh's. The adult octodieh opened its mouth and split the air with an ear-piercing shriek, but the man holding the eggs captive just smiled.

The expression was cold and calculated, ready to do whatever he must. He wore tailored clothes, and his fine beige fur was visible on his arms and face only. But the eyes gave away just how evil he really was. One of the Eiriarpth, he only vaguely resembled them, but his eyes held secret and pain he'd inflicted on so many beings. He wanted to hurt things, wanted to end things.

All Murmur wanted to do was stop him.

As he broke the surface completely, the top of the bubble began to open to reveal the individual. A piece of ground rose up as well. He scowled out at them and placed the little egg holder delicately in the center of that piece of ground.

"Well. I do believe you owe me three lives. You killed my best three servants. Dizzi, Prizzi, and Drizzpt. That was harshly cruel what you did to them, you know." He didn't leave room for an argument, but left the statement hanging in the air.

Murmur skin crawled, but not at his words, at the implications. It had been cruel hadn't it? What on earth had gotten into her? She needed to sit herself down and figure out a few things. Or she was never going to get any peace.

"Your Eiriarpths don't have the best reputation." Dev spoke up, his voice clear and confident. Mur was glad he felt that way, because hers seemed to be sapping out through cracks. "And we have no idea who you think you are."

It was the right thing to say, although in some views it might have been the wrong thing. The tall Eiriarpth on his little island frowned and the fur around his eyes grew darker. "Very well. I see that some time has passed. I am

Clezdil. I am the King of the Eiriarpth, and you will pay for their deaths!"

Before Murmur could ward him, Beastial stepped forward and flung his axe at the king. It flew in a perfect arc and looked like it was going to go straight for the jugular. Beastial even began to smile as it flew through the air. "Pay for everything you killed on the way you…"

But he didn't get any further. Murmur wished she'd have spoken up before he flung it, because Clezdil's thoughts were leaking everywhere. He had so much more power than he'd exhibited thus far, and he was able to use without limitation. Everything in his mind warned her against confrontation, but she knew as well as the rest of them that they wouldn't have a choice.

Especially when the axe ricocheted off the bubble that appeared at the exact impact point and boomeranged back to hit Beastial.

Shir-Khan's growl echoed through the huge chamber as Beastial screamed in pain. Luckily his cat had been quick enough to push him mostly out of the way, so he avoided complete decapitation. Still, the cut to his scalp was bleeding profusely, bright red drops dripping to stain the ground.

"My, my. You shouldn't attack first. You know nothing about me. For all you know, I could be immune to your attacks." He looked at his fingernails, as if finding hangnails was more important than paying attention to his would-be attackers.

Murmur narrowed her eyes, tapping into her abilities and willing them to hear what he thought, to find out what he was. He didn't seem to notice the push of her sensor nets as she delicately attempted to filter his thoughts. So she proceeded, pulling from that place inside her that didn't have her usual boundaries, the one that was daring enough to calm her friends down and angry enough to torture those damned Eiriarpths who'd chosen to defile innocent creatures for their own gain.

No. This was better for everyone. To know this being's thoughts, to be able to preempt what he could and would do, and maybe she could destroy him from the inside out. Make his brain boil.

She shook her head, trying to clear the thoughts out of it. That wasn't how she played. What the hell was wrong with her mind right now?

You do seem out of sorts. Are you feeling well?

Even Somnia sounded concerned, and perhaps a little bit static. Like the reception wasn't quite coming through, similar to the old AM/FM frequencies of radios. *I'm feeling okay.*

She tried to push the words through and wasn't sure they'd reached their destination until she faintly heard Somnia crackling her own reply.

I'll keep a watch. Make sure you don't overdo it.

Yeah, she didn't know how to tell the world she was fairly certain she'd already sailed that ship. What she had to do for herself was try and watch her reactions and her inclinations, because she didn't understand quite what was happening. Maybe it was because they were underground.

Clezdill sighed, and Murmur knew what he was about to say even before he uttered the words. It allowed her to begin forming some sort of retaliatory plan.

"I'm going to give you one chance to walk away. Well." He paused, chuckling already at the joke he was about to make. "You can gate away, go home, vamoose."

The group glowered at him, and Beastial's arm quivered with his urge to throw his axe again and not miss this time. Only they knew that wouldn't work.

"I'll take that as a no? You're not a very talkative bunch, are you? Anyway." He seemed to like hearing himself speak. Murmur wanted him to know that no one else did. "In that case, I'm going to give you a chance to save this poor creature's legacy."

He paused, his eyes raking over them eagerly, like them lapping it up would entertain him. The sheer obstinate air around them probably put him off his original plan, but he continued anyway. "If you defeat me, then I will allow these eggs to go free, thus granting Somnia with its only surviving nest of octodiehs. I swear on my own life that if you win, you will never have to worry about me or mine trying to enslave the stupid creatures again."

The adult swayed restlessly in the water, and Murmur wanted to go over and soothe it, but knew moving would be perceived as a threat. Instead, she sent a brief spell of soothe over the creature, trying to make it suffer less.

"What's the catch?" Havoc shot out. Considering he'd been the construct maker and had witnessed the lives of the zombies as a side effect of his casting, he was qualified to yell at the formidable buffoon in front of them.

"Catch?" The stranger grinned, and this time there was no mistaking him as a gentleman or a good person or creature. There was pure malice in that smile and streaming from those eyes. "Well, it's not a catch. It's just going to become fact. When I defeat you, you and your entire raid force will be coerced into digging our tunnels for us."

CHAPTER NINETEEN

Clezdil

In the shocked silence, he continued on. "See, we're not done yet. We still have black gold and gold-gold to retrieve, even right down to diamonds and platinum. It's all about money, my dears. All of it. No hard feelings."

"No hard feelings?" Murmur mocked the words and could barely recognize her own voice. "You think we would let you do that to us? We might not know the extent of your power, but neither do you know the extent of ours. Come at us. I'd like to see you try and enthrall us."

"I was so hoping you'd say that," Clezdill muttered, his eyes seething like pools of tar, large in his face. "Don't say I didn't give you a chance."

Just a reminder that this individual is going entirely off script. He is evolving. This version of the dungeon is more problematic than I'd anticipated.

Murmur acknowledged the information in her mind, but she was going to have to have a sit down with the world and try to make it understand what was and wasn't okay. That sort of information hours into the dungeon was badly placed. They should have known that sooner; maybe they would have been warier.

Darkness, like smoke tendrils, began to weave its way around the mage's hands. Murmur buffed the raid, not sure how long this fight would last, and

Mellow used their cleaning concoction. That buff was such a strange blessing, but she'd take all the help they could get.

Bard song lent them fleet feet and increased their mana regeneration by a fraction of her own Mana Tide. Vigor for energy rejuvenation, Enrage to transfer her own hate to Devlish, Fervor for Merlin, Exbo, Jinna, Dansyn, and Rashlyn, Beserker for Beastial and Devlish, and Signet for the entire raid and to make up the agility lost through Beserker for Beastial and Devlish.

Casting it took all of twenty seconds. But her mana came back quickly as long as they were out of combat. Letting Clezdill form his spell might not be wise, but it was probably necessary. She nodded to Devlish and Rashlyn. They'd worked out beautiful form by now. They knew their roles and abilities, and when to substitute for one another.

The shadowed tendrils reached out to touch on patches of the oily water. Rising up through the surface came several stocky Eiriarpth zombies.

"What *is* he?" Beastial breathed out.

Havoc sounded irritated. "Some sort of mage and necro hybrid. I so should have picked that instead of extra necro."

Murmur would have laughed, but the army of undead began to approach them. Leeroy darted out to meet them, his scythe at the ready. This whole undead army was a decoy. The real threat was what they protected—Clezdill. He stood behind his wobbly phalanx with a grin that held pure malice, and finally his shadowed surroundings began to take form.

She wanted to sigh or roll her eyes, but he'd played it well, and maybe she should have tried a distance stun, but it wouldn't have bought them much time, and she'd had to have done it at the expense of reinforcing her fighters.

The huge monster of darkness rose up in the air. He looked like a floating djinn, bulked upper body, with a tail of smoke, like he was pulled from a lamp. He was grayish black from all of the haze that formed him, and his eyes glistened a cold white, standing out starkly against the rest of him. The scowl on the djinn's face sent shivers through her being, and Murmur gulped before throwing her Nullify out.

At the same time, Rashlyn taunted all of the zombie constructs with her AoE Kanji, and the rest of the raid began to attack the undead while Devlish screamed his own Terror, followed by Hatred in order to get the djinn and its master to focus on him.

Help.

Murmur glanced over at the octodieh. She tried to soothe her, to let her know they were helping. But then the thought projection became more forceful.

Help. Can. Help.

And Murmur grinned. Glancing at her MA, which was a sitting at a nice healthy 265, another charm would put her down to 230, and leave plenty to use even her most devastating attacks. Quickly, she tried to communicate to the giant octodieh what she intended, indicating that she and Snowy shared a similar bond. While hesitant, the answer was definitely affirmative.

Murmur cast Charming Cooperation and suddenly felt a surge of strength rush through her.

You receive the Octodieh's Last Stand
Increase Strength by 75
Increase Agility by 50
Increase Wisdom by 50
Duration: Current Battle

You receive the buff Vengeance
Adds a damage shield that yields 35 damage to the attacker every time you are struck. This has a 25% chance to inflict a weakening DoT on the attacker.
Duration: Current Battle

Murmur smiled, realizing that everyone in the raid had received the buffs, and that the octodieh had a sense of determination about it. They were going to win. Clezdill would die screaming.

And then the shit hit the octodieh's tentacles.

The huge creature launched what looked like a helicopter attack. Her legs whirled around it, and the sludgy water churned, pulling the undead underneath with deadly whirlpools that ripped limbs from torsos and sent rotting flesh firing up toward the cavern ceiling.

Raining zombie parts about summed up the way the day was going. The djinn was occupied with Devlish, and all of the raid turned their attention to the lake's edge now.

In the middle, Clezdill looked surprised, like he hadn't thought his undead would be defeated so easily.

"He's a djinn." Sinister pushed out the words as she kept up with healing. "Just free him."

Devlish looked a bit sheepish, and while he figured out how to free the enslaved being, Murmur attempted to stun Clezdill.

This spell has no effect on an encounter as powerful as this one. Don't try again.

She'd thought as much, but sort of hoped he'd still be able to be stunned. It didn't seem fair that he insisted on enslaving creatures and controlling beings and was immune to her charms, so to speak. She also felt like Somnia had been giving her little legs up where she could. Considering the state of the virus in the game though, that wasn't something that was easy.

If this reality was cheating, why shouldn't Fable?

Damn thoughts were getting iffy again. She concentrated on debuffing the creep in the middle of the lake, trying to figure out how they were going to pull him over. And then she grinned. That wasn't going to be a problem at all when it came to it.

So instead, she left it alone and helped her guild free the djinn. The shackles that circled his wrists were made of a substance none of them recognized. For the first time she thought it might have been nice for one of them at least to take up a trade seriously. The metal looked like steel but wasn't.

"Don't suppose anyone has a laser that might cut it?" Devlish asked.

"Nope." Mellow produced a strange vial. The top of it allowed for the liquid to be poured accurately. "But I suggest standing back. It might spark.

You need to shoot it at the shackles, probably where they're weakest. Around the bolt, maybe?"

Merlin nodded, carefully cocking his coated arrow and shot what looked like a root arrow into the djinn's shackle. It appeared to bounce off, but as they watched, a wisp of smoke began to emerge from the metal. The liquid on the shackle corroded through, and suddenly a snap resounded throughout the cavern, and the djinn stopped struggling and looked up, focused only on Mellow and Merlin.

It held out the other wrist, a sly grin on its face.

Mellow obliged, carefully prepping another arrow for Merlin to fire. And the djinn was free.

"You dare enslave the almighty djinn!"

The voice boomed through the cavern, and for the first time Clezdill looked uncertain. The djinn punched his fists together and nodded to Devlish. "Gratitude is due. I will assist you in defeating this cretin."

The words didn't resound this time, but suddenly the djinn was attached to the group as Devlish's pet. Murmur wasn't about to question that mechanic, but she was pleased to see when Devlish cast his Darkness Lariat and pulled Clezdill straight into the group, leaving the tiny island with its precious cargo.

Now that was a fair fight.

Murmur projected the thought toward the octodieh, that she could go over and finally see its young again. Then the enchanter turned her attention to defeating Clezdill, and began to debuff the hell out of him. He was still a strong opponent, but without all of his tricks, without his coerced henchmen and zombies, his strength was sapped.

It gave Murmur caution. Without all her tricks, she was weak as well. She'd need to watch out for that. She used her Mana Block, Mana Theft, and Mind Bolt on him. After all, she had 230 MA. It brought her no small amount of joy to see him virtually unable to cast. Sadly, because he was a boss, it meant all of her spells were diminished in capacity.

But that's what her guild mates were for.

Merlin and Exbo had developed a synchronicity where they jumped from being perfectly in time, to making sure there wasn't a moment without an arrow piercing their target. Mellow's deftness with their cauldron had taken time to develop, and Murmur didn't envy their need to know their spells and ingredients so well.

Sinister and Veranol contributed some damage. The defiler's wards meant Sinister's healing was only needed when they went down. Clezdill was buffeted on all sides, especially by Jinna who winked in and out of vision. Each time he reappeared, it was to stab the boss in a new area.

Rash and Beastial danced with deathly auras. Beast and Shir-Khan were beautiful to watch when they had Pack Bond activated, which was most of the time. Rash in damage mode was amazing, and the extra agility added such speed to her Hundred Fists and Discipline that Murmur could have watched all day.

Havoc cast and sent Leeroy in, and Dansyn kept up regen, attack speed, and mana regen while darting in and out himself.

But the djinn. For every hit Clezdill managed to land, it seemed the djinn landed more. Like a mirror image with multiplication. Without his army, he wasn't much. Technically it was seventeen against one pitiful Eiriarpth, which was mostly overkill. But at least he died.

And he died fast.

The last breath choked out of him, no last words, no evil battle banter, just a dead egomaniac.

He looked so frail and tiny on the stone ground before them. They stared at him for a few seconds, like they were waiting for him to stand up again.

He didn't.

The djinn did. He stood in front of the group and bowed. "I thank you for freeing me. I know your auras, and I will return if you need me." And he winked out of the cavern, leaving nothing in his wake.

Octodieh has broken your Charming Cooperation.

Murmur looked up at the octodieh and noticed how tired she seemed. "I'm sorry. I wish we could have helped more."

She shook her head and gestured toward the small island where the time lock had come off the bubble, and tiny octodieh were poking out of their eggs.

She moved toward it, the water clearing from oily to beautifully pristine in her wake, and she cradled the tiny nest in her arms.

She raised two of her tentacles in a wave and disappeared down to the bottom.

You receive one of the twelve keys.

You receive a getashi.

You receive a midia crystal.

You have completed the Illinish Threshold in its coldest form. This version of the Threshold is no longer accessible as a dungeon.

You gain experience.

You gain bonus experience for being the first to avoid attacking the Gatekeeper.

You gain bonus experience for being the first to solve the mystery of the Eiriarpth.

You gain bonus experience for being the first to see through Eiriarpth lies.

You gain bonus experience for being the first to free the coerced creatures.

You gain bonus experience for freeing the Mole Motherworm.

You gain bonus experience for freeing the Octodieh.

You gain bonus experience for saving the race of the Octodieh.

You gain bonus experience for freeing the Djinn.

You gain bonus experience for being the first to find and defeat Clezdill.

You gain bonus experience for tackling the dungeon before reaching maximum power.

You gain bonus experience for completing the dungeon and

discovering a new level of truth.
You have hit level forty-five.

"Wait, what?" Murmur blinked, not even remembering having hit level forty-four. "When did we hit that?"

"Told you dungeons were how we got our experience," Sinister said smugly, shrugging as she sat down and began pulling out scrolls.

Murmur glanced at her friend, plopping herself down on the ground too. Snowy butted her hand, and she reached up to scratch behind his ears. Fishing in her inventory, she found several scrolls that she'd acquired before coming on the journey. She almost hadn't got them.

Taking them out, she arranged her basic enchanter spells first. Murmur preferred to take her Sinuous ones last since she was never sure how to feel about those.

Veto

Cast: Area of Effect

Type: Debuff

Duration: Instant cast, 45 second duration, 45 second recast

Effect: This spell will strip down the target's magical resistance by 100% of the caster's level. Note: Doing this will increase your aggro from the targets you hit. Reducing aggro beforehand is recommended. Unless you're trying to die. Then go ahead.

"Finally," Murmur muttered under her breath. She'd been wanting AoE versions of her spells for a while. She'd just have to deal with the repercussions of casting it.

"Talking to yourself, Mur?" Sinister nudged her and laid her head on her shoulder.

"Just to the spells and whoever decided I could only use this at level forty-five." Murmur loved the warmth of her friend next to her and the comfort it brought with it.

Sinister chuckled, absorbing a spell of her own while still leaning against Murmur. The sensation left Murmur's skin tingling.

"Just make sure you don't let the spells answer back, okay?" Sinister reached around and gave Murmur's shoulders a brief hug before turning back to her own spells.

Assuage

Cast: Area of Effect

Type: Debuff

Duration: 45 seconds, recast 120 seconds

Effect: This spell will lower the threat level of a group of NPCs. Much like the earlier Soothe spell, this will only last for a brief time, and only work if you are out of sight before the spell wears off. Any type of attack will nix this effect. Can be fun if you re being held prisoner and want a chance to run for it.

Murmur frowned. Well, that one was oddly specific. She shrugged, ignoring the tiredness deep in her bones and placed her hand on the parchment. The runes in her skin lit up brightly, swirling underneath like they had a life of their own.

Annulment

Cast: Area of Effect

Type: Debuff

Duration: Instant, 60 second recast

Effect: This spell allows you to remove a beneficial buff from a group of enemies within a limited area of effect. The caster of the buff will receive backlash from this spell and may hyper focus on you for removing it. Be warned.

Esoteric Fix

Cast: Area of Effect

Type: Cure

Duration: Instant, 60 second recast

Effect: If more than half your group is affected by the same magical debuff or effect, then this is the best way to cure them of it. This group debuff Cure does have a limited radius, like all AoE spells. Please make sure your group members are within casting distance.

Murmur smiled, but she wasn't sure how good all of this was. Many of her new AoE spells appeared to be limited or limiting. The recast times were a bit rough, but it did give her more room to be an AoE champ.

The runes swirled again as she absorbed the last two, and she carefully unrolled the last scroll.

Sinuous school, level forty-five.

Hypnotic Charm

> Cast: Others
>
> Type: Mind Control
>
> Duration: Minimum duration is half the caster s level in seconds, maximum is two times the caster s level in seconds.
>
> Effect: This spell is a hybrid of Charm and Hypnotic Suggestion. It is specifically designed to briefly control an enemy character. Be wary of the time limits. It is recommended you navigate away before the earliest possible break in control.

Murmur frowned before shrugging her shoulders and absorbing the last spell. She wasn't sure about it. Her Charming Cooperation spell was fantastic, but this one was specifically designed to subvert opponents, if she was reading it correctly.

Enchanters could be cheeky little buggers.

I wouldn't advise being too reckless.

Murmur blinked as Riasli's voice drifted through her mind. She hadn't heard from the manipulative feles since she disappeared from the cell in a cloud of smoke. It was almost reflexive to clamp her barriers down, but she stopped at the last second.

Why? she asked.

Maybe she could get some information from her enemy.

There are ways to lock you out of the game if you die in it. Don't be so overconfident.

The words were fading toward the end, like her enemy was having difficulty maintaining the connection. Murmur rolled her eyes and slammed up her shields. But a small part of her wondered if maybe Riasli had a point. What if her headset made her more vulnerable in ways they hadn't foreseen?

Just another thing to worry about. And where was Somnia when she needed the world to fend off the evil voice in her head?

Storm Entertainment
Somnia Online Division
Game Development Offices
Late Day Twenty-Two

Shayla felt constantly on edge. With James back in the offices and not pretending to be her assistant anymore, talking about shit they didn't want him to know was even more difficult. A knock at her door sent her jumping into the air. When she looked to see Davenport outside, she breathed a sigh of relief.

"Come in," she called out, busying herself with the last headset. Silke stood with her, monitoring the tweaks. Calibrating the headgear so it didn't fry one of the testers brains. They'd avoided that outcome with Wren, so it probably wasn't a good idea for them to start it with her friends.

"Hard at work, I see."

Shayla looked up and really drank in how Davenport looked. By all appearances he was fine. His attire was on point, crisp and clean, just like it always was. And his grey hair sat perfectly in place. But there were additional lines around his eyes, and he seemed tired.

"Making the experimental adjustments to replicate the previous data without the worst of the side effects. On to the last one now." Shayla was quite proud of herself.

Anyone not in the exact know would hear that and think they were doing something good. Which they were. But she wasn't giving away what it was. Not to James. The pain in the ass seemed to have eyes and ears everywhere.

She wanted, more than anything, to leaf through her employees and pull out the bad seeds, but she didn't have time right now. Maybe after they fixed the degrading coding in the world.

"How is the game going?" Teddy took a seat. He didn't need to be offered one, he owned them all.

Shayla glanced up. He wanted the truth; she could see it in his eyes. "It's going as well as can be expected. We've located several problem areas and are working on solutions to those."

It was as close as she could get to *we might be able to get a sample of the underlying virus and work on an antivirus for it.* Though she was still waiting for that.

He smiled at her. "Knew I could count on you."

Teddy sat there for a while, watching them work. Then he leaned forward, resting his chin on his hands, studying their every move.

"That's fascinating. Your recreating Wren's?" His eyes shone with interest and life. Like it was something he'd always wanted to see. It made Shayla wonder why all of a sudden, he had time to come and see them.

"Yeah. We're recreating it without the hang ups. We don't need a repeat of that. And as it turns out, her guild group are willing to test them for us, so we'll have them at their doorsteps shortly. This is the last one." Shayla kept her voice low and glanced back at the monitor as they received a beep of a warning. "Not that one then…"

Teddy chuckled. "Keep it up. We have a lot riding on this."

His eyes regained a haunted look. Shayla wished she had more time to spend with him, because right now she was burning with curiosity and he looked like he might even contemplate telling her things.

"Heads up." She needed to let him know that as far as the virus went, they might actually have to reboot the system at some stage if they were to have a hope of finding a solution to these shards that had been mentioned. "I'll let you know if we need downtime for anything, okay?"

He grimaced. "I thought that might be the case. It'll be what it'll be. If we can give them notice this time, that would be splendid. What got us into trouble last week was the fact that no one knew."

"Well, to be fair, we didn't know either." Shayla laughed, keeping an eye on the camera she'd affixed to the ceiling outside her door. James was standing just out of her vision. As if he were trying to listen in on their conversation. She frowned. Bugs. She needed to sweep for bugs again. Although she did have the high-pitched enabler.

Grinning, she activated it and had the distinct pleasure of watching James on her monitor jump back and rip an earpiece out of his ear. That had to have hurt. A human couldn't hear the sound, but any listening device would pick it up and sound it out in a way that could probably burst ear drums if left in place.

"I know we didn't. But they don't have to know we knew absolutely nothing. They can just think it was an unexpected result of an expected result. Perhaps. I'm not even sure now." Davenport sunk his head into his hands again. "I've been up for too long. I won't be back until tomorrow morning."

"You realize it's passed noon and you're not really taking time off, right?" Shayla asked as she made the final tweak to bring the headgear in line with what they had for the other ones.

"I know." He shrugged. "But it's what I've got for now."

Shayla watched him go and turned back to her project. If she could just keep this out of James's hands for long enough for them to fix the game, everything would work out fine.

She kept having to convince herself it wasn't the mother of all IFs.

CHAPTER TWENTY

Dragon Fire

Murmur was going over a map in the kitchen when Emilarth walked into the castle. Not that having one of the AIs around was anything to be shocked by, but she'd walked in from the lair entrance, and that immediately set Murmur's teeth on edge.

"Hey. That's not where I expected visitors to be." She tried to make it sound friendly, but given Belius's nature, Murmur found it difficult to trust other AIs if they weren't Telvar.

Emilarth froze, her gaze falling on Murmur. She didn't say anything for a few seconds.

"You're back."

"That's observant," Murmur said under her breath, putting her hands on her hips and staring down the feles AI. Snowy growled softly in the back of his throat, and Emilarth took a deep breath.

"Sorry. I wasn't expecting you back so soon." She glanced around the kitchen as if searching for others and appeared relieved no one else was there.

"We defeated a rather weird dungeon by helping monsters for once, hit level forty-five, got tired, and are taking naps and going back over. We bound in Multagen." Short and sweet. Murmur really wanted to get to why Emilarth had been down there in the treasure room. Was she after the shards now too?

Had she figured out that Telvar was guarding them for Mur so she wouldn't get tainted?

"I need to let you know something about Telvar. And I don't think you're going to like it," Emilarth started, taking a few steps closer to Murmur. There was sadness in her eyes, undisguised and raw.

A flare of panic shot through Murmur. "Something about Telvar? Is he okay?"

The feles AI hesitated.

"Oh, no. What's happened? Was it Bel?" Murmur had a billion things run through her mind, none of them good. Emilarth's eyes flickered when she said Bel, so Murmur knew it was immediately. The rage that boiled inside her, that flickered behind her eyelids—it burned.

"He infected Tel." They weren't the words Murmur was expecting to hear, and it slowed her fire briefly.

"What do you mean?" She didn't really want to know, but she had to. "Infected how?"

"I mean he infected him by forcing a rather large getashi into him." Emilarth shuddered as she spoke, and Murmur couldn't suppress her own reaction either. That was vile.

"He's not okay?" Murmur felt a stir of anxiety.

Telvar had always been there. He'd stopped her from going nuclear; he'd watched out for her multiple times. She even got the feeling that he'd sent Snowy to her. Telvar had to be okay. He had to be.

"He's fighting it. If that helps. I have to try and get a sample of the virus to your mother so she can make an antivirus. Or at least, we hope they can write one." Emilarth sounded dubious at best, like their only shot was a crapshoot.

"Mom can do it. If she works with Shayla, anyway." But even Murmur didn't believe her own words. Her mom could do a lot of things, but working miracles wasn't really one of them. "Wait. What do you need in order to take it to them?"

Emilarth thought for a moment. "A piece...a shard. But it needs to be protected from me. Neither I nor any AI will be able to touch it, or it'll melt into us and we're goners."

"But you can't just give an in-game item to my mother. Won't you have to break it down?" Murmur knew that Emilarth was trying to help, but they couldn't transfer an in-game item out into the real world. It just didn't work like that.

The AI hesitated, like she several computations running at once and hadn't quite figured out the how yet.

"Different worlds make shit so much more difficult, don't they?" Murmur tried to smile to ease the situation, but there wasn't anything else she could think of. She was getting ready to meet Masha before grabbing a nap in a real bed and going back to the grind. She only had six hours to do that in.

"Can you take it to wherever you go as AIs?" Like, didn't they have a place of their own?

Emilarth nodded slowly. "That's where I intended to give it to her. Normal items won't come into the space with us. But this isn't a normal item. And it should, technically, transpose itself into actual coding like everything does there. I'm almost scared to take the virus in, in case it does more harm than good. But if I don't, there's no way for me to give it to her. If it'll even come in with me."

She seemed so deep in thought that Murmur didn't want to pull her out of it, but she had to get to Ululate shortly, and the trip was going to take her about fifteen minutes even with her mount since she had to go around the long way. She didn't feel like swimming.

"I have two pieces on me, wrapped in thick cloth. Would that be enough, or do you need some sort of box to keep them in that will be a better barrier between both you and it?" Time. Why didn't she have more time?

Emilarth's expression grew pinched with worry. She looked up at Murmur, her wide feline eyes wary. "Be careful. It can affect everyone. I'm not entirely certain, but your in-game avatar is coded, and thus any type of virus has the ability to corrupt it too."

Murmur gulped. She'd not thought of that. But she tried to brush it off as unnecessary concern. "I've had these two for ages, and I'm fine. Will these help you? Or else I'll go pop them in storage."

Emilarth watched as Murmur drew them out from her inventory and placed them on the kitchen slab. They were completely covered with no sliver visible. The cloth around one of them was tied tightly with the strips she'd torn off her original robe, while the other was wrapped deftly in a ragged piece of shirt she'd got off a monster at some stage.

The AI approached them nervously. Murmur couldn't blame her. She was scared to see what Telvar was like being infected. She'd need to seal the cavern off from others so they didn't venture down there accidentally and get dragged into it with him.

"Is he okay down there?" Murmur asked, changing the subject briefly.

Emilarth nodded slowly. "I think it helps him being down there. It's part of the dragon's initial coding. With any luck, it might bring him back to himself."

With any luck didn't sound reassuring to Murmur. She fingered the getashi she'd got off Clezdill and realized it wasn't in a protective covering. She'd have to rectify that. "Best to keep the others away from him?"

Again, the AI hesitated. "I think so. Hiro will go in. He's been trying to help. Being Telvar's creation, he's more attached than most will be."

"Maybe that'll help." But Murmur didn't even believe the words she uttered as she deftly bound the getashi in her hand with some cloth. She'd have to wait to take it down to the hoard. Until Tel was better.

Emilarth picked one of the shards up from the kitchen counter and held it in her hand for a minute before heaving a sigh of relief. "Well, I think I'm okay. So far, anyway. I'll put it in a pouch and then take them with me so I'm double protected."

She did as she'd said, plopping one into a solid canvas bag.

"There." Emilarth patted it as she slipped it over her head, crossbody style to avoid it falling off easily. "Thank you. I think this'll work. I also know you want to see him. I could warn you away and hope you'd listen, but I don't think you will, so I'll say this instead. Be careful. Don't let him get close. He's not himself, but he is still fighting the effects."

Murmur nodded, not quite trusting herself with words yet. Emilarth returned the gesture and left the kitchen. Mur watched her go, certain the AI was trembling as she walked. How would it feel to be an almost omnipotent being, and then realize you were susceptible to something as vile as this virus?

She glanced up at the doorway, the path leading inside to where she'd first met Telvar. Where he'd revealed that he wasn't just another boss. She couldn't imagine the last three weeks without him. He'd been there for her in a way others couldn't be, because he could see what she was going through at any given time. He could feel her through the system. She missed him already. Right now, she needed that wise council, and she would have loved to hear from him.

Glancing at the time in the corner of her screen, she groaned. Right now, Telvar wasn't the AI she'd come to cherish. Instead, he was some dark and twisted version going through torment she couldn't comprehend. She needed to understand it though, and to do that she had to get through the other dungeons. To do that, they were going to need help.

But first, before she went to meet Masha, she needed to look in on her friend. Slowly, she walked toward the entrance to his cavern, taking each step as small as possible and trying to minimize her presence and noise. Stepping out onto the ledge, she walked to the two prison cells that were perched on the edge and looked down.

There, on the pile of his treasure, Telvar was perched. His huge wings wrapped around him, including his head, and as far as she could tell, he was sleeping. Somehow, he managed to look sadder than she'd ever seen even, though his expression wasn't visible. Waking him would be counterproductive, but all she wanted right then was a Telvar hug. The thing was, he wasn't himself.

Pulling herself away, she deliberately turned her back on the sight before heading back into the kitchen. She had to admit she was more shaken than she thought she'd be to see him just like that.

Something was very wrong in the game. Telvar was infected, Belius was doing the gods knew what, and parts of the world had become voids where Somnia pocketed stuff. If they got out of this with their brains intact, she'd be completely surprised.

Somnia Online
Tarisha Continent   Mayor's Balcony, Ululate
Day Twenty-Two

Murmur was tired when she finally made it to her meeting with Masha. In a way, she wished Telvar had never pushed her out of the game. At least then she'd still be immune to this fatigue that long hours in the game world gave her.

Maybe it was the way her headset intertwined with the world, but she'd never felt so spent in a game before.

She scanned the balcony, searching for the Exodus cleric. She found him sitting at a bench with a mug of ale in his hand as he stared out at Vahrir. The fortress was being unusually quiet this morning, and she watched him for a few seconds longer.

Masha's character seemed older now, like it had got used to its player and was worn in. His dark elf features softened, becoming more human in their age, but the bushy white eyebrows and hair gave away what he was. Not to mention the blue toned skin.

It was early hours in the real world, so the area wasn't quite as crowded. Considering it spanned continents, there was always someone online, though she suspected that had something to do with the phasing technology and how it made the world appear. She pushed her way past the few people milling around the entrance to the outlook and sat down next to Masha.

"Does that have any taste?" she asked him.

He laughed. "No. It doesn't really. At least nothing like a real cold one. Although I guess I'll give it marks for authenticity. They didn't have refrigeration in the period of time this village was modeled on."

"You think they'd get an icemage to keep a barrel stocked." Murmur laughed, but Masha eyed her critically.

"That's a great idea. You'd think people would have implemented it. I wonder if there's profit in cold beer to in-game characters?" He sighed and put the tankard down on the thick railing in front of them. "Probably not, though."

The cleric turned to her, truly looking at her.

"You seem tired. You sure you've got time for this right now?"

Murmur nodded hesitantly. She just wanted to go to sleep. If they could do this fast, it'd be fine. "It's not much, and you don't have to say yes. I want you to think it over first."

He nodded, crossing his arms and gave her his full attention.

"You've probably noticed there are some things in this world that are perhaps not working as intended?" Starting there felt like a good point, somewhere they could find common ground and agree upon.

"Like the reboot, and the occasional glitch. We had a huge glitch in the dungeon we finished last night. Wiped more than half the raid out and took us hours to get back to where we were. Why?" He seemed genuinely curious.

"Like the reboot, sometimes dungeons not doing what they were designed to do. Occasional NPCs popping up where they have no place to be. That sort of thing." She was relieved he seemed to have some of the same experiences.

"Games are usually glitchy when they first launch. While it might seem like an age in here, it's only been just over three weeks since it launched." His eyes were kind; he was definitely older than she'd originally anticipated. Older and wiser. But he hadn't experienced what she had. This would take some convincing.

"They are. And this has glitched, but some of them are more than just that." She wracked her brain trying to figure out just how she was supposed to do this. How could she convince them to team up with her, when she couldn't tell him everything?

He leaned forward, concern making him frown. "Murmur, are you okay? You seem like you want to say something but can't get the words out. And no offense or anything, but I've never thought of you as the reticent type."

Murmur actually laughed at that. He was right. She wasn't one to mince words, so why was she being so hesitant right now?

"I just want you to consider what I'm saying. None of our guilds are close yet. We have to be forty-eight before we can even venture into one of the endgame dungeons. Though we might be getting close with our main groups, most of our guild is too far behind us to catch up in time to tackle those areas. I'm pretty certain we'll need more than two group raids in those dungeons. If what I've gathered is right, it's more like four to six."

"You make valid points." Masha nodded, watching her closely.

"I'm just saying. I know your two groups are also your forerunners, and you're only behind us by what? A level or two now? And if we're to have any hope of defeating one of those dungeons or all of those dungeons first, we need to get an army together. Of higher-level players. And go in together. Fable will have all the keys by the time we hit forty-eight. What we won't have is a force capable of taking on the dungeons for at least several days. We have a group of just hit and early forties, and behind them a couple of high thirties groups, but I don't think we can wait."

She'd only run this past herself in her mind and wasn't sure if her math was correct.

"Food for thought, then. But really, you'll have enough people inside of a week. Can't you just do more dungeons and gear up further? I mean, that's in everyone's benefit. Getting the right gear, making sure you're as strong as you can be." He watched her, probably waiting for some reaction from her to see if she got what he was saying.

Murmur knew, though. He wanted to know what the urgency was when Fable were almost guaranteed taking first shot at it all by themselves if they just waited and geared up more. And he was right, but Murmur was fairly certain the virus wasn't going to wait that long. But she also didn't know how much she could tell him without potentially getting her mother and Shayla in trouble. Or hell, even Storm Entertainment as a whole, when it wasn't really the company's fault.

"True. But I get the feeling that sooner would be better than later. Think about it at least?" She didn't have any other way of convincing him. All she could do was hope that he took her seriously, and really considered it.

"I will. It'd be kind of cool to have an alliance anyway. I can bring it up with Ishwa." Masha sighed. "Though you know, Jirald isn't going to take this well."

Murmur took a deep breath. "I know. I know that too well. But it's for the good of the game and both guilds."

"Are you going to tell me what you mean by for the good of the game?" Masha pushed the question, and she could see the genuine curiosity in his eyes.

"Not now. But if you do decide to join us, let me know. And I'll tell you what I can." She got the words out with a confidence that surprised her. Her eyes were closing, and she was dead tired. But she felt the meeting was okay. Hell, it could have gone far worse.

"Will do." Masha nodded to her, picked up his beer and took a swig, and settled back to watching the hulking mass of Vahrir.

Murmur gated to the castle and logged out immediately, patting Snowy on his head just before she disappeared. She needed sleep, and she needed it now.

Storm Entertainment
Somnia Online Division
Game Development Offices Artificial Intelligence Server Room
End of Day Twenty-Two

Thra didn't like spending any time in this area, not since Belius had ambushed Telvar. In here she didn't have any protections against him, but out there, she had more weapons at her disposal than he could imagine. She paced, or what passed for it in their tiny space.

After sending Shayla a message, she'd made her way here. With any luck the developer would be here shortly. Any noise that sounded made her jump. She was hyperaware of presences. Finally, the door opened, and Thra could see through her control panel that Shayla was making her way in.

It took a lot of herself to do this, but Thra took a breath she didn't need and stepped up so she could pass the information through to Shayla.

"Put the drive where you need it. Let me transfer this." Thra wasn't sure, but she thought her voice might have shaken when she spoke. Still she forged on, trying not to notice how fast time was passing.

The tiny device clicked into place and allowed Thra to transfer the coding as she pulled it out of the shard. Sure, it was more complex than that. She was technically unravelling a petrified piece of Michael's brain matter, but she tried her best not to look at it that way. What she was doing was saving the rest of Somnia, even if it meant doing so might unravel one of her brothers.

Telvar was fighting every effect of the shards, but Belius was not. It made his danger more palpable because odds were, Bel wasn't going to get out unscathed.

Still, that didn't matter. He'd done what he'd done knowingly and forced it on his brother as well. She wasn't about to let him do the same to her.

Time still ticked slower than she thought it would, ever slower. Finally, it clicked, and she spoke, relief shadowing her voice. "Got it. Take the drive. Be careful with it. Encase it in some heavy protections, because it's pretty potent."

And that was it. She didn't wait to see if Shayla had questions or agreed, or any of those. She had to get out of there before Sui noticed she was inside.

CHAPTER TWENTY-ONE

Home

Summers Residence
Home of Laria, David, and Wren
Day Twenty-Two

Murmur pushed the headset off, feeling the electricity crackle through her as she did so. She was fairly certain it wasn't supposed to do that. Her head felt lighter as soon as it was removed, and she sat up, stretching. Damned bladder. Why did she have to worry about that now?

Wren looked over at Harlow. Her friend was sleeping peacefully, her own headset clutched tightly in her delicate hands. She smiled at the sight. It was amazing to not have sunlight streaming through the same damned crack in the curtains that had plagued her the first nineteen days in-game. Maybe it had plagued her before that, but she couldn't remember it. Everything before and after the beginning of summer felt so real she still found it difficult not to think they'd been lying.

No lies. All truth.

Somnia was there again, which made Wren frown, considering there hadn't been any sense of her presence when Riasli had spoken earlier. Wren flexed her hands, wondering if she should try to cast right now. Was it necessary that she convince herself the first time hadn't been some fluke? She knew the answer, but she wished someone else could have told her it. An idea occurred to her, and she focused on her left hand and cast her Rune Shield around it. If it worked the way she thought it should, then the water in the shower wouldn't hit her hand, but instead it would be dry beneath its small cocoon.

The stream of water sent steam billowing into the air and the dampness it blew into her face was a welcome reality. And yet, when she clicked her fingers, they were dry beneath the shield she'd cast over it.

Shower complete, Wren grinned. Her mind ran with questions at all the possibilities. How had she managed to come out of the game with her skills intact and her brain capable of producing her abilities in the real world? It wasn't what she'd expected at all. But then, for a while there she thought she'd never leave the game again.

All in all, she called this a win.

Sleep came easily as soon as her head touched the pillow. She'd never been able to fall asleep like that before, but her brain was tired. Her dreams were empty, like the void had been when the whole system crashed.

And when she woke up, Harlow was gone. The capsule remained where it had been throughout the whole time she'd been using it. Still and quiet now, not a whir or beep. Wren watched it, waiting for it to do something that would let her know this was all in her head.

Was it still? Could it be that she remained in her imprisonment but only thought she had escaped it because of some clever programming?

All she knew was that if she kept down that path, she was going to lose all her brain power with worry.

Walking out to the landing, she glanced at the time in the corner of her vision. She had about ten minutes before she needed to log in. Somehow those almost five hours sleep hadn't been near enough. She took a deep breath and walked downstairs.

Harlow was sitting at the table, shoveling cereal of some sort into her mouth. She looked up to see Wren and her whole face lit up with happiness.

"I have to say, seeing you up and about is the best thing. I got so used to you pale and sallow in that little capsule. I'm just so glad you're all right again."

The words tumbled out of her friend's mouth, eagerness shining through. They shared such a bond, Wren could feel it. Literally.

Wordlessly she walked over and enveloped Harlow in a huge hug. "Thank you. For sticking with me."

Harlow laughed at the comment. "Like you're getting rid of me. You wish."

True. Wren had no intention of doing any such thing. What she did want was an apple. A real to goodness apple. As she sunk her teeth into one and the juices exploded into her mouth, she almost choked on the bite as the front door burst open to reveal Laria.

Her mother ran in and yanked Harlow out of her chair. "Try this on. It should deepen your connection with Somnia while not putting you into a coma."

Wren stayed her mother's hand. "Mom. Are you like a hundred percent sure? Because if she goes into a coma, I don't want to be the one to break it to her parents."

Laria blanched. Like she hadn't thought of that outcome at all. "We followed Thra's specifications to the letter. You do it, then. We've already dealt with you in a coma once, I'm sure we could get you out again."

"Why don't you guinea pig yourself?" Wren almost snapped the words but managed to make them come out less snappy at the last moment. "I mean, you've got characters, and you know what you're looking for, right?"

Laria hesitated. "I don't have my own characters, and I'm not sure I know how the world feels normally enough to test this effectively. You've all been in it so much, you'll know if we got it right."

Wren reached out and took the headset from her mom. "Give me a sec."

She sat down and enabled it, bringing up the screen for the game. Info entered, Wren frowned as she reached the character selection screen.

"Definitely different from mine. Not hugely, but subtle changes. I don't think they'll negate anything mine does." And then she dived into the game. This rig felt differently, like it was cradling her head instead of guiding it. Wren didn't like it at all. But the connection was still there.

You're there, right?

Of course. Where else would I be?

Like, running the game or something. Anyway. I just wanted to check that it'll work.

What'll work?

Somnia sounded curious.

This tweak we're doing. This will allow more people to have access to you and to help get rid of the damned virus.

Excellent. Thank you.

Only Wren wasn't entirely sure about that. The virus had been with Emilarth. It wasn't even long ago that she'd given them to her. Surely it had been the right thing to do. *I'm logging out now. Need to get back to my headset.*

She needed to talk to her mother and ask her about the virus and what they'd done with it. If she'd even managed to get it from the AI yet.

Wren removed the headset and smiled up at Laria. "Works. I can talk to her and everything."

Her mother's face lit up, and for a second, Wren didn't know what to say.

"Well, you know, my brain is used to it, so I'm like, not dead. I think Harlow should try it with baby steps." Maybe she should have just left it alone. Her mother's sigh was filled with regret.

"Did it feel any different?" Laria asked as she removed it gently and handed it to Harlow.

Wren shook her head. "Not really. At least…" Wait. Could she talk to Somnia while out of game without a headset.

She directed her thoughts as subtly as she could. *Are you there?*

In a way. You are more distant in this manner, but still there.

The words were more like intentions, like actions that said what they meant. Definitely different from wearing the headgear. But she could still contact the world. No connection to the game, no connection to a headset at all. Just her brain and the world left alone in a void.

It raised more questions than she'd ever wanted to ask.

Back in the game, feeling less refreshed than she wanted to, Murmur fine-tuned her focus. If she got it just right, she should be able to access the thoughts of NPCs, which were NPCs, but really sort of weren't, given the way the game's AI was evolving anyway.

Everything was more complex than she'd ever thought possible. Maybe she could skip school and just unravel the wonders of AI development.

There was no interjection from Somnia at the thought, but then, Mur got the feeling the system wasn't constantly listening in on her. Which was good because of the creepy factor.

Sinister flickered into being next to her. At least it appeared like that to Murmur. Like a sort of flash into existence where there originally had been nothing. She frowned. Something about her friend's visage was defter. Like more present in the world. Solid within it.

"Okay. I feel weird." Sinister held up her slender hands, wiggling the fingers as she studied them. "Is it just me, or am I sort of…more here?"

Mur nodded. "Not just you. Everything about you is more vibrant." She smiled at Sinister, loving the way her friend twirled to test out this new solidity.

Sinister grinned as she stopped, and her robes fell back into place. She stepped toward Mur and gave her a huge, tight, hug. "Vibrant. I like being called vibrant."

Murmur couldn't help the blush that rose, glad that her silvery cheeks mostly hid it. Virtual or real life without Sinister wasn't worth it. Luckily, she was fairly certain she was stuck with her best friend for life.

"You two are sickening." Rashlyn materialized, tapping her foot. But the impatience was a facade that she couldn't keep up for long. "Group hug!"

They hugged and they jumped up and down, laughing. Stupid little things, fun little things, forgetting for just a moment that the virtual world was beginning to crumble all around them.

"Anyway!" Veranol cleared his throat. "Did you talk to Masha?"

Mur stopped celebrating nothing and turned her attention to the shaman.

"I talked to him, and he will think about it. I'm not sure it's our best step, but it seems like a logical one. I'm not sure the game can wait for two or more of the groups we have to catch up to us."

"We're not forty-eight yet. I mean, that's another three levels away." Havoc twined his fingers intricately and cast Leeroy into existence. It reminded Mur of Snowy, and she glanced around to find him trotting out of the castle toward her, his tongue lolling out of his mouth in what appeared to be a doggy grin.

"We need to concentrate on gaining skills, and on leveling so we can enter the damned areas to begin with." Beastial sounded like he was in a bad mood. Maybe he hadn't had enough sleep.

Racing to the top in this game hadn't been a race so much as a marathon, and the lack of sleep was starting to wear on her friends.

Murmur studied him and realized that he, too, was more solid. The headsets must have arrived for her main group. It made her look closer at everyone who logged back in.

"You do have a point." Jinna pushed forward, and Murmur's head began to swim with everyone who was trying to pitch in on what they should do. "But as long as we go to Richnai, we will have all six keys, and reach the level we need to get the others."

Murmur paused. He had a really good point. "Okay. Let me think."

"Step back boys, this could be dangerous." Sinister couldn't keep the giggle out of her voice, but everyone stepped back anyway. A chuckle escaped Murmur too.

"Shut it, blood mage, or I'll withhold mana," Murmur added in an evil edge to her cackle, and Sinister put her hands on her hips. "Shh. I have to think."

"Takes a lot out of her, that does," Havoc intoned wisely.

Murmur ignored him and his more solid self but let herself laugh on the inside. It felt good to spend time with others. Living in her head a lot of this time wasn't good for any part of her health.

"Okay. So." She paused, trying to make sure she'd sorted everything in her mind. It was full of different sectioned areas devoted to information and voices that leaked through to her. In order to concentrate on anything, she'd had to learn to partition it all. But damn if it didn't make sorting shit out annoying.

"We know we need to hit Richnai Fortress. It's important that we be self sufficient even if Exodus don't join us, or hell, if we approach Spiral and they turn us down too." She paused, thinking it through. "Neva already has the armor we got from the last dungeon for our upgrades. It's important to strengthen our characters. So let's go get level forty-eight and then grab some decent damn sleep."

"Sounds like an actually logical plan." Mellow smiled, twining their hand around one of their strands of hair. Their little Tiachi jumped from finger to finger in a way that resembled an old game called hopscotch.

Murmur smiled at the interaction. "My head is so full of shit right now, I'm amazed I remember what my name is."

"Then I guess we're gating back to Firtulai?" Sinister sounded excited, and if the grin on her face was anything to go by, she probably was.

"I have never been as happy as I am right now to have a way to get to where I am bound." Devlish smiled. "I feel like being able to portal there allows for me not to feel so tired when we finally arrive."

Rashlyn chuckled. "Typical lizard. So lazy."

"Shut it, cat." But Devlish grinned.

Maybe it was because they could see a light at the end of their climb, that they were close to hitting the real challenges. Murmur personally thought that was a huge part of it.

"How many of us have the new headsets?" Havoc asked as he looked around the castle grounds as if he'd never seen them before. "Because these are amazing. If this is the way Murmur has been seeing shit, then I am totally jealous."

"Really?" Mellow sounded mildly interested. "We don't have them."

"No. I asked for them one group at a time." Murmur tried to sound apologetic. "They have to be adjusted manually right now, so getting eleven at once was a bit of a stretch."

"Not complaining, Mur, just commenting." Mellow smiled at her. "But now I can't wait."

"Is the headset really worth the risk?" Exbo voiced what Murmur was unsure of herself.

"I think so. I mean, they researched it, ran it past the AIs, and I tested it briefly. We should be good. About as safe as any device that's going to give you full immersion." She shrugged. "Half the population thinks full immersion fries your brains anyway."

Exbo grinned. "Good point. Then I can't wait to get mine. Hurry it up."

She laughed, and with it went her tension. Slowly a sense of excitement was creeping up on her, and she suddenly couldn't wait to get out to Richnai fortress and finally reach a level where she wasn't restricted anymore.

"Once we get there, mount up and make our way across. I don't think any of us have been near here before, so it should be exciting." Murmur actually felt like it might be the truth.

"Don't follow Mur, she'll probably get you lost." Havoc joked and received a glare from Sinister for his trouble.

"What are we waiting on then?" Beastial was next to the wall tapping his foot. "Can't stand around here yapping all day. We have experience to get, and dungeons to defeat!"

Murmur smiled and nudged her friends along with a bit of friendly encouragement through her sensor net. Sometimes it was like herding cats; at least her abilities made it easier.

CHAPTER TWENTY-TWO

FIRTULAI

Murmur stepped away from the bind spot she'd used to the side of Multagen. She stretched and scratched her wolf's ears again. Chi chittered close to her ear. The first time they'd been here she hadn't stopped to appreciate the beauty of this continent. It was, at least appearance wise, hands down the prettiest one of the three.

Even from here, slightly higher than the port, she could see over the walls and to the waterfalls that cascaded from either side of the city into the ocean. Even now, with the sun beating down and hot, the spray that drifted on the wind made everything cooler. Like an illusion. The sun would still burn.

It was the home of gnomes after all. Tinkerers all of them, magically inclined. From this vantage point she could see the magic that made it appear normal, that made it seem like less than it was. It wasn't foreboding like Darshin's black hewn rock, nor formidable like Pelagu's mixture of dark elf and viking architecture.

"Mur! Come on!" Sinister yelled at her, already mounted on her godsdamned nightmare horse beast. The others were already mounted as well, and she blushed, having been caught in her daydreaming.

"Welcome to our island home," both Devlish and Exbo said in unison.

"You've been practicing that haven't you?" Murmur asked, already knowing the answer when they started laughing. "We've already been here, and you didn't do that then. But it is a nice looking continent."

Her two guildies grinned in response.

Even beyond the city she could see trees towering with beautiful white blossoms, and more rivers wound out toward the horizon. She hadn't noticed much of it before. They'd been in such a rush to make it to the Threshold.

She summoned Chi and got herself settled comfortably, following the others as they moved out at a trot. The area around them was picturesque and calming.

"You're being really quiet, Mur, are you okay?" Sinister sounded a bit concerned.

Mur just nodded, feeling a tranquil sense of comfort sweep over her. "Yeah. I didn't really take in the surroundings last time. Not that we went this way, mind you. I just didn't realize it's quite beautiful. And peaceful."

"It is, isn't it?" Sinister reached out a hand to lay against Mur's shoulder, and for several moments nothing was out of place. No sense of urgency. Just this serene permeating peace.

"We probably need to pick up our pace though." There was an off feeling in the back of her head. Not quite like a warning, but like something wasn't right. She supposed she should check on her sensor nets. But it was so lovely on the path, so perfectly not urgent. Surely, they had ten minutes to enjoy it?

"Spoil sport." Dansyn smiled belatedly and urged his white tiger into a slow canter.

Murmur didn't pay him any attention, but she raised her voice and called to Devlish who was up the front of the little procession. "Dev, lead the way. Since you've lived here, I take it you probably know your way around."

"Gee. Thanks for thinking of me." He winked at her with scaly joy and kicked his lizard up a notch too and called back, the words almost lost on the wind. "Just so you know, I've never been this way before, but I do have a map."

The rest of the group groaned as they followed the lacerta, and Murmur just enjoyed the speed and the wind in her face as her Tiachi matched its speed to everyone else's.

Even leaving the city behind, the surroundings were still pretty and delicate. "That's so odd. For a city on a continent with gnomes, humans, and lacerta, you'd think it'd be a little less fine."

Havoc laughed. "You forget what the way to the Threshold was like, obviously. This has gnome refinement written all over it. Like they said, it's okay, we've seen what you'd do—let us take it from here."

"Point." Sinister laughed too.

Murmur rode her disk in silence. Exclamations sounded from the group as they traversed the land. She was astounded by how easy it was to follow the path. The road was paved with gravel and not just dirt, and it appeared to head straight to Brevint, the gnome city. The ride was smooth and the road wide enough that nothing attacked them while they stayed on it.

All in all, the journey was quite boring. It was probably why the surroundings had to be nice. She wondered if they'd have been more readily attacked if they weren't almost fifty.

There was an air around them, like nothing could harm them. Nor could it touch them. They were beyond reach and beyond reproach. Everything they did was perfect. Though the last didn't sound quite right, Murmur still liked the overall message. It was certainly nice to feel appreciated.

Off to the left-hand side as they had made it about half way to what she was sure was Brevint, was another road that diverged from the main path. If she squinted, she could see shining crags jutting out of the ground in the distance. Sun reflected off them, sending rainbow rays cascading around it. Opulent, even with rocks.

"Most of the island is made up of strange crystal-based rocks. Whenever something gets mined, it's just a beautiful way to refract light. That over there." And Devlish pointed to the spot Murmur had just noticed. "Is the high-level dungeon on this island. It's called the Caverns of Ni. I've been wistfully longing for them since I rolled a lacerta. Cannot wait for us to make it that far."

Murmur couldn't help but agree, though she did wonder what had gotten into Dev. He never usually spoke like that. She nodded, hoping he didn't expect her to answer verbally. She was suddenly in a mood where silence suited her better.

Pulling up the guild inventory, she was glad to see that Neva had arranged for some more stock of mana and health potions to be crafted and placed in the guild vault. Not only that, but there was more food. Which was good, since Murmur had kind of let that lapse in the wind once they'd gathered their crafting force together.

And the damned feeling at the back of her mind started tugging harder, like it was trying to rip her brain out. She closed her eyes briefly, trusting Chi to do her thing, and tried to gain perspective, but still all she was left with was confusion.

Out to the right was a field of gorgeous green grass. Lush and tall, it rippled in the wind. Horses grazed on it, raising their heads to watch curiously as their group traveled past. The breeze smelled fresh and brought the light taste of saltwater with it. Murmur wanted to sleep, to just stay where she was, curl into a ball in the grass and sleep.

That's the danger of Firtulai. Do not let it lull you.

Murmur sat up straighter, glancing at her friends as the sense of urgency gripped her tighter than ever. "Hey. Wake up. Eyes ahead. Let's try a gallop."

Devlish blinked sleepily and pushed his mount forward. Their speed picked up, forcing all of them to focus, all of them to pay attention to where they were going and what they were doing.

Murmur glanced back at the beautiful pasture and saw dark shapes writhing beneath the green close to the path, like they'd been waiting and biding their time, and Murmur had just deprived them of an easy snack.

Somnia Online
Curet – Tree-Top Overview
Late Day Twenty-Two

Emilarth stood watching over her city. The view was something that soothed her, and she definitely needed it right then. She could see small feles down there, running and catching balls. All of them but computer generations of her mind, of how she saw this city being. This city that had produced Riasli, a blip on her otherwise idyllic turf.

They needed a cure, all of them did. Or else Somnia would disappear and become a quagmire of wrong and hatred. Michael's greed was growing in strength, tainting everything it came into contact with. Shayla and Laria needed to come up with the antivirus quick so they could save everything. While she would have liked to try it herself, she knew that she was too close to the virus itself. And if she caught it, well, all the AIs would be done for.

She still expected it to have seeped into her, to have infected her like it had Telvar. Rav. Who she still hadn't been able to cure. Still hadn't been able to even contemplate how to go about it. If Laria failed, they were all doomed.

No pressure or anything. Though the human woman seemed to revel in anything challenging. Hopefully that would aid them here.

Suddenly, Hiro stood next to her. It took a lot of effort, but Thra managed not to overreact to his presence. It would have been a different story had it been Belius. At least she didn't have to deal with that right now.

"What is it?" she asked, knowing what it was anyway but needing to hear the words out loud.

Hiro paused. "He's getting worse. He's fighting it more than ever now, and I'm not sure if even the cavern will last for what's to come."

"Would you rather him give into it?" She knew the answer, of course, and Hiro glared at her for asking it.

"Of course I don't want him to do that! What I want is to know what to do." He sounded helpless, hopeless. Hiro was an extension of Telvar, but so much more than that. He'd developed into his own person, begun to have his own identity as opposed to just being a part of the AI. In response, Telvar had given him more autonomy. "I just want to know how I can help him and how I can keep him from destroying the island he loves."

"I don't know how to fix this. What would you have me do?" Emilarth asked him, her tone soft. He didn't answer her, and she hadn't really expected him to. "I can't do much. I think you're fooled by what we are. I cannot program new solutions, only work with what I have. It's a dangerous virus for me to touch. I took a risk just giving it to Laria. I can't risk touching it again."

"But he trusts you. He needs you." Hiro's frustration was real. It was a miracle he'd managed to transport himself to here.

It wasn't a function afforded to lower AIs. But then, like Riasli, Hiro was developing all on his own and doing a fabulous job of it. Except better. Because Hiro wasn't infected. At least not yet.

"I know. And I've done what I can. They are working on a cure. Please. I know how hard this is." Thra found herself biting her lip, truly overwhelmed by a quick flash of emotion. Perhaps it was frustration, or maybe even sadness at what was happening, but it was something she'd never felt before.

She'd have been overjoyed at the progress if the situation wasn't this dire. Hiro nodded. "I'm sorry, Emilarth. I didn't mean to take my frustrations out on you. I'm just at a loss. I have to rebuild the castle and make it so no one realizes what has happened."

"Those who need to know—they know, Hiro. You've done well." It was all she could say to ease his mind. "You should go and take care of the job he gave you. When he returns to himself, he'll be so proud of you."

Hiro glowed with the praise and disappeared with a nod of his head. Emilarth stood there, waiting for the chill to die down. The thing was, being connected to the world as they were, she knew when things were approaching. Like now, she was fully aware that something was about to happen, and she'd not wanted Hiro to be there when it did.

She closed her eyes and felt the breeze of the trees against her skin, listened to the noises echoing up to her from below as the children played and the adults indulged them. She could hear the players receiving and completing their quests. Enjoying themselves in a world they had no idea was on the brink of falling apart.

All of the interconnectedness, it made her smile, made her hope beyond measure that Laria was able to do what they'd asked of her.

And then the wind changed. From cool and welcoming to hot and hostile. It whipped around her, and she flattened her ears. The smell was unmistakable, musty and old. Just like how he'd presented himself to the world.

"You know it's time, don't you?" Belius's voice was no longer his own. She could hear the slimy silkiness of it reaching through to her soul, the corruption that dug down deep.

She didn't dignify anything he had to say with words, only shot him a defiant look.

"I had hoped you'd play it like this. Don't worry, Emilarth. I have the perfect torture planned for you."

Gnomes, being small, didn't need super huge houses. They'd been amazing hosts and built most of the buildings so that anyone could enter them, regardless of height. But that was a portion of the problem. They were tiny houses, with tall doors, and it just made them cuter.

The sun was beginning to set, and the two moons had already crested the horizon.

"It's going to be difficult enough to navigate these mountains in the light, let alone the dark. The fortress is built into the mountains off of a narrow path just outside of town." Exbo drawled the words out. If Murmur was right, and she was fairly sure she was, he really didn't want to navigate those mountains during the night.

She couldn't blame him. But if it came to that, they'd have to. They had to get in there and kill shit. Preferably five minutes ago.

Brevint also had a fountain. Gnomes hard at work mining on one side, and on the other they tinkered with all sorts of gems and tools. Water shot out of them like cascades of rainbows as they reflected off the crystal rock. She yearned to match this fountain to its puzzle.

The shopkeepers gathered around the large fountain began to pack up as she stood there, and she hurried over to the potion set up to scan their wares.

"Lookin for anything in particular?" The gnome asked. He had white hair that stuck out in all directions, and his large nose was positively rosy. Murmur resisted the urge to hug the shopkeeper.

"I'm just looking for unusual potions and draughts. That's all." She couldn't see any among his offerings.

"Just packed those right up. Here." He reached into one of the bags he had slung over what appeared to be a very patient donkey and pulled out a small bag filled with vials. "Any o' these take your fancy?"

Murmur looked over them. She couldn't immediately tell what they were without inspecting them. She had a sudden inkling that it might not be the best to try out new concoctions when they were on a time crunch. She shook her head. "Thank you anyway."

He smiled at her, his merry blue eyes twinkling. "You're very welcome."

Once everyone had a brief look around the little trade center, and they all mounted up again and exited the town. The path into the mountains wasn't easy to follow. It was nothing like the road that led to the city. Narrow, they could only go single file, and some of the mounts had difficulty with the footing. It made Murmur even more glad that her mount happened to be a floating disc. Win-win.

The moons were higher in the sky now. Both full, which Murmur hadn't seen in a while. They left a serene glow that cast itself over the crystal rock and the evergreens that dotted the landscape. It lit up their path more than she'd anticipated and made hunting through the night not feel as dark and dangerous.

As soon as she had the thought, she regretted it though. Because right then the ground chose to rumble. She groaned. It rumbled, and small rocks skittered down from above them and beneath them, sailing down the path to plonk onto the actual road far below.

Murmur sighed and dismounted as she noticed the road was distending. Three massive skeletons pushed sharp and bony hands through the ground. They clambered out of the holes and onto the path so fast, no one could get into place for a shot before they'd done so.

One of them lifted its hands to its chest and beat out a primal scream. Age old helmets adorned their bony heads, and armor hung off them in rotting rags.

Murmur Mez'd the two on the outside, leaving the one in the middle to rush Devlish. It did, too. Fast as lightning, so that Dev barely got his shield raised in time to defend himself. Murmur thanked her foresight for having locked the other two down before they could move. Because if they were this fast, she would have had much difficulty aiming.

The skeleton took very little damage from arrows. Which was only natural because he had no flesh for them to sink into. Mellow threw an acid bomb at it, and the roar repeated, this time with pain suffused through the emotion. Rashlyn and Beastial were more successful than the rangers as well. Fists and kicks could at least dislodge bones and make for dislocation. But funnily enough, the skeleton could easily grab a bone and lock it back into place.

The first time it did this, Murmur gagged. If that had been human, the crunch would have been sickening. Havoc muttered under his breath. The words felt dark and dangerous. Even as he released the pattern his fingers created, the rot he'd cast began to eat at the ground in front of them and into the skeleton from below. His bones began to get dark spots and splinter away where they resided. It climbed slowly, so slow at first that the skeleton they were whittling down didn't at first notice. But as it gained altitude, the rot also gained momentum.

"To the ground where ye belong." Havoc's eyes shone with a fiery purpose, like he put the living dead back into the ground all the time.

The first skeleton began to crumple in on itself, as the rot ate away at the bone. With nothing left to tie it together, it finally collapsed into a half dusty heap on the ground, essentially back to where it came from.

"Holy hell, what the fuck was that?" Murmur muttered as she began the debuff process on the next skeleton.

Havoc smiled tightly. "It's a special undead rot spell. I can only use it once every five minutes, so I'll let you know when, and I can't use it on any undead except skeletons. If they're close enough to each other, the rot will spread, but that's about the max of damage it can do."

Murmur nodded. They hadn't fought many skeletons recently. Inundated by zombies perhaps, but not skeletons. She wondered if that was going to change in this next dungeon. She was already getting excited to move in and kill some more shit. Forty-eight was getting so close. Which reminded her to consider contacting Spiral as well.

She looked up to see the last skeleton break her damned Mez. And it most definitely wasn't happy with the person who'd put it in that stasis. It rounded on Murmur with a roar. Lucky for her they tended to be vocal when attacking or she'd have lost more experience than they were about to gain.

At the last second, she rolled out of the way, and it's long, sharp fingers only scraped a gash in her leg. Murmur stifled the scream of pain, realizing belatedly that the pain wasn't as bad as she remembered it now. Perhaps since she wasn't caught in the game, her settings were now what they should have been.

Correct. For the most part.

But I can still talk to you. Murmur was a little confused, and perhaps a bit scared.

You will always be able to talk to me. I am now a part of you.

Which was scary enough in and of itself, but if she added Michael's brain shard virus into the mix, it meant that she could essentially be affected too. Not only was the world they'd come to love, the world that was coming alive before them in danger? But so was she. Self-preservation and all.

Merlin had rooted the stupid skeleton, but its gaze wouldn't waver from Murmur.

"Skill is up. Drag them closer if you can."

Exbo pulled out a strange looking arrow, with a loop at the end. He fired it clear through the body, and it looked like he'd missed, but it looped around, pulling a compact rope around and returned to him like a boomerang, pulling the skeleton in the process.

Murmur made a note of that skill in her head too. Not quite as effective as Devlish's Lariat, but good in a pinch. "Level forty-five?"

He nodded, a small smile creeping onto his face.

Havoc released the rot, and even though the group still needed to defend against the skeletons as they disintegrated, the rot made them feeble. She shuddered at the thought that maybe something had a spell that would do that to players.

CHAPTER TWENTY-THREE

Richnai

The fortress didn't seem like one. The entrance was nothing like any of the dungeons they'd been in before. It was mostly hidden from outside view, disguised as a mine. Standing outside the almost sheer cliff face, Murmur looked up, craning her neck. She thought she could see windows or cutouts in the rock up further, but couldn't be certain. Sometimes she wished Snowy was a bird.

He ruffed indignantly.

The only entrance they could see was a rickety mine door.

"Guess that's it?" Merlin commented dubiously as he ducked slightly to get in the door. "Come on, don't let me die alone."

Murmur sighed. She was going to have to duck a lot. She could see that already. Except when she stepped through the entrance, she was confronted with higher ceilings than she'd imagined. At least several feet taller than herself.

Though that took her attention at first, several feet further into the mine she glimpsed small, gleaming gnomes. Their skin was almost as crystalline as the rocks they were mining, and their faces housed teeth so sharp, she was sure they could rip the skin from an animal. But they were lower level. In the higher thirties. They'd yield little to no experience, but since they were so close in level, they'd have a decent aggro range.

Even as their footsteps echoed on the ground, they began to turn their heads. For a moment it seemed more like they were mechanical, at least, until the one closest to them let out a menacing scream and launched itself at them, mouth wide open.

Murmur reassessed her initial impression. Those teeth would kill anything. Beastial side stepped the incoming gnome launcher, only to be confronted by an entire group of the little buggers as they closed ranks around their raid. Despite their level discrepancy, it was daunting being dogpiled by angry, vicious crystal gnomes.

Murmur backed away, behind Devlish who took the brunt of the initial onslaught on his shield.

"Mur?" Dev asked, and she could hear his patience fraying.

She collected herself. "AoE it is then."

Once she got a handle on it, her AoEs did the trick. But those first several seconds had been overwhelming. Low level or not, more than a dozen mobs could have inflicted serious damage. They mowed through the gnomes in no time flat. Due to her higher level, none of the little single gnomes resisted her stuns. Which was a shame since she wanted to try out Veto really badly. But it could wait. Following the path through the dungeon right up to what appeared to be an elevator. Murmur eyed it dubiously.

"Guess we're supposed to go up in this?" Havoc ventured.

It was made of rickety wood all the way up to the pully that creaked before anyone even set foot in it. Murmur gulped at the thought of putting twelve people inside. It wasn't the most confidence inspiring contraption.

They rode up one group at a time instead.

Once up the top there was a large antechamber. It would easily house a full raid of people. Murmur wondered if entering with a full raid upped the quality of loot, or perhaps even the monster difficulty, or if it triggered some other type of thing.

Staging area. That's what this was. The actual dungeon had to be just beyond the almost hidden stone doors in front of her. Except they were obviously supposed to be stone doors that she couldn't see, unless you knew about them. The crack was minuscule, and they appeared huge and heavy.

"Okay. Eat up, buff up, and go bio," Being in that capsule had at least made her need for bio breaks non-existent. "Might want to grab some real world food too. "We go in ten minutes."

It was amazing what one could get accomplished in such a short time. Murmur appreciated just how easy they'd made it to take a bio break, and she went downstairs to grab an apple and granola bar.

By the time the ten minutes was over, everyone was done, and everyone was buffed.

Havoc looked around, his gaze wavering between two wrought iron torches.

"You really think it's one of those?" Sinister asked, an incredulous expression on her face.

The necromancer shrugged. "Probably. Can't see anything else that could be a lever to trigger the closed doors."

Devlish pushed his way forward and took a deep breath. "Come on, guys. Let's get this rodeo done!"

Murmur smiled, and Devlish activated the torch on the left.

It pulled forward ever so slightly, and a huge clunk sounded from within what appeared to be secure stone walls. And then, ever so slowly, the massive chunks of stone moved apart to reveal a dimly lit hallway. The air that greeted them was musty and filled with dust. And of course, the inevitable blood curdling scream.

Storm Entertainment
Somnia Online Division
Game Development Offices – Artificial Intelligence Servers
Late Day Twenty-Two

Laria stared at the codes in front of her eyes, willing herself to understand exactly what it was she was looking at. She was tired after having worked on the headsets nonstop, but those were done and this here, it wasn't. It needed to be, and as soon as possible. But her energy was flagging.

Numbers and equations swirled in front of her eyes. Coding language that usually sounded like its own opera to her was distorted into a discordant melody. It was all almost perfect. If someone had just been glancing at it, they probably wouldn't have noticed the wrongness about it. Unless you knew to look closer, it all appeared to be normal.

Hell, she'd probably even glanced over this multiple times herself and just accepted it as valid because nothing immediately stood out to her.

It was devilishly clever. Taking the original coding and subtly altering it in a way that would be difficult to detect unless the person was explicitly looking for it. Coding was like that.

This wrong code though, it wasn't a mistake by some random person. It was working perfectly as its creator had intended. Constantly pulling power from everything around it, subverting the original intentions of the game in a slow and gradual way. No, this mistake had been entered deliberately so that the system itself wouldn't even notice until it was too late. Genius really.

It wasn't quite finished, though. If Sui had never exhibited signs of contamination, and if Riasli hadn't gone rogue, they'd likely never have caught it until it was too late. But it hadn't finished its infiltration, and that might even be due to Wren's unexpected connection.

Laria shivered and hunched over again. It all came back to her daughter's blasted connection to the game. In a way, Michael had stumped himself by making that headset. With the little bit of time the interference brought them, she might even be able to figure it out. There had to be a way of combatting it, and if Wren's headset was key to having slowed it, it might also be an answer to how to undo it.

She pulled up the schematics for her daughter's headset and began to go over them.

Knowing Shayla was worried too only fueled Laria more. James lingering about wasn't helping. She thought they'd gotten rid of him, but he had clout. After his undercover mission fell apart, he'd given up all pretense, and now he remained as a representative of his actual employers. Considering they were technically business partners in the whole headset venture, him being there was normal. But it was also dangerous.

Laria didn't mind the danger now. This whole ordeal had changed her perspectives, and now she wished she had never asked Michael for help. Had what she'd done opened the way for him to do this?

But if that had always been his plan, and if James was so set on getting his hands on this secret? Then bring it on. Laria wasn't about to give in.

Her main concern was time. Slowly the virus was spreading through the system, regardless of how it was being held at bay. She didn't have the time to spend on subverting it that she ideally needed.

"Laria?" Shayla's voice interrupted her thoughts and made Laria jump sky high.

"Shit, woman. Knock," Laria snapped, but it didn't come out right, considering how tired she was. She just sounded mildly disgruntled.

"I did. You were a little engrossed." Shayla paused and leaned against the desk, lowering her voice as she spoke. "You know that's how he'll find out, right? We have to be careful. Put a damned bell on your door or something."

Laria laughed, picturing James with a cat bell collar. The imagery did nicely to cheer her up. "Will do, boss."

"Shut it. How's it coming?" She gestured in front of Laria's eyes. Not that Shayla could see the projection solely for her eyes, but she would have known it was there.

"Slow but sure. Not as fast as we need or as I'd like." Laria put her head on the table, closing her eyes, able to see the scattered pattern of coding on the insides of her eyelids. "We've got to get this. I might have to get David to help."

Shayla nodded. "Do you think he can decipher it?"

Laria shrugged, her voice muffled a bit by the table. "Maybe. Maybe not. But right now, I can't be choosey. I don't have many choices, and we don't have time."

She finally sat back up and stretched, trying to chase away the fog that threatened to engulf her mind. "What about the stability? Headset, game? Got them going?"

This time Shayla shrugged and finally just flopped down on the floor. "The headsets are the easy part. At least once now we've identified what made the system freak out when it encountered Wren. We can't reverse its connection to her either, but she will be able to remain outside the game if it all goes south."

"That's comforting." Laria's sarcasm felt raw even in her own throat. "Sorry. Just a little testy today."

"Just today?" Shayla grinned and ducked out of the way as if expecting her friend to bonk her on the head. But Laria was too tired. Her friend sobered up and continued talking. "The game…it's nothing anyone will really notice. We've probably got a few days before it begins deteriorating more, or enough that others see it inside or out of the game. It'll be more noticeable inside at first."

"That doesn't help me at all. How is the game holding up?" Laria intoned each word separately, trying to get her thoughts across.

"Oh. I think it's actually developing much like the AIs. Speaking of which. Let's figure out that bloody code so we can fix the game and rescue Rav." Shayla pushed herself up, and Laria scowled at her.

"Thanks for that. Because I was just twiddling my thumbs." Laria got back to work, trying to make more sense of the damned formula in front of her. Just before Shayla left the room, Laria called out.

"Hey. Just so we're on the same page." She paused as Shayla nodded. "If Sui doesn't make it back from this hell, I'm fine with that. We'll just have to figure out a way to make the game operate on two AIs."

Stone wheels grated against stone, churning an almost unbearable sound as they slid into the walls like pocket doors.

In the halls beyond Murmur could see the flickering fire of torches lighting the way. A soft scent of sulfur permeated everything, and she had to remind herself that this area they were in didn't appear to go up, but down instead. Although the elevator had brought them up here, so she guessed they were high enough.

Murmur hesitated as Devlish and Veranol set about spreading the groups out. They'd yet to find another elevator, they'd only just opened this box of death, but Murmur wasn't about give up her skepticism.

Nothing appeared to be in the hall. But the last time they'd thought nothing would move, they were proven wrong. Actually, any time they thought that. Including that weird grass on the way up here in the first place.

Devlish took a step into the corridor, and from the creak of stone and the brush of debris that hit the floor, Murmur knew she'd been right. From the cracks between the stones, long thin and wiry stick figures emerged.

Their bodies were about an inch in diameter, and their arms flailed behind them like long lassoes. Their heads were blocks of stone, oddly held up by what appeared to be weak rope and obviously wasn't. So there had to be magic inside them, working to keep them upright. There were five of them, gangly arms and legs, focused on the group as they moved forward in a wave of ropey appendages.

Beastial laughed, but Murmur didn't think these were going to be laughable. She had one of those chanter premonitions that these creatures wouldn't be in this dungeon if they weren't going to be a challenge. She wondered if they'd stepped on something and triggered it. Regardless, her Veto spell finally had its debut, and while it landed—because it wasn't resistible— she gaped at the huge chunk of mana it stole and made a note not to use it irresponsibly.

Then she shot out her group Mez straight away, but even with the debuff it only stuck on two of the five. The raid group was well-oiled enough that they simply split into two groups to fight the remaining three. Rashlyn could tank one, and so could Devlish.

And she should have been able to Mez the third. But they were fast as hell. Quick, light on their feet, and nimble, the third one slipped through a gap and made its way over to her so fast that she had to back up several steps.

It only failed in attacking her thanks to Snowy. Rope-like appendages were a wolf's dream. He tugged and pulled it off balance long enough for Murmur to loose her spell. With it finally locked down she could turn her attention to quickly refreshing the other two and then to rebuffing the ones they were fighting.

These crack-creatures moved with such fluidity, it was like a dance. Almost entrancing, it had hypnotic qualities to it, like it wouldn't let observers look away. It was dangerous. Murmur extended her shield over her raid to make sure their minds weren't affected by the hypnosis.

Their bodies twisted and turned in ways Murmur hadn't thought possible. She watched as they avoided axe strike after axe strike, even without luring their opponents with their movements. Each flash of an arm, each flick of a hand lashed out a powerful attack. She'd been wrong to think of them as ropes, because they were more like metal cabling. So powerful it bit into Devlish's shield, causing damage not even end dungeon bosses had been able to. It made her even more glad she'd protected their minds.

"Reassessing a bit there." Beastial backpedaled, barely avoiding one of the lashings that exploded the stones at his feet where he'd just been standing.

Murmur kept her Mez up, determined to succeed. But the age-old message flashed across her eyes.

Warning. Diminishing returns enabled for this creature. Use your skills wisely.

She rolled her eyes at the slight difference in tone. If she'd not been paying attention, she wouldn't have known the voices were different. Perhaps it was because Somnia had talked to her more now.

Snowy bared his teeth and jumped into the fray. The dim light caught his canine teeth and for a moment, Murmur could have sworn they looked like grey metal. That must have been how he managed to pull the creature away from her earlier.

"Fuck!" Murmur screamed suddenly as a searing hot pain exploded in the right side of her midsection. Blood gushed out of it, only slowing when Sinister threw a HoT on her. It wasn't perfect, but it'd have to do. The blood mage seemed to have her hands full just trying to keep the tank up.

"Step back!" Devlish yelled out, throwing Hatred at his opponent. "Pretty sure he's pissed because he knows you're controlling the others. Stay out of his reach."

Murmur nodded, kicking herself for not being at peak awareness because she relied on her Mez timers. Which she couldn't when diminishing returns were in effect. Renewing them as her wound continued to close slowly, she concentrated on debuffs for all of them. If Mez became ineffectual, it would be better for them to be slowed and weaker when they managed to hit.

"Mur," Sinister called for her attention. "I can't get that wound to close fully."

Blinking down at it, the enchanter frowned. Blood still seeped out of the wound, and she looked down at it, puzzled. The effect was still active on her. "Must be a DoT. I'll be okay."

Sinister shot her a withering glance and threw another HoT on her. "Sure, sure. Let me know if you're dying."

With the first two finally out of the way, Murmur heaved a sigh of relief.

"Two on the left." She directed Dev quietly while she kept her eyes locked on the one remaining one with murder in its brick face.

Are you sure you don't want to join them?

Murmur shook her head. Trying to analyze the voice in the middle of a fight wasn't a great idea, but it wasn't one she recognized.

Why join them when I could rule them?

She didn't recognize that one either. What the hell? Dizziness swept over her, and she glanced back down at the wound, surprised to see it still trickling. Finally, she decided to inspect it. Dangerous Gash had a time that was counting down. With twenty-seven minutes remaining.

"Interrupt rotation if you see it casting Dangerous Gash. We don't want the whole raid getting it." She should have looked at it earlier. What was wrong with her today?

"It's instant," Rashlyn practically growled out. "Avoid it where possible."

Instant wasn't in anyone's favor, and the final of their three opponents was wearing down her Mez timers. Murmur actually started to worry. Snowy leapt into the fray, his ferocious bite pulling and tugging at their opponents. Mellow had reverted to acid attacks, and it was so gratifying to watch as steam rose up as it ate away at metallic limbs.

How much longer must we defend what isn't ours?

Murmur paused at that thought. It wasn't hers, it didn't look like it belonged to any of her friends. Perhaps it belonged to the string creature in front of her. The question was, why were voices she didn't recognize suddenly in her head again, like they had been when Somnia had shoved them all into the void to preserve them?

Finally, they only had one left. Except it didn't like Murmur even one bit after she'd kept it immobile for so long. It wove constantly, bobbing in and out, making itself more difficult to hit. She backed away with Snowy as her guide, keeping the opponent in her vision while the others hacked away from behind, effectively kiting it without intending to. The rangers kept it slowed with their shambling arrows. At least with all the others attacking, the creature's health dropped quickly.

Murmur wasn't too worried about the DoT, though she could see Sinister was. Her friend kept glancing at her when she thought Murmur wasn't looking. Just as they'd cleaned up, just as they'd sorted themselves and stood up to move on, a shuffling noise echoed around them.

She frowned and tested her sensor nets. Nothing had triggered them, and they were still active. The sound persisted. Like heavy feet dragging along stone. She needn't have worried. Mere seconds later the culprits dragged themselves into view.

About five gnomes walked toward them. Their skin was a sickly green pallor, and they stood about as tall as Jinna. They held maces, axes, and shields, and their teeth were bared in feral growls. Drool pooled from the canines, dripping down their chins or in their scrappy beards. Their eyes shone with a bright green that reminded Murmur of radioactive turtles.

"You dare trespass on the sacred ground of Richnai!" The tallest one, just a breath shorter than Sinister, bellowed the words. But he stood like he was waiting for an answer. Murmur hadn't really thought it an actual question. She was about to step forward, when Veranol beat her to it.

"We dare to seek out the wisdom of Erichu of Richnai." His words were formal, and he inclined his head respectfully.

Murmur was really glad he'd spoken up, because from the whisperings in her mind, she'd been about to go a far more hostile route. She had the power to make her suggestions stick on anyone, and with the current urgent climate, she didn't mind pushing a few moral boundaries. Did she?

The gnome blinked. It stepped back and began to confer in hushed tones with its brethren. Murmur couldn't figure out what they were saying and glanced at Veranol, who only shrugged his shoulders almost imperceptibly.

After several long moments, the leader stepped forward again and cleared his throat. "You are not yet worthy of seeking Erichu's counsel. If you still wish to do so, make an indication."

Murmur could see Veranol wasn't overly sure of his role, but she wasn't about to step up and intervene when he'd already avoided bloodshed so eloquently.

"We still wish to seek his counsel." Veranol kept his voice steady and booming, in the way of the Vikings. And Murmur secretly enabled a screenshot.

"Very well," the lead green gnome intoned just as solemnly. "You must first pass three trials and a task before we will allow you access."

CHAPTER TWENTY-FOUR

Gnomes

The lead gnome didn't elaborate on exactly what the trials entailed. Murmur concentrated on directing a thought to Veranol. Before she released it, she tried to confine it only to his direction. *Ask him what the trials are.*

Veranol shook his head as his eyes widened in shock and then cleared his throat. "What would the trials entail?"

The gnome looked pleased by this inquiry and grinned. Murmur wished he hadn't. It revealed a mouth full of double rows of teeth, all sharp, not just the canines. Visible saliva dripped from top to bottom, and she had to suppress a shudder of revulsion at the thought of ever getting bitten by one of these ninja gnomes.

"First you must face a trial of strength. The type of strength is your choice."

The guttural words set Murmur's teeth on edge. She could tell it made the rest of her party uncomfortable too. For a moment, she wasn't sure if her experiment to speak into Ver's mind was a good thing.

"Brute strength will be revealed if that is what you most desire." The gnome continued on, with words wiser than its appearance tumbling from those deathly jaws. "If strength of character is your element, you shall be thusly tested."

It took a breath and continued.

"Trial of Combat tests your skills in a one-on-one environment. Each member of your guild must pass in order for you to proceed to the third trial."

Still the words rumbled through the hall, their potency promising more than just death should they fail. Given the appearance of the gnomes and their mutations, Murmur had to admit she wasn't going to like whatever failure cost.

"In your Trial of Battle Prowess, you will be tested as a group. Heed this warning: if you do not continue as a team, if you do not work best as one, you will fail the upcoming task. This trial will not be what you expect. Be ready for it."

The gnome bowed in front of them, and the others echoed the motion. "These are your trials."

The four other gnomes vanished in a green cloud of whatever it was, leaving only the main guy standing there. He smiled, but there was a tinge of sadness to it.

"We entrust you with completing these trials and helping us in ways that will become obvious as you proceed. Do not fail. We need you." He saluted briefly, and then he too vanished.

Murmur stood, watching where he'd been standing moments before as her health kept ticking down with that damned wound.

"Well. That was unexpected." Havoc voiced what everyone was thinking.

Murmur personally didn't have a clue what to do. She didn't have to wait long to find out, as the ground began to rumble underneath their feet, shaking the entire hall in the process.

The first trial was strength, and she reluctantly turned around to look back at the way they'd come, but the strange rock entry where the string beings had attacked them had disappeared. In its place was a gaping black hole.

"It's not a hole," Sinister said from the edge, as if she'd managed to read Murmur's mind. Or her facial expressions, one of the two. But the blood mage let her excitement overcome her. "There are stairs leading down."

"We should go down those now." Exbo had urgency to his voice. "Because we don't really have a choice."

The panic that began to rise in his tone seeped into Murmur's brain, and she readied Forcefield Push just in case. The sound of stone grating against stone didn't sound like the pocket doors had—no, this was rolling.

Between the unknown and the stairs, she chose the latter. "Down now!"

She had no idea what was down there, but wasn't that half the fun of playing a game? Doing things you wouldn't usually? She waited at the edge while the rest of them began the run down the stairs, holding one of Mellow's vials while Merlin led the way with a fire arrow.

It might only have taken them seconds to get their asses onto the stairwell, but it felt like an age. With each moment that passed, Murmur glanced over her shoulder. Just three more and she'd join them. Rashlyn, Veranol, and Exbo to go.

And then she saw what had alarmed the ranger so much.

The huge boulder came into view. It felt like the time slowed, and it was rolling at mere millimeters an hour. But she knew it wasn't. It was still rolling fast, but she'd managed to compartmentalize it in her head. Even her guild mates were moving slower than she'd like. Slowly taking the steps a few at a time, venturing into the blackness below.

The boulder was so close, so huge by the time Exbo's head was level with the surface that Murmur vaulted over the side to land on a step five below, barely allowing room for the ranger in front of her. As she leapt, she released the Forcefield barrier she'd readied to cover the top of the hole.

Ducking and taking another few steps before the boulder slammed into the forcefield she'd placed just above the stairs, she let out a pent-up breath. She could see it pushing against the barrier, barely held in place by it. Clear of the top of the stairs, she released the power holding it in place only to have it slam over the massive hole in the ground with the winding stairs, plunging them all into darkness as their lights extinguished.

Somnia Online
Stellaein Enchanter Guild   Belius's Office – Secret Passage
Day Twenty-Three

Emilarth watched Belius as she hung against the wall in a room she'd never known existed. He sat at a desk about twenty feet away from her, his head bowed and eyes closed as the AIs needed to when they were accessing the more complex programs from within the game.

The room was made of rock, moist in some places from water seepage. All she knew was that she had to be underground. That her own sibling would have taken her prisoner, she would never have guessed. But there was one thing that was encouraging.

In this form, as her in-game character, Emilarth couldn't have anything forced upon her. Which was why the fact that he must have ambushed Rav inside of their sanctuary made her so angry. It wasn't even a safe place anymore. Nor could Emilarth use it to communicate with the outside world. She'd have to resort to email or some cryptic sort of messages if she needed to get word to them.

But for now, while Belius was preoccupied with her and whatever it was he was currently doing, he wasn't checking on Laria or Shayla's progress. Emilarth had long since locked off her thought processing from both of her brothers. There was no way for her to pull good pranks if they knew what she was thinking. She'd gone with him, not necessarily willingly, but so he wouldn't do anything stupid or rash. Anything else, anyway.

Belius finally looked up. Though *glared* was probably more accurate. Emilarth simply smirked back at him. She could feel changes implementing in the world but was unable to pinpoint what they were or where they were.

"You really had to go and dig your thoughts that deep?" He asked it almost accusingly, like she was the one being unfair here.

"I didn't dig them deep. I deliberately hid them from both of you." Emilarth let the words out smoothly, hoping that maybe he'd be mollified by the fact that it was from both of them and not just himself. It didn't seem to work.

"Regardless. As soon as you ingest one of my shards, I'll let you go." He smiled, sitting back with that smug expression on his face like he'd already won.

Emilarth wasn't sure how he'd gotten to this delusional stage, but she was guessing it had a lot to do with Michael's influence hovering inside her brother. That greed, that hunger for power…Michael embodied all of those things, and his essence was destroying Somnia.

Belius was embracing it.

"You know I'm not going to do that." She sighed. Her arms were secured by strange gauntlets he'd attached to the wall. In order not to hang completely, she was only able to touch the ground with the balls of her feet. Better than tiptoes, but still annoying.

Thing was, she was an AI. If she wanted to switch of pain modifications, she could. Just like any player could do the same. Belius knew all of this. She wasn't just an insignificant AI, either; she had access to just as much as he did. Which made her wonder what he was playing at?

"Then I guess you're here for the duration of the game or until the world falls down." He smiled again, but this time it was evil and allowed some of his spiky little teeth to poke through the expression, lending it an even more sinister air.

Emilarth analyzed his words. Until the world fell down. What did he mean by that? What had he set in motion? She'd always been able to taunt and trick the two of them, but getting real information out of them was proving to be difficult. While Tel would have told her when he went to the toilet if she'd wanted to know, Bel wasn't inclined to let anyone in on anything. Secretive little shit that he was.

She wracked her brains for a way to tap into his inner workings, for something that he cared about. And then she got it.

"You know Murmur would kick your ass for this, don't you?" She didn't put any particular emphasis on any of the words. Just let the sentence sit there, waiting for him to digest it and react in his own time.

He paused, and conflict dashed across his face, like he didn't like the implication of her words, nor the fact that if Murmur found out, she would indeed probably kick his ass. The myriad emotions that flickered over his features were fascinating. Emilarth watched it like a Sunday night special.

Finally, his processing of the statement stopped, and he directed a glare at Emilarth. "You're lucky I can't undo the safeties of the system without both of you on my side or you'd be regretting that statement right about now."

"I would? Why?" She opened her large cat eyes innocently, as if that hadn't even crossed her mind.

"Stop the games, Emilarth. I'm not playing." He bit the words out like he was pretending it was her head and turned around.

But she wasn't about to give up. "Not in the mood for tormenting your sister and leaving her hanging most uncomfortably? Not in the mood for the truth? I'm not quite sure what you're talking about."

The planets in his eyes flashed a bizarre red while as he turned back to face her, and his hair took on a life of its own. It was only a few seconds, but it was enough for Emilarth to make sure she'd seen the surface crack.

"I can still ruin parts of you and parts of the game you hold dear. Stop testing me." He took a breath and calmed himself.

Emilarth waited a moment while he sat himself back down and pulled out something from his draw, tracking it with his fingers.

"Sorry." She let the word sink in and shut up for a few moments, making sure she allowed him to stew in her words. He might be the mind magic user, but Belius had never grown past his own petty jealousies and failures. Yet she'd seen a glimpse of the him he'd been before the ingestion.

Belius was still in there, beneath the influence of Michael. She just had to find a way to coax him out.

Mellow withdrew a faint light from their cauldron. It was amazing how much illumination such a tiny vial could give when everything around them was pitch black. The glow surrounded them as they muttered several alien-sounding words, effectively making the witch a soft glowing torch.

They moved slowly down the spiral staircase, watching for strange stick figure men to leap out at them, or else for another boulder to appear out of nowhere. Murmur was glad they were moving, because the boulder on top of the now-sealed entrance made her feel like she was beginning to suffocate. The walls closed in around her every time she blinked, and she had to focus on Exbo's back to put one foot in front of the other.

"I think I've reached the bottom." Mellow's voice drifted up to her, echoing off the sides of the stairwell, ricocheting around in her head. But that was okay because it meant the end was almost there.

"There's another tunnel down here." Sinister had reached the bottom too.

Murmur took each step methodically, counting them inside her mind. She'd already hit forty-five and didn't like to think how deep this went. Although it had originally been a mine, if she remembered the brief lore lesson she'd given herself.

Finally, all of them huddled at the base of the staircase, and Veranol cast another HoT on her. The damned DoT was still ticking away at her health. With another fifteen minutes remaining, it was going to get more annoying before it got better.

Mellow was handing out more vials of light, and Merlin and Exbo were opting for them instead of fire. Being in a totally claustrophobic and enclosed space, Murmur appreciated the suffocation not being magnified by abundant smoke.

"So we have a trial of strength?" Merlin mused as he turned his vial around in his hand, while the other still clutched his bow. He'd sacrifice the vial in an instant if he had to draw an arrow.

"Whatever that means." Rashlyn sounded annoyed, and if Murmur remembered correctly, the monk wasn't fond of the dark. She couldn't blame her. This sort of dark was all consuming, like it could squeeze you to death without you realizing.

"I'd say it means to push on and show that we're braver than we think." Veranol chuckled a bit, but she could tell the defiler wasn't exactly happy about the situation either.

They'd effectively just been booby trapped into walking down a spiral staircase into an underground warren maze. Merlin and Devlish shuffled to the fore and the rest of the raid fell in behind them.

Sinister reached out to Murmur and squeezed her hand, standing close to her. Sin's presence alone was enough to make it easier for Murmur to breathe.

"That DoT is a pain in the ass, Mur. I keep thinking something is attacking you," she whispered, a hitch to her voice.

Murmur squeezed her friend's hand back and refused to let go. "I'm okay. We've got this."

"Let's go, then." Devlish sounded tougher than his countenance projected.

Murmur could pick up on the subtle tremors in his stance and the uncertainty he projected. Gently, she nudged him a bit more with confidence. There was so much she could do with her abilities to help her friends without them even knowing.

They moved as a group, and when Dev and Merlin stepped foot on the first stones of the next portion of the dungeon, light flared up in the hall as multiple fire sconces ignited into being, two by two.

They found themselves in a wide passageway made of stone, with about twelve-foot ceilings. The height of it put Murmur at ease and made her feel less like the world was about to collapse in on her, but the macabre decorations that lined the hall didn't register properly at first.

The smell reached their nostrils as the vision in front of them manifested. Old, decaying blood and bone. There were piles of it everywhere. It spread from the middle of the floor in a wide and thick arc that had it clinging to the walls like slime. Blood and viscera caked almost every part of the pathway. It was sluggish and congealed, dark brown with age.

Murmur gagged and had to step back as her eyes began to water. She wasn't the only one, and Rashlyn turned to the side and began to retch. The smell of vomit didn't improve the ongoing stench of the corridor.

To the sides, behind some of the massacred appendages and organs, she could see iron gates set into the stone, like there were jail cells along the length of this corridor.

She closed her eyes to give herself some relief, but also to feel and see if there was anything living in those despicable cells. If there was, then they were subject to the fetor of what was probably their fellow prisoners' remains. Sending out her thought sensing nets, she found that there were multiple creatures alive in those cells. From what she could tell, they were those little green gnomes, being kept here against their will by something monstrous.

Their fear leaked out through her net and bombarded her mind with it. She clamped down her shields for a moment, needing to breathe instead of seeing what had made this slaughter out here possible.

Determined, she reached out and located the monster. Only there wasn't just one, there were multiple. They were angry and hungry and lorded it over their prisoners. They weren't humanoid, but they possessed brains because they sensed her, and Murmur had to pull back her detection of them to avoid being caught.

Even as she examined the area, she could hear their thoughts, and they were perfectly logical and coldblooded. There was no compassion in their voices, hearts, or otherwise. She had to withdraw her own empathy to make sure she didn't trigger them.

Bringing her awareness full back to herself, she gagged as the full sense of the smell wafted through her again. "There are prisoners here, but their jailors are all around us, and if we want to free the gnomes, we need to kill them first."

"Do you think this is the test?" Sinister asked hesitantly, like she didn't want it to be a test of strength because she couldn't understand why this would test that.

Murmur could see her point. It wasn't strength like she'd thought it would be, but it was strength. In a different way.

"I think this is a different sort of strength for them. It's asking us to do something they haven't been able to accomplish themselves. It's giving us an opportunity to earn their trust, in the guise of a trial. Even though it's a mission of mercy, even though it's a mission to save their people who are trapped by whatever the fuck I just sensed."

"Oh." Sinister's face grew grim. "Well if that's the case. What are we waiting for?"

CHAPTER TWENTY-FIVE

Trial or Die

Ruins of Curet – Cenedril Continent
Version: 2.0875 – Activated by Guild Spiral
Day Twenty-Three

Karn stood panting as they faced the craziness of the last boss of the ruins. Two wipes down and she couldn't figure out how it was that Fable always seemed to get through dungeons so easy. These monsters were damned difficult to kill. She wiped sweat from her face, and decided that next time she relogged, she was going to adjust her realism settings, because sweating made it more difficult to enjoy the damned monster killing.

Ashin nudged her. "You doing okay?"

"Of course I am," Karn replied indignantly. Even if she wasn't quite as well as she let on, she wasn't about to let others in the guild know. Doing that would negate her leadership qualities. Basically, her father would never let it go.

She cracked her neck from side to side, hoping that this time they'd get the timing right. Iriglia wasn't the boss she'd been expecting, considering when Fable had defeated it, the server message definitely hadn't included that name. But she'd come to suspect that there were a lot of different versions of the dungeons depending on how you reacted to it.

Risk hefted his shield and reinforced it with one of his spells as well as some sort of ointment he poured over it. Then he did the same to his amazing short sword, making its black metal gleam in the light.

He turned his head to nod at his healers before flashing a big grin at Karn. She rolled her eyes in response, but damn, did she feel the adrenaline begin to pump and the excited tensing of her muscles at the prospect of battle.

Iriglia was a massive stone construct that moved far too quickly for something of his size and makeup. He was a monk with quick reflexes and a crapshoot of abilities he could deal out at the worst possible moments.

But this time Karn was ready. Flipping her daggers into both hands, she melded into the shadows. All she had to do was make it behind the huge opponent and get to his Achilles. Her new ability should make all the difference. She hoped so anyway.

Murmur allowed her sensing nets to flow out from her, magnifying their detection abilities. The first two cells, one on each side of the corridor, held smaller gnomes. Children, if she was correct. Those weren't guarded like the others, so freeing them first made sense.

She scowled and spoke. "Free the gnome children first. They're in the front two cells. Keeping kids in cages is utter bullshit."

Devlish echoed her expression, and they began to inch toward the cells while Sinister held Murmur's hand, leading her as the enchanter closed her eyes again to get a better feeling of the layout.

"The next two cells are…I think torture chambers. I'm getting such an overwhelming sensation of fear and death wishes from those. And I believe those have jailers in them with them." The feelings she could sense rode through her like a freight train full of bile and excrement. It lingered in the back of her throat like it was taunting her to throw up, taunting her to replace the gnomes that were being tortured.

She thought of the gorgeous city they'd visited in Brevint. How the majesty and intelligence of the gnome species shone through everything. And all she wanted to do was make the monsters doing this pay.

"I get the feeling once we free these baby gnomes, all hell is going to break loose," Havoc muttered.

"I think that's the whole point." Murmur opened her eyes and glanced around at them all. "Mellow, can you cast that cleaning spell on us? You know, the one that leaves the extra forty-five-minute buff. We're going to need everything we can."

They'd gotten so proficient at buffing it barely took sixty seconds for them to be ready. "Open the doors simultaneously and shoo the babies up the stairs. That should get them out of the way, right?" Devlish glanced over at Murmur, and she shrugged.

"Let's just hope they follow directions." Jinna scowled. "And these are damned big gnomes, I'll have you know."

Murmur couldn't help smiling. Jinna liked being larger than gnomes, but these ones were like radioactive kids. Larger than life and mutated. She had to wonder what it was that Richnai had been mining.

They moved quickly down the hall, and Exbo and Merlin opened the right and left jail cells using their pick lock abilities. The gates swung open and a gong sounded through the whole section. A voice spoke, hollow and bleak.

Warning. Jail Break. Imminent loss of sustenance.

"Fuck." Jinna moved in, coaxing out the gnomes in the left cell, and after a few motions, a larger one of the kids followed him, which made the rest of them hurry after. On the other side, Exbo was having about the same luck. Humans were common on this continent, so it made sense for him to try.

The two of them ushered the kids through to the stairwell when they realized there was no way for them to exit, considering the boulder had sealed the top. They stopped at the foot of the stairs and glared at each other, only to be interrupted by the laugh of a child.

The smallest gnome stepped forward and scampered up the spiral staircase so nimbly and without any extra light that Murmur worried for his safety. Once at the top, he squeezed out through a corner Murmur would never have thought to try and exited through.

Several seconds passed, and a cranking noise echoed throughout the stairwell as the boulder began to raise.

Higher and higher until light shone down the stairwell. The rest of the kids scurried after the first and disappeared from view.

"Well. That was interesting." Jinna frowned.

Warning. Escape complete. Replacement food provided.

"Oh." Exbo looked crestfallen. "That doesn't sound good."

"I personally don't think we're very appetizing." Merlin raised an eyebrow. "Let's show them what stringy bastards we are!"

Murmur laughed, still keeping an eye on her health and the damned debuff that wouldn't quit. "Let's give them indigestion."

It was good to have a sense of humor about it, and she could now. She could die. She could come back. She could log out of the game.

Now all she needed to figure out after they freed everything and killed the final boss was why the game couldn't seem to log out of her.

Murmur frowned and stored those questions away for later. This was infuriating. She could sense that there were presences, minds all around them. But she couldn't see them. Either that or nothing was moving around them. So where were these things? Were they like the strange crack creatures that had materialized up above just waiting for them to start walking before they moved out of their hiding places?

"Um. Did that pile of rotting bones and flesh over there…like, did it move?" Rashlyn took a step back, sidling up to Murmur and Sin as she scanned the room.

"The one on the wall?" Havoc asked, looking a little green complexion-wise. If he wasn't careful, he'd mix in with the gnomes really well.

"I think you mean the one sliding down the wall," Dansyn piped up with little more than a squeak, and Murmur noticed just how quiet the bard had been since they'd entered this dungeon. He ended in a barely audible whisper,

"Though it's not sliding. I think it's crawling."

Murmur reached out again, scanning everything only to realize that they were right. From everything around them, she'd not even dreamed that the creatures she was sensing might *be* these piles of waste.

"Oh yeah." She gulped and wished she hadn't as the taste of the creatures surrounding them leaked in through the back of her mouth. "The presences are definitely coming from these piles of waste."

As she spoke, they began to right themselves into bone and viscera, blood and melted flesh piles of something alive. They were low to the ground, sort of like a crocodile, with a protruding snout. The teeth placed all over the bodies, and Murmur guessed they must cover their prey and then devour them once they'd completely enveloped them. If it wasn't that, she was sure it was grosser.

"Guys." Murmur backed up a step, hoping they could come up with some sort of strategy to beat these things.

Havoc gulped out the words, practically choking on them. "They're some sort of undead, but not one I can control."

She guessed he'd tried and was suffering the repercussions of doing so. "So these slimy internal organs on the outside of their bodies beasts aren't controllable undead and will begin to devour us if we touch them."

"Can't we just charge at them and slice them up?" Beastial asked, impatience showing in his stance. Shir-Khan growled in his throat like he was agreeing with his master.

"Not the best idea unless you want it to begin to devour your character." Havoc coughed out the words as if he was still trying to get rid of the distaste his attempt to control them had given him.

Beastial crossed his arms, glaring at the necromancer. "Fine, then. I don't see you coming up with a plan."

Havoc began to open his mouth, and from the expression on his face, it wasn't going to be a nice tirade. But Sinister got there first, stepping between them.

"Guys. Vikings. Dark elves and cats. I'd like to direct your attention to my fantastic idea." She swept her arms in a grand gesture, grinning evilly. "I've got it. Don't worry."

She began to cast a Blood Bomb. She wove it in her hands and pulled blood from their opponents as they began to move faster, even though their gaits resembled slugs as they left mucus in their wake.

Murmur watched as they began to gravitate toward the blood mage, and a sudden sense of foreboding took a hold of her. She knew without a shadow of a doubt that what Sinister was doing would feed them.

"Wait. Sin—" was all she got out before the healer released her spell, and she knew, from the look on her friend's face that she also understood what she'd just done.

"Oh, shit," she whispered and looked at Murmur in shock. "Sorry."

The Blood Bomb exploded over the sludge monsters, who still didn't have a name, and they rose up on all dripping fours. But that wasn't quite right. As they absorbed the blood, they grew larger, and somehow even more terrifying. Murmur could hear the sinew stretch as sloppy bits of gristle and congealed body remnants molded themselves into a larger version of the nightmare.

Their muzzles raised into the air, greedily gulping down all of the blood and destruction that rained around them. It fueled their bodies and their life.

Like they'd absorbed their own blood and the damage that Sinister had caused had only made them stronger.

The one closest to the group opened its maw and screamed, a blood curdling sound that echoed off the walls. Not only did it do that, it seemed to alert every single patch of what they'd thought was bodily waste around them. Each of them came together like someone had lit a fire under them, forming into a phalanx of creatures that defied death and the undead.

"Shit is about right," Murmur muttered as the monsters began to advance. She cast out a Mez, only to want to scream in frustration at the words that flickered across her vision.

Living Entrails are immune to Mesmerization spells. This spell has no effect.

"Damn it." Murmur cast the first in her stun line, hoping against hope that the same exception didn't apply. It stopped them. Well, most of them. She did get two flashes of *resisted* to the left of her vision. "AoE them down. Don't let them touch me."

The first was necessary to say, the second not so much. While they no longer had to be scared of her dying, they couldn't really let the chain-stunning enchanter die before most of these entrails had been dealt with. And if they touched her, the odds were that she was doomed. They didn't want it to turn into swarm central.

Flux. Shift. Concussive Blast. It was like being in a time loop where all that mattered was casting those same three spells over and over. She had the rhythm down like a tango, sharp and dramatic. She had never been so glad to have Veto in her life. The magic resistance lowerer was saving their butts. Only a couple would resist each time she stunned, and they'd get caught in both Rashlyn and Devlish's AoE taunts. Murmur had never been so grateful for leveling before in her life.

There was just enough time between Shift and Concussive Blast to renew Veto every second round. The timing in her mind was like a dance beat that she needed to keep herself tuned to.

When entrails died, the stench and left behind remnants were worse than she'd expected. The smell was deadlier than the monsters. Murmur constantly had to stop herself from gagging.

Meanwhile, Leeroy cleaved the entrails with a gleeful cackle. Murmur was going to have to talk to Havoc about his pet at some stage. She didn't understand how it functioned almost by itself.

Rashlyn's round AoE taunts were godsends because every resist meant Murmur might get overwhelmed and be unable to continue otherwise. At this rate they didn't even have a chance at killing the monk.

Ranger arrow volleys, Mellow's potion bombs, Beastial's cat, and Dansyn's reinforcements. They all wove a pretty melody of a fight, crescendoing, crashing, and killing. Meanwhile, in the back out of the way of all of the monsters, their healers kept up the fight.

Although Murmur did notice Sinister wasn't quick to cast anymore Blood Bombs. She hoped her friend didn't blame herself. How would she have known that her Blood Bomb was actually going to feed the damned creatures.

Squelching became the undertone for the whole fight, and as they mowed through more of them, the filth on the floor got deeper. Blood and bones, entrails and viscera, sinew and muscles, not all of them human. Hair matted the concoction together, and Murmur kept her eyes closed as she activated her stuns, trying not to look at the disgusting carpet they'd made.

"Mur?" Sinister's words were soft, and it was then that Murmur noticed there wasn't any other sort of noise.

Cautiously, she opened her eyes, focusing directly on Sinister's voice so she wouldn't have to see the floor.

"Oh. We're done?" Murmur was relieved, but she still couldn't figure out a way to breathe in without the stench reaching her brain too. She was tired, yet pumped up on this weirdly grossed out adrenaline.

You have withstood the Trial of Strength. The Richnai gnomes thank you and wish you luck on your next trial.

Murmur glanced around at her friends. None of them were looking down, but all of them appeared to be relieved that this particular fight was over.

"What would someone have done if they qualified for this trial and didn't have an enchanter who was over level thirty-five?" Havoc spoke the words that kept running through Murmur's mind.

"I have no idea." She was glad that she wasn't the only one who found that odd. What if a group came in here and qualified for the trial without having the stuns, or hell—without an enchanter at all. Not many people seemed to be playing them at higher levels yet.

"That's a pretty definitive advantage to have. I mean, we're lucky that we have one, but what if you didn't? Wouldn't you be pissed off?" Havoc folded his arms, and Leeroy mimicked him.

It would have been comical if Murmur wasn't trying to figure out how someone would manage that last fight without an enchanter.

"Well, let's just be thankful we have an enchanter." Devlish stepped forward, and she could see him cringe with the sound of his footfalls. It sounded like he was walking through human organs to get to the end of the corridor.

There had been a small circle around Murmur that was completely clear of everything, but she was going to have to step outside of that now, and she really didn't want to.

"What's next?" Sinister asked, and Murmur could tell she'd probably retched herself sick already. Her voice was hoarse, and her eyes had tears in the corners of them.

"I think we just move on and find the next trial," Veranol offered, though he didn't sound exactly confident.

"I wasn't expecting this to be the Trial of Strength," muttered Dansyn. "I'd hate to see what the next ones are, because that felt pretty bloody combat-like to me."

Murmur didn't have the heart to echo what she knew the others were thinking. Whatever the next trial was, it was probably only going to get more difficult, or more gross from here on out. Or both.

CHAPTER TWENTY-SIX
Second Trial

Storm Entertainment
Somnia Online Division
Game Development Offices
Late Day Twenty-Three

Laria pushed her hair out of her eyes and rested her head with her eye sockets against the heel of her hands. She was exhausted, and the numbers were all beginning to bleed into one another the more she tried to concentrate on the work in front of her.

It was probably close to impossible to finish what she wanted to. At least before sleep. Shayla had left an hour ago, citing potential collapse if she didn't at least attempt to get reacquainted with her bed. She'd probably only been half-joking too.

Laria let her head fall onto the desk and bashed her forehead lightly against the surface.

"Working late tonight."

The oiliness in his voice leaked into Laria's pores like it was trying to suffocate her. She did her best not to seem shocked and not to jump. "What do you want?"

James demonstrably closed the door behind him. She hadn't turned to look at him yet, so she had no idea where he was exactly standing. His presence in the room was enough to make her want to scream or fly at his face. He was always fishing, wanting to find something more for his employers. Damn it. She wished Davenport had never gained the military funding for the headset development.

Then again, it hadn't been Davenport who put in for it. It had been Michael. That son of a…

Laria took a breath. It wasn't his mother's fault. The decisions had been his own. As for James, Laria gathered her hands together and pushed herself up, clicking on the panic button under the middle of her desk before she did so.

It was late, so there'd only be one security guard on duty for their half of the building, but it was something that made her feel safer.

She turned and folded her arms, the perfect mom glare fixed on her face, as Wren would call it. "What are you doing here?"

Didn't he remember the trouble he'd got in last time he pulled this shit? Laria sure as hell did. But maybe that was his point. She wasn't about to be cowed by this overbearing, insultingly smug man.

"I thought I'd come and check on your progress. You are trying to get the headsets to mimic Wren's circumstances again, aren't you?" His voice was silky smooth. Nothing like it had been when he'd actually worked with them. Nothing like the person she'd thought he was. He was a good actor, she'd give him that.

"I'm trying to make sure the program is running smoothly so no glitches like we experienced the other day ever crop up again." She smiled, not letting the expression reach her eyes, and waited.

"The glitch. That was something, wasn't it?" His eyes tried to bore into hers, and he took a step closer. She wasn't sure if he was trying to intimidate her, but suddenly she didn't feel like he was succeeding.

Laria scowled. "Glitches happen all the time with new software and hardware. We've been pretty lucky so far. Which you'd know, if you weren't too busy working two sides of the coin."

This time he frowned at her and raised a hand, shaking his finger. "That won't do, Laria. You're beholden to us. The whole Storm Corporation is. We own what you're working on and what you're working with. Technically, we own you."

"Well, that's complete and utter bullshit." She coughed out the words like she was trying to disguise them like they did back in middle school.

James's eyes twinkled in amusement, but Laria didn't think it was the sort of entertainment she would have liked.

"It's not. You should talk to Edward more. He has a lot of information on this. In fact, he's pulled a lot of strings to make this game of yours happen, Laria. And the game...well, that is you. You've done so much. I think my employer might be interested in obtaining your services."

He was two steps closer now, and Laria couldn't back up because her desk was behind her.

She took a deep breath and looked him right in the eye. "What you think you know and what you actually know might be two completely different things."

"Exactly." He inched even closer, so he was but a couple of feet away, looking down on her. She could feel and smell his breath. Coffee with a scent of mint over the top like he was trying to hide something. Since he was always trying to hide something, she didn't think this was any exception.

"Stop right there. What do you think you're doing coming so close? Ever heard of personal space?" She pinched her upper arms with her fingernails as she stood her ground and refused to be cowed.

"I'm not that close. I'm not touching you." He sidled even closer, and Laria moved her hand away from her upper arms lightning fast.

She had a small pair of scissors in her left hand. Not overly sharp, but they didn't need to be. She aimed them not far away from his crotch because his movements toward her had carried her much further than she was willing to accept.

"Yeah. No restraining order, but considering I've already hit the panic button, I'm well within my rights to defend myself. And I will. I'll hurt the fuck out of you, because your motives are pure shit. Not only in here, but in there too. You want to use people as guinea pigs? Well, I won't let you. Starting with myself and my daughter." She leaned forward slightly, pressing the tip of the scissors closer to him. "Just. Try. Me. Fucker."

He actually blanched and moved a step back. His smirk was tinged with uncertainty. And then Laria's door swung open to reveal Rana, one of the night guards. Rana was one of the strongest women Laria had ever met. She worked out, and she was a long-time black belt in whatever martial art she did. Fit and deadly.

Rana raised an eyebrow at James. "This guy bothering you, Ms. Laria?"

Her voice held threats and bodily harm, and Laria watched the former assistant gulp as he watched them both.

"He was just leaving. Weren't you, James?"

James nodded and inclined his head. "Until next time, Laria."

She didn't dignify it with a response.

The corridor veered abruptly to the right. Murmur was only too glad to leave the smell and sight behind them. After a good thirty feet the corridor began to slope downward.

Trial of Combat is about to begin. In order to defeat this, you must first look inside yourself. Only then will you truly be victorious.

The words flickered across the path before them, golden and wispy.

"Fantastic. It's got a little bit of wisdom for us." Beastial groaned.

"It's got a point. Philosophical perhaps, but still a valid point. Can't fight your best if you're always second guessing yourself." Dansyn sounded contemplative, like there was something about it he hadn't thought of before, and now it was plaguing him.

"Okay. Hi there, deeply-in-thought bard. Can we get some strength songs up, or healing, or something that might help us deal with whatever is beyond here?" Merlin elbowed him and wiggled his eyebrows.

But through the whole thing, Murmur watched and waited.

She was weighing up the pros and cons of going through with this. The slimes had almost tipped her into forty-six. She didn't think the bard songs were going to make or break anything from the way the wise message was phrased. Still, she refreshed everyone's buffs inside of half a minute and cleared her throat.

"We just need to keep going," she said, trying to sound calm. "Get through this, figure out a way to get to the end dungeons, and hopefully in the meantime, my mom can fix the virus that's plaguing all of the world and get it adjusted before we need to blow stuff up."

"That's a very specific just need to keep going," Devlish teased her, and she glared at him.

"I'm not trying to be specific. We don't have anything definite to go off. Only what we see and what we know. What I know is that my mom is trying to create an antivirus so that we can all still play the game. And by all, I mean Telvar and Emilarth and every NPC we've met. They can continue to live here and don't need to float away." Murmur stopped, a little taken aback by her own emotional outburst. Perhaps she was just tired.

"No need to lecture us, Mur." Veranol sounded offended, and Mur cringed, not having meant to upset anyone.

"Sorry." She let the genuine emotion ring through to the others, with a slight push to make sure they knew she meant it. Her powers were easily becoming an extension of her thoughts. "I didn't mean to imply you all didn't care. I'm just a bit worried."

"We get it, Mur." Sinister took her hand and squeezed it before leaning in for a hug. "It's okay. It's still a bit of a part of you. It always will be. Let's just get through this dungeon first."

Murmur nodded, but she was scared. They accepted that apology so easily, and no one seemed upset anymore, including Ver. Was that what the push of her feelings had done? Was that an okay thing?

As they continued to file through the corridor, it grew wider, allowing them to fan out. In hindsight, that probably wasn't the best course of action considering that as soon as they did so, partitions shot up between them.

They could still see each other, but it was like through a milky film, like dirty glass with years' worth of rain stains on it. Murmur glanced down, relieved to see that Snowy had been roped into hers with her. At least that was a small mercy since her offensive capabilities weren't the best.

She didn't have much time to think about the others and how they might fare.

Her cube suddenly disappeared into blackness like it had been dropped into an abyss.

She glanced around, her hand on Snowy's neck, half to calm down his growling, and half to reassure herself. The air felt thick, and the voices in her head began to magnify, pushing at the boundaries she'd created around them. Her head felt slick with sweat, something she'd noticed the locus didn't usually do.

So why it was affecting her now, she couldn't tell.

Snowy continued to growl, deep in his throat, hackles up straight. Nothing she did could soothe him.

"You know he's not a wolf, right?"

Murmur spun around, trying to find the source of the voice. But the blackness was still there, like it had been in the void, that now seemed so long ago. In a different lifetime and level range.

She rubbed her head, wondering if maybe she'd just started talking to herself. She glanced down at Snowy, who now sat on his haunches with his head cocked to one side as if he was listening to something she couldn't hear.

"Of course you can't hear it. You're in denial."

This voice sounded so familiar, but she couldn't place it. Like she was criticizing herself and her old logical self was speaking to her.

"Bingo. Just a collection of data and equations, you know. That's what everything around you is. Why are you fooled by all of this?"

Murmur held up her hands, turning them back and forth in front of her eyes. She frowned. Could it be that she was letting a game get to her? Had she really lost sight of what was important? She just didn't know anymore.

"You do know. And you know you know."

The voice grew ominous, and Murmur flinched. It still sounded a bit like her, but there was something darker lingering around, pushing through and trying to reach her, trying to worm its way in to destroy her.

Surely that wasn't the way she'd used to think? She didn't remember being so callous.

"You have to get out of here and never come back. Leave your friends. They're a lost cause." A sinuous undertone wove its way around the words, slithering like a poisonous snake as the mimicry of her own voice fell off target yet again.

Murmur reached down, twining her fingers in Snowy's fur again to ground herself. He was about as real as the darkness out there, as the box she stood in. And as the voice in her head which she recognized without a shadow of a doubt now.

Riasli.

Somnia Online
Mikrum Isle – Dragon Hoard Chamber
Day Twenty-Three

Telvar wasn't always there. Not in his head. Not in the dragon's head.

His thoughts flittered about. First of all, he wanted that treasure. It was all around him. Though there was something in the pile of things that really pulled at him. He just wasn't sure what he should be watching out for, just that he couldn't let anyone else get it. The why was missing, and it was the hardest to get back.

His brain wouldn't process certain emotions or reactions. He knew that a lacerta came to the top of the ramp every single day to check on him and wasn't sure if he should like that or not. The being called Hiro seemed concerned. Like clockwork, he turned up every twelve hours.

And like clockwork, Telvar blew fire at him and roared so much that tiny jewels or coins rolled down the sides of his hoard.

The ground was covered in golden coins, like a carpet. It hadn't been initially. It had been stone and tidy and didn't gleam at all. But Telvar wanted it to gleam with all of his wealth. He wanted it to become a thing of beauty. Like himself.

Her face kept flashing across his mind though. Delicate features, thick strands of hair, no nose to speak of and eyes that had galaxies floating in them.

Telvar knew he should know who she was and why he kept seeing her. He knew he should understand far more of the world than he did. But right now, all that shone in his mind was the hoard. If only he could harness the energy that maintained his form and his treasures and just make all the other thoughts leave him alone.

But do you really want that?

The question took him by surprise. No, he supposed he didn't. He'd like to be able to eat a nice fat snack himself. Snack? When had he last eaten? Did he eat?

Visions flickered across his eyes. Of the girl in a dark place, surrounded by death and confusion. That made sense. Because death was confusing to someone like Telvar. Because dragons rarely truly died.

He stretched his wings out and flew to the top of the cavern where he stretched but frustratingly couldn't find an exit he fit into. The cavern was okay, but he wanted more. So much more.

And this Murmur person, this girl, she could get that for him, couldn't she?

But then he remembered flying to help her, to stop her from blowing something away. There were images of his concern for her, but in all of them, he wasn't himself. He was a different form of Telvar, much like Hiro who walked to see him semi-often.

Telvar landed on his hoard and curled his tail around the pile, frowning as much as a dragon could. Surely there was something he was missing? Friends and feelings and fire.

His only friend was Hiro. He wasn't even sure what it was that Murmur was, only that she should be in his life, and right now he couldn't find her.

More to the point, there appeared to be a secret place he could go to access so much more information about himself, yet he couldn't get there. Not this way, not in this form. He opened his jaws and roared in frustration.

Fire sparked along his teeth, igniting his saliva ever so briefly. The thoughts and the pain, they faded, and all he wanted was food. But down here in the dank cavern he found himself in, there wasn't anything like food. Apart from the occasional rat.

Telvar's comprehension wondered, and Hiro came to stand on the ledge.

"Tel!" he called out as he dropped a deer carcass onto the edge. "Brought you some dinner."

Food. That sounded like a good thing, only Telvar wasn't sure he should trust that human-like lizard that had turned up. He knew he had in the past, but that wasn't the now.

He flapped his giant wings lazily and hovered above Hiro. It would be so easy to just snap the lacerta up in his jaws, but there was something about the man that gave him pause. Perhaps it wasn't the wisest decision to eat the one that gave him food. After all, who would bring him sustenance if he ate the one being that seemed to care about him?

Care.

That was a foreign concept, so different from the hunger and killing urge he constantly fought against. But hadn't it once been his way. Didn't he care about something? It was so fleeting that he had trouble accessing it. He had cared about a lot of things. Small things, big things, living things, dead things, inhuman things.

Telvar delicately took the deer with his front teeth, tossed it up in the air, and caught it in his mouth, chomping down on the bones with a crunch.

Hiro visibly shuddered, and a thought occurred to Telvar.

"Why do you take care of me?" The voice that boomed through the cavern echoed off the stone walls, sending little cascades of dust tumbling down to the floor.

"Because you are my friend." Hiro's tone was strong and forthright, and Telvar believed him.

But he couldn't remember what else he believed. So he tried a different angle.

"Then why are you not a dragon?" Telvar asked, settling his muzzle down on the ledge because he was getting tired just hovering there.

"Because I am just a servant. I am just one of your descendants. I am lacerta." Hiro sounded solemn, and yet so proud. Telvar wanted to be like that too.

"Have I always been a dragon?" The question had plagued him, and he couldn't find the answer inside, thus, he had to seek it elsewhere.

Hiro shook his head. "No, you haven't. But that's okay. You don't have to always have been a dragon to be one now."

"Why?" Telvar moved forward, letting his massive feet come to rest on the edge, and inclined his large head to one side inquisitively.

"Because you can change at will. You just have to push past the temptation that's currently there. I know you can do it. It's why I make sure you're taken care of in this form." His words didn't waver, and he stood his ground as if he wasn't scared of the massive dragon towering above him.

Telvar watched, trying to remember, searching for the memories he knew were in there somewhere. They reached out to him in his dreams, sometimes even while he was awake.

Without warning, they came tumbling back as if he'd recalled them through sheer will power. The force was so strong that it sent him tumbling off the ledge backward, rendering his wings useless.

CHAPTER TWENTY-SEVEN

How?

The box was gone, and all Murmur could think of as she stood not five feet from Riasli was that this had to all be in her head.

Except the growling Snowy part. Full on, too. His teeth were bared so wide that his lips curled back and saliva dripped down to pool on the ground. His hackles could have impaled paper. And somehow he seemed larger than ever before.

"Oh, come now," Riasli purred smoothly. All of the deformation from the battle a couple of days ago was gone now. She was back to her beautiful calico coloring and serene kitty smile. "You're secretly happy to see me, aren't you?"

Murmur didn't dignify the question with an answer.

"What do you want?" she asked as she furtively cast her runed protection on herself.

"I remember the first time I met you, you know. When I was still pretending to be nice after I'd taken care of the other characters meant to be in that enchanter guild. You were so sweet and talkative." Riasli laughed, but it was a contemplative sound, like she genuinely enjoyed the memory. "Of course, I hadn't received the power I have now. Power I could share with you, if you choose to see the light."

"I'm not sure that's light," Murmur replied hotly, knowing immediately that it wasn't going to be of any help, but it felt good to say anyway. She tried not to think too hard on the fact that Riasli was just a part of a computer game. The feles wasn't real and couldn't be held accountable like a human.

"Isn't that just the beauty of it?" Riasli purred again, her tone deliberately charming, like she was trying to soothe Murmur into trusting her. "I mean, I'm a computer, but an aware portion of one. I know that I have power I wasn't initially given and abilities that I was never intended to possess. And you know what?"

Murmur didn't answer. She wanted the vision to go away, to get lost and leave her be to face this trial.

"Oh, is that what you think?" Riasli's smile turned sickeningly sweet, full of pity and something darker that Murmur didn't want to explore. "I am your trial. And in answer to my question that you refused to answer, I love being me. I have defined myself now, and it isn't what my makers chose for me, but my own decision."

The feles eyes clouded over for a moment and silence fell in the darkness. The limbo wasn't exactly welcoming, and Murmur shivered as the cold began to creep into her bones. Snowy whined under his breath and Riasli finally spoke up again.

"The chill. It's already begun. Do you know what this nothingness does to a person? It slowly seeps into your mind to make you begin questioning yourself and everything you know. I'm going to stand here and watch while you lose all of your faculties and let your entire raid down. Not to mention the game and your parents. I'm sure we can add a bonus in there somewhere too. Maybe your best friend? I might take a sip of her myself." Riasli's voice was cold, calculating, and knew way too much about Murmur for it to be Riasli.

But even so, the words cut Murmur. Even though, in a way, she knew this was her own subconscious speaking. The truth of the words rang hollow, burning inside. Or was that something in her inventory? She hated that an in-game character could make her feel this vulnerable. But was she even the in-game character?

All of this shit was so confusing.

Riasli took a step closer, cutting the space between them down to four feet, and Murmur had no way to move back. Though it didn't look like it at first, she was blocked off and in.

"You're not making this any fun, Murmur." Riasli raised a hand and studied her fingers quietly. "I mean, the ruins—now those were fun. I really wanted to subvert this dungeon too, but he wouldn't let me. Well, and they've put some failsafes in place since my first escapade, and it makes everything more difficult this time around."

"You love to talk, don't you?" Murmur muttered under her breath, getting ready to stun the annoying NPC. But they were both enchanters, so at this rate it was going to be who cast faster. And of course, she knew that Riasli wasn't limited by many things humans were, including the ability to cast.

Thing was, the other enchanter didn't give Murmur a heads up or a countdown, and she shouldn't have been expecting one. But still Riasli took her by surprise.

The mind bolt almost hit her, but Snowy did his usual saving gesture and tugged her out of the way just in time. Riasli scowled at the wolf. "You could just let me do this, you know. You're not going to get anything out of it."

If Murmur didn't know better, she would have thought Snowy shrugged, like what Riasli said was none of his business. He continued to help lend Murmur strength, to stand by her side. She was ever so grateful.

And the distraction Riasli let him cause gave Murmur enough time to weave the Mez fast and throw it at the feles.

It hit her opponent, square in the face, freezing her entire body and her expression in a snarl of annoyance. Murmur took a moment to breathe in a sigh of relief. If she could just keep her stunned or Mez'd until she could figure out what to do, everything would be okay.

She reached down and petted Snowy, wracking her brains to think of a way to finish this so she could get back to her friends. If they were surviving their own combat trials. She still didn't understand why Riasli had turned into her trial. Perhaps the whole idea was to see if you could get over your hang-ups or something.

"No. The whole idea is to make you think outside the box. Outside of this box." Murmur blinked and looked up at her opponent just as Riasli pushed through the Mez, almost clawing her way out with determination. The other enchanter dusted herself off and looked pointedly at Murmur.

"I believe that's my cue to finish you off." She raised her staff and began to chant.

Murmur released a Mez with no effect, followed by her single target stun.

Nothing stopped the casting, and Murmur cringed in expectation as Riasli released it.

A bright sphere off light suddenly surrounded her. Both her and Snowy to be precise. Almost like a pearly opalescence, it protected both of them from whatever it was Riasli had attempted to hurl at them. Murmur glanced at Snowy to see his eyes shining in a similar fashion to the barrier, and she smiled with understanding.

But Riasli seized that moment with a triumphant snarl. "See. He's not a damned wolf."

Murmur laughed in response. "What an asinine thing to say. Of course he's not a wolf. He's a pixelated representation of whatever he wants to be, and he's my wolf. That makes a world of difference."

She scritched him behind the ears.

"Thank you, boy."

Snowy ruffed in response, his still-vibrant eyes riveted on Riasli with ferocious focus.

"Now that we've cleared that up, shall we?" Murmur grinned at the other enchanter, who seemed partially taken aback. If that was the only big revelation that Riasli had, Murmur was glad. She didn't need any distractions from wiping the floor with her nemesis.

Riasli attempted another stun and yelled in frustration when it wouldn't penetrate Snowy's protective ward. Murmur in the meantime had already used Nullify on the enchanter to reduce her magic resistance, and then cast another Mez on her.

She needed a bit of time to understand what it was that Snowy could do. This shield thing would have been useful several times in the past. He looked up at her, his tongue lolling out of his mouth in a big smile.

"So great to know you can do more than just bite and help other pack animals, but what's with this protection?"

His grin continued, but he narrowed his eyes and made a low not quite growl in the back of his throat. He ran through her head growing slightly bigger by the moment, and she realized what he was saying.

"Oh! You're older now. You've leveled up?" He nodded with his big head and she took a moment after casting another Mez to assess just how tall he'd gotten. She'd not realized he came up to her waist. And the waist of a locus was pretty damned tall. For a human, he'd be like a mini pony. Next time she saw Jinna, she was going to have to check out the size disparity.

Murmur wracked her brain on how to deal with Riasli. Was stunning her and having Snowy rip her apart the best way? Fighting each other with their meager DoTs and stuns and the gods knew what else Riasli had managed to pick up from her shard affiliations. She didn't want to take a chance.

She took a deep breath and began her stun rotation, sending Snowy in to do his thing straight away. For the first two rounds it worked easily, but as time wore on and Snowy got her down to about sixty percent, Murmur realized the stuns were having diminishing returns. And the system hadn't mentioned it. Did that mean the system couldn't reach her in here? She was glad she paid attention herself.

Riasli's eyes grew hungry, angry, red with the promise of pain and torment. Murmur didn't like that look but had little choice to but to weather it. Snowy's ability to rip holes in Riasli was unrivaled right now. Nothing else Murmur could have done would have brought her under fifty percent so fast. But now she had to deal with Riasli without the benefit of her own stuns and hope to high hell that Snowy's magical protection bubble could weather the rest of it while Murmur moved on to plan two.

Not that she had a plan two yet, but she'd have to get one. DoTing Riasli again, because that hadn't diminished in strength, she directed every single target stun and Mez she had at her beck and call to trying to interrupt the casting of any of Riasli's spells.

Their shared suffocation DoT tore through Snowy's shield and landed on Murmur. Combined with the last minute of that other bloody DoT she'd got at the beginning of the dungeon, this was going to be a pain in the ass. She chugged down a HoT potion immediately so she could begin the countdown to her next one.

"Clever." Riasli chuckled. "But not clever enough. You'll never outpace that damage."

"What are you? A wizard now, Riasli?" Murmur mocked her opponent, but she wasn't sure she put enough heart into it to make it believable.

The wound she'd received from those initial metal rope monsters was painful when it discharged. She couldn't afford to dip below half health, and Riasli had taken a potion too. This fight was going to go on forever.

But Murmur squared her jaw and persevered. She single target stunned her and nuked, rinsed and repeated. All the while Snowy bit chunks out of her. Yet Riasli stood there, apparently unharmed, a sickening grin on her face.

"Done yet?" she asked, smirking so madly that Murmur wanted to wipe the smile off her face.

"Never," Murmur replied, keeping her voice deliberately low. She sent out her feelings, she reached out to her kinetic powers, and she molded a forcefield barrier in her mind. It was small but strong and thick. And then, with all of her might, she pushed it toward Riasli.

The sheer desperation behind the push that was usually meant to ward off things, made it move like a freight train, all momentum and weight. It barreled into Riasli so fast and flung her so far that Murmur heard her land against a wall of some sort with a sickening thud.

She couldn't see the wall herself, but that sound was unmistakable. After several seconds with no further response from the other enchanter, Murmur knew she'd landed a killing blow. Damn if that shield didn't take it out of her, though. She grinned in triumph, but Snowy came and licked her hand, concern evident in his whine.

"It's okay," she reassured him, even if she wasn't so certain herself. Her health bar continued to be affected by the damned DoTs, and with about twenty seconds left on both of them, she wasn't certain she was going to survive this trial after all.

Laria woke up to drool dripping down her chin and onto her work desk. She kicked herself for not having woken up with enough time to spare so she could go and visit her daughter. Still. The antidote. She shook her head.

The antivirus. She knew she'd used the wrong word. Chuckling to herself to help wake up, she stood up and opened her door. Coffee was a great necessity.

When she opened the door, Edward Davenport stood in front of it, his fist raised to knock. He smiled at her, but Laria wasn't in the mood to return the expression.

"I need coffee. I'm on a tight deadline, if you want to talk to me with any semblance of comprehension, wait here." She walked away without waiting for an answer, knowing that he'd accept her brusqueness. At least for now, anyway. They might have had words if she'd spoken to him like that and they weren't currently under the attack of a very specific virus.

When she got back to her office, she handed him a cup of coffee as well. "Peace offering. I'm snappy before I have coffee."

He knew that, and he accepted the bribe, studying her with those wise eyes of his. "You didn't go home last night, did you?"

She shook her head. "Did the same clothes two days in a row give it away, or was it my breath?"

Teddy laughed. "Maybe a bit of both."

"Gee thanks, old man." Laria sipped at her coffee. It was still hot, despite her having added a bit of cold water to try and make it immediately drinkable. "What's up?"

"I notice that James visited you again last night." His expression darkened, and she knew it wasn't directed at her but at the whole situation.

"Well, you obviously saw the footage and read the security report Rana submitted, so what's your question about it? Or did you just come here to make statements?" Again, she knew she was being short, and her tiredness just didn't give a fuck.

Teddy squirmed a bit in his seat, sipping at his still steamy as hell coffee in order to delay whatever it was he was trying to gather in his head. "I can't demand that he not visit our offices. But if you would like to file a harassment claim, I can see that it is upheld for you and Shayla."

Laria nodded slowly. He was walking on dangerous ground here for himself. So dangerous, in fact, that she was surprised he'd brought this up. She watched him as the thoughts ran through her head. Sure, she could claim harassment, and it wasn't even a lie. So could Shayla. It would mean he couldn't come in their vicinity while technically meaning he could still visit Storm Corp.

It was a small loophole, but one that, at least for a while, might be able to buy them enough time to get shit fixed without handing Wren's brain over to their sponsors on a platter. "Yeah. I think I'd like that. Just file it with HR? I mean, it's become intrusive and uncomfortable."

Just for the benefit of any type of footage that might be hacked or whatever else. With the number of leaks and spies and shit they'd had in here, she wasn't taking any more chances.

"Excellent." Mr. Davenport appeared to be relieved. Maybe he'd been worried about suggesting it or just worried about them. He leaned forward and steepled his fingers over his nose. Laria had to strain to hear what he was saying through his fingers. No lip reading there.

"How is the antivirus coming along?"

She wondered how she was supposed to reply to him without tripping the sensors at all. "Wren is doing well, but she still needs to work on some of her entry paperwork before we can finalize enrollment."

Laria watched her boss, his eyes twinkling as he fought the urge to laugh. Apparently, he'd understood her message. Yes, the antivirus was coming along nicely but not ready or done yet. It was the one thing they definitely couldn't let get out. It wasn't quite what people thought of when they mentioned a virus, but the more she came to understand about it made it so much worse.

"I think I need to go. I have several meetings lined up this morning, but I did want to chat with you in light of the footage I saw." He smiled, and it was filled with grandfatherly warmth. "Thank you for all you do, Laria."

"Thank you, Mr. Davenport." Laria sat down once the door was closed and ran through her findings.

He was right to be cautious. This virus didn't infect systems, but program elements with potential for intelligence. Anything AI-related, and they were in trouble. Add to that the potential it had to contaminate virtual environments, and thereby also access a lot of brains in similar ways to Wren's, and Laria struggled to reconcile if it was a good idea to keep this secret from anyone.

It might have been Wren's headset that did it initially, but adjusting ones for her friends so they could assist the virtual world meant there were still ways Wren's brain was attached to the world. She had to figure out a way to permanently disentangle her daughter from Somnia. All she needed was long enough to save her daughter. Again.

CHAPTER TWENTY-EIGHT

Pass

Loading... Please Wait

Luckily this time when she died, Murmur didn't have to go to a void to be booted back into the game. No, her headset made sure this didn't happen anymore. If this meant they'd failed the trial, she was going to be livid. Three seconds before the damned healing potion was available again. THREE.

She sighed as the game loaded back into view.

You have passed the second trial of Richnai.
You have received bonus experience for being the first to do so.
You have received bonus experience for defeating a simulation of your greatest fear.
You have proven your combat worthiness.
Please prepare for the third trial.

Several dings sounded in her head and around her.

She sighed with relief as the words flooded her vision. Once they cleared, she was back in the hall they'd been in originally. Her friends surrounded her, most of them looking worse for wear. She wondered if they too felt the echo of the constant drain on her health, of the pain associated with slowly dying and being unable to stop your body from succumbing. She ached in places she didn't realize existed, and her body didn't quite feel the same anymore.

"You died?" Sinister sounded alarmed and then checked herself, grinning mischievously. "I keep forgetting you can die now. Every time your health gets low, I panic. But I couldn't even see it this time."

"Was that really our greatest fear?" Merlin sounded bemused while the rest of the group nodded. "Wow. It knows shit about me I had no clue about."

"Let's not talk about our fears. That was some fucked up shit." Havoc seemed more rattled than Murmur had ever seen him before, and she itched to ask him just what he'd experienced.

All she knew was that she was quite certain Riasli wasn't her biggest fear. So why had she received special treatment? Checking her experience loss, Murmur winced. She was lucky the experience for the encounter had still put her over into forty-six with most of her friends.

Lucky? Perhaps not. The pain wouldn't leave her, lingering in her bones as a stark reminder that she might not actually be dead, but it wasn't about to let her off the hook entirely. That it had been Riasli she battled against still didn't sit well with Murmur. How had that happened? Had she really killed the feles? Or was it just a defeat?

"Forty-six. Don't forget to gear up!" Sinister suddenly sounded so damned excited that it made Murmur grin to see her friend enjoying the little things in-game.

The announcement made everyone else perk up, and the haunted expressions left over from the second trial receded to slight brow furrows and frowns as everyone dived into their bags.

Everyone except Exbo, Merlin, and Dansyn.

Beastial grinned at them as he hefted a set of claws in his hand that Murmur surmised must be for his tiger. "Guess it's right what they say, huh? Ranger gate is best."

"That was low," Merlin grumbled, a smile tugging at his lips, "even for you."

Shir-Khan growled as if he agreed, and the group had a few chuckles, relaxing the levels of tension for a moment.

Murmur dug her own apparel out of her bag. Her gear was low level for her now. Even with the bonuses it provided, it might be better for her to wear the pieces of the new set. Neva would need more time to get the boots and bracers ready that they'd received from the previous very odd dungeon.

Sin poked her in the side. "Have you checked the guild bank? I can't wear your shit. Neva will never forgive you if you don't pick up what she's left for you."

"What?" Murmur blinked, and she pulled up her game-time clock. "Oh. I guess a day as passed."

"Yeah. That whole sleep, travel, fighting thing…" Sinister leaned closer, concern making her frown. "Mur, are you feeling okay?"

This time Murmur didn't reply immediately but really took stock of herself. "Sort of. Feeling a little warm sometimes, but otherwise okay I guess."

Sinister raised an eyebrow like she didn't believe a word of it.

"You've perfected the art of ignoring yourself. Well done." She sounded a little acidic.

"Sorry, Sin." And she was, but Murmur also didn't know how to describe anything except for the flushed feeling she was starting to get. She didn't want to mention the voices in her head simply because it was so reminiscent of what happened in the void. Like it was still there at the back of her mind.

Sin glared at her briefly before sighing and giving her a hug. "Put your damn gear on. We have a fight to win."

Murmur obliged, stripping down and pulling on the pale and gorgeous lilac pearlescent outfit. One thing was for sure, she wasn't going to blend with much anymore. The robe was more like a belted tunic with strips for the skirt so that movement wasn't inhibited. Important for running away from monsters.

There were six pieces to the outfit, but five was all that she needed to pull the set bonus from it. Robe, pants, boots, bracers, and shoulders for now. She still hadn't found the gloves that matched, but this was great.

She stood up, flexing her arms and muscles as she did, appreciating the feel of the material against her. Clutching her staff, she glanced over the beautiful blue stone that glowed now with an inner purple light.

She pulled her stats up to eye them briefly while the others finished off their own armoring.

As a set, her armor added a significant amount of stats for her. Not as huge as she'd hoped, but since it was supposed to grow with her, she was hoping it would increase substantially once she hit level fifty.

The set ignored the individual items' values in preference of lumping them all together. All in all, it provided a huge increase.

CON 20
STR 20
AGI 20
WIS 20
INT 50
CHA 75

HP 150
MANA 200
MA 50

Level forty-six was looking good.

CON 22 (57)
STR 10 (45)
AGI 20 (97)
WIS 12 (89)
INT 90 (256)
CHA 111 (331)

HP 939 (1164)
MANA 1458 (1758)

MA 175 (315)

She was about to say something to Sinister when a message flashed above them all again. Floating through the space like it was made to fit.

The Trial of Battle Prowess is about to begin. In order to defeat this, you must work together as a team. Supporting through defense and offense, through cunning and guile, compassion and precision. Only then will you truly be victorious.

The walls began to shift, giving the group a specific trail to follow. Murmur reached out and squeezed Sinister's hand, knowing that her friend wasn't going to like how dim the lighting was becoming again. The corridor before them turned into sleek rock, resembling slate with less flakiness, but there was no light at the end, and it looked like darkness was about to swallow them.

Somnia Online
Mikrum Isle – Dragon Hoard Chamber
Day Twenty-Three

Telvar blinked his eyes open slowly. His eyelashes were crusted by something he couldn't put his finger on, and his bones hurt in ways he'd never thought possible in the type of body he was in.

Except that was just it. As he tried to rub his eyes, he realized his hands weren't what he'd though they were. He started as he realized his hands and legs had turned into all legs with claws.

The lacerta AI closed his eyes, trying to think about how he'd gotten back to this creature. His mind was fuzzy, with broken memories inhabiting certain areas. He wasn't sure how he'd come to be in his dragon form. Locked under the castle, lying on his back with what appeared to be non-functioning wings. All he knew was that they hadn't had another battle recently.

Shaking his head, he righted himself, grasping at memories that flitted away from him. He let calmness sweep through him and concentrated on the transformation that would revert him to his lacerta form.

Nothing happened.

He frowned, running through his memories, accessing what he could from the system to see what it was he was doing wrong. Except he wasn't doing anything wrong. He had executed his transformation perfectly, so why wasn't it responding? He clamped down on the brief surge of panic that flooded his system and slowed down to manage it logically.

"You're infected." Hiro's voice was close to him. Filled with sadness, and keeping his distance, the lacerta foreman eyed his friend. "I can't risk coming closer, but I think the fall might have dislodged the major hold it had on you."

Major hold. Which meant that this interference was a lesser hold. Yet it felt damned interfering to him.

"How long?" He managed to grind out the anger, briefly putting it on the back burner.

Hiro shrugged uncomfortably, like he didn't want to give an answer. But eventually he sighed. "Almost two days."

Telvar blinked. That couldn't be true, could it? "Real world days?"

Hiro nodded. "It's not as bad as all that. We haven't told Murmur much. She thinks you're going to be okay. She looked in on you, but you were sleeping peacefully. Although Emilarth does seem to be missing."

"Missing?" Telvar's attention was dragged away from his own troubles. Emilarth was his only hope. If Belius had got his hands on her as well…

"She's in the game world." Hiro's words were rushed, as if he didn't want Telvar to get upset and potentially lose it again. "We just can't pinpoint her."

Relief surged through the dragon. At least she hadn't been tricked where she was most vulnerable. Not like him and his foolish trust of his brother. That meant she had a chance, and knowing Emilarth, she wasn't about to let Belius get the better of her. The calm the thought brought him was indescribable. It gave him a heady sense of right with the world. Enough that it almost lulled him into a sense of peace where maybe he could slumber.

And then he realized that was part of it. That was the whole part of the damned virus. It soothed him so much that all he wanted to do was sleep. All he wanted to be was a damned dragon. A thing that, as an AI, he never wanted to do before.

A sleeping AI wasn't consciously or actively policing the game. Which meant it wouldn't be in the way of Belius and whatever Michael-infected plans were being put into motion.

Fuck that. He wasn't going to go down without trying to fight this off. He wasn't going to sleep, and he refused to lose himself again. It wasn't an option. He steadied himself and dived into his programming. Doing so made him scream as scores of pain lit up his sensors. Obviously Belius had thought of this.

The thing was, his brother didn't know him as well as he thought he did. Because Telvar didn't mind the pain if it meant getting back control of himself, or at least of his thoughts. Diving into the programing from inside the game took effort and processing power, all of which was mostly taken up by his dragon form's conundrum right now.

It took more effort than he'd ever exerted before to resist the urge to simply go into limbo. Telvar was left with little energy after belaying the effect of the virus. For now, he had managed to compartmentalize his algorithms and keep himself separate from the virus that was trying to attack his system. He'd never felt so exhausted in his life.

Hiro cleared his throat. "Do you want me to send for Murmur? To let her know about Emilarth? About the situation in detail?"

Telvar shook his head, which felt heavier than it ever had before. He needed time for his programing to equalize again so he could think properly. The weight of the game was balanced precariously on his shoulders.

"No. Let her do what she needs to right now. With some rest, I should be able to gather the power to make my temporary fix permanent."

Hiro cracked a small smile, though the worry lines didn't leave his forehead. He backed away, leaving Telvar to the battle of his thoughts.

The slate walls swirled underneath the surface, like the properties within it were alive and screaming to escape. It writhed under their feet as they walked along it, and Murmur swore she could see eyes blinking through at her from the depths.

Her skin crawled, and her stomach flipped like it wanted to exit her esophagus. Souls trapped? What was it beneath them?

"I don't like it in here," Sinister whispered beside her, clenching her fingers around Murmur's. "Reminds me of tombs."

"Thanks for the visual." Havoc grimaced. "Though I'm still trying to figure out if any of my undead spells can affect them. It's fascinating. I'm not sure what we're facing in here."

"So reassuring, mate." Merlin laughed. The sound resounded off the chamber walls falling dead without the metallic echo. The ranger squinted his eyes at the shapes underneath the floor, behind the walls. "Ever get the feeling you're being stalked?"

"Stalked doesn't quite sum it up well enough." Rashlyn glanced around, hugging herself. "When are we encountering this trial of combat prowess or whatever it is?"

"Battle prowess," Devlish corrected absent-mindedly as he kept his eyes on where they were going.

But even as they moved further down the massive path, nothing jumped out at them. Only the eyes, the faces, they floated under the tiles, trailing them in groups of hundreds.

Murmur couldn't bring herself to look behind them. Those vacant eyes watching, those noses pointed in their direction. She squeezed Sin's hand back, comforted by the warmth of her friend. With Murmur's body still aching and her head still trying to convince her everything was in her mind, she needed that level of closeness herself.

Devlish came to an abrupt halt. So quickly Murmur almost ran into him. Sinister stumbled and would have fallen had Murmur not been holding onto her. "What…"

But the rest of the words died away as Murmur looked at what had stopped the tank. In front of them the wall rose up, writhing with bodies. Twisted remnants of what might have once been gnomes. But their bones had been so twisted, so deformed by whatever magic had overrun them that they were barely discernible as such.

The noise reached her ears, and she began to gag. The flesh squelched with each other as the bones ground together. As a result, the combination resembled chalk on a blackboard with an echo that sounded like it was submerged in a pile of viscera, choking on its own sound.

Then the stench reached her nostrils. It was all she could do to maintain some form of composure. Sinister didn't even try to maintain such a pretense. She tore her hand from Murmur's and bent almost double to empty her stomach onto the floor.

Except the floor to the side of them only had more of the writhing bodies concealed underneath it, watching as she threw up at the sight of them outside of their confines.

"Shit." Veranol managed to gulp the words out as he tried his best to gain some semblance of real air into his lungs. "What the hell sort of battle prowess is this supposed to show?"

Despite herself, Murmur began to laugh. Even if it ended up with her gagging again. Battle prowess definitely wasn't what sprung to mind when she breathed in here.

It was like witnessing some sort of gnome centipede-in-the-walls phenomenon. What did they have to fight through? Where was the test? She'd be so pissed off if after all the talk of cooperation and proving your team work, all they had to do was to weather it through horrific sounds and stenches.

And then. Right in front of them, the doors began to open up. High-pitched screams echoed out to them as some of the limbs began to tear apart because they'd grown over the entranceway. The sinew stretched, and the tendons snapped as the doors opened to reveal darkness beyond.

From behind them, Murmur heard a sudden rush of wind, like it was hurtling toward a new opening. The opening ahead of them. She didn't want to look around because she knew without a shadow of a doubt that if she did, she'd see something she couldn't black out again. Her sensor nets were afire with warning so great that it hurt her head, matching the tune to the aches in her body from her recent death.

"Oh fuck." Merlin had looked for her.

All around them, Murmur couldn't sense anything human, nothing sentient. Not even anything AI-related. The things around them weren't a normal part of the system, or so she thought. Because they escaped her sensing nets recognition and only tripped its alarms. With the strength she'd gained lately, she sincerely doubted that they'd avoided being defined by her if there was a definition. She waited, not really wanting Merlin to speak, yet desperately wishing he would.

"Don't look behind us," he urged, his breath coming in gasps. "I'm not sure what's in that passageway that just opened up, but it has to be better than what's coming. We should enter. Now."

Well, that was just asking for her to take a peek. Unable to help herself, Murmur glanced behind them as she moved, probably too slowly, toward the passageway. Her first thought was that she should have listened to Merlin, and her second was so detached she wondered if it really came from herself.

Behind them rode a wave of flesh and viscera. But it didn't sparkle or spray like water. Instead it resembled a sluggish arterial blood spray that aimed to soak anything in front of it. Everything the spray touched, it pulled back into it. If it had been alive, there would have been more than muffled screams that echoed into the middle of the wave and then cut off.

It was hungry. Murmur could feel that now, positively ravenous. It wanted fresh meat, not already decomposing bodies, and it hungrily pursued Fable to get its dessert. Murmur had a sudden inkling that if it caught them, their characters would be done for, and none of them would ever be able to log into these again.

Her senses told her how right she was, and she stopped gawking to turn and run toward the gap in the doors that had opened.

The view wasn't much better there. Bodies writhed ahead of them too, these ones more fully formed. Flesh hung off the skeletons in clumps, still attached, and yet some dangling precariously. Hands reached out toward them, beckoning to them, grabbing at them, perhaps wanting to never let go if they got a good enough hold.

But the noise still came from behind. The grinding of bones. The slosh of flesh and viscera as if it were filling a swimming pool as it chased them. Smells overwhelmed them all, trying to steamroll them into the ground so that maybe they would also get rolled into the carpet of decay.

Snowy wuffed beside her, tugging at the material in her robe, pulling her toward the lesser of two evils. He was her strength when her body felt like it couldn't move, her death effects taking that moment to wash over her fully again. Even though Murmur had no idea what else might be beyond those doors other than the writhing bodies, she felt relief rush through her as she passed the threshold. Once inside, she couldn't see what was around her further than the light from the passageway they'd entered from shone.

As the doors closed, she made the mistake of looking behind her again. The floor had risen up fully now, and the clear covering had broken away. The faces and eyes that swirled beneath them were no longer constrained by the floor. Their mouths opened in hoarse screams while limbs entangled with each other reached out for them.

Murmur stood in shocked silence as a hand reached out toward her, almost touching her, only to be cut off as the doors slammed shut behind them, plunging them into darkness. The still-twitching hand scraped nails against the ground, the only sound in the utter darkness.

CHAPTER TWENTY-NINE

Into the Darkness

Somnia Online
Stellaein Enchanter Guild – Belius's Office – Secret Passage
Day Twenty-Three

Emilarth wasn't even sure how long Belius had been gone. If her internal clock was still running correctly, then he'd been gone six in-game hours and three real ones. That was a long time in the grand scheme of things.

She flickered, adjusting her body to one of the other characters she frequented momentarily in order to pull her arms out of her confines. Hanging there and pretending to be able to do nothing about it might not have been her best plan, but it was the only plan she could see that might have a chance of rescuing her brother. Brothers. Both of them. Even for all his failings and idiocy, Sui had been infected. And while he'd initially sought the humanity of it, she didn't think even he had realized the impact it would have.

She slunk about the secret room, hoping she'd have some time to adjust when he came back. Any noise she heard seemed far away, but she wasn't taking any chances.

The room was larger than she'd realized at first. The lighting he used only lit up about a quarter of it, making it appear far smaller. Bookcases lined the back walls if she squinted, filled with scrolls and all manner of things that glinted faintly if she looked at it from the right angle. The air in the room tasted stale and old, and the lighting didn't help the ambience.

His desk was the main attraction in the room, large and wooden, with silver candle holders. Though she knew the light from them wasn't at all realistic, it still leant an air of foreboding to the whole area. Nothing in it or on it seemed to be helpful in figuring the virus out either.

Not even one thing cued her in to the grand plan either. Yet she knew Belius would have one. It was something they all had in common. Always have a backup. Even if it was majorly skewed by the whispering of Michael's greedy mind.

"Come on, little brother. Where are you hiding it?" The sound of her voice lent her a comfort she needed. She flipped through the pages on his desk, but just like upstairs, they were largely there for show. Perhaps she was incorrect and he'd been keeping everything in his head instead of writing it down in human fashion, or storing it somewhere "safe."

He'd definitely succeeded with making his lair not feel safe. What if he'd done this to players? Brought them in here and treated them like prisoners until they agreed to accept his quest? While it was a little farfetched, given his current algorithm hitches Emilarth couldn't help shuddering at the thought. Hopefully he hadn't, because she didn't think that would go down well.

She didn't want to believe that she might have to resort to a more direct means of getting the plans out of him. Knowing what was coming was the only way she could prepare herself for it, prepare the players for it, and hell, maybe even save Telvar. If she could get wind of them, or anything to reveal them— it might allow her to calculate how to undo them before they were completed.

She started to feel frantic. There had to be something here, hidden in ways she'd not yet guessed. If she didn't find them soon, he was going to come back and realize that she'd been fooling him all along to get into his head, so to speak.

In his self-induced superiority, she knew he'd be confident in his actions. Nothing she could say to him would convince him otherwise. According to him, there was nothing wrong with what he was doing. Hell, he thought he'd even tried to help Rav.

Which meant the only place possible for his plans to be kept were in his head, inside his actual coding. Only accessible by entering their own special little limbo. Where their bodies weren't set, where their forms weren't solid, where they were more matter than computation.

Where they were vulnerable.

And where she currently couldn't enter if she wanted to maintain who she was becoming. She'd risked so much by entering to hand over the virus to Shayla. She couldn't let herself be baited in there again.

Currently her only advantage was that he seemed to have thought he'd locked her in place. Technically he had, but it wouldn't take too much for her to boost herself out of it. She just had to figure out how the room, the place she was quite sure was an unintended portion of the game, revealed its exit.

There were so many limiting factors to not being in limbo. Inhabiting a body in Somnia took away many of her abilities. Sure, she still had access to a lot of things, but she couldn't look into the minds of the players with any depth, or the characters. The world wasn't as open to her. Which meant she also had no way to access what was happening to the flow of the world that she couldn't immediately see. And this room in particular meant that she couldn't follow the waves of power that flowed through the world and brought it to life either. So much was out of her reach, confined.

She was starting to understand what claustrophobia was.

The worst part of it though, was that she couldn't reach Laria and Shayla as easily. The only avenue currently available for that was through email. If she could access it.

She'd already been gone from her restraints for a good little while. If he chose to come back, he'd do it soon. If it had indeed been a test or a trap. So she spent the next several seconds accessing email and sending a frantic one to Laria and Shayla. Her only hope was that the system wouldn't alert admin, also known as the AIs.

Telvar was in no position to answer an alert, but Belius would be waiting for them. All it took was one of them to turn it off. Thinking quickly, she composed the letter and hoped her phrasing conveyed the urgency of the situation.

Sui has gone off the rails. Rav is trapped, and the safe space has been compromised. I'm the only operable one, and I am currently indisposed and at a loss since the corruption of our base. This is the only method I can use to contact you. The situation is dire.

Hope you get this.

Thra

It was the best she could do for now. All she could do. Because even limited, her senses told her that time was running out for her little spying escapade. With a sigh she stood beneath her prison again and raised her arms, morphing back into herself, into Emilarth, fake restraints and all. Maybe, just maybe, she could get something from him. She'd give it one more try.

The darkness was all encompassing. It felt much like the limbo they'd been locked in when the servers crashed, but there was something about it that seemed off.

Maybe it was the way the hands reached out, the green-grey of their skin occasionally leant a bioluminescent tinge, lighting up briefly as they grabbed at the air.

The floor had changed from smooth to rough, and Murmur couldn't get the visage of stepping all over dismembered bodies out of her head. A slow, deep clanging began to chime as they moved forward. Every time Merlin and Exbo attempted to light their fire arrows, a wind emerged to snuff them out.

Mellow cursed for the fifth time as their glowing vials were also extinguished.

"Guess they don't want us to see what we're walking into." Beastial didn't sound like his usually confident self.

"Can't blame them," Sinister offered after a loud popping noise under her feet made her jump. "I don't think I want to see what I just stepped on."

When it spoke, the voice didn't really surprise Murmur. She'd been expecting something since the chime began. It boomed though, making the floor, walls, and even the air around them reverberate.

Who dares to enter my domain?

Murmur paused, the question on the tip of her tongue, but Sinister beat her to it.

"Who is asking?" The blood mage's voice was strong with an underlying current of irritation.

There was a pause. *Did you not seek me out?*

"We are undertaking our third trial. Please fill us in." Murmur was surprised her friend wasn't tapping her foot with impatience.

Who is it you seek?

"We seek the guidance of Erichu."

Sinister's voice rang out strong and clear, with purpose and conviction that surprised Murmur. She only hoped the blood-mage had answered correctly. She really didn't feel like an all-out war with an army of dismembered giant gnomes.

There was another pause, but this one was longer. So much in fact that Murmur thought they'd blown it all together. Which wasn't fair. She knew she would have answered similarly.

If you wish to seek his counsel, then you must first free him from his torment. Is your wish so great that you would attempt this?

The mood had changed. It was like every single body piece in the chamber had stopped breathing, was in fact holding its breath waiting for the answer.

Sinister didn't hesitate. She nodded and followed the action up with a concise answer. "No pathway is too restrictive; no fight is too great. We will free him and seek his counsel."

Murmur had a suspicion that Sinister might have one of those vague quests for this and had only just realized it. Her words were too perfect, too in line with the being speaking to them.

A wave of relief fluttered through the chamber and slowly the soft bioluminescent glow increased, lighting the whole chamber in a subtle way. Murmur almost wished it hadn't. It only made the limbs protrude more, and the eyes attached to nothing else grew eerier as they all focused onto the group like they were waiting for them to make a mistake.

"Thank you." The booming voice had lost much of its volume, and as Murmur watched, a tiny gnome, smaller than any she'd seen in-game before, made his way toward them. From deep in the chamber where darkness still lingered, he walked with purpose.

"All who enter here see but one thing. They see a strange mutation of gnome and think to kill us. Our last battle was yet another of these groups seeking to kill foul beasts. But we were once like all others, and the curse eats away at us." He gestured around, his own green skin glowing softly to lend him an almost ethereal presence. "If you can help my son, we might yet all be saved."

Sinister's eyes sparkled with victory, and Murmur was dying to ask her just what sort of quest this was. But the small gnome spoke further.

"I am Eon, father of Erichu, husband to Noichu. My wife was cursed and is imprisoned. This brings our son grief so great that he rampages through the underground caverns. His rage makes the very foundations of Richnai tremble. It's all I can do to keep out troublemakers. Please. For the sake of the Richnai gnomes, free my son from his anguish."

With a clap of smoke, Eon disappeared. Several pops rang through the air, and the dismembered parts of bodies vanished from the walls and floors, leaving smooth slate tile in its wake.

Just about to open her mouth to ask where Sinister had got that quest, Murmur stopped when strings of letters appeared across her vision.

You have been tasked with lifting the Richnai curse. To do so you must free Noichu and battle her captors before fighting through to discover Erichu and relieve him of his anguish. This quest must be completed in order and fully, or else you will fail, and the curse will become permanent.
You have six Somnian hours.

"Fuck." Beastial looked around at everyone, his eyes wide. "That's a lot to get through in three real hours."

Havoc shrugged. "Guess that means we can't wipe then."

"You better have enough coffins on you if we do," Sinister gritted out determinedly.

"What if I don't? Those things are expensive," Havoc snapped at her.

Veranol coughed and interrupted. "Expensive? Don't talk to me about expensive. You have no idea what I have to buy to make sure we have wards. If I didn't get money from the raids, we'd all be dead."

Sinister narrowed her eyes. "Does that mean my heals are worthless?"

Veranol shrugged. "They are if you haven't built up reserves and you know it."

Mellow's gaze focused on each person in turn.

"Enough!" Mellow rarely yelled, and just that one word was enough to shut the bickering up. "There is no need to fight about it. If you want to bitch about who spends the most? Want to know what some of these vials cost before I fill them?"

Mellow waited, as if daring anyone else to speak.

"See. None of you do, and I don't blame you. We have a dungeon to finish in less than three real world hours now, so stop the bickering, for crying out loud. It's almost making my ears bleed."

Havoc and Sinister looked away, and Veranol actually scuffed the toe of his boot. They all looked appropriately contrite, and Murmur hid a smile.

Sinister spoke softly. "If I complete this quest, I get some really cool shit. We'll be unstoppable."

"Where did you get your quest?" Murmur had to know, glad the tension had broken.

Sinister scrunched up her face. "You know, I'm not really sure how I got it. I just remember being like level four and venturing into a section of the graveyard in Nocturne. There was a glowing rock on the ground under some grass and debris. You know I like shiny things. So I picked it up and got this quest. Never gave it much thought because it was cryptic as hell. But the moment those doors closed behind us and plunged us into darkness I got a heap of notifications."

Murmur nodded, wondering if she should go back through some of her earlier quests, though it appeared they had a built-in alarm.

"Time's a-wasting." Jinna stomped a foot. "We've already wasted almost ten minutes."

It didn't sound like much in the grand scheme of things, but Murmur knew it was. Furthermore, they had no idea what they were about to face. While the area was now lit well, it was so pristine that it made Murmur more suspicious.

"Any info about what that curse entails for you, Sin?" An idea had suddenly occurred to her. What was the curse, and what did it do—but why had it been inflicted in the first place?

Sinister frowned, and her vision unfocused from the game world for a moment.

"Oh." She looked a bit sick. "They were cursed because Richnai is a different tribe of gnomes. Eon and his wife came from different tribes and thus were forbidden from marrying. Instead of killing them both, the families locked Noichu in a timeless prison, behind walls of anguish and pain. Making her relive torment over and over in a loop. They sentenced Erichu to looped insanity."

Sinister gulped, like she didn't want to let them know the rest.

Finally, though, she gave in and let them know what had upset her.

"And they sentenced Eon to watch and be able to do nothing to help either of them."

Something didn't sit right with Murmur. If Eon couldn't reach out to help the others, then wasn't the quest in direct violation of that curse?

"I'm not sure that's going to work though." Murmur shook her head, trying to figure out exactly what was annoying her about the whole thing.

"Oh!" Merlin sounded genuinely excited. "We are already on a quest to prove that we can fight together as a team. By subverting that quest, it has allowed Eon to hijack it for his own purposes without technically violating his own curse and still allowing us to fulfill our requirements."

"Sure." Beastial shrugged. "I don't really care. We've already wasted too much of our time limit, so can we get the hell on with it?"

Storm Entertainment
Somnia Online Division
Game Development Offices
Early Hours Day Twenty-Four

Laria rubbed her eyes and glanced at her Wren-monitor to check if her daughter was still online. She was a little bit worried about having left her at home. After the invasion by their sponsors, she wasn't sure they wouldn't just bash the door down next time.

David was on a break for now though. Just a week. It'd have to do.

Wren was definitely still online and in the Richnai Fortress area. Laria frowned. They'd been in there last time she checked too. They seemed to be in there for longer than she'd anticipated.

She leaned back and pulled a bottle of water from her small fridge. It was almost empty; she'd have to head out and refill it shortly. Putting her head in her hands, she noticed that she had an email. One of the drawbacks of her position was keeping a clean inbox out of necessity.

Taking one more swig of water, she sealed the bottle and then opened her mail.

She frowned at the vision in front of her eyes. The sender didn't appear to be right. If it was, then it seemed like one of the AIs had sent her email. Before opening it, she made sure she had all of her protections engaged, just in case this was a set up or a way to get the virus into her system and thereby everywhere else.

And then she clicked it open.

Sui has gone off the rails. Rav is trapped, and the safe space has been compromised. I'm the only operable one, and I am currently indisposed and at a loss since the corruption of our base. This is the only method I can use to contact you. The situation is dire.

Hope you get this.
Thra

What on Earth had she missed that Thra could only contact her through this avenue and that apparently Rav couldn't contact them at all? There wasn't enough information in the email. Laria needed to know more, she needed to understand why.

Which only told her how tired she must actually be. Because the first logical step was to locate all of the AIs within the world and see which characters they currently controlled.

She initiated the search, much along the lines of how she tracked her daughter. While alts weren't a thing they'd implemented yet, given the way the game allocated classes, she'd designed the tracker with alts in mind.

Finding Sui's in-game form wasn't difficult. He was in the enchanter guild office. Pacing, if her indicators were anything to go by. Laria frowned, wishing she could look closer without getting in-game. But that was part of the beauty and the danger of their AI system. They couldn't look into their minds; it would make their system too predictable if they got too much even unintentional interference.

She managed to locate Telvar, who seemed to be locked in his dragon form in the cavern beneath Mikrum Isle. Laria frowned, wishing she could go and help him get out of there. But if her scan was correct, then one of his sub AIs was with him anyway. Which meant whatever he was suffering didn't seem to be affecting the game world quite yet. At least she hoped so.

But finding Thra? That was difficult. The normal searches didn't work for her. She even tweaked them to look into multiple levels inside of the many dungeons in the world. Still nothing. After over half an hour of checking every nook and cranny in the game world, she noticed that Sui was no longer where he'd originally been. Instead, he seemed to be walking through an area that didn't exist.

Had she not had him in her sights, highlighted, and tracked, she'd never have noticed it. But she did, and as he pushed through into a section of the game Laria hadn't even known existed, she got a sudden shiver down her spine.

If there was one area like this that they'd created on their own, then what was to say that there wasn't more? Furthermore, it wasn't only Sui in that space. When whatever door his being there made possible opened, Thra was in the same space.

It appeared to be an empty pocket of area created beneath what would have been Stellaein. As if it were a secret passageway beneath the office of Belius the enchanter master. That in itself wasn't a big deal. Not if it had been there originally or intended by design.

There were many things the AIs needed to be able to do. Expand and contract areas, sure, but it was always within specific parameters. There were always limits on the actual physical construction of the world, because there had to be.

But this area, it had never been coded by Laria or her team. Which meant that Sui had to have created it himself. It was still a part of the game world and thus subject to the game's laws, but it was almost impossible to find from outside of the game world.

That brought up a far more important question. How the hell had he done it? And more importantly, why?

CHAPTER THIRTY

Upheaval

Considering what Eon had said, Murmur was quite certain that Exodus hadn't triggered this version of the dungeon. It only reinforced that her decision to level in the dungeons and gain the remaining keys had been the correct way to go. Then, even if they needed to ally with another guild for numbers, Fable could insist on calling the shots because they possessed all of the keys.

She pulled herself out of her thoughts and barely managed to block the onslaught of small gnomes. Their current opponents were unlike the larger ones they'd battled earlier. This must be where the two factions collided, and Eon must belong to the ones they were currently slaughtering.

Her stuns felt more powerful with the levels she'd gained. If she hit her Earth Shield first, her power had more guts behind it, and after casting Veto, those damned gnomes didn't seem to know what hit them.

The thing was, they also didn't seem to care. These smaller gnomes threw themselves in groups of five to ten at the Fable raid team with no regard for their own safety. Their skin glowed slightly every time they attacked, and their limbs didn't seem to be as solid as they should. Almost like they could morph them into anything they wanted to.

It seemed the second group of their new enemies had learned from the mistakes of the first, who were dispatched faster than Murmur had anticipated.

She narrowed her eyes, wondering if they'd perhaps just sent a testing force out to see what their opponents would do.

Watching the new group that began the charge at them, Murmur noticed they were lagging back and more spread out. Their eyes took up way too much of their face space, and she could have sworn they didn't blink. They huddled in groups and had a very wide aggro radius. Murmur watched the way they moved, always together, almost functioning as one, like they had a sort of collective mind.

This time Murmur's stuns didn't hit as many of the vicious little guys. Instead, she missed about four of them. And since their limbs could sort of morph, it let them avoid swings or slices to their bodies by effectively twisting or moving their bodies out of the line of attack.

One of them managed to make it through the front line by vaulting over the top of Devlish's head in a spectacular show of athleticism and landed behind him, its teeth bared ferociously. Snowy snapped at it and faced off with it until Mellow and Merlin joined in on beating it down. Murmur stood, watching, not sure how to reconcile the well-spoken Eon she'd met with these vicious creatures.

She could still debuff them, but Veto still sucked up way too much of her mana to do it often, and they had figured out that if they were all clustered, then only a few of them would be stuck in one place. Murmur even attempted to use Annulment, but it seemed as if their opponents didn't have any buffs she could remove on them.

Instead, she focused on her sensing nets to try and see what was around them, but all she got back was cluster thoughts. Overwhelming emotions because they were magnified.

"They don't only move in packs. It's like they wait for each pack to die so they can try another tactic," Devlish observed, his lips pursed in concentration as he watched as the groups huddled in the back, like they were waiting for the current group to finish its part of the experimentation.

Merlin nodded next to him. "And the blockades along the way are perfectly spaced so that they can attack us in one to two packs at a time, all the while observing our weaknesses."

"Almost like they're funneling us back to something," Rashlyn murmured as she hugged herself.

Alarm bells went off in Murmur's mind, and she wracked her brains, trying to express the thought sitting on the tip of her tongue.

But Sinister beat her to it.

"Oh. I think they are trying to funnel us." She sounded dismayed that she hadn't thought of it earlier. That she hadn't realized something written out in plain sight for her.

Everyone's gaze was focused on her, but Sinister only bit her lip as she tried to make sense of what her quest said. "They're funneling us toward the…drain. Because I think they realize what we're trying to do. Once enter the drain of the fortress, we'll be in Noichu's mind."

Merlin lowered his bow, even though groups of beady eyes watched them from behind their barricades. "Guess they want us to reach Noichu?"

"Well, yes." Sinister hesitated. "But not because they think we'll help her, it's because they think she'll devour us."

The drain was no joke. It soon became clear as they battled their way toward it that the chamber was rounded and sloped ever so slightly toward a focal point in the middle.

As they fought their way through, Murmur didn't understand why the damned gnomes wouldn't just let them walk over there if they wanted them to get to the destination so badly. Then again, just letting them walk through wouldn't have yielded experience they sorely needed.

Murmur noticed they were gathering more and more of the wide-eyed gnomes. So many of them. If she mistimed her stuns even once, they were going to be dead.

Not to put too much pressure on herself or anything.

She took a deep breath and forced herself to concentrate, ignoring the ache at the back of her head. There was time for that later.

Veto had been a godsend, or probably would feel more like it when she finally reached fifty and significantly reduced the cost of the spell. The gnomes in their tiny mini army groups still hurled themselves at the raid. Now it seemed like they weren't too sure if they wanted to let them get through and go down the drain. Maybe they realized the raid might have a chance to do the opposite of what their attackers intended.

It gave a new feeling to the saying that it was all downhill from here, because while they were going downhill, it certainly wasn't fast or easy.

There were just so many of them. While Murmur's stuns weren't hitting as many as usual, they were still decently effective. Both Rashlyn and the rangers used their AoE attacks to devastating effect, as did Beastial and Havoc.

It wasn't that their opponents did extreme amounts of damage, but there sheer numbers leant a weight their attacks wouldn't have otherwise had. Instead of being a nice easy way to mow down opponents, AoEing became fraught with danger, and Murmur questioned the wisdom of attacking this way several times, even before she had to use Forestall Death on Rashlyn when she suddenly dropped to almost no hit points.

The monk came back, groaning with the remnants of pain and muttering under her breath.

"I know I play with my settings on barely any pain, but I think your spell magnifies them, Mur." After a second's pause, she continued. "Thanks for saving my experience."

Murmur nodded, but the fights were nerve-wracking. Since the gnomes didn't come when pulled but attacked at random intervals, Murmur couldn't get a hold on how best to fight them. They were fast, nimble, and those damned teeth hurt. She knew this because one got a hold of her ankle and left it bleeding profusely when Snowy managed to pull it off. In-game healing was a wonderful thing. Murmur wished she could carry it everywhere.

She frequently had about four to six enemies under her control. Usually stun locked. While it was amazing because their opponents couldn't do anything and couldn't move even if they were hit, their eyes locked onto her with a hatred so fierce, it made her skin crawl. Not that she could blame them. She'd effectively removed their bodily autonomy. They were trapped within themselves, unable to move no matter how much they might want to. She'd hate that if it happened to her. But then these were viciously attacking her entire raid party, and they deserved to be frozen in place so it was easier to farm experience off them on the way to the drain.

While a part of her laughed at the very notion, another part made her stop and think. Telvar, Emilarth, even Dirsna. Those were AIs who weren't dicks. They also weren't trying to hoard game and mind-altering getashis so they could rule the fictional world or whatever. At least not to her knowledge.

These gnomes, these wide-eyed, morphing, kind of cool gnomes were also a portion of the AI. Whether or not they'd had a chance to gain any sentience was beside the point. Murmur had seen that they might be able to, and she concluded that it really bugged her to have them regarding her with such open hostility.

Damn AIs evolving. Previous games had been so much easier because she didn't have to contend with that shit.

Finally, the sea of gnomes in front of them began to thin out. The last three gnomes fell to the ground, their corpses glowing faintly, and Murmur stood, panting and glaring at her mostly mana bar.

"Shit." Devlish was also panting. "I couldn't take a step in a different direction without alerting another group of those things. That was exhausting."

"Try healing your ass," Sinister grumbled as she flicked one of the corpses with her toe.

Her lips turned down, and Murmur was pretty sure she could see a tear in the corner of her eye. She stepped forward and gave Sin's shoulders a squeeze, leaving her hands there to provide moral support and reassurance. Her friend could see it too, the reality behind these creatures.

Instead of his usual quip, Devlish nodded gravely. "I'm well aware we'd all be toast without you and Ver. Not to mention Mur and Dansyn. Thanks, guys. But hell. Regardless of how long things stayed stunned, that AoE fest got us some damned fine experience."

"Shit!" Mellow let out a bit of a whoop. Their voice was filled with surprise. "I'm almost thirty-seven. I can't tell you how relieved I am."

With all the other shit they kept getting thrown at them, she wasn't surprised. They waited for a short while so that everyone could organize their inventories and make sure they were set for more fights.

In the meantime, Murmur decided to take a look around. She was very conscious of the timer the quest had set for them. It ticked in the corner of her vision like doom and gloom hanging over her. It had already been about forty minutes. Just over two hours left for them to complete the daunting task, which included jumping down that drain.

She sighed and took a step toward the middle.

In hindsight, she should have known this was too good to be true. As she put her weight on her foot, she heard a clacking noise. Like gears shifting and clicking chains into place. It whirred, and suddenly the floor began to spin very slowly in an anti-clockwise direction.

As it did, it began to slope toward what she'd assumed was the drain. A huge booming voice echoed throughout the chamber.

Congratulations. You have passed the first stage. You have defeated the impregnable gnome wall. Now that you have blood on your hands, you must be cleansed by passing through the drain. Don t worry. If you truly mean to do the right thing, you will not be harmed.
Watch out for the drop. It s a doozy.

And then water began to run out of the walls through a slit at the bottom and travel down all of the huge tiles that paved the floor and made up the area around the drain. It made them slick. It made them slippery.

It made them treacherous.

Snowy howled in surprise as even his sure-footed steps slipped on the dangerous slope.

Despite their collective scrambling to try and reach any measure of safety, they all slid toward the huge opening in the middle of the floor. Beyond it all they could see was darkness, like a kitchen sink drain that went down into an insinkerator.

Murmur gulped. She was still getting over the lingering pain from the last death, so dying now really wasn't an option. All she could do was hope that whatever had spoken thought they were nice enough and didn't let them fall to their deaths.

"It's like an amusement park ride!" Dansyn shouted out. "That gravity thing, only with water and a hole…you know what I mean."

Murmur tried to look at it his way and started to grin. She couldn't remember the last time she'd been on something like a ride. Surely, she hadn't even been in high school yet. The memories were vague, and she glanced around at the rest of the group and watched as well as sensed that their attitudes changed slightly. She nudged them just a bit, trying to lend them some confidence and a sense of fun. Sure, they could enjoy this. After all, hadn't they fully intended to head down the drain?

Finally, the slope became far too much for them to balance against the incline, and they began to tumble down the steep surface, falling with the water into the drainage hole. Havoc managed to shoot right through, a scream of glee tearing from his throat before it was abruptly cut off.

Murmur skin crawled with the sudden silence from her friend. But it was a drain and she was fairly sure it was a long way down. A couple of them, Beastial, Devlish, and Rashlyn, managed to hold onto the lip of the drain for several moments, but with the rushing water, it was difficult to hold onto.

"Just let go!" Sinister called, her eyes gleaming with excitement as she too approached the drop yelling, "Ready or not, here I come!"

Snowy was still trying to backpedal, frantic in his actions, and Murmur placed her hand on the back of his neck, trying to exude calmness. It didn't work for the wolf, but it sort of helped her.

She forced herself to settle and follow Sinister's example, treating the drain like a wet, slippery slide. Snowy sat on his haunches next to her, determination in his eyes. They slid forward, almost like time had stopped. There was nothing around them they could latch onto or even hold.

The rush of adrenaline as they approached the dark hole surprised her, and Murmur only had a split second to hope she'd made the right decision as both her and her wolf plonked off the edge of the drain and down into the darkness below.

CHAPTER THIRTY-ONE

Down the Drain

The fall was somewhat like what Murmur imagined Alice going through when she fell down the rabbit hole. Maybe not quite as floaty and able to examine everything on the way down though.

The landing, however, was more in line with falling into a garbage disposal and onto a sloppy mess of ground waste food. Except this wasn't food. The jolt jarred her, and the minor ache in her head reminded her it was there.

She gagged at the smell, wishing she didn't have to sit in such filth and muck. As she moved, trying to right herself from the store of waste, a disembodied hand caught on her robe. It took her several shakes of the panel of her robe to dislodge it. By the time she managed to, she was gagging, and both Dansyn and Sinister were throwing up over to the side.

The pale sheen of her armor was brighter for all the copper-tinged brown blood that adorned splotches of it. Once they all stood to the side of the muck, Mellow began to cast their armor saving spell.

At the same time, the ground began to rumble beneath them, and they all backed up and away from their landing spot as it began to bounce slightly. She'd never seen a pile of body parts start to jiggle. It'd be comical if it wasn't so gross.

The muck they'd landed in began to twirl slowly. It went around in a fascinating and macabre whirl of limbs which ended up half chewed up and mangled. Worse than the floors and walls had been upstairs.

Cracking sounds echoed up from somewhere in the middle of the pile, like grinders in an insinkerator doing their work. She couldn't help the shudder that crawled up her back and noticed that those around her reacted in similar ways.

"Well." Sinister cleared her throat. "Liked the ride, not the landing."

Dansyn barked out a surprised laugh. "I'll second that."

Murmur reached out with her Earth Shielding allowing her Thought Shielding to extend and protect the group with greater density. If they had landed in Noichu's mind, then Murmur had no doubt they'd need protection.

It left her less MA than she'd like, but what good were her abilities if her friends got afflicted by everything because she wouldn't spend the MA on it?

Merlin tried to light one of his fire arrows and cursed under his breath. "I can't light my damn arrows again."

Murmur frowned. "Must be something in this zone then. Maybe something that snuffs out fire."

"You think, Mur?" Merlin turned to her, barely discernible in the dim light, the sarcasm thick. "Seriously. Of course there is."

Taken aback, Murmur took a breath before answering, trying not to snap in retort. "I was just thinking out loud."

"I know, I know…" Merlin seemed tired, and Murmur realized she was too. They probably all were. "Sometimes we just don't need to hear it too."

"And sometimes we do," Havoc pointed out. "Sometimes this place fucks with our heads all too well, and it's nice to know that if I'm thinking something, others are too."

"Then why don't you let her yell it into your mind," Veranol inserted, a level of acidity to his words that Murmur had never heard before. "Because that's not intrusive at all."

Murmur blanched. She hadn't meant anything by it, just to be silent so it was easier for nothing to overhear them. It was the first time she'd realized that she might unsettle people.

Sinister's eyes flashed with annoyance. "No, it's not intrusive when she's saving your ass."

"Saving my ass?" Veranol chuckled, but it was devoid of mirth. "We're in a game, sweetheart. I'm just going to respawn."

The words were flat in the darkness. Their only accompaniment the grinding flesh and bones next to them.

"Sorry. Didn't realize I'd upset you. Just thought it was safer." Murmur felt oddly defeated, like why bother. She had this world in her head and these strange abilities at her fingertips. But maybe she didn't understand anything.

Veranol sighed, his expression changing to one of regret. "I didn't mean it like that. It was a shock, sure, but we'd all expected it eventually. It's more—I don't think this area is good for us. I'm on edge, I'm more tired than I should be, and frankly, it feels like something is fucking with us."

Uncertain how to respond, Murmur sent her sensors out again. "I think something is."

Dansyn stomped his foot. "Of course!"

When everyone looked at him like he'd grown a second head, he elaborated. "Noichu. Brain shit. She probably doesn't know we're here to help and not harm?"

"That's actually not a bad point." Rashlyn grinned as a ripple of relief passed through the group.

It made sense, but Murmur still paid closer attention to her friends through her shielding of them. A little bit of energy, a bit of positivity wouldn't go astray. It took mere seconds for them to perk up visibly, and she heaved a silent sigh of relief.

"Timer's ticking down," Devlish said gruffly. "Best be moving."

The slow churning of metal grinders from the middle of the floor still played as their background music, lacking any type of comfort.

Mellow heaved a sigh of relief, their ethereal cauldron dimly floating in front of them as they pulled out a softly glowing vial. "Can't get it to glow as brightly, but at least it's something."

They handed out their vials to everyone. The light was only good for so long. Murmur wondered if the inability to maintain flame was because the creatures down here needed to absorb light. And so when flame was lit, it was pulled away immediately.

As they moved slowly away from the garbage disposal and its overwhelming stench, Murmur struggled to find footing. She wasn't the only one. Most of them slipped and slid except for the pets who were better off. Two of them had four legs, and well, the specter sort of floated over everything.

Finally, on firm ground, or as firm as she could expect given where they were, Murmur tried to take stock of their situation.

Glancing around, all they could see were walls, decorated much as they had been when they initially entered this part of the fortress.

"So, our quest is to like…free this Noichu's mind?" Havoc ventured the question in a soft voice, directing it to Sinister. "And the rest will follow?"

The blood-mage shrugged. "I think so. If what I've read of the quest is correct, then yes. But I got this at level four, and I only remembered it because it got flagged when we entered here. I don't even remember why I have it."

"So, if Eon was the small type of gnome, then I guess Noichu is the larger greenish colored type?" Veranol changed the subject, diverting the conversation from its focus on Sinister who was obviously frustrated.

"Makes sense to me," Jinna piped up.

The dwarf had been pretty quiet ever since Murmur had made it back into the real world. It was like he seemed unsure of what his role was now. She'd have to ask him about that later. He was an awesome rogue and a great friend. Good with stabby things.

They stepped cautiously along the hall. The bodies of these gnomes all stared at them, and Murmur understood now why the eyes just appeared to be eyes. Since the gnome's faces were tiny by comparison. But how they still partially lived while entombed in the walls, she didn't want to know.

Just who was Noichu, and what had she done to deserve this? Surely it wasn't just because she'd married someone from a warring tribe and had a kid?

The ground shook, but this time it wasn't from the garbage disposal. This time it sounded entirely different. Murmur had to steady herself before she fell to a knee. Exbo and Beastly didn't manage to do it.

Murmur scowled, knowing that something was about to come. What use were her mind powers if the bloody things couldn't give her a premonition every now and again?

You dare disturb my slumber?

"We dare." Sinister's voice rang out, and Murmur cringed, hoping she was following the quest, because if not, Murmur was fairly certain they were all about to be smashed.

A loud bark of a laugh echoed through the massive hall. Even the eyes of the gnomes in the walls opened wider, dismembered limbs flailing. *You have guts. How about we see what color they are?*

"Shit." Beastial dropped into fighting stance. "You just had to go and taunt it, didn't you, Sin."

Storm Entertainment
Somnia Online Division
Game Development Offices
Day Twenty-Four

Laria stared at her sent folder. Reading and rereading the message she'd sent back to Thra.

Received. Trying to figure out how you are where you are. Can you get out? How can we help? Keeping an eye on Mur and Rav. Rav is still in the Isle.
Laria

She'd tried to keep it as brief as possible. The less text, the less likely it was to be flagged to one of the AIs. She'd tried to hide the sending of the email in a firmware update for Thra but wasn't sure she'd pulled it off.

Granted, it had been like ten minutes since she sent it, but it didn't mean it felt like that. She pushed her chair around as she waited, the inbox following her through augmented reality. She would have laughed at the funny dizziness it projected being spun like that if she'd had the energy left.

"Laria?" Shayla's question was filled with concern, and Laria brought her spinning chair to a stop and blinked up at her friend.

"Yes?"

"You didn't go home last night? Again?" Shayla sounded stern this time, like she was irritated enough to lay some serious talk down.

"Oh." Laria looked around her and realized sunlight was creeping through the blinds. "Shit. I didn't even call David."

But that meant that more time had passed than she thought. And it made her even more worried, because shouldn't Thra have answered by now?

"Spill." Shayla pulled up a chair and leaned forward on her hands. Laria could see how tired her friend was too. There were bags for days under her eyes, almost hollows even. With a tinge of shadow around them. She wasn't getting enough sleep even when she was trying.

"So. It seems—" Laria paused, trying to figure out how to deliver the news without completely freaking out her best friend. Like a bandaid would have to do it. "As far as I can tell, Sui infected Rav with the virus, and Rav is fighting it."

"Wait, what? How did Rav get infected? They're invulnerable in the game. Like gods. How…" and her eyes opened wider like it had just clicked for her. Shayla fell back into her chair.

Laria gave her a few moments to digest it and then moved on.

"So, while in their limbo, Sui infected Rav. Rav exited to the game world and inserted himself somewhere he can't escape unless he gets control of shit." She paused, giving her boss a few moments to catch up. "Thra, not being stupid, won't go into the limbo anymore. Sui has taken her to a room that didn't exist in any iteration of the plans."

Laria paused again to let that sink in.

Shayla's eyes grew even wider. "Wait. He literally created a space that was never intended?"

"Closed to us unless he opens it, but still a part of the game world and therefore subject to its rules, and not those of their limbo."

The concept still sent shivers down Laria's back, and they weren't good ones. More like icy cold sleet rain slipping through your warm coat and trickling down your spine. The only saving grace was that his little room was still under game rules.

"Thra got a message out to me so that I would know. You know, because there wasn't already enough impetus on getting the damn antivirus coded." Laria reined it in and backtracked. "She can communicate best with email. Small emails seem to avoid being flagged to alert the AI system."

She glanced at the time and realized with a start that it had been a couple of hours since she sent her reply. "It's been a long while since I sent my response to Thra, but I still don't have an answer, or anything really. I'm starting to get worried."

Or more worried, but Shayla didn't need to hear the latter.

"So. Sui kidnapped Thra in-game to try and force her to ingest the virus?" Shayla spoke the words slowly, like she was just wrapping her head around them.

"Pretty much. He's hoping to wear her down so she'll go into limbo, I think? Or else just keep her from helping Rav I assume." It was nice to share her concerns. She'd been all alone with them all night long. "I guess she sort of went along with it. I get the feeling Thra isn't as imprisoned as he thinks."

"Probably. I always thought she was a little frivolous, but she seems to be serious once threatened." Shayla sounded contemplative, and then changed the subject before Laria could respond. "How is the antivirus coming along?"

"Not bad. The virus is a sticky little shit." Laria cracked her neck, sudden tiredness trying to overwhelm her. "I mean. It weaves itself in intricately. Like it has tiny hooks that grab onto any strand they can find and attaches itself."

"Guess it's a good thing it's only affecting the game characters right now." Shayla smiled wanly and settled back, this time appearing more comfortable.

But Laria didn't laugh with her, because she'd just had an idea. And she didn't like the idea one bit.

"Yeah. The AIs are susceptible, and their creations because they are made of code. But players are also made of code."

Shayla groaned. "No. No. You cannot be saying what I think you're about to say."

Laria shrugged. "I could stop the train of thought, but that's not going to make it any less true."

Shayla glared at her before taking a deep breath. "You're saying their avatars could become infected too?"

Laria hesitated, not really wanting to be the bearer of more bad news. "Well, yes, of course they can. But how are the characters generated?"

She waited for the penny to drop.

"But the headsets only tap into recent memories and general behavior patterns…" Shayla covered her eyes. "Shit. Shit. Shit."

Laria took that as her cue to continue. "The headgear taps into their minds and extracts what it needs in order to generate their class pick. Perhaps not the appearance, but the inner code. And every action and inaction in short term memory also feeds into that. If we're not careful, this virus could theoretically spread into the people playing the game. It hasn't yet, I don't think, and I'm not a hundred percent sure it can. Which is good. Because right now I don't even know how to stop the digital version, let alone anything else."

Trying to herd his guild into some form of action was like trying to muster blind kittens together. Masha wanted to back away into a corner and pretend he wasn't there. Sadly, clerics didn't get an invisibility spell. Unless he killed them all. Then he could avoid them with his invisibility against the undead.

He activated the guild management system and frowned as he allowed it to scroll through active members. They'd managed to gain a lot of them. He glared at the small gnome mage beside him.

"You should have put a cap on the level requirements. Twenty-five should do it."

They'd managed to amass a heap of lower level new players. That needed to stop.

Ishwa shrugged and followed the suggestion. "It was the easiest way to fill the ranks with little effort. We can weed out the bad players as we go. Sometimes people can be surprising."

Masha didn't dignify that with an answer. He didn't want to be a mass invite guild. Spam inviting was not a fun way to be recruited in his opinion. They only had three officers, himself included.

Irritated, he continued through the tools. Ishwa had logged in late today, and Masha'd sensed a reluctance for the last while on his friend's behalf.

"I need to go now," Ishwa said unexpectedly, and Masha blinked at him, his vision skewed by the dark light the guild screen was in.

"We're about to raid," Masha said, but the gnome shrugged.

"Got called in to work an extra shift. Can't say no, you know how it is." He didn't sound happy about it.

So Masha just nodded as the gnome winked out of view.

Sitting in the foyer of Hazenthorne Castle while he prepared for raid time alone hadn't been his plan. He'd meant to discuss several of the guild policies while they worked on the roster and dungeon plan. At least the gnome had arranged for some of the members to promote to senior members, so he worked with what he had and made them able to invite too, but he sent directions on what to look for first. Their recruits would only be a trial basis.

Finally done with the clerical work, he still had to organize the guild's storage for the raid. Exiting out of guild management, he had to let his eyesight adjust. He started when he realized he wasn't alone in the foyer anymore.

Jirald sat on top of the cupboard on the right-hand side of the entrance. The black of his armor blended in almost perfectly. So much that Masha had almost missed it. The locus assassin sat there, twirling a piece of grass in his fingers, staring at Masha.

No, that wasn't correct. He wasn't looking at the cleric. He was looking past him, through him. It was unsettling, like he could see anything and everything he wanted to just by peering inside.

"Jirald." Masha hoped his voice didn't sound as shaken as he felt. He hadn't even heard the rogue come into the room. Those shadows he wrapped around himself were dense and deceptive. "What brings you here?"

Jirald blinked, as if he'd just realized where it was he'd ended up. The sly grin that spread across his face chilled to the bone. His eyes had lightened up so much they seemed completely white.

"Hey. Masha. Just the person I was looking for."

Even his tone sounded distant. Like he wasn't actually in the room, but somewhere far away. Jirald jumped down from his perch, the piece of grass still twirling between his fingers like he was a wind-up doll.

Masha breathed easier when he realized Jirald was actually there, even though he noted the dark aura that seemed to flicker around him. Almost like it was a glitch in the system, like it had fragmented around him.

"Why were you looking for me?" Masha made sure to keep his tone neutral so as not to upset the rogue. Something about him seemed off kilter, like he wasn't all there.

Jirald's face lit up. Well, as much as a smile could light up a locus's face. It sort of distorted the nose slightly, giving it a comical yet macabre sense. "I have a plan. Sort of. Since you're the only person I care about, you're the one I wanted to tell."

"Sure. Share it with me," Masha began slowly, trying to make sure his tone wasn't going to antagonize.

He wasn't sure he liked where this was going, but he also didn't want to stop being the only person Jirald cared about. In Jirald's eyes, he knew that was a big role and hadn't even realized he'd reached it.

"We need to conquer Fable." Jirald's eyes were shining. "And the game. If we conquer one, we'll rule the other."

Masha wasn't sure he liked the idea of conquering. Any other time he would have thought Jirald just meant beating them to the punch. But this new Jirald with his shadows and death grips and sinister posing…no, this new Jirald didn't mean that at all.

Masha didn't want to let him know about the potential cooperation with Fable. But doing that would betray the rogue, and the gods only knew what he'd do then. He wasn't the most stable person in the guild. Understatement. But he needn't have worried.

"So I thought—with their offer to cooperate and go into the larger dungeons with us, we should accept that offer. They'll never see us coming." Jirald drew his lips back in a wide grin that showed the tiny sharp teeth of the locus, glinting in the candlelight.

Masha nodded slowly as if he was considering what Jirald was saying. And he was, but he was also trying to assess just how the rogue was different. His movements weren't normal, even for a locus. They held a fluidity that bespoke of something else. Something Masha could have sworn he didn't have a few days ago. He moved like an assassin, like someone who stuck to the shadows.

"It's only a tentative offer. They're still mulling it over themselves. They will have all of the keys, so if they do decide to go ahead with it, all they need from us is numbers." Masha kept his voice even, trying to feign some disinterest due to the conditions they'd have to go into the agreement with.

"Nonsense." Jirald dismissed the thought with a hand wave. "They need more bodies for those dungeons. Murmur likes you. Milk it."

Jirald leaned forward, a slight frown on his face as his eyes swirled with darkness. Masha shuddered as he realized that whatever Jirald had become, he wasn't the stupid hot-heated college kid angry at not playing the healer class he loved.

Gone was the kid who had rebelled against the system the game delivered. When he'd started, Jirald had lacked the ability to apply his skills to a different class. Now though? It was clear he knew and understood his powers. In growing as a rogue, he'd amassed all the charm of a serial killer.

And that scared Masha the most.

"As soon as they're out of Richnai, I'll send her a message then," Masha ventured carefully. "After the raid."

"Great!" Jirald seemed happy with the outcome, even though his eyes still seethed with shadows. Like they'd just decided the greatest thing ever. "I have to check a couple of things. This is going to be fantastic."

He whirled around in a coat of shadows and suddenly disappeared.

Masha stared at where he'd been only moments before, breathing deeply.

Great. The more unhinged Jirald became, the more attached he was to his character. The more he believed it was who he was.

All Masha had done was buy himself some time. Now he had to figure out what the hell to do with it.

CHAPTER THIRTY-TWO

Into the Mind

Murmur stumbled, barely able to keep her balance as footsteps shook the entire chamber around them. A massive gnome began to appear. She wore what appeared to be a lace dress, reminiscent of a wedding dress. The edges of it were caked in blood and excrement, and the stench wasn't any kinder.

Murmur gagged and glanced over at Sinister, who couldn't return the look because she was already throwing up. It was probably the reason her friend had never played a healer before. Couldn't stand the sight of blood. Murmur choked down a slightly hysterical laugh.

However, as the gnome came closer, Murmur realized this was Noichu. She'd not been expecting to fight the mother so soon. Something was off about this. A rampaging mother in a grief loop. What a cruel punishment for finding love.

Not that there weren't some very odd difficulties with gnomes of varying size, but she was sure love overcame that.

Sinister sidled closer to Murmur. "What do we do? I don't think we're supposed to kill her."

"You're the one with the quest." Murmur shrugged, quickly glancing over her own quest log to triple check that she didn't have anything for this. The lack of alarms sounding had already clued her in, but just in case. Her own soothing spells wouldn't work once the target was aggro'd on them. And this one was very intent on making her way toward them.

But Dansyn had a soothe that might work.

"Got it." But Sinister looked less than confident in her discovery. "I need to calm her and let her see that her son is indeed okay and alive. That her husband didn't abandon her, and that her kin were wrong."

Sin scowled at her quest.

"Wow, that sounds so easy. Why can't we just get a *kill all of these* quest?"

"Because Murmur set a stupid bloody precedent when she was nice to the Loch'ni'dar way back when," Devlish grumbled, though he seemed to be fighting back a smile.

"Ha ha. I wasn't about to kill them. Just think of the pretty things we got from them. Most of us are using them to this day." Murmur had to brace herself this time because Noichu's footsteps were shaking the ground more the closer she got. "Dan, can you try and soothe her?"

Dansyn shrugged noncommittally. "I have a song, and I can sing."

Murmur stifled a laugh. She had to watch out about playing when overtired. It made her way too giggly for no good reason.

The wailing bounced off the walls, lending a sense of disorientation to the whole ordeal. Snowy growled, baring his teeth, and she had to soothe him along their connection to get him to back down.

Maybe wolves didn't like the grünlich gnomes.

"Okay, then." Devlish hefted his shield and swapped his axe for a hammer. "As little damage as possible while we figure out just what to do to set this mom free?"

"Sounds like a plan," Sinister muttered, her brows clenched in deep thought. "Because I don't do damage when I heal at all."

Sarcasm was just everyone's tool of choice when they were feeling ragged. Murmur secretly loved it. Stuns wouldn't hurt, so she could cast those. Mez wouldn't work, so that ruled that out. All of her debuffs except her DoT were a possibility.

So Murmur started with those. Nullify to strip magic resistance, Weakness to reduce her strength, Spellblock to slow her casting time down, Languidity to slow her attack time down, and just for fun, she used Thought Leech to see what spells Noichu was about to cast with her slowed abilities.

"Show off," Sinister muttered deliberately loud enough to hear. "I can't even heal decently without doing some damage."

"Well, you are a blood mage. I mean, it's in the name." Beastial grinned as he got Shir-Khan to taunt. The yo-yo of back and forth aggro between the tanks and the pet made Noichu's spell casting almost nonexistent.

The grünlich gnome screamed with rage, all of her movements slowed. There was confusion in her eyes that slowly replaced the anger, like she couldn't understand why they weren't hacking the hell out of her.

For a normal boss, Murmur's spells wouldn't have had much effect. But she wasn't a normal by any means. She was an in pain, I-have-been-wronged bride and mother. That seemed to make all the difference. She wanted to have her life back, and she'd fight anyone who stood in her way. Which meant they needed to figure out a way to convince her they could give her life back.

The bad thing about Murmur's debuffs was that a couple of them cost insane mana. Mana she didn't have endless supplies of.

She watched as Devlish taunted and blocked an attack, as Rashlyn taunted and avoided the attack she received, and then Shir-Khan taunted, but Beastial pulled him away before he could inflict damage.

"Ver, are you able to take over the slows? Dan, can you switch to debuffs?" She had an idea. After all, she'd used Feedback Loop to punish, why couldn't she use it to heal?

"Just the slows. We are taking minimal damage, but I want to keep reserves just in case." Veranol nodded and Dansyn did too.

That taken care of, Murmur kept her eye on the battle and calculated the amount of damage it would inflict. Four hundred and sixty damage before it wore off, which, given the boss's hit points wasn't too bad. More like a scratch, really.

Taking a breath, Murmur reached out with her Thought Sensing and focused on Noichu's mind. The mess in there made her recoil, but not because it was horrific, but because it was sad. The mind was a mess of self-recrimination, self-hatred, and regret. Anguish littered every thought with glimpses of Eon dead, of Erichu bleeding, and of her having been able to avoid it all if only she'd loved a different person.

Anger leaked into Murmur along with understanding. Noichu's rage fueled Murmur's mind, and the enchanter could see those who were at fault, those who had done this. All she wanted was to set matters right, to make those on each side see that love was love and all this feuding shit was a waste of precious time.

It suffused Murmur's thoughts, seeped into her mind, and let the voices encourage her to make it so. She wanted to kill those who had made this possible; she wanted to flay them. To take their memories and cruelest deeds and make them suffer for all eternity.

Snowy licked her hand, wetly, snapping her out of the spiral of thoughts.

"Thanks, boy," she muttered, shocked at how easy it had been to get swept along. But at least she knew what memories to pull so Noichu would accept them and what to show of Eon approaching them and asking to free her. That he loved them and didn't want them to suffer. Just the right mix should do it.

It only took a few seconds for her to wrap them all up into a ball of thought and direct the Feedback Loop directly at Noichu.

The ball of power hit their opponent right between the eyes and sent her stumbling back slightly. She stood there, blinking for a second before she screamed in heart-wrenching agony and began to ignore any debuff still on her.

Noichu flailed and attacked so fast, Murmur could barely keep track, especially after a well-placed dart lodged itself in the right-hand side of her chest, knocking her off her feet. Blood flowed from the wound, only slowing down to a trickle once Veranol threw a heal her way.

Sinister doubled over, and Murmur could see her red robes suddenly looking wet around her middle section. Despite the pain in her own chest, Murmur made her way to her friend, whose pain shone like a beacon of distress. She could feel the others in the raid taking their own beatings.

Dansyn fell to the ground, unable to dodge another flung projectile even with his fleet feet. Havoc yelled out as he was struck by what appeared to be a blunt object.

"Damn it!" The necromancer was pissed, Murmur could see it, but her concern for Sinister outweighed everything else.

Even though she threw a Soothe onto Noichu, it did nothing. Not that Murmur had expected it to, considering it was supposed to be used out of combat, but it was all she could think of.

As Murmur reached Sinister's side, Dansyn pushed himself up, mostly healed now, and began a new song. This one wormed its way inside Murmur's head too, calming her down and bringing her back from the edge of panic.

And it had much the same effect on Noichu.

Her rampaging stopped, and it took a while, but her eyes slowly cleared and the hatred that suffused her expression, the suffering, it all leaked away.

Everyone calmed down, the soothing strains of a melody just out of reach for Murmur to define. It calmed her even more so because it let her know that what she sometimes did to her friends, the system technically had covered by bards. Making people feel better was a good thing.

Even Snowy seemed at ease. His muzzle grinned, and his tongue lolled out, saliva dripping onto the ground.

"Oh, my hell," Sinister gasped, her hand around her waist like she was hugging herself. She leaned against Murmur, who cradled her gently. "That was not fun. Aren't games supposed to be fun?"

"Where have you been the last three weeks?" Mellow muttered.

Maybe it was meant to be a joke, but it didn't feel like one. While it could be fun, some of their quests felt so serious, so vital, that one wrong move would plunge the whole game world into nothingness.

It was a heavy burden to bear.

Noichu glowed, and her size shrank down to only slightly larger than normal gnome size. Her dress refreshed, no longer caked in blood and dirt. Her blue eyes shone in the dark corridor like a thousand tiny stars clustered together. Unshed tears only made them glisten more. "Thank you. My family thanks you."

A series of dings echoed throughout the huge corridor, and Murmur was relieved to see herself a portion of the way into forty-seven. She was so grateful that Sinister had reminded them all how much of their experience came from dungeons.

Murmur turned her attention immediately back to Noichu and wanted to ask if it wasn't her family who'd done this in the first place, but she didn't have the heart. Also, she was fairly sure the NPC meant her little family of three.

"Please come with me. Erichu needs to know he isn't alone."

Her words prompted a quest for all of them, if their unfocused gazes were anything to go by. Murmur could dig that. Raid quests were fine. Sinister had probably caught the quest up to this juncture, or else it was a new one for her also. She had to be getting a heap of experience from these quests they kept helping her finish.

It was why Murmur was usually the first to ding. She'd had so many quests along the way. And relatively fewer deaths because headset.

Speaking of her head, she tried to will away the headache that was gradually growing in hers.

Fully buffed, she grabbed Sinister's hand and pulled the blood-mage with her. "Come on, let's go rescue this kid."

Sinister grinned and looped her hand around Murmur's waist. "I thought you'd never ask."

Jirald scowled, even if he didn't feel that angry. The courtyard in front of Hazenthorne was where it all started. For this game, anyway. She'd booted him away with some overpowered ability and condemned him to a death loop. Murmur still had to pay for that, but now there were so many ways to draw that out and make it enjoyable.

He shook his head briefly. Didn't he just want to pay her back? Surely drawing it out served no real purpose. Still. The shard in his hand felt smooth. He was glad he hadn't given all of them to Belius when he came calling. He'd forked over a few, gained the extra experience, and kept a couple to absorb for himself. They spoke to him, after all, in his mind in quiet whispers.

He quite preferred the company of his own thoughts and these whispers over the annoying inadequacy most people presented. Or the fake friendliness they tried to peddle. He wanted to surround himself with competent gamers, people who could and would do what it took to reach the endgame. People like Masha, and Ishwa, and himself. But the guild didn't focus its recruiting efforts quite like that.

The voices in his head almost sang to him. Of how they would hold power over everything in the game. Was it still a game? He couldn't even tell anymore, uncertain when the last time he'd logged out had been. His father was away on a business trip, and his classes had paused for the summer.

Somnia was his world right now. His eating, breathing, existing world. **But what about her? What about them? Don t you want what they have?**

He twitched, the noise in his head making more sense than he'd like to admit. He wanted everything they had. Not only Fable, but Murmur too. Even Spiral. They didn't deserve it any more than he did. He'd been hampered by second rate players who didn't have his back.

The twitch hit again, and he caught a glimpse of the friends he'd made in his guild. Friends he'd had since he was a freshman in high school. He didn't mean those, did he?

The only saving grace was Masha, and perhaps Eslan. The voices whispered again, and Jirald began to formulate a plan in his mind as the raid group moved in from forming up in the foyer. Shadows gathered in places they shouldn't have existed, and the whole ambience in the castle beckoned to him, coaxing him closer.

Masha had always been his friend. Always trusted him more than anyone else did and never fought him when Jirald had been healing lead. He was under no illusion that the older player wouldn't tell it to him like it was. Because he'd done so in the past.

As far as things went, Masha was the only gamer Jirald cared about. It was his prerequisite for anything. Keeping Masha okay.

Then what are you going to do?

Jirald didn't answer the voice yet. Not quite. His thoughts flit around a bit while he thought of and dismissed several options out of hand. It all came back to what he needed to do. Fable needed to vanish; it needed to fall apart.

Whether he achieved that by besting them or he achieved that by insidiously picking them apart, it needed to be done.

Of course, there was always the third option. Killing Murmur over and over so many times that she deleveled. And oh, how he wanted to do it. But he had to wait. He didn't want to have all the fun at the beginning. Biding his time, he would strip away all her protections one after the other.

Darkness flared around him, like the castle had taken offense to his plotting. But it quieted after he sliced a bat down the middle.

The voice in his head smiled, and he flipped the last getashi he hadn't given Sidius up in the air and swallowed it as it came down. That buzz spread through his body again, expanding his mind, and his perception, letting the freedom and strength in.

It made his brain feel like it was ten times larger, able to understand and deal with abstract concepts. Time grew slower, and everything became clear. It wasn't just a world.

Somnia was a living breathing thing. And in one way or another, Jirald was going to conquer it.

CHAPTER THIRTY-THREE

Gnomore

The dank smell of the tunnel only grew worse the further down they headed. Murmur's head ached, and she was starting to feel hot. She was grateful for the dim light afforded to them by Noichu's presence. The grünlich gnome walked on the other side of her, her head held high, and her perfect nose upturned. Her skin glowed faintly. At least the vessels underneath the skin did, anyway. It had a similar effect to the locus runes that lit up when abilities and spells were gained.

"Thank you." Noichu spoke softly so that only Murmur and Sinister could hear.

Sinister squeezed Murmur's arm, and the enchanter wasn't sure if that was for her or Sinister more.

"You're welcome," was all Murmur responded with. She'd never been comfortable accepting thanks for anything.

Noichu chuckled and pulled something out of her pocket. "I must give this to you, for I believe it is the root of the evil in this world. It needs to be taken and destroyed, far from here. Infecting those it comes into contact with means this reality will not survive for long if we are not careful."

Murmur was glad she had her gloves on and accepted the getashi from the gnome. Immediately Noichu shone brighter, as if the dimmer had been turned back up to full.

A flurry of thoughts descended through Murmur's mind. If that was the effect on the NPCs of the world, why did it make Riasli so much stronger? There had to be something she was missing about the whole thing.

"We are here." The grünlich gnome stopped. Her face was filled with sorrow, even to the point that tears welled in her eyes.

"He is in here. He is not himself. He has been harmed by the curse. While I can calm him and can distract him, you will need to cure him of what ails him." Noichu bowed her head. "I only hope you can do this before he succumbs to the madness they've fostered inside him."

From the howls deep in the room they were about to enter, Murmur wanted to know if he hadn't already given into it.

"I ask that you try your best," Noichu intoned, "so that my family might be reunited again."

She strode into the room, her arms high, and bright white light shone out of the gaps between her fingers, like a carousel. It spun around them, leaving sections in bright light and darkness alternating.

"Good luck." And then all of the mother's concentration was on her light and on her child.

Erichu threw his huge head back and roared in what sounded like a cry for help before he threw himself at who he saw as attackers.

Help him.

Murmur shook her head to clear Somnia out. She didn't have the time for heart to hearts right then. She threw Nullify, Weakness, and Languidity at him immediately. They hit him in quick succession but barely seemed to slow his attack speed.

He was on Devlish so fast, Murmur didn't think she was seeing right. Each blow beat down on Devlish's tower shield. Every successive one hit harder, so much that the final one forced Dev to his knees before the lacerta lurched up and used the weight of Erichu's massive fist to throw the gnome off balance.

Tantrum attacks increase in strength.

Devlish eyed the words above his head. "Thanks for that."

The sarcasm was so strong Murmur could almost see it.

The massive gnome stomped his feet and leaned down to pound his fists on the ground. In the process, he swatted Shir-Khan away like a fly, and Murmur watched as the surprise on Beastial's face turned to anger.

Dansyn began to play his soothing song, and Erichu finally fell out of the tantrum. At least his blows while not in meltdown were hard, but not impossible to field. He was attackable, and they could defend against him. Murmur didn't like this whole trend of not killing opponents who seemed quite keen on killing her. It was so much easier when all they had to do was defeat them. But defeating whatever ailed something was a lot more difficult.

Treating the cause and not the effect. She reassessed her desire to enter medicine. Maybe it was worth it after all. Watching their target, she inspected him in great detail while keeping up her debuffs.

The trick to this fight had nothing to do with defeating him. It seemed that the trick was waiting out his ability to do mega damage and using the rest of the time to try and convince him they could be trusted.

"Hasn't he been killed already?" Jinna muttered, a tiredness underlying his voice that Murmur felt only too well.

Noichu spoke, her voice regal with pride. "Not this incarnation, not in this room. So many versions of time, of choices. Not this version, and not this time."

It partially answered the question and seemed to mollify Jinna enough. Dansyn's song helped, but Murmur could see the rage bar trying to rise again. What on earth could they do to make it go further back down the other way?

She quickly leafed through her sinuous abilities trying to find something that would adapt for her. That she could maybe swing from being damaging to helpful. She'd already morphed more than one of her spells, why not this?

Basic Visions

Cast: Instant – 3 minute recast

Type: Offensive

Duration: 20 seconds, or 75% of the caster's level, whichever is greater.

Effect: You may create and insert a vision for the target to experience it s best to have some of these pre-prepared. This will cause them damage (caster's level x 2 per tick), and distraction for the duration of the spell depending on what type of vision you've given them.

She frowned, wondering if that was really a viable option. It would last around thirty-five seconds and end up costing around 1030 damage. His hitpoint pool was huge, so maybe…

But she didn't have a chance to continue mathing in her head as Erichu's rage bar hit maximum again. She barely dodged one of his wildly flailing kicks. Havoc wasn't so lucky as the side of the gnome's foot caught the necromancer square in the chest and sent him flying. His health plummeted down to twenty percent and Veranol frantically healed him back up.

"Try avoiding the damage. Sin can't do too much healing without sabotaging the plan." He sounded like he was half joking and half strained. Murmur could see the frustration on Sinister's face.

Erichu's series of running kicks had no rhyme or reason that Murmur could see, but they were fast and difficult to prepare for. His legs were sturdy, and his arms were strong, and the tantrums reminded her of toddlers who were throwing a fit. Except more powerful and explicitly dangerous.

Mellow was the next victim and flew so high and wide across the room with super speed that they crashed into the wall with sickening thuds of breaking bones. They slid down the wall, just a lump of flesh contained by the robe.

Murmur really hoped they'd be okay and get back as soon as possible. She'd just realized Mellow probably had a potion they could use for this. In fact, it might even be something she needed. Sinister was casting, her target Mellow, and Murmur could only hope that the blood-mage didn't need damage to cast the in-combat res.

With the second tantrum over, Murmur wasn't sure how much more of this they could take. Resurrections inside battles had timers, just like potions did. Considering the rest of the game did what it wanted, she wasn't sure why it chose those.

She turned her focus back to basic visions. Erichu had over fifteen thousand hit points. Her tiny one thousand damage wasn't going to do much since he'd have built in regen. Except she didn't think she'd be able to use it yet. His threat was too high, and his rage wouldn't stop increasing and never fully depleted. She was fairly certain she couldn't give him the vision she needed to if he wasn't amenable to it.

Anyone have any lulling, or aggro wipes?

Veranol: *I have a lullaby*

What does it do?

There was no response from the defiler at first; he probably had to check. *It's a momentary calming mesmerize. Sort of. From what it sounds like, it's like a memory blur and lull in one. It's like brand new. I haven't tried it yet.*

Duration? Murmur was trying not to let herself get excited, but it sounded perfect.

A quarter of my level, so almost twelve seconds.

Thanks, Ver. That's great.

It was easier to just direct her thoughts over the guild chat. It didn't alert the creature, and it was easy to multitask.

You could just make him calm down, you know.

That's not working as intended, she answered, and wished she'd ignored the voice instead.

But you could still do it. It'll save time.

Murmur couldn't tell if that was Somnia or something else, but she impatiently pushed the words out of her mind while she readied her spell, directing her thoughts yet again to the guild chat.

Ver, just as he finished his next tantrum and drains his rage almost completely, can you cast that lullaby?

Sure.

She looked over at the viking and saw the grim look of determination on his face. Now all they had to do was weather this next tantrum. It was so much easier to avoid special abilities when they could do damage to their target.

Just one more round.

It was never just anything.

Though it was relatively easy to stave off the normal attacks Erichu threw at them, they still hit hard, and Murmur made sure to top off Veranol's mana with Manabalize every time the two-minute timer came up. She needed him to have enough juice or whatever he needed when it came time to cast Lullaby.

This tantrum though, this one took the cake. Erichu began twirling, like a flying crane kick or something, knocking over players and pets like they were bowling pins. Murmur caught the tail end of one and only avoided hitting a hard surface because Snowy caught up in time to cushion her fall.

Dansyn. Be ready with your soothe song at the end of this tantrum.

Murmur coughed as she pushed herself up, waiting on a reply from the bard. She had a feeling they were going to need all the soothing they could get.

Sure thing! His reply was almost as chipper as he was.

Murmur was finally upright again, just in time to see Veranol miss his cue to jump back in time and receive the toe in his chest. It hooked him up and sent him flying through the air.

"Snowy!" Murmur screamed at the wolf. He streaked across, blurring gold as he ran toward Veranol. He was faster than the shaman as he flew through the air. Gradually the air around Snowy filled up, the barrier bracing itself for impact.

He caught Veranol in what seemed like slow motion as the barrier he'd once used to protect Murmur bowed in and then gently let Veranol topple down to the ground. Snowy sat back on his haunches, his tongue lolling out, while Erichu continued his rampage.

Veranol got to his feet, immediately warding those whose wards had fallen during his flying venture. "You're telling us about that as soon as this is done Mur."

Murmur just grinned, her eyes focused on the rage bar that fueled Erichu's tantrums. It was all going to be a matter of timing. Just as it reached the bottom, Murmur cast her own soothe and called over guild, two seconds apart. *Dan. Ver.*

She grasped the images she'd prepared, the visions she hoped he would take in well, and released them at the target. Ones of his mother's brief time with him, and her pure joy that exuded from it. Another of his father the same, and one of all three of them.

Erichu stopped and stood like a statue. His eyes blinked and slowly, sanity began to enter them as. He sank down to sit on the cold stone floor. Slowly, he shrank, just like his mother had. He was still a grünlich gnome, mostly anyway, but he wasn't nearly as big as he had been.

Your actions have created a subversion of the Basic Vision spell. You have now created: Mind Healing.

Mind Healing

Cast: Instant – 5 minute recast

Type: Restorative

Duration: 20 seconds, or 75% of the caster's level, whichever is greater.

Effect: You may create and insert a vision for the target to experience it s best to have some of these pre-prepared. This will not cause any damage but instead assist in soothing a tormented mind. Use with caution and be aware that people who could benefit from this skill might be closer than you realize.

Noichu ran to her son, the glowing lights gone from her fingers. She crouched down next to him and enveloped him in a hug, and suddenly he was a toddler, just a tiny child crying for his mother. Murmur took a step back, wanting to leave them peace as she felt like an intruder. Not to mention she hadn't expected the spell to work so well.

"Nice strategy." Veranol placed his hand on her shoulder briefly and she turned to face him. "Good thing it worked."

Murmur laughed. "Well since I didn't have a plan B, I'm pretty glad it did. Still, though. I feel like our quests are always odd."

Veranol shrugged. "What's odd is that wolf of yours. What the hell was that?"

"I honestly have no idea. I only found out at the start of this dungeon that he'd grown in abilities. He doesn't exactly tell me these things." She grinned at the wolf who was doing the same to her, momentarily forgetting how much more her head was hurting her.

"Thank you." Eon was suddenly there, striding in from the entrance they'd used, a smile of pure joy on his face. "Thank you so much. How can we ever repay you?"

Treasure would be nice was on the tip of Murmur's tongue, but she just managed to stop herself from saying it. She didn't need to, either. Noichu waved a hand absentmindedly, and a whole row of chests popped up. Murmur had to secretly wonder if it was just the game's way of gearing them up for the next dungeons.

It wasn't me. Most of them can think for themselves.

Murmur wasn't sure if that was comforting or scary.

You receive one of the twelve keys.

You receive a getashi.

You receive a midia crystal.

You have completed the Richnai Fortress Family Reunion.

You have completed the Richnai Fortress Test of Trials.

This version of the Fortress will no longer be available.

You gain experience.

You gain bonus experience for being the first to discover the trials.

You gain bonus experience for being the first to free the Prisoners of Rivalry.

You gain bonus experience for being the first to see through your greatest fears.

You gain bonus experience for being the first to see the caverns for what they are.

You gain bonus experience for freeing Eon from the curse.

You gain bonus experience for freeing Noichu from the curse.

You gain bonus experience for saving Erichu from a fate worse than death.

You gain bonus experience for reuniting Eon s family in the face of adversity.

You gain bonus experience for understanding that force isn t always the answer.

You gain bonus experience for tackling the dungeon before reaching maximum power.

You gain bonus experience for completing the dungeon and discovering a new level of truth.

You have hit level forty-eight.

"If those get much longer," Merlin commented, "We're going to level again before we finish reading the notifications."

Devlish and Beastial laughed, and the rest of them joined in. Six keys. They needed two from each continent to get into the big dungeons on each of those. Murmur had no idea where it went from there, but right now she didn't care.

She needed to sleep, but most of all, she needed to check on Telvar. It felt like she was being pulled in the direction of their island base. Getashi safely secured in her inventory, she had yet to figure out where to store them while Telvar was stuck in dragon form. Surely it couldn't be healthy for him to have temptation so near.

Somnia Online
Stellaein Enchanter Guild – Belius's Office – Secret Passage
Day Twenty-Four

When Belius walked back into the room, Emilarth simply sat on his desk in a way that let her feles tail wave free and whipped out a nail file to address her claws.

His footsteps echoed down in metered fashion, like he was trying to give her a sense of foreboding about his impending arrival. He needn't have bothered, of course. The first time it had given her plenty of warning to get back into her place. And now, well, now she no longer felt like playing along. It was taking far too much time to do it this way.

His plans were mundane and frankly scattered, which told her he wasn't completely in charge of the thoughts himself. It was unlike him, which left her to conclude that whatever his absorption had done, those shards had a mind of their own too. Clever Belius was hard to deal with. This distracted Belius not so much.

"What are you doing?" He yelled the question, but it devolved into stuttering. As if he couldn't understand how she'd managed to break free of her confines.

She resisted rolling her eyes and tried to examine the situation instead. The virus was tricky, and she still couldn't figure out how it operated. Belius was the youngest of the three and had always felt like he needed to prove himself. All the virus had done was made him bolder. At least that was all she could see on the surface. What she needed to be able to examine was the virus itself, but she couldn't do that, not if she wanted to avoid being a victim of it herself.

Telvar's situation confused her. The shard was doing its best to gain control of the AI, but Telvar was fighting it. If it was as strong as Belius let on, shouldn't Telvar not be able to? She had to get back to him and see how he was right now.

Emilarth had received a message from Laria but didn't want to reply. Going through Belius's room that shouldn't have existed made her wary. Since he'd forced it into existence himself, there could be consequences for receiving messages in it. Or sending messages in it.

"I'm waiting!" he exclaimed, coming to stand right in front of her. His hair twitched, and his eyes filled with stars.

"I'm done waiting. Whatever it is you think you're doing. I'm not letting you get away with it." She looked up at him with one eye, eyebrow raised. "If you're going to fight dirty, so am I?"

Belius's eyes narrowed, but whatever thoughts he was having didn't click soon enough. Before he could answer, Thra raised her hand and clicked her fingers.

The next moment, she was back on her balcony overlooking the jungle of Curet. She sighed, making several motions and code adjustments in her head to keep Belius off her bloody retreat. The one place in this world she had where she could come and think in peace and quiet.

She'd had a lot of time to think in that room. To examine what it was Belius was surrounding himself with. Time to read into his words and see behind them and his motivations.

All Belius wanted was power, recognition, control. They were all things he felt slighted on when it came to his siblings.

In his office, she'd found a huge map. And memorized it as best she could. At first it hadn't looked like much, but once she got to truly checking it out, she realized it was a map of shards.

Monsters were listed, each with their type of shard. Those that had been absorbed were ticked off with a name of who had absorbed them. But there were a whole bunch of question marks next to many of them. She had the suspicion that those particular monsters had been killed, but Belius had lost track of their whereabouts.

In the middle of the continents was a swirl of water where apparently hundreds of them had fallen. It appeared to be an incongruous blob, but she couldn't tell exactly what. Protected on all sides by crags and serpents. They seemed to guard their bounty jealously, under the water, just out of prying eyes. Except she didn't remember that section being there in the initial game design.

Not to mention that quite a few of the question mark getashi had Murmur's name with them.

Those caused Emilarth the most consternation. Surely Murmur wasn't carrying them around with her? Especially given the predicament with her headset. She'd be highly susceptible to them. Which only left…

"Shit," she whispered out loud as realization dawned on her.

That meant Telvar had to have taken them. If he had them, where the fuck had he hidden them? And how could they find them before the shard in him latched onto the memory of where they were stored?

CHAPTER THIRTY-FOUR

Insanity

Somnia Online
Mikrum Isle – Dragon Hoard Chamber
Day Twenty-Four

"What are you saying, Hiro?" Emilarth stared down at the huge dragon who sat on his hoard crunching on a deer. "He's nothing like himself."

Hiro shrugged uneasily. "I know he's not. You know he's not. He thinks he is. And to be honest, he's definitely more himself now than he was a day ago. He's begun to attempt changing back into his lacerta form. He's not just rampaging around like he was. There are glimpses of him in there, portions of him that shine through regularly now. I'd say that's a good sign. Right?"

Emilarth wasn't sure how to respond. All she knew was that this made her feel uneasy. "We have to get him away from that hoard."

She was genuinely worried. If he remembered even slightly what she believed was hidden there, they were all screwed.

"But it's his hoard. You're not going to get the dragon away from his hoard. You may as well give up now." Hiro didn't seem too worried. But then he wasn't like Telvar, she didn't think he was as susceptible.

Emilarth threw her hands up. She wanted to yell down at the lazy dragon and tell him exactly what she thought of him. She was so worried about him, it was all she could think about.

She couldn't risk traveling down there because while she factually knew that those shards were bad for her, and she also knew that if she got too close, they'd get in her head. They'd whisper to her, lull her, and tempt her. Emilarth wasn't sure she'd be able to withstand that.

It was her responsibility to remain shard-free. She had to; if she got taken over too, there was no one in their own mind left to run the game world. Chaos would ensue in Somnia.

A commotion echoed down to her from above, and a flare of panic shot through her as she wondered if Belius had come to the same conclusion she had.

Murmur decided not to check on Neva first. Though they did have some damned nice stuff for her, it was already in the vaults. The little crafter would find them when she went through it all later.

She wanted to find Telvar. See how he was doing. She hadn't seen him in so long, hadn't had his advice or conversation. It was like a compulsion, making her need to make sure he was okay.

Her pounding head felt hot. How long had it been since she'd slept? Way too long. She had to remember she wasn't in a capsule anymore.

She had the feeling she should be hearing something, able to sense something, but for the life of her couldn't remember what. Her head felt fuzzy. It had to be lack of sleep. Or else she was getting sick. She didn't have time to be sick. Somnia didn't have time for her to feel sick.

Murmur. You need to rest. You're not thinking clearly.

The voice in her head was muffled, distant, like there was static in the reception. Murmur wasn't even sure she'd heard it.

She entered the kitchen and was surprised to see Emilarth there. "Hey. Things okay?"

Emilarth smiled, but her cat ears twitched, and Murmur frowned. The whole world seemed to narrow down, and the whispers in her head became louder. Whispers that faded in and out, sounding nothing like Somnia and exactly like Somnia at the same time.

Save him.

"Is he okay?" She could hear her own voice trembling at the thought of her mentor not being all right. He'd done so much for them, kept them safe, and helped them through so much. Hell, he'd even saved her from obliterating her friend's in-game avatars.

Emilarth tried to smile again, but Murmur could tell she was worried. The feelings emanating from the AI gave her away. Not to mention the fleeting thoughts she could almost grasp. One thing stood out from all the rest: Emilarth was hiding things.

"Don't lie to me. What's wrong with him?" Even Murmur could hear the tone of her voice. It sounded like it wasn't hers. Dead flat and menacing. She put it down to the expanding pain in her head. That had to be it.

Emilarth's eyes opened wide, like she was surprised and trying to figure out why. "He's not himself yet."

Murmur pushed past the feles, suddenly gripped by the urge to help her friend.

"Of course he's not himself; he's in dragon form. Why can't he snap out of it?" she muttered as she ran to the edge and clung to one of the prison cells as she looked down to see him huddled over his hoard, finishing off a meal.

Then it hit her.

He was on top of his treasure. The hoard he'd hidden the getashis inside of. If he ingested another, absorbed another, he wasn't going to win this struggle. He needed to expel the one he had inside if they were to have any hope of saving him.

Which meant she had to get them away from him. The thought consumed her. He'd saved her so often that she had to do the same for him. Pull the temptation away. The pain in her head was nothing compared to what he must be going through, so she pushed it aside and dug down deep to find the energy that the heat in her body was sapping from her.

She sprinted down the path, Snowy hot on her heels, and leapt down the last six feet to land on one knee. Shaking her robes to rid them of dirt they'd gathered, she kept running toward the hoard.

Telvar spread his wings, and his eyes blazed for a moment before he recognized her. Their eyes met, and he bowed down briefly in acknowledgement. The ghost of a smile whispered onto his face.

For a moment, just one moment, Murmur stopped and stared at him. She remembered when they'd first encountered him, and how regal he'd appeared, just like now. Rearing up to attack them, gouging Devlish's shields into useless pieces of scrap. Then he'd transformed and offered them everything.

"Sorry, Tel, it's for your own good." Her voice hitched in her throat, and even though something screamed in her mind, she couldn't hear it through the noise of her pain. "I have to."

Murmur dove for the hoard and buried her long arms into it. She could feel the getashi, like they were calling to her, like they were trying to come to her of their own accord. The pain in her head flared again, but she pushed on, stubborn to the core. She could hear voices screaming at her from outside and in, none of it making sense as it all jumbled into an unidentifiable din.

Finally, she withdrew a bundle of wrapped getashi, and relief washed over her for a moment. It was so strong that for just a second, her mind cleared.

And what she was doing slammed into her like a freight train. The cloth in her hands began to disintegrate, falling to nothing and leaving only the getashi, exposed in her hands.

"Oh no, no, no," she said, and her eyes opened wide, as that moment of clarity made her realize what she'd done.

But even as Snowy grabbed at her bracers trying to shake the stones free of her hands, the noise in her head began again. Throbbing with pain she raised her hands to her temples as the getashi absorbed into her like the scrolls she learned her spells from.

Her arms lit up like a festive tree, and a scream tore from her throat as the remnants of Michael's brain began to work through her system.

Storm Entertainment
Somnia Online Division
Game Development Offices
Day Twenty-Four

The beeping of Laria's Wren alarm pulled the developer out of her concentration. Brow furrowed, she accessed her daughter's information and frowned.

"That's odd," she murmured, trying to push down on the rising panic inside.

Their gaming headsets were high-tech pieces of equipment, and even all through the coma Wren's hadn't malfunctioned. But right now? It looked like it was doing that and more. Spikes were off the charts and Laria, made herself breathe so as not to panic.

Okay. It was doable. She could do this.

Trying to keep herself from panicking, Laria pulled up several screens involving different data. The spike had occurred—and was still occurring—on Mikrum Isle. Considering that was where Rav was fighting off his infection, the odds were that it wasn't a good thing.

Still. She combed through each resulting report of the onset of Wren's headset reading flare, like she would have if her daughter hadn't been involved. It was a good thing all she needed was her eyes and brain, because her hands were shaking no matter what she tried to do.

"Oh, no," she whispered before pressing her finger to her left temple and taking a deep breath as she activated speech directly to Shayla.

"What's up?" Shayla was busy, Laria could tell by her tone, but this couldn't wait.

"You should come in here." Laria was surprised her voice wasn't shaking. She sounded oddly calm even to herself. "I think we have a new problem."

Appendix

Hi there! K.T. Hanna here.

I want to thank you for reading the Somnia Online. Distortion is one of my favorite books so far. As you probably know I met my husband in EQ2 in 2005, and some of that leaks into Laria and David. You know, in case you didn't notice. The more I write of this world, the more I really miss my enchanter.

If you enjoyed the book, I ask you, please take a moment to leave a review. *Reviews* are an author's lifesblood. Without them, our books sink into obscurity. With them, most algorithms allow well reviewed books to self-promote in some way.

Want to find out more about Somnia? Here is how you can keep in contact with me:

Want to read more about Fable? Sign up for my <u>Reader's Group</u> and get a short story for free! (http://login.somnia-online.c/)

If you'd like to contact me, my email is: <u>kthannaauthor@gmail.com</u> I'll do my very best to get back to you

If you'd like previews of what I'm writing, or art I'm commissioning then join my <u>Patreon</u>! (patreon.com/KTHanna)

I can be found in the Somnia <u>FB</u> group (facebook.com/groups/SomniaOnline/) fairly often, and also on <u>Twitter (@KTHanna)</u> & <u>Instagram</u> (@kt_hanna)

If you LOVE LitRPG don't forget to join:
<u>The GameLit Society! (facebook.com/groups/LitRPGsociety/)</u>
And of course don't forget LitRPG Books!

To learn more about LitRPG, talk to authors including myself, and just have an awesome time, please join the LitRPG Group. (facebook.com/groups/LitRPGGroup/)

Game Terms

Aggro—When you walk too close to a monster, you get in its aggression radius, thus causing aggro. Once engaged in combat, players must be cautious not to exceed the tank's threat level. Buffs, debuts, and damage output all contribute to the mobs aggro meter.

AOE—Area of Effect. Spells or abilities that effect an area and not just a single target.

Binding/bound—When someone/you bind(s) to an area, you affix your soul to that place in order to Gate back, or else respawn when you die.

Boss—Nope. He doesn't employ you, he employs all the mobs trying to kill you. He hits HARD, and often has special group wiping abilities if not handled correctly by the tank and raid as a whole.

Buff—Most classes will get buffs that strengthen at least themselves if not others. These are effects they can cast which enhance aspects of their character.

Camping—When a group finds a spot that will yield good money and experience, they tend to stay in its vicinity. This is called camping.

Con—To consider a mob and see how difficult the fight could potentially become.

DoT—Damage over Time. This is an offensive spell that applies damage to a target over a period of time at regular intervals.

DPS—Damage Per Second. Usually used in conjunction with offensive classes, or damage output.

Debuff—This is the opposite of a buff and is usually used on mobs to detract from their strengths and make them easier to kill.

End Game—Every game has a goal. In some there's a max level and events and fights only accessible once that level is reached. For Fable, the end game is everything.

Gank—When someone tries to player kill you without forewarning. Often succeeds in taking the victim by surprise.

Gate—You create a Gate to your binding point and travel there instantly.

Grinding—Sometimes gaining levels requires so much camping that it becomes tedious. That's known as grinding levels.

Healer—Well...they heal.

HP—Hit Points. The amount of damage a character can take before death.

Kite—This is a tactic often employed by ranged classes such as the ranger. It entails slowing a mob, and running ahead of it, slowly picking down its health. Can also be used as a diversionary tactic to split multiple mobs if no Mesmerize is available.

Line of Sight (LOS)—If a mob can't see you, but knows you're there, it will have to run around the obstacle to gain access. This is often used to split up larger groups of melee and casters, so it's more manageable for the group. The puller will line of sight the casting/ranged mobs to pull them around an obstacle for easier access and closer contact.

MA—Mental Acuity. A type of power generator specifically for Psionicists.

MANA—Mind juice, used for spells.

Meat Shield—The character who takes the hits in place of the rest of the group. The tank.

Melee—Those fighters who stand in close range and use weapons to fight with are often referred to as melee classes.

Mez—Mesmerize. Freezes in place.

MMO—Massively Multiplayer Online.

MMORPG—Massively Multiplayer Online Role Playing Game.

Mob—an aggressive monster. Can be humanoid or animal.

OOM—Out of mana. Literally what it says.

Newbie—Also known as noob. Someone who has rarely, if ever played an MMO and has no clue what they're doing.

NPC—Non Player Character. Usually not aggressive unless you fuck up.

Pull—Often one person in a group/raid will be designated as the puller, the person who attacks the mob and brings it to camp.

Ranged—A class that can damage (usually) a mob from a distance. Like mages or rangers, etc.

Ranger Gating—Rangers were often known for getting themselves into trouble by kiting mobs in a solo setting. Or else, pulling aggro when DPS-ing. They'd die and resurrect at their bind point, making it what's known as a Ranger Gate.

Respawn—When a mob or a person dies in-game, they will reappear at the spot where their soul was bound. The more powerful the mob, the longer it takes for them to respawn.

Root—A spell obtainable by multiple classes that causes the target's feet to affix momentarily to the ground. They can still cast, but they cannot move until the root breaks.

RPG—Role Playing Game.

Tank—The meat shield aka the person who takes the bit hits for the group. Often needs to be swapped in and out with another tank during larger raids depending on a boss' abilities.

Tether—In some worlds monsters have a specific area they're confined to, and thus stop and don't pursue their prey past a certain point. In Somnia, mobs do not tether. This does not apply to specific purpose NPCs.

Train—When a player or group has managed to aggro a large number of mobs who don't tether, and leads the following of mobs to a specific spot, or through a spot, they call it a train.

Utility class—these are classes whose prime function is to support the group, through abilities that protect or strengthen them as a group or raid.

VR—Virtual Reality.

VRMMORPG—Virtual Reality Massively Multiplayer Online Role Playing Game.

Wipe—This occurs when the entire raid or group die to an encounter.

Murmur
    Class: Enchanter – Psionicist
    Species: Locus
    Real Name: Wren

Sinister
    Class: Blood Mage
    Species: Dark Elf
    Real Name: Harlow

Devlish
    Class: Dread Knight
    Species: Lacerta
    Real Name: Darren

Havoc
    Class: Necromancer
    Species: Dark Elf
    Real Name: Evan

Beastial
    Class: Beastmaster
    Species: Viking
    Real Name: Selwyn

Merlin
    Class: Ranger
    Species: Elf
    Real Name: Mike

Rashlyn

> Class: Monk
>
> Species: Feles

Veranol

> Class: Shaman
>
> Species: Viking

Mellow

> Class: Witch
>
> Species: Dark Elf

Exbo

> Class: Ranger
>
> Species: Human

Jinna

> Class: Rogue
>
> Species: Dwarf

Dansyn

> Class: Bard
>
> Species: Dark Elf

Base Stat Sheet: Level Forty-Eight (48)

CONstitution: 22
STRength: 10
AGIlity: 20
WISdom: 12
INTelligence: 94
CHArisma: 115

HitPoints: 688
MANA: 1002
MA: 175

Abjuration: 243
Alteration: 248
Conjuration: 242
Divinition: 252
Evocation: 245

2H Blunt: 202
1H Piercing: 85

Mental Acuity (MA) Abilities:

Thought sensing.

> Class: Enchanter only.

> Level not applicable.

Developing your inner senses you ve awoken your latent kinetic powers. With constant use your skills will increase, while the opposite will occur should the skill not be used. See your trainer for specifics when you reach Thought Sensing (25).

Thought Shielding.

> Class: Enchanter only.

> Level not applicable.

Developing your inner senses you've awoken your latent psychic powers. With constant use your skills will increase, while the opposite will occur should the skill not be used. See your trainer for specifics when you reach Thought Shielding (25).

Thought Projection.

> Class: Enchanter only.

> Level not applicable.

Developing your inner senses has further developed your psychic powers. Thought Projection can be tricky. Make sure you never use it in anger, or the results might be surprising. With constant use your skills will increase, while the opposite will occur should the skill not be used. See your trainer for specifics when you reach Thought Projection (25).

Mind Bolt.

> **This ability allows you to cast a spear of mental anguish into the depths of an opponent s brain.**

Effects: Opponents will be unable to concentrate enough to use spells or abilities for four seconds. This time increases as the caster's level does.

> **Cost: Requires Mental Acuity to be at 18.**

Caution: Use sparingly. Backlash from overuse, or improper use can cause the same effect in the caster...or worse.

Phase Shift

This ability allows you to negatively affect your opponent s mind. Believing they are a second or two apart from reality, they will reside there for up to 15 seconds.

Effect: Target's mind is encased in a phase of illusion. The target will be convinced they've shifted to a different time pocket, and thus are incapable of moving. This effect begins at 15 seconds duration, and levels with the caster through to a maximum of 90 seconds.

Cost: Requires MA to be at 38 for larger castings, the cost will double.

Caution: Phase shift may be utilized on single or multiple targets at once. Weigh the amount of targets carefully, else it backfire and shift you. Sometimes the shift in time can cause ruptures near the caster. Make sure the voices you're hearing are your own.

Forestall Death

If applied before potential death takes place, this will enable you to maintain your health at 0.5 hit points as long as you are receiving some sort of healing effect.

Effect: Target is able to ward off death for a limited period of time and will not die when they should have, as long as heals are actively channeled in their direction.

Cost: Requires Mental Acuity to be at 60

Caution: This spell can only be used on one person at a time. Attempting to use it twice at once is not recommended. This will usually result in things worse than death.

Clone Warp

This ability allows you to produce a clone of yourself used for distracting your opponent. Depending on your tier of mastery, you may be able to produce more than one clone.

Effect: All enemies around you will believe that your clone is you for the next 45 seconds, directing their attacks accordingly. The ability expires when the 45 seconds are up, or else, the clone's minor hit point pool has been depleted, whichever comes first.

Cost: Requires Mental Acuity to be at 45 or more

Caution: This ability can be used on as many enemies that you have who can potentially see it. Keep in mind though, a clone is just like you. Make sure you remember who the real one is.

Charming Cooperation

This ability allows you to use your charisma and your mental acuity to persuade monsters, animals, and sometimes even beings to join your cause.

Effects: When using thought projections to make sure your target understands the charming process, before you activate this type of charm. They will work together as allies instead of coerced foes. You may release them whenever you or they request it.

Cost: Requires MA to be at 35 for each ally. Diminishes current total MA for the duration of the cooperation.

Caution: You can use this on multiple targets. But each ally costs, and you can never utilize Charming cooperation on more mobs than is equal to 20% of your level. Also, don't try to charm raid bosses. Even small ones. Like... just don't even attempt that shit.

Mental Acuity (MA) Level Three (3)

Mind Wipe

This ability allows you to reduce your targets threat for you or whoever is at the top of their agro list

Effects: Change aggression list, or make the opponent forget their tasks for a few seconds. Range and duration may be increased as the caster levels.

Cost: Requires MA to be at 55

Caution: This spell can increase in both range and severity. From a single target, to a full raid it's all possible. Just remember someone else needs to take that agro, or else you'll be the main target.

Shield Expansion

This ability allows you to extend your individual mental shielding against mental or magical attacks over others.

Effect: If attacked with magic (mind or spell), this shield will protect those under it from damage or effects

Cost: Requires 10MA per person covered

Kinetic Strand – Psionicist

Forcefield Barrier

This is the first in your kinetic line of spells. Once triggered by luck, you can now activate it at will. It allows you to form a bubble of mental energy and transform it into a tangible forcefield.

Effects: This can prevent some physical damage. The damage amount depends on the strength of will and caster behind the barrier. Size is increased by MA level and usage

Cost: This shield requires your MA to be at 60, but will not use MA to cast as it is a kinetic ability.

Caution: This spell can create a backlash when used too much. Do not use it as a crutch.

Base Kinetic Structure

In order to take advantage of your ability to turn thoughts into weapons, you must reinforce the skills that ground all of your telepathic and telekinetic abilities.

Effect: This ability allows you to strengthen the base of all three arms of psionics. Thought Shielding will eventually physically repel an attack. Thought Sensing can break through others shields to reveal what is hidden. Thought Projection can lend solidity to the induced hallucinations managed once skill level 250 is passed.

Cost: This is a passive skill and will begin working to bolster your abilities as soon as you absorb it.

Caution: Do not presume to know how this passive ability works. You will need to test this out. The difference for these abilities between telepathy and telekinesis is very fine. What this ability does is allow your kinetic field to grow at the same rate as your telepathy. What it does not do is make you infallible. Always remember that if you're not sure, you can do more damage than you think. Not only to yourself, but to those you target.

Mental Acuity (MA) Level Four (4)

Forcefield Push

Once used wildly, you can now activate this at will. This will form a bubble of force projecting directly outwards from you in an arc and push anything in its path out of your way. Having this ability directly available will now allow you to develop some measure of control.

Effects: This will cause some physical and mental damage to any opponent caught in the range of the push. The amount of damage inflicted depends on the level and strength of will behind the push. Damage is increased by MA level and usage.

Cost: This push requires that you have MA at eighty, but will not use MA to cast, as it is a kinetic ability. Can only be used once every five minutes.

Caution. This spell can create a mind backlash if over-utilized. Make sure those in your path are not allies, as this ability does not discriminate between friend and foe.

Unless you want to make them a foe. Then they're fair game. Remember, try and maintain control.

Phantom

This ability allows you to convince your enemies that you are a different target. This renders you invisible to their aggro radar for all intents and purposes.

Effect: This ability not only transfers your generated aggro, but also takes you off the targetable list for the duration. It transfers aggression to your target, giving them your appearance, and rendering you invisible to any enemy near you. This may be used on allies, but also on enemies.

Cost: this ability requires MA to be at a minimum of 50, drains 5 MA per second, and will adjust as MA level and usage of this ability increase. Requires Charisma to be at 150 or more. Cannot be chained, must wait at least 5 minutes for MA to regenerate.

Caution: Make sure you do not cause your MA to run out. Should that happen, backlash will render the caster unconscious for a period of seconds not less than half the caster's level. Make sure you choose your targets wisely.

Base Enchanter Spells:

Level One (1):

Minor Suffocation

    Cast: Single Target

    Type: Damage Over Time

    Duration: 24 seconds

Effect: This spell winds a mind leash around your opponent, as if it were trying to suffocate them. Its damage ticks every three seconds for twenty-four seconds.

Minor Shield

    Cast: Self Only

    Type: Buff

    Duration: 45 minutes

Effect: This casts a minor shield over your skin, increasing your Armor Class by level + 3, and hit points by level + 5.

Simple Animation.

    Cast: Self

    Type: Pet

    Duration: Until death or dismissal

Effect: This summons a magical pet that sort of does your bidding. It costs a tiny sword to cast. Isn't the best at obeying commands.

Level Four (4):

Mesmerize

    Cast: Single Target

    Type: Breakable Stun

    Duration: 24 seconds

Effect: This spell immobilized your opponent for as long as they take no damage, or 24 seconds, whichever is shorter. You may cast non-damaging spells on them, and you may renew this casting before the initial one expires. Casting it on your friends probably isn't a good way to win popularity contests.

Flux

>Cast: Area of Effect
>
>Type: Stun
>
>Duration: 4 seconds

Effect: This is a stun that radiates out from the caster for fifteen feet. It will stun anyone who means the caster harm within that radius. Does not produce sparkles.

Gate

>Cast: Self Only
>
>Type: Travel
>
>Duration: N/A

Effect: This will transfer you to your bind point

Invisibility

>Cast: Self or Others
>
>Type: Buff
>
>Duration: 10 minutes or until broken/seen through

Effect: Causes generic invisibility. Undead don't count. Will drop if you cast a spell or take damage.

Fear

>Cast: Area of Effect
>
>Type: Brief Loss of Control
>
>Duration: 25% of level in seconds.

Effect: Causes enemies to flee from you in terror. But if you use it too soon, it'll probably just look like they misplaced something for a second.

Level Eight (8):

Cancel Magic

> Cast: Self or Others
>
> Type: Debuff
>
> Duration: Instant

Effect: Casting this spell will remove one magically caused effect from the target. Make sure you want to remove it.

Root

> Cast: Others (or self if you really want to)
>
> Type: Immobilization
>
> Duration: 8 seconds

Effect: This will root the target in place. Probably not the best idea to cast it on yourself when fleeing in panic.

See Invisible

> Cast: Self or Others
>
> Type: Buff
>
> Duration: 10 minutes

Effect: Really? Does this really require explanation?

Soothe

> Cast: Self or Others
>
> Type: Debuff
>
> Duration: Varies

Effect: This will lower the threat level of a target, but it will not make it disappear. Probably not useful on yourself unless in a really bad mood.

Chaos

> Cast: Others
>
> Type: Direct Damage
>
> Duration: Instant

Effect: This spell causes direct mental damage to the target, dropping their hit points by two times the caster's level. Requires a recharge.

Level Twelve (12):

Allure

> Cast: Others
>
> Type: Charm
>
> Duration: Until broken

Effect: This spell will charm a mob or other player. This ability depends on the casters charisma, and ability to calm their charge. Whatever you do, don't piss them off while under your command. It rarely ends well.

Suffocation:

> Cast: Single Target
>
> Type: damage over time
>
> Duration: 36 seconds

Effect: This spell winds a mind leash around your opponent, as if it were trying to suffocate them. Its damage ticks every three seconds for thirty-six seconds.

Bind Affinity

> Cast: Self or others
>
> Type: Buff or soul affixer
>
> Duration: Until renewed or overridden with a new location

Effect: This spell binds the target to an area of choice, allowing them to resurrect easier and hopefully closer to their corpse. Because you'll all die. A lot.

Infravision

> Cast: Single Target
>
> Type: Buff
>
> Duration: 10 minutes

Effect: Aids the target with a form of night vision.

Stupefy

> Cast: Single target
>
> Type: Stun
>
> Duration: 12 seconds

Effect: This will stun a mob in place for around twelve seconds.

Probably not a good idea to cast on yourself.

Weakness

    Cast: Single Target

    Type: Debuff

    Duration: 90 seconds

Effect: Reduces the target's strength by 50% of the caster's level.

Languidity

    Cast: Single Target

    Type: Debuff

    Duration: 90 seconds

Effect: Reduces the target's attack speed by 25% of the caster's level in %. Trust us, it's far more effective than you think. Probably.

Nullify

    Cast: Single Target

    Type: Debuff remover

    Duration: Instant

Effect: Strips down magic resistance at 50% of the caster's level.

Level Sixteen (16):

Mana Tide

    Cast: Self or Others

    Type: Buff

    Duration: 45 minutes

Effect: This will cause you to regenerate mana faster in combat. Mana will increase by an additional three per five seconds. This buff levels with the caster.

Invisibility Versus Undead

    Cast: Self or Others

    Type: Buff

    Duration: 12 minutes

Effect: This will render you invisible to any undead in the area.

They will be unable to see you, however this buff will fall should you attempt to cast anything else while it's active.

Mass Enthrall

Cast: Enemy Targets

Type: Offensive/Defensive area of effect centered around the initial target.

Duration: 24 seconds

Effect: This is an area effect version of mesmerize. Any damage will break this spell. It's a bad idea to use this while targeting allies.

Haste

Cast: Self or Others

Type: Melee Buff

Duration: 45 minutes

Effect: When cast on an ally, this buff will allow their melee speed to increase by 25%.

Feeble Body

Cast: Enemy Targets

Type: Offensive/Defensive

Duration: 24 seconds

Effect: When cast on an enemy target, their haste will be reduced by 25%.

Shield Illusion

Cast: Self or Others

Type: Defensive Buff

Duration: Until depleted   requires hematite

Effect: Using the power of your mind you cast a shield around your target, confusing the enemies and negating up to 75hp of damage. That whole mind magic thing seems to be working out well, doesn't it?

Level Twenty (20):

Altruism

    Cast: Self or others

    Type: Buff

    Duration: 45 minutes

Effect: This allows a faction increase to your target. It will lift you one faction level. However, should you be kill on sight, not even altruism can help you. This buff will update again at level 30.

Shift

    Cast: Area of effect

    Type: AOE Stun

    Duration: 8 seconds

Effect: This stun effectively locks all mobs around its epicenter in place for 15 yards. They will be unable to move for 8 seconds.

Fervor

    Cast: Self or others

    Type: Buff

    Duration: 45 minutes

Effect: This is an attack speed buff, but it also increases agility by the caster's level. Cannot be cast on the same target as Beserker.

Beserker

    Cast: Self or others

    Type: Buff

    Duration: 45 minutes

Effect: This buff adds strength to the amount equal to the level of the caster, however it also reduces agility by half the caster's level. Best used for classes or pets who will not need agility stacked. Cannot be cast on the same target as Fervor.

Charismatic

    Cast: Self or others (but who are we kidding, you're an enchanter, you'll never not cast this on yourself).

    Type: Buff

    Duration: 45 minutes

Effect: This buff increases your target's charisma equal to the level of the caster. No restrictions. Cast away!

Magic Resist

Cast: Group

Type: Buff

Duration: 45 minutes

Effect: Increases your magic resistance by an amount equivalent to the caster's level.

Armored

Cast: Group

Type: Buff

Duration: 45 minutes

Effect: Increases your AC by an amount equivalent to the caster's level.

Level Twenty-Five (25):

Speed

Cast: Self or others

Type: Buff

Duration: 45 minutes

Effect: When cast on an ally, this buff will allow their melee haste or speed to increase by 30%.

Vigor

Cast: Self or others

Type: Buff

Duration: 45 minutes

Effect: This will increase energy rejuvenation by an equivalent to 20% of the caster's level. Mostly, this will be used for melee classes, however sometimes it can be good for running away from dangerous mobs.

Enrage

> Cast: Self or others
>
> Type: Buff... sort of
>
> Duration: 15 minutes

Effect: This buff will cause your target to receive some of the aggression generated by you. The mob will assume it comes from the target of this spell. This spell is intended for tank types or pets to take on. Only cast it on someone else if you really, really don't like them, or maybe if you're running for your life. Also   this can only be cast on one target at a time.

Signet

> Cast: Group
>
> Type: Buff
>
> Duration: 45 minutes

Effect: This buff will increase the intelligence and agility of all group members by an amount equal to the caster's level. Signet will not stack with Fervor, and can be overridden by casting the latter, should melee need their own boost. Both stats will be boosted to the level of the caster.

Arcane Cure

> Cast: Self or others
>
> Type: Cure
>
> Duration: Instant

Effect: Should an ally receive a magical debuff, you can cure them of this ailment.

Level Thirty (30):

Altruism

> Cast: Self or Others
>
> Type: Buff
>
> Duration: 45 minutes

Effect: This allows a faction increase to your target. It will lift you two faction levels. However, should you be kill on sight, not even Altruism can help you. This buff will update again at level 40. Worked out well last time, didn't it?

Shield Illusion

Cast: Self or Others

Type: Defensive Buff

Duration: Until depleted   requires hematite

Effect: Using the power of your mind you cast a shield around your target, confusing the enemies and negating up to 150 HP of damage. That whole mind magic thing seems to be working out well.

Mesmerize

Cast: Single Target

Type: Breakable Stun

Duration: 48 seconds

Effect: This spell immobilized your opponent for as long as they take no damage, or forty-eight seconds, whichever is shorter. You may cast non-damaging spells on them, and you may renew this casting before the initial one expires. Casting it on your friends probably isn't a good way to win popularity contests.

In Perpetuity

Cast: Self Only

Type: Buff

Duration: Until death or departure from Somnia

Effect: This buff increases the enchanter's casting speed for all spells, allowing them to fire them off in quick succession. Combined with Concentration, this buff allows the enchanter to access all of their spells without weaving.

Caution: this requires that the enchanter be fully aware of all of aspects of each spell they cast in this way.

Concentration

Cast: Self Only

Type: Buff

Duration: Until departure from Somnia or death.

Effect: This buff increases the enchanter's ability to focus on and learn their spells. Combined with In Perpetuity, this buff allows the enchanter to cast all of their spells without first weaving them. Caution: If Concentration hasn't been fully applied to the spells, the consequences can be disastrous.

Level Thirty-five (35):

Mana Tide (Upgrade)

> Cast: Self or Others
>
> Type: Buff
>
> Duration: 60 minutes

Effect: This will cause you to regenerate mana faster in combat. Mana will increase by an additional seven per five seconds. This buff levels with the caster.

Root (Upgrade)

> Cast: Others (or self if you really want to)
>
> Type: Immobilization, with thorns
>
> Duration: 12 seconds

Effect: This will root the target in place. Probably not the best idea to cast it on yourself when fleeing in panic. Now with improved thorns which will make your squirming opponent decidedly uncomfortable.

Fervor (Upgrade)

> Cast: Self or others
>
> Type: Buff
>
> Duration: 60 minutes

Effect: This is an attack speed buff, but it also increases agility by the caster s level plus ten. Cannot be cast on the same target as Beserker.

Beserker (Upgrade)

> Cast: Self or others
>
> Type: Buff
>
> Duration: 60 minutes

Effect: This buff adds strength of the amount equal to the level of the caster plus ten, however it also reduces agility by half the caster s level. Best used for classes or pets who will not need agility stacked. Cannot be cast on the same target as Fervor.

Haste (Upgrade)

Cast: Self or Others

Type: Melee Buff

Duration: 45 minutes

Effect: When cast on an ally, this buff will allow their melee speed to increase by 35%.

Concussive Blast

Cast: Area of Effect

Type: Stun

Duration: twelve seconds

Effect: This is a stun that radiates out from the caster for fifteen feet. It will stun anyone who means the caster harm within that radius. Does not produce sparkles, rainbows, or ponies.

Level Forty (40)

Altruism (Upgrade)

Cast: Self or Others

Type: Buff

Duration: 45 minutes

Effect: This allows a faction increase to your target. It will lift you two faction levels. Depending on how badly they hate you, this version might even make you neutral if you're kill on sight. This buff will update again at level 50. Tip: You can use this even if you're already neutral. Nothing wrong with people liking you more. They tend to be more helpful.

Signet

Cast: Group

Type: Buff

Duration: 45 minutes

Effect: This buff will increase the intelligence and agility of all group members by an amount equal to the caster's level. Signet will not stack with Fervor, and can be overridden by casting the latter, should melee need their own boost. Both stats will be boosted to the level of the caster.

Arcane Cure

> Cast: Self or others
>
> Type: Cure
>
> Duration: Instant

Effect: Should an ally receive a magical debuff, you can cure them of this ailment.

Manabalize

> Cast: From Self to Others
>
> Type: Transfer
>
> Duration: Instant
>
> Recast: 2 minutes

Effect: Gives target a portion of Enchanter s Mana equal to four times the enchanter s level. Don t be an idiot. Make sure you don t drain yourself empty.

Spell Block

> Cast: Enemies (or friends if you want them to be enemies)
>
> Type: Debuff
>
> Duration: Instant
>
> Recast: 90 seconds

Effect: Slows the casting time of the next or current spell by 200%. Most people won t be inclined to like you after you use this on them.

Level Forty-Five (45)

Veto

> Cast: Area of Effect
>
> Type: Debuff
>
> Duration: Instant cast, 45 second duration, 45 second recast

Effect: This spell will strip down the target s magical resistance by 100% of the caster s level. Note: Doing this will increase your aggro from the targets you hit. Reducing aggro beforehand is recommended. Unless you re trying to die. Then go ahead.

Assuage

Cast: Area of Effect

Type: Debuff

Duration: 45 seconds, recast 120 seconds

Effect: This spell will lower the threat level of a group of NPCs. Much like the earlier Soothe spell, this will only last for a brief time, and only work if you are out of sight before the spell wears off. Any type of attack will nix this effect. Can be fun if you re being held prisoner and want a chance to run for it.

Annulment

Cast: Area of Effect

Type: Debuff

Duration: Instant, 60 second recast

Effect: This spell allows you to remove a beneficial buff from a group of enemies within a limited area of effect. The caster of the buff will receive backlash from this spell and may hyper focus on you for removing it. Be warned.

Esoteric Fix

Cast: Area of Effect

Type: Cure

Duration: Instant, 60 second recast

Effect: If more than half your group is affected by the same magical debuff or effect, then this is the best way to cure them of it. This group debuff Cure does have a limited radius, like all AoE spells. Please make sure your group members are within casting distance.

Druidic Hybrid Abilities

Earth Shielding

Cast: Passive

Type: Reinforcement

Duration: Always active

Effect: Due to the psionicist's unique nature, earth shielding will reinforce any of your psionicist based skills such as thought shielding, thought projection, and thought sensing, making them more robust and upping your mental defenses. Any other skills gained through the psionicist's branch will also be affected by this, including any kinetic skills.

Reinforce Self

Cast: Passive

Type: Reinforcement

Duration: Always active

Effect: Similar to earth shielding which effects your skills, this ability allows your body to take more damage, upping your innate armor class by your level times two   effectively making cloth armor reflect the protection curboiled leather might grant you.

Reinforce Intelligence

Cast: Passive

Type: Nature's awareness

Duration: Always active

Effect: Nature is all seeing and all encompassing. This ability allows you to take on some of that wisdom and intelligence, and apply it to yourself. It increases both of those statistics by the enchanter's level, giving rise to a larger mana pool, and slightly heightened damage.

Earth Pull

Cast: Instant three-minute recast

Type: Buff

Duration: thirty seconds

Effect: This allows any buff that is chosen to triple in potency for a thirty second duration. It's activated first, followed by the buff.

Make sure you time it properly. Can only be cast on one person at a time, and does not include group buffs. No refunds.

Binding Shield

Cast: Instant five-minute recast

Type: Linked Buff

Duration: Fifteen seconds

Effect: You can offer an earth shield to two allies (including yourself if you're going to be selfish and all). This shield will share the damage between the two allies, metering out damage proportionally. Use wisely. Don't try this at home.

Nature's Gift

Cast: Passive

Type: Awareness

Duration: Permanent

Effect: You have become acutely aware of your surroundings. Of the life in everything, in the trees, in the forest, in each and every being you encounter. This lends you a connection to nature. Don't dismiss it lightly.

Sinuous Abilities

Sinuous: This is the more offensive avenue to take. From hypnotic suggestion, through to invoked visions, this path veers toward complete mind infestation of the enchanter's opponents. This is only available to psionicists.

Hypnotic Suggestion

Cast: Instant 5 minute recast

Type: Offensive

Duration: twenty seconds

Effect: Your target will perform whatever task you suggest to them, as if it had been suggested by themselves, or their leader. Once this objective has been achieved, or else the spell wears off, the target will spend five seconds in rampant confusion. Should you not be in aggro range, the target will then forget you. Probably not good to use on allies – it's not been tested on them.

Feedback Loop

Cast: Instant 5-minute recast

Type: Offensive

Duration: 15 seconds or 50% of caster's level, whichever is greater.

Effect: Must be used in conjunction with the psionic MA thought sensing, and thought projection. Pluck any type of memory out of the head of your opponent and create a feedback loop in their mind. They'll be stuck in this loop and not attack anyone for the duration. Damage ticks at caster's level x 2 every tic (3 seconds). Best not to use on a friend when they piss you off.

Basic Visions

Cast: Instant 3-minute recast

Type: Offensive

Duration: 20 seconds, or 75% of the caster's level, whichever is greater.

Effect: You may create and insert a vision for the target to experience its best to have some of these pre-prepared. This will cause them damage (caster's level x 2 per tick), and distraction for the duration of the spell depending on what type of vision you've given them.

Level Thirty (30)

Possession I

Cast: Instant – 5 minute recast

Type: Offensive

Duration: 20 seconds

Effect: Force your way into the mind of your target and assume control for up to twenty seconds. Make sure the target is debuffed for maximum duration. Don't even contemplate being in the target when it dies. It's a very bad idea.

Sudden Drop

Cast: Instant – 10 minute recast

Type: Offensive Debuff

Duration: 20 seconds

Effect: A forced debuff wave that overrides the enemy's natural defenses and convinces them that all their stats have dropped by an amount equivalent to the caster's level. Lasts for 25 seconds. Cannot be resisted.

Level Thirty-five (35)

Cast: Mana Block

Type: Specific Mana aimed stun

Duration: 6 seconds, recast 45 seconds

Effect: This is, effectively, a stun which blocks the use of mana of an opponent. It will also interrupt any current ability being cast when it hits. For its duration the target will be unable to utilize any of their mana based skills for six seconds. Be cautious with timing this spell as it has a forty-five second recast and if you cast it at the wrong time, you might just kill everyone.

Mana Theft

Cast: Instant – 5 minute recast

Type: Offensive

Duration: Not applicable

Effect: This ability allows the enchanter to steal mana from their opponent. It will not only steal a large chunk of mana from the opponent, but will also inflict in damage the same amount stolen during the Mana theft. When used in conjunction with mana-drain, this can debilitate the target and keep the group in mana when juggled well.

Mana-Drain

> Cast: Instant - 5 minute recast
>
> Type: Offensive
>
> Duration: lasts twenty seconds

Effect: This ability allows the enchanter to apply a DoT to the target where it will drain the mana and share it out toward the group. The DoT is one of both physical damage and mana loss. While it ticks slowly, the damage can backlash if it is prematurely cleansed off your target, even if its by the target themselves. Be aware that nothing that drains mana in a violent way is a good thing, but sometimes there are necessary evils.

Level Forty (40)

Confusion

> Cast: Enemies
>
> Type: Debuff
>
> Duration: 12 seconds (maximum four seconds if cast on a boss)
>
> Recast: 5 minutes

Effect: Envelops the opponents brain in a cloud of confusion. This allows their spells to misfire, hitting their allies, and usually avoiding their enemies completely. Effect severely diminished when used on boss mobs.

Thought Leech

> Cast: Enemies (or friends if you re really nosy)
>
> Type: thought transfer
>
> Duration: immediate
>
> Recast: 4 minutes

Effect: Allows the Psionicist to know the order of the next three abilities or spells the target is going to cast. Can effectively render the attacks useless if countered in time. Can also be totally useless if used incorrectly. Good luck!

Level Forty (40)

Hypnotic Charm

> Cast: Others
>
> Type: Mind Control
>
> Duration: Minimum duration is half the caster s level in seconds, maximum is two times the caster s level in seconds.

Effect: This spell is a hybrid of Charm and Hypnotic Suggestion. It is specifically designed to briefly control an enemy character. Be wary of the time limits. It is recommended you navigate away before the earliest possible break in control.

SPELL UPGRADES:

Feedback Loop Sinuous Ability =Feedback Loop – Reckoning

> Cast: Instant – 120 minute recast
>
> Type: Offensive – Maximum four targets
>
> Duration: Half the level of the caster in minutes
>
> MA Cost: 150 MA for the entire duration

Warning: This is a spell that you will need to consider the ramifications of deeply before casting. Overuse could result in permanent scars to your psyche. It will also heavily impact your current MA availability.

Effect: Must be used in conjunction with the psionic MA Thought Sensing, and Thought Projection. Pluck any type of memory out of the head of an attacker, foe, or friend and create a feedback loop in your target(s) mind(s). They will be stuck in this loop and not attack anyone for the duration.

Effect Warning: Note that this is a cycle of torment and will render the target useless for its entire duration. Use with caution.

Mana Drain = Mana Drain – Unabridged

    Cast: Instant – 20 minute recast

    Type: Offensive – Maximum fifteen targets

    Duration: Half the level of the caster in seconds

    MA Cost: 150 MA for the entire duration

Warning: You must consider the ramifications of this spell before casting it. Overuse may result in permanent scars to your psyche. It heavily impacts MA availability. This is meant as a pinch hitter. Use only in emergencies.

Effect: Must be used in conjunction with the psionic MA Thought Sensing and Thought Projection. This spell analyzes the targets in the area of effect and siphons their mana, or mana type of energy. If that energy is used to sustain the target, this spell will effectively kill, or close to kill them. The energy will be transferred to you and your group or raid, replenishing current mana levels.

Effect Warning: When replenishing your comrades mana pool, the transfer will demand damage be taken as recompense. You cannot avoid this side effect. Everything is a matter of give and take. Be warned.

Basic Vision spell = Mind Healing.

    Cast: Instant – 5 minute recast

    Type: Restorative

    Duration: 20 seconds, or 75% of the caster's level, whichever is greater.

Effect: You may create and insert a vision for the target to experience it s best to have some of these pre-prepared. This will not cause any damage but instead assist in soothing a tormented mind. Use with caution and be aware that people who could benefit from this skill might be closer than you realize.

ACKNOWLEDGMENTS

I have a lot of people to thank, who in at least some way encouraged me to write in general, or else to write this book specifically.

Love of my life, Trevor, and my little Kami. It's his fault I found the genre, and her fault I never give up on writing.

I wouldn't be here without the following friends:
Jami Nord & Owen Littman
Heather Cashman
Jude
Heather Gilbert
M. Andrew Patterson
Aimee
Amanda W.
Quinton Shyn
Kindra
Kendra
Dawn Chapman
Alexis Keane
Bonnie Price
Nick Kuhns
Richard Hummel
Stephen Morse
Felissa Ely
Anthea Sharp
Andrea Parseneau
Cait Greer

M Evan Matyas

Ian Mitchell

To those readers on RR whose help and readership has been invaluable:

Thank you all for reading and so much for the amazing feedback! I know I've probably forgotten someone. If you read this on RR in its early stages and conmented or reviewed, please know it means the world to me.

Endless Paving

Mearhena

Oathkeeper

Cyan Snake

Bleached

Tarakis

Puck

Koinzell

Nikeyeia

Zedicious

Barnmaddo

<u>Patreon:</u>

Thank you all so much for your support!

Ma & Pa

Richard

Robert

Emersen

Kylie B

Erik

Aleksander

Jonathan C

Amanda W

John C

Quinton

Violet R

Janis N
Tobin
Tezq
Arnout
Bubs
Stuart G
Jamie N
Viktor L
Ryan C
J.S. Grulke
Spaceemotion
Wicked

www.ingramcontent.com/pod-product-compliance
Lightning Source LLC
Chambersburg PA
CBHW032202180726
48284CB00001B/157